IN THE HEAT OF PASSION

If ever there was a moment to let Cassandra go, this was it. Her body was pressed close to his. Holding her had made sense when she was tormented by fear. Now he did it only because he couldn't bring himself to release her.

Her lips parted, to question, to chastise; Max wasn't certain. But then he was certain of nothing but the overwhelming desire to taste her again.

Max lowered his head. His lips grazed Cassandra's and he heard her tiny gasp. She shuddered, but not from fear.

And then he was kissing her. Thoroughly and deeply as he had before. Her arms were wound about his neck, her fingers digging into his silk jacket. He tasted the salt of her tears, the remnants of her fear; but there was more. Heat and passion. Overwhelming, all-consuming passion. It flowed between them, surrounded them like the waters of the pool. Max felt as if he were drowning in her.

The kiss deepened. Cassandra was swept away by it, dazed. She wanted to drop to the ground with Max . . . touch him everywhere . . . lose herself in the heat and strength of his body. . . .

* * *

Advance praise for *SPLENDOR:*

"Captivating, enchanting, a feast for the senses. Everything Ms. Dorsey writes is infused with freshness."

—*Romantic Times*

Books by Christine Dorsey

TRAITOR'S EMBRACE
WILD VIRGINIA NIGHTS
BOLD REBEL LOVE
THE CAPTAIN'S CAPTIVE
KANSAS KISS
SEA FIRES
SEA OF DESIRE
SEA OF TEMPTATION
MY SAVAGE HEART
MY SEASWEPT HEART
MY HEAVENLY HEART
SPLENDOR

Published by Zebra Books

SPLENDOR

CHRISTINE DORSEY

ZEBRA BOOKS
KENSINGTON PUBLISHING CORP.

ZEBRA BOOKS are published by

Kensington Publishing Corp.
850 Third Avenue
New York, NY 10022

First Printing: February, 1996
10 9 8 7 6 5 4 3 2 1

Printed in the United States of America

To Madonna and Frank for rearing her . . .
To our son Ben for finding her . . .
And to Dori, for being the daughter-in-law
mothers dream of.
And fathers too . . . As always, this one's for Chip.

One

Once upon a time in a peaceful kingdom far away there lived a beautiful queen. But alas the fair queen was troubled. . . .

The vision was upon her again.

Gasping, Cassandra shoved aside the counterpane and threw her legs over the side of the bed. She opened her eyes, praying the dream would fade . . . knowing in her heart it was no dream.

They were still there, the people, her people. Men and women, children, screaming, fleeing the onslaught of mounted soldiers. Trying to escape the fire-breathing guns and flashing steel of sabers. Trampled beneath the pounding hooves.

"No, stop!" Pale hands covered her face, trying in vain to erase the images. "Please."

Gradually the scene before her eyes faded. The screams and frenzied shouts evaporated till they were but echoes. Then naught remained but the faint odor of brimstone.

Slowly Cassandra allowed her fingers to drift down her face. Her cheeks were wet from the tears she hadn't realized she wept. When her eyes could focus, clearly perceive the everyday trappings of her bedroom, Cassandra let out her breath.

She stared at the tapestry hanging from the wall. A white unicorn with a golden horn, the symbol of her country, frolicked on a sky blue background. Fluffy clouds framed the beast. Cassandra loved the tapestry. It had hung by her bed since she was a child and always made her smile. But now the mythical animal seemed to mock her.

"Do something," it seemed to say. "Save those who depend upon you."

But what could she do? Besides, there was no danger. No armed troops roamed Breslovia's soil. Her country had a long history of peace and neutrality.

Yet what of the visions?

As if on cue, Cassandra's gaze snagged on a flicker of light reflecting off the gold mirror frame. Her vision blurred. Her heart pounded and she could feel herself begin to tremble. It was happening again.

"No, oh, no. Please."

She scrambled from her bed, not even bothering to grab up a cloak before lifting a corner of the tapestry. Behind the woven silk, a door built into the stone wall opened slowly, silently, when she pulled a small lever.

Cassandra slipped into the corridor. It was dark, but she knew the way. Even running from the vision as she was, she knew every step, every turn in the long, descending tunnel. Her bare feet padded down the passageway hacked into solid rock for some distant ancestor. Some king or queen who'd ruled Breslovia before her.

The tunnel seemed to go on forever. But not even its comforting darkness could blank out the scenes of horror from her mind. So she ran faster, harder. Gasping for breath, trying to escape the unescapable.

She could smell the damp earth, could vaguely sense the wavery lightening of the tunnel's end. But the splashing tumble of cascading water was drowned out by the cannon fire and screams reverberating in her head.

Sticky with perspiration, Cassandra plunged forward into the waterfall that hid the tunnel entrance. The cool water engulfed her, soaking her thin cotton nightrail, but it did not purge the horrific images.

"Try to think of something else," Cassandra admonished herself as she tossed back her head, allowing the crystal droplets to pound her face. But it did no good. She could still see them, hear them . . . feel their fear.

Then, suddenly, another sensation overwhelmed her, clawing away at the visions. Her relief was short-lived. Cassandra swallowed, stepping far enough forward on the slippery rock ledge to look about. For she could swear someone watched her.

Blinking water from her eyes, she scanned the area. The moon was full, gilding the feathery willow trees that lined the glistening pool at the base of the falls. Somewhere in the night an owl hooted, and Cassandra let out her breath. She was letting fantasy blur the sharp edges of reality, much as mist softened the landscape. There was no one here.

No one knew of the secret tunnel but her. She was safe.

Yet the feeling that eyes followed her every move would not dissipate.

And then she saw him.

Cassandra stood still, as still as he, wondering if the stranger was real or another vision conjured up by her mind. Tall and muscularly built, he leaned against an oak's trunk near the reed beds by the pool's edge. Moonlight blazed on the open white shirt he wore, and caught the shine of his boots. His face was in shadow, but she could sense his eyes. They stared at each other for what seemed like long moments while her visions of death and destruction ceased. And all the while water tumbled over her body.

He was the first to move, pushing his shoulder off the tree trunk and taking several steps toward the pool into the moonlight before squatting down. His eyes left hers long enough for him to pick up a twig and toss it into the swirling water; then they were back, searching hers.

"You are real, aren't you?" he finally said in a low deep voice. "For I should feel quite foolish conversing with a figment of my imagination." He paused. "However lovely."

Because she was thinking the same of him, wondering if

she had conjured him up as a way to fight the awful visions haunting her on this night, Cassandra smiled.

His responding grin made Cassandra's toes curl.

"Do you speak, Mistress Water Nymph?" The man accompanied his words by pushing himself to his feet and taking several more strides in her direction.

"Of course. But I'm no more water nymph than spawn of your imagination."

"I can see that now." His voice was even lower than before.

He was perhaps two rods from her, near the end of the ledge where she stood. He extended a hand toward her, and the spray from the falls quickly wet his sleeve. But he appeared not to notice as he stood, waiting.

His hand was large and well formed, the fingers long, and Cassandra could do no more than stare at it. She should turn around and retreat into the tunnel, she was certain of that. Even if he chased her she would find her way through the labyrinth better than he. Yes, that was what she should do. But though her mind made the decision, her body seemed unable to carry through.

Even when he moved closer.

" 'Tis obvious you're chilled. And I do have a cloak at your disposal." He motioned back toward the tree, where he'd originally stood. Cassandra could see something on the ground, though she couldn't tell what.

His boots splashed in the water.

Cassandra could see his face again, found herself beguiled by his expression. Without waiting to weigh the consequences her arm lifted. Before she could draw in a breath his hand, warm and firm, encompassed hers.

He drew her toward him till she was pressed against his wet hard body. Only then did he back up toward the shore.

Cassandra could barely breathe. Close up he seemed so much taller, so much broader. He was overpowering. One of his muscular arms held her to him, pinning her body to his. Her flesh tingled and she felt lightheaded. When his thumb lifted her chin

Cassandra looked into blue eyes as clear and deep as the pool behind her.

"Isn't this better than shivering beneath a torrent of water?"

His voice, his words, were as soothing as the feel of his embrace. As the mesmerizing tug of his eyes.

She needed to pull away from him. To grab the cloak and cover herself. To return to the castle. There was a part of her mind that preached prudence. But though she tried, Cassandra could not make herself move away.

His fingers trailed down the side of her neck, catching a sodden strand of hair and brushing it back. Then his hand followed the flow of her hair, finger-combing it till it curled to the small of her back. And Cassandra could only melt against him.

"I've heard legends of maidens who live in the sea and tempt mere mortals with their beauty." His warm breath wafted across her cheek. "But I ne'er thought to find one 'neath a waterfall."

"I'm . . ." Cassandra hesitated. It was obvious he didn't know who she was. He was a stranger to her kingdom. Yet if she told him there would be no more seduction. Naive as she might be, Cassandra recognized seduction.

Desire strummed through her like heady wine, and driven as she was by the need to forget the visions of destruction, she was momentarily thrown off balance.

Then the moment to tell him . . . to stop him . . . was gone.

His mouth descended, covering hers in a kiss that seared her soul.

His lips were insistent, shaping hers, spreading and opening them to receive his tongue. His first thrust sent Cassandra's hands to his shoulders. He was all bulging muscles and hot skin. So hot the layer of wet fabric covering him seemed to sizzle.

She had never felt such as him. Didn't know that touching another could be so erotic.

When he lifted her, his mouth never left hers. They were

moving, to where Cassandra didn't know. Nor did she care. Her arms wrapped around his neck, her breasts pressed to his chest, and she let the fever seize her. Let it keep the haunting memory of the visions from her mind.

Only when he reached the oak tree did he put her down. And then only to scoop up his cape and snap the thick folds. The black fabric floated over the fern-covered ground, swirling the mist. It made a fine bed for her to lie upon.

She sighed when his body followed hers, welcoming his weight . . . the strong feel of him.

She waited for his lips to cover hers again, but instead they slid toward her ear, nipping and warming. He swirled his tongue along the soft crescent. Cassandra moaned and his mouth surged lower, finding the ridge of her collarbone, tasting.

He rose on his elbows staring down at her, and Cassandra felt bereft of his weight. Her arms lifted, tangling with his mane of dark, unfettered hair. Pulling him back to her. He hesitated, touching the curve of her shoulder while the muscles of his supporting arm corded sensually beneath the filmy fabric.

"You're shivering, my water nymph."

"Cassie," she whispered. "My name is Cassie."

The last of her name he tasted as his lips again covered hers. Then he was dragging his hands down her body, pulling the sodden nightrail over her head.

Cassandra expected embarrassment to overwhelm her, for no man had seen her thus. But there was none. Only the sweet oblivion of his scorching touch as he skimmed his mouth down over her breast. She moaned, unable to stop herself, when he sucked the puckered crest into his mouth. She was melting.

"Ah, Cassie, you taste so good." His mouth moved lower, blazing a path between her ribs and all Cassandra could do was sigh.

She'd never known such sensual pleasure . . . didn't know it existed. Her mind seemed to have abandoned her. She could not think, only feel. The moist heat of his mouth. The carnal abrasion of his whisker-roughened chin as he inched lower down her stomach. The delightful tickle of his hair as it fell across her fevered flesh.

Above her the narrow leaves swayed in the breeze, a dreamy counterpoint to what was happening to her. It was as if she were floating on the clouds of her tapestry rather than lying on the ground. Floating. Swaying. Carried forth on the sensual tide of the stranger's magical mouth.

He drifted lower, feasting on the arch of a hipbone, sliding along the juncture to her thigh. Cassandra's eyes shot open and she pushed up on her elbows when she realized where his mouth was. But he only glanced up, his gaze meeting hers over the expanse of her naked body.

"Let me," was all he said. Simple words that she seemed incapable of disobeying. And as soon as his tongue touched her fevered flesh Cassandra had no desire to stop him.

She drifted down, her head falling back onto his cape, then twisted from side to side as he worked his magic. He was no longer slow and gentle, but insistent—hungry. He licked. He stroked. He sent waves of pleasure washing over her.

Then his large hands dug beneath her, lifting, spreading, opening her more completely to the ravages of his mouth. Sending her over the edge of some mystical chasm with his exquisite torture.

Cassandra cried out, the sound mingling with the eternal fall of water, as the tremors crashed over her, scrambling her senses. She was whirling, skimming high above the earth, sailing into the heavens.

Max was going to burst, explode, if he didn't divest himself of his breeches. He'd been hard and throbbing since he first glanced up to see her appear magically beneath the waterfall. Her gown was transparent, the water molding it to every curve and swell of her luscious body.

Desire, carnal and lustful, had clawed at his body, like a giant cat. It was still prowling.

At first he thought he was dreaming, still wasn't certain this was real. Mortal women simply didn't have such perfect skin, such softness. They didn't smell as sweet or taste as erotic . . . or respond so intensely.

Max pulled away long enough to unfasten his breeches. Dream or not he wanted nothing more than to sink into the hot oblivion of her. His pulse raced as he slid between her open thighs. His first thrust impaled her. She arched, reaching for him, clutching his shoulders.

Everything about her was exciting him. Her creamy breasts, hard and pebbly from her release, seared his chest. Her hands tugged at his shirt, baring more skin to skim across hers. And her hips surged to meet his, matching every thrust as he sank deeper. Drowning. Drowning in the exquisite torture of her body.

As the explosion came he drove himself harder, plunging, lost in the molten ecstasy of her body.

"Cassie." Max felt her tremble, felt the subtle squeeze as she climaxed with him.

Tremors gripped him, leaving him weak and bone tired. With a satiated moan Max sank down heavily, garnering just enough energy to roll onto his side. He gathered her close, a smile tilting his mouth when she came willingly, resting her cheek on his chest.

Cassandra came awake by slow degrees. She'd been dreaming. The most sensual, erotic dream imaginable. Her body tingled just thinking of it. She sighed deeply as she stretched her legs, only to freeze when her foot rubbed against something muscle-hard and hairy.

Cassandra's eyes popped open. She barely managed to stifle a scream when she noticed the man sprawled out beside her.

In the pale pewter dawn she could see him clearly. The man

from her dream . . . Nay, it had been no dream. He lay on his stomach, one large muscular arm draped below her breasts. Her bare breasts.

His face was turned toward her, his eyes closed, thick dark lashes fanning his cheek. But she could remember those eyes, those clear blue eyes. She could remember everything that had happened . . . everything she had done.

How could she have?

Cassandra squirmed, trying to wriggle from beneath the man's arm. His breathing changed. Hers stopped. A groggy groan vibrated from deep in his chest, and Cassandra bit her bottom lip. Please don't have him awaken, she silently pleaded to whichever saint looked after fools—one of which she certainly considered herself.

She wasn't sure how long she lay there doing her best not to move, watching his face for any sign that his eyes would open. When he finally seemed to settle deeper into slumber, she again tried to extricate herself from his hold. This time she moved more slowly, breathing deeply only when she managed to slide free of his arm.

Pushing herself to her feet, she grabbed her nightrail and splashed into the pool. Hurriedly she climbed onto the ledge and dashed through the waterfall, leaving the stranger behind.

Returning to the castle . . . and her husband.

Two

"I gather you didn't sleep with the queen last night."

Albert, Grand Duke of Breslovia and consort to Her Royal Highness Cassandra I, waved away the servant who fussed with his lace cravat. "I wasn't aware my . . . sleeping arrangements . . . were your concern."

"Really?" Cardinal Sinzen, advisor to the queen and elder brother of the Grand Duke crossed plump hands over his ample abdomen.

The gesture was lost on the Grand Duke who studied his own reflection in the gilded mirror, before turning, satisfied, toward the cardinal. "You know the woman bores me."

"Bores you?" The words sliced through the air and into Albert. He continued to meet his brother's hard stare only by reminding himself that it was *he* who was the Grand Duke. *He* who married the queen.

Albert's chin was firm, his voice nearly so, though a bit petulant. "She lies open beneath the sheets like a royal sacrifice barely able to summon up the mildest of responses."

"Unlike your darling Madam Cantrell who screams her pleasure at your barest touch."

Albert lifted a jeweled snuff box, more to admire his long slender fingers than the twinkling rubies, jerking his head toward his brother's smirking face. There was too much assurance in those pale eyes, and a shiver ran down Albert's spine. He would not put it past Sinzen to spend the nights with his fleshy body cramped into a tiny alcove and one eye glued to a peephole. Watching him. Watching him with Nicolette.

A slow smile curved Albert's thin lips. "Do you enjoy watching what you seem unable to do? Does the sight of Nicolette's lush body, open to passion, make you wish for more than your young boys?"

The cardinal's expression never changed. "It makes me wish my brother were not so insufferably stupid." Stepping forward Cardinal Sinzen cut off any blubbering response Albert might make with a lift of his red-robed arm. "Your position is tenuous . . . will remain so until you beget an heir on Her Highness. Need I remind you of our ultimate goal—of the reason you married Cassandra—or who arranged the match?"

Nicolette's constant admonishments to be strong and stand up to his brother paled before Sinzen's wrath. Albert fidgeted with the snuff-box clamp, thumbing it open only to clamp it shut again. Again and again. Spilling finely ground tobacco onto the gilded surface of his dressing table. "I think the bitch is barren," he finally managed to mumble.

"Her Highness," Cardinal Sinzen emphasized the title as he took another step forward, noting the film of perspiration glistening on his brother's upper lip, "mayhap is unable to bear a child. However I can count on one hand, nay with one finger, the number of times you've bedded her in the last fortnight."

"I don't—"

Grasping his brother's shoulder, pleased by the flinching of muscle beneath the puce satin, the cardinal softened his expression. "You need not enjoy the mating, Albert, nor must she." His fingers tightened. "Consider it the price you must pay to sustain your lofty position. You do take pleasure in being the Grand Duke, do you not?"

"Yes, of course, but—"

"Then it seems such a small price to pay for the life you lead. For the opportunity you've been given to restore the throne to our family . . . to the rightful family." Cardinal Sinzen loomed over his brother. "Your son, a Martinette, will be king. Imagine that Albert. After over three hundred years Martinettes will again reign over Breslovia."

Albert was far less concerned about his son's life than his own. But he never said as much, not when his brother's fleshy face shone with excitement about the throne passing back to their family. He simply nodded, grateful the cardinal's anger had abated. Thankful that anger hadn't reached the intensity it might have.

It was difficult to imagine the two men in the dressing room of the Grand Duke's apartments had emerged from the same womb. Where Albert was tall and lean, understandably proud of his face and form, his brother hid the bulges caused by consuming too much food and wine beneath long flowing robes. He could not camouflage his pumpkin round face, however, though he tried with a fancifully curled wig.

Temperament and intelligence separated these men nearly as much as appearance. Yet they were united by blood. Sinzen reminded himself of this as he patted his brother's cheek.

"You do know Albert that all this depends upon you. *I* depend upon you."

Albert's lower lip settled into a pout, but only for an instant. Then he nodded.

"That's excellent. Then you shall do what needs to be done. It isn't as if you will be saddled with her forever. Get her with child and your job will be complete." The cardinal's smile was chilling. "Then we need only wait for nature to take its course. When your son is born, the Queen . . . well, the Queen shall be of no further use."

Albert swallowed, though his mouth felt dry. It was his wife whose life was threatened. A fact that bothered him not at all. He didn't like to be so easily controlled by his brother. As if they were still children.

Albert may have grown taller and stronger, but he feared defying Sinzen. No matter how often Nicolette told him he could.

* * *

Not so much as a glimmer of surprise crossed Kanakareh's bronzed features as he opened the door. But then Maximilian Hawke expected as much from the Seneca brave. The man's steadfast calm was nearly legendary. Which was only part of the reason Max frequently tried to fluster him.

But this was not one of those times. Arriving at their rendezvous a day late and covered with mud from the road was due to accident rather than design.

"Well, do you intend to admit me or must I stand here dripping on the good tavern keeper's hall floor?"

The door swung wider, then closed behind him. "I expected you to be here when I arrived—was not that your plan when you rode off ahead of the coach?"

Max shrugged out of his dirt-encrusted jacket. " 'Twas. Unfortunately the horse I rented at the last inn had other ideas."

"You allowed the horse to throw you?" There was a change in expression now. Amusement tilted Kanakareh's wide mouth.

Not that Max could blame Kanakareh for this reaction. Riding was as much a part of Hawke as breathing, which was one of the reasons he'd chosen to abandon the coach that carried his trunks in the first place. After days of bouncing around in that poorly sprung contraption, he'd decided to rent a mount and enter Breslovia's capital astride. Instead he lumbered in during a chilled rain that had turned the roads into a quagmire.

Max moved closer to the fire in the grate. "Perhaps we should keep this incident between us." A needless admonition. Kanakareh could be counted on for his discretion and loyalty, as well as his unflinching expression. He had proved himself to Hawke many times since their first meeting.

When the warmth began seeping through his damp shirt, Max took a moment to glance about the accommodations arranged for them. His dark brows lifted. "I am pleasantly surprised." The room where he stood was a large, well-appointed sitting room with tall windows marbled by the incessant rain. Several doors opened off it to the right. "Are the other rooms as fine?"

"Nearly."

"Perhaps we shall enjoy our stay in Breslovia after all." A fleeting memory of the beautiful goddess from the previous night was interrupted by a knock at the door. "I see the landlord is prompt." He pointed the buxom maid to a bedroom door, then followed as she instructed several young boys in the arrangement of the brass tub. More boys followed with pails of steaming water.

By the time the tub was full and the boys gone, Max had stripped off his soiled waistcoat and shirt. A fact the maid did not miss. Her sloe eyes traced the contours of his broad chest, and her smile broadened.

"Ye'll be need'n help with your bath, I'll wager." She allowed her gaze to drift down to his muddy boots, then slowly up the soiled breeches. "And I'm just the gel who can help ye."

"I'm quite certain you could," Max said with a grin. The girl was pretty enough, and it wasn't difficult to read the meaning in her dark eyes. She fluttered her hands toward her bodice as if to show him how small and delicate they were, despite her lot in life. And Max fought a surge of temptation. Kanakareh could retire to the tavern below to break his fast while Hawke enjoyed the skimming of those deft hands over his body.

With a sigh he shook his head. "Nay, though I do appreciate the offer. I imagine my bath will proceed at a quicker pace if I see to it myself."

Her lips parted. "If you're sure, govenur . . ."

"Regretfully, I am." Max dug in his waistcoat pocket and tossed the girl a gold coin, which she caught and examined only long enough to discover its worth before stowing it between her ample breasts.

"Me name's Missy, govenur. If there be anything I can do for you—"

"I'll be sure to send for you," Max declared as he guided her from the room. When he turned back Kanakareh only shook his head.

"What?" Max met the Indian's stare. "I sent her away, didn't

I?" Catching the heel of his boot in the bootjack by the hearth, he pried one foot loose. "Besides, she's harmless enough."

"I doubt that could be said of any female where you're concerned, Hawke."

Max shrugged, then pulled off his other boot. "You make me regret ever telling you that sordid tale about the Earl of Northford's wife." When Kanakareh simply folded his arms and retired into the sitting room, Max continued. "I was young and a bit irresponsible." He peeled off his breeches and climbed into the tub, making a sound of contentment as the warm water sloshed around his hips.

"All right," he called into the other room when Kanakareh still made no response. "Perhaps I was more than a bit irresponsible. Cuckolding your commanding officer is not the best way to advance one's military career." He sank down farther in the water. "I know things were looking pretty grim before I received this royal summons, but I have a feeling about this." Cupping his hands, Max tossed water in his face.

"You had a *feeling* about the French regiment at Cross Creek."

"And we won, didn't we?" Max blinked toward the open door between the two rooms to see Kanakareh staring at him.

"All right, perhaps I did manage to stop an arrow. But all in all I think it was a good campaign." He had been commended for his actions that kept the French and their allies, the Huron, from swarming over a small fort protecting the headwaters of the Ohio. He'd been promoted too.

Max rubbed his palm across the puckered scar on his thigh. It was still tender. But no more so than the memories of what happened later. When the lies and allegations had begun circulating about him. When his military career . . . such as it was . . . had come to an ignoble end.

"What did you say?" Scooping soft soap from a crock Max set about scrubbing his lean body. He would not dwell on the past.

"I only questioned what has troubled me since you received

the letter. What could the Grand Duke of Breslovia want with you?"

"I don't know." Max rarely questioned fate. He only knew that the royal summons was greatly appreciated. Since his forced resignation from the British army he and Kanakareh traveled from place to place, most recently staying at a friend's villa in Italy. But by the time the message from Breslovia had arrived, their welcome was wearing thin.

And there weren't many options open to him. Returning to England was out of the question. His father had made it clear he wished no part of his wayward son. Though not court-martialed, even a hint of treason was too much for the Duke of Belmead to tolerate.

Max had considered signing aboard a ship bound for the Caribbean, and trying his luck there. But the prospect wasn't that appealing. And now, thanks to the Grand Duke Albert of Breslovia, perhaps he wouldn't have to. At least not for the present.

Max stood, realized he couldn't reach the towel and stepped from the tub. Wet footprints marked his path as he crossed the room. "Were you able to discover anything about Breslovia's army?"

"There is none."

Max flicked the linen toweling behind his back. "None?" Admittedly he knew little of this small country nestled in the foothills of the Alps. It wasn't strong militarily, or he would have remembered something of it from his education. Much of the other information the tutors had poured into his head was forgotten.

"There is local militia and the Imperial Guard. Their duty is to protect the Queen and her family."

"Queen?" This was the first Max had heard of this. "I thought the kingdom was ruled by the Grand Duke." He swiped the towel across his chest. The shirt he pulled over his head absorbed the remaining water droplets.

"There is a queen."

Though Max couldn't see him, he could imagine Kanakareh's expressionless face. "And no army."

"Breslovia prides itself on its neutrality in all conflicts."

Wonderful. A peace-loving country with no army. Sounded like heaven . . . unless you were a soldier.

Searching through the chest Kanakareh had brought in from the coach Max found breeches and weskit. Gone were the days when he could afford a valet.

"Is that all you learned from gossiping with the locals?" he called through the open door. The only response was a grunt which could have passed for a laugh. Gossip was hardly the term used to describe how Kanakareh came by his information. He simply said nothing. Most people assumed he could not speak their language and talked around him as if he were no more than a piece of furniture.

Max found this amusing since he knew of Kanakareh's ear for languages—the brave had picked up French from the Huron and spoke it better than Max who'd been tutored in it by a Frenchman his father hired.

"I find it preferable to discover what I can about a situation before walking into it."

"I quite agree," Max mumbled. It was a wise philosophy. Unfortunately, it was one that Maximilian Hawke, second and disowned son of the Duke of Belmead, rarely seemed to follow.

By the time the appointed hour to meet with the Grand Duke arrived, Max was groomed and garbed in a suit of blue silk only slightly less grand than that of the footman who showed him into the gold and crystal anteroom at the palace. If he could have worn his regimentals Max would have felt more at ease. But that was no longer an option.

Max pushed up out of the gilt chair and, hands folded behind his back, strode the length of the room.

He tried not to delude himself . . . at least not too much.

Besides a penchant for pleasing ladies—a questionable talent at best—Max's only attribute was soldiering. And that was open to speculation depending upon whom you spoke with. Certainly Lord Northford had nothing good to say about Max's ability to lead men.

So why had the Grand Duke of Breslovia sought him out, not to mention sent him a sizable purse of gold? Why had he asked him to travel to the capital, Liberstein, with all haste? Max was still pondering these questions when the mirrored door opened and a powdered doorman in scarlet livery bade him follow.

It had been years since Max lived at Salisbury, the county seat of the Duke of Belmead. But even after being sequestered in the wilds of North America, he remembered what luxury was, and he'd never seen anything quite as splendid as this palace. The floors were marble, the ceilings intricately carved and painted. And everywhere you looked there was gold.

The walls in the wide hall were covered with frescoes in deep, rich colors. Vivid green meadows. Autumn-crowned trees or white-crowned mountains of such scope and beauty Max felt the air to be crisp and frosty.

Such were the vistas that greeted him as he followed the footman through the wide passage. But it wasn't until he passed the crystalline mural of a waterfall that he was tempted to pause . . . to reach out and touch.

It was the waterfall from last night. He recognized it even though he'd viewed the lacy willows and sparkling water only in misty moonlight.

The scene brought memories racing back. The smell of damp earth. The woman's silky skin. Her taste. The feel of her body enveloping him.

Until this moment Max had nearly convinced himself last night was a dream. A conjuring of his mind. The perfect fantasy. How else could he explain to himself the beautiful goddess who had appeared from nowhere to give herself to him with such passion?

"Ah, so you're a lover of the arts as well as a military man. You are Maximilian Hawke, I presume?"

Max glanced around to see a porcine man smiling at him through fleshy folds of fat. "I am," Max replied, adding a hasty "Your Grace" as he noticed the man wore the robes of a cardinal.

"I am Cardinal Sinzen. Shall we join the Grand Duke? The mural was painted by Marcel Rubert," he explained while they continued down the hall. "It is a masterpiece, don't you think?"

"I fear my appreciation of art is limited to what appeals to me."

"And that fresco does?"

"I'm fond of waterfalls."

"Ah, then perhaps you can visit this one someday. It's on the palace grounds I believe." When Max said nothing the man gestured toward an open door to the right. "I believe the Grand Duke awaits us."

If the Grand Duke was interested in Max, or anything other than surveying himself in the tall gold-framed mirror, Max would have been surprised. His Highness was tall, with even features women probably found appealing and a mouth seemingly curved in a perpetual pout. He nodded and lazily lifted his fingers when Max presented his best bow. Then he settled into a large scarlet-cushioned chair.

Cardinal Sinzen indicated a seat to Max before resting his wide form on a settee. "We, the Grand Duke and I, are pleased you could accept our invitation to visit Breslovia."

"Thank you." Max leaned back in the chair. "Though I must admit I'm a bit perplexed about why you asked me to come."

Cardinal Sinzen's face wrinkled in a smile. "Ah, some of that refreshing candor for which you're known."

Max merely lifted a brow.

"My comment surprises you?"

"Amuses perhaps." If he was known for his candor at all, Max doubted many described it as refreshing.

"As it happens the Grand Duke and I are forthright as well. You've made a long journey, and you deserve to know why." Sinzen paused, steepling his short stubby fingers." We would like you to be the commander in chief of Breslovia's army."

What? Max leaned forward, wondering if he'd heard correctly. "I don't believe I understand."

"It's quite simple." This from the Grand Duke, who appeared bored and seemed to wish the interview over. "We need someone to build up and train the locals, and we . . . that is, my brother seems to think you are the man to do it."

Brothers? These two were brothers? Max took note of that as well as the sharp look Cardinal Sinzen shot the Grand Duke.

"What His Highness says is essentially true," Cardinal Sinzen said in a tone that implied he wouldn't have worded it in the same manner. "Breslovia's army lacks leadership. Leadership you can provide."

Max had the sinking feeling he was shooting himself in the foot—he could almost feel the burning pain—but he couldn't help asking. "What makes you think I can train an army?"

"I was the one who made that decision," Cardinal Sinzen responded. There seemed to be no more pretense of including the Grand Duke. "However, it was a choice I did not make lightly." He smiled again, but this time Max found the expression chilling. "There is very little about you I do not know."

Max swallowed. "One would almost believe you've been spying on me." The words were spoken low and without a trace of humor, yet Cardinal Sinzen chuckled.

"My dear sir, you can't possibly believe I would offer you such a post without making the necessary inquiries." The Grand Duke rose and wandered toward a bank of windows. Cardinal Sinzen seemed not to notice. He leaned back, crossing his hands over his ponderous belly. "I know you trained large numbers of savages in the Americas. Made them into a formidable fighting force."

"Most of those *savages* already knew more about fighting than I—or the entire British Army for that matter."

"Perhaps. Yet you are the one who brought them together. Inspired them if you will."

Max couldn't help smiling. "If you've spoken to anyone about my military career, you know it has not always been stellar."

"Honest to a fault," Cardinal Sinzen said. "Actually, though, I've decided you are just the type of commander we need."

Max let his gaze drift toward the Grand Duke who by now was examining a gold-framed miniature he wore on a chain about his neck. He must have noted the silence for he glanced up and dismissed the two men with a wave of his hand. "I'm in complete agreement, though most of the military affairs are handled by the Prime Minister."

Which Max took to be his brother, Cardinal Sinzen. The cardinal confirmed Max's speculation with his next words.

"Of course you will be in charge of the army if you accept the position . . . reporting directly to me. And I in turn report to the Grand Duke."

"I've been led to believe Breslovia doesn't have an army to speak of." Max wasn't certain why he was erecting obstacles when he should be down on his knees thanking God for this opportunity.

"True enough. Which is what we'd like you to see about changing. Earlier I mentioned your work with the savages. Though Breslovia's citizens are quite civilized, their military training is sadly lacking. Your mission will be to change that."

Max didn't know what to say to that. He had worked well with the Seneca. And together they had won a decisive victory over the French at Cross Creek. But as military careers went, his was overshadowed by the failures. Max wondered if Cardinal Sinzen knew that. Wondered if he should tell him. Discovered it wasn't necessary.

"Let us speak with candor here. We are interested in your expertise in training a group of men with little or no military experience. We intend to make it worth your while. And we know you have nowhere else to turn." Cardinal Sinzen smiled again. "You need this position Mister Hawke."

Max wanted to argue. To rise and stalk to the door, slam it in the faces of Cardinal Sinzen and the ever-silent Grand Duke. There was something about them he didn't like. They made his skin crawl in a way it hadn't since he'd been captured by the Huron.

But as much as he hated to admit it, Cardinal Sinzen was right. He did need this offer. Refusing them was unthinkable. Besides, he'd been wrong about people before. Perhaps the cardinal wasn't that bad. And Max had known men as vain as the Grand Duke.

"Are you going to tell me what's troubling you?"

"Nothing is amiss. Why do you ask?"

Lady Sophia pulled Cassandra into a windowed alcove, away from the crush of people in the palace ballroom. "Because you haven't listened to a word I've said."

"Of course I have. You were discussing Lady Dupont's gown, wondering if her décolletage could be any lower before her breasts spilled forth."

Sophia smiled. "It is shocking."

Cassandra lifted her fan in mock surprise. "I was of the opinion that nothing shocked you."

Sophia's expression sobered. "Well, your contention that you wished to pull Madam Cantrell's wig off and sit upon it did. I could hardly believe what I was hearing—that you were expressing a deep-felt desire to expose her bald head to everyone."

"What are you prattling on about? I never said that." Cassandra's gaze flashed toward her husband's mistress who stood beside the Grand Duke, one hand resting possessively on his arm. She might have thought of doing such a thing in the past. But no more. And she certainly would never voice such an intent. But her friend Sophia was shaking her head and laughing.

"Perhaps you didn't say it. But you did agree . . . when I said it."

Cassandra tilted her head. "I never—"

"You did. Right before I pulled you in here. I suggested you might wish to try it and you said, 'Of course, Sophia, that sounds like an interesting idea.' "

"I obviously wasn't paying your words any heed."

"Which is exactly my point. You've been distracted all evening. All day really. This morning you barely touched your chocolate. And you know how you usually enjoy that."

Cassandra turned to stare out the window. Mirrored in the glass were the dazzling gowns and jackets of the dancers. All gaiety and light. Cassandra shut her eyes. "I had the vision again last night."

"Of the soldiers?"

"Yes." Her voice was little more than a whisper.

"Oh, Your Highness, I'm sorry, truly I am. If I could do anything to help you know I would. But you must stop worrying about that. You know as well as I that it won't happen. Look." She turned the Queen to face the ballroom. "Everyone is happy. As they've always been. Dancing and laughing. See Lady Dupont and her silly gown. There is no conquering army." Her fingers squeezed over her friend's hand. "It is simply a bad dream that you must forget."

When Cassandra turned her head toward Sophia there were tears in her eyes. "I don't want to see these things. I try not to think on it." She swallowed. "When I was very young I envied Simon his ability to . . . to see things that were not there. It seemed such a wondrous gift to peek into the future, to know what would happen before anyone else. I told him as much once."

"And what did he say?"

"That I spoke with the voice of a child." She grasped her friend's hand. "Sophia, I do not wish to be a seer. But since my father and brother died, since Simon disappeared, the visions have been upon me. At first only once in a while and barely strong enough to cause notice. But now . . ."

"Have you spoken to the Grand Duke?"

"Nay, he would not care to know."

"You've no doubt the right of it there." Lady Sophia snapped open her fan and smiled as one of her suitors strode by. He would have paused to join his beloved had not she turned her attention back to the Queen.

"Will nothing stop this? A spell perhaps?"

The memory flashed through Cassandra's mind. Of broad shoulders and blue eyes. Of the shattering pleasure that had made her forget. But she merely shook her head. There was no way she could tell even her friend and confidante about what she'd done last night. Her lips parted on a sigh. "I don't know."

"Well, we must do something. I fear this is affecting your health. You're so pale. Did you sleep at all last night?"

"A bit." In the arms of a stranger. Cassandra took a deep breath. "But you are right. I can not allow this to continue. Perhaps I should speak to Albert. If I assure myself that all is well with Breslovia, then perhaps I shall be able to rid myself of these visions."

"Cardinal Sinzen is the one you should speak with. From what I understand Albert can barely be bothered. But look, here is Cardinal Sinzen heading our way as I speak. And who is that sinfully handsome man at his side? Certainly no one I've ever seen before. Do you know who he is, Your Highness?" Sophia glanced back toward her friend. "My God! Are you all right? Someone help me. The Queen is going to swoon."

Three

If he'd given thought to his actions things might have been different. Not significantly to be sure, but at least he wouldn't have nearly dropped the Queen.

But Maximilian Hawke rarely tiptoed on the path through life.

One moment he was being led by Cardinal Sinzen across the ballroom to be presented to the Queen. The next he heard a frightened female voice wail that the Queen was about to swoon.

It seemed the most natural thing to rush forward and sweep the lady into his arms before she landed on the parquet floor.

She was tall for a woman and, despite the billowing gown of silver lace and hoops, lighter than he'd expected. When he held her high against his chest she gave a small cry, of relief or surprise, he wasn't sure which. All he knew was the sound caused him to look down into her face.

And that was when he nearly dropped her on her royal rump.

"Oh, my God!"

His arms tightened as did hers. She clung to him, obviously afraid he would bobble her again. And all he could do was stare.

Last night the moonlight had allowed him only fleeting glimpses of the woman from the waterfall . . . the woman he'd made love to. Yet there was no doubt this was the same woman.

"Oh, my God," Max repeated, his voice lower now. He'd made love to the Queen of Breslovia. The blasted Royal Highness herself. Max shut his eyes as he heard the excited voice of the Grand Duke who was pushing through the crowd. No more cuckolding generals. No, now it was a goddamn monarch.

"What's going on here? Cassandra, are you all right?"

She couldn't speak. She opened her mouth to say that she was perfectly fine—except that this man, this stranger she had slept with the previous night had somehow reappeared and was holding her against him. But not a sound came forth. Which was probably good considering the gibberish she might have uttered.

"Take her into the hall." Cardinal Sinzen's ponderous form was nudging people aside while he signaled for the Imperial Guards. They rushed forward, splitting the crowd of splendidly garbed lords and ladies as majestically as Moses parted the sea. "This way. Come. Come," the cardinal ordered, jolting Max from his stupor.

Max strode through the multitudes, the Queen in his arms. Several maids hurried before him, opening doors and ushering him into a small room dimly lit by a single branch of candles. Cardinal Sinzen waddled in his wake.

"Lay her there. You!" The cardinal pointed to one of the maids, causing her to dip into a deep curtsey, her hands fluttering. "Find Doctor Williamson and send him immediately."

"Yes, Your Grace."

"Nay." Cassandra pushed up on her elbows, shoving aside the masculine arm that was still draped across her waist. "It isn't necessary to disturb the royal physician. I am quite all right." At least she would be as soon as the stranger moved away from her. Just looking at him made her heart race and her stomach quiver.

"Yes, Your Highness." The girl settled into an even deeper curtsey. "As you say, Your Highness."

"Are you still about? I told you to fetch the doctor. Now do it immediately or suffer the consequences of my wrath."

The girl looked from one to the other, her face as red as

the chaise upon which the Queen lay. Apparently deciding she feared the cardinal more than the Queen the maid turned and hurried from the room.

"Your Grace." Cassandra tried to sit up, but ceased her struggles when her husband's brother flattened his palms on her shoulders. "I'm all right," she said again, but it was obvious no one paid her any heed. Several servants were busy lighting a fire in the small ornate stove and flooding the room with candlelight.

There seemed nothing to do but lie quietly and wait until Doctor Williamson confirmed that she was perfectly healthy. Cassandra sighed, turning her head to the side.

He was still there.

Cassandra could see his dark blue breeches and the well-muscled calf that she knew needed no padding beneath the silk stockings. As she watched he bent down so that his face, that handsome face with the sensual mouth, came into view. Last night she'd committed the planes and contours to memory, but she'd thought—wished—never to see it again.

He was staring at her, concern in the depths of those clear blue eyes. And unless she was mistaken that concern was more for himself than her. Still, his voice was low and sympathetic when he spoke.

"Is there anything I can do for Your Highness?"

Cassandra wished to tell him he'd done quite enough already, but she didn't, for at that moment Sigmund Williamson came bustling into the room.

"Out, all of you." He pointed a bony finger toward Cassandra. "Except for you, of course."

Max had no choice but to exit the room. As the door closed behind him, Cardinal Sinzen caught his eye. "I'm afraid you haven't seen the Queen at her best."

"What? Ah, no I suppose not. Though she cannot be blamed for taking ill." Max was still trying to decide what had just transpired. Or more importantly what had transpired last night. Why in the hell would the Queen of Breslovia choose to dally with him in the middle of the night? And what would be the consequences for him?

"You sent for me?" Lady Sophia's skirt swished through the doorway to the Queen's private apartments. She paused when she saw her friend resting against a bank of pillows propped on the high tester bed. "Oh, Your Highness, you look so dreadfully pale. Are you all right? Is it true, the rumors I've heard? If so I congratulate you. I do hope you won't have a difficult time, though by the look of you I imagine you shall."

"Shall what? Goodness, Sophia, whatever are you chattering on about?"

"Why, your pregnancy." Sophia lifted her wide crimson skirt and climbed the steps to plop herself on the side of Cassandra's bed. "The palace is buzzing with the news. I have even decided to forgive you for not telling me first, even though we pledged as children to never keep secrets from one another. Of course that was before you became queen, so perhaps it doesn't hold. However, I think—"

"Stop." Cassandra sat up, flipping back the mounded comforters and sliding off the bed. She landed on her bare feet with a thud.

Sophia twisted around. "Are you certain you should be bouncing around so?"

"First of all I didn't bounce. At present I am walking—pacing, if you prefer. And in the second place I am not going to have a child."

"Are you sure? Lady Lowdry seemed very certain. She'd heard it from Miss Sarah Henderson, who heard it from her sister Catherine, who is betrothed to Doctor Williamson's son."

"Though it is certainly difficult to refute such knowledgeable gossip, I fear I must. I am not enceinte."

"Are you sure?"

"Yes."

"Then why did you—"

"Faint?" Cassandra would have laughed at the expression on her friend's face if she weren't so upset. "In all truth, I was not on the verge of swooning."

"Cassie, I saw your face. It was white. As if you'd seen a ghost."

Her nightrail and robe swished around her softly as Cassandra stopped in her tracks. Her father had called her Cassie, and her brother. And because Sophia was her friend and cousin, her companion since childhood, she too occasionally used the nickname.

Yet it was the stranger's voice she heard in her mind, saying the name as his body covered hers.

"Your Highness, what is it? I know something is wrong. Is it the vision again?" Sophia had her now by the hands, guiding her back to sit in a brocade chair near the unicorn tapestry.

Cassandra squeezed her eyes shut, then opened them to stare into her friend's worried face. "There is something upsetting me . . . something besides the vision. And I need your help."

"Anything, Your Highness. You know you but need ask."

"Thank you." Cassandra took a deep breath. "I want you to take a message to . . . to the man who carried me out of the ballroom. I don't know what his name is."

"But why—"

Holding up her hand silenced her friend. "I can't tell you why. I can only say it is very important to me . . . and that you must be discreet. No one at court must know of this."

"Cassie."

"I mean it Sophia If you do this for me there can be no further discussion of it, with me or anyone else." Cassandra softened her next words with a smile. "I know that is asking quite a bit."

Sophia stood. "You won't even tell me—"

"No."

"Not ever?"

"Ever is a long time. But you should not agree to help me thinking I shall change my mind. 'Tis highly unlikely."

Sophia's sigh was heartfelt. "Oh, all right. This shall probably be the death of me, knowing there is some wonderfully juicy tidbit of gossip I'm barred from knowing. It is juicy, isn't it?"

"Sophia."

"Sorry. What is the message?"

"Tell him . . . tell him to meet me where we met before, tomorrow night after the musicale."

"You've met him before? When? How? Who is he then?"

"Sophia."

Lady Sophia Stivelson clasped her hand to her mouth. "I forgot. Don't worry. I don't even care to know the answer to any of those questions. It was simply habit." She paused, glancing back at the Queen. "Unless you wish to tell me, that is. No, no. I can tell you don't. I shall take the message to him immediately."

"Only to him."

"Yes, only to him. But, Your Highness, please try to get some rest."

"I shall," Cassandra promised, though she did not climb back into bed when her friend left. There was too much chance the vision would be upon her again . . . or that she'd dream of the handsome stranger.

"Well, aren't you going to say something?"

"It is not in my place to chastise you for your indiscretions. I am not your father."

Max scowled at his friend, then abruptly stood, walking toward the window. It was dark outside, the moon shrouded by clouds. "My father would have plenty to say about this," Max mumbled more to himself than Kanakareh. But then his father wasn't speaking to him so perhaps not. One of the last correspondences he'd received from his father was through the Honorable J. Landon Farnsworth, Esq. It hadn't exactly been a statement of disinheritance . . . but close to it.

His allowance was cut off, as was any communication with his father or brothers. "Until such time as you can manage to execute your life in such a way as to not embarrass both yourself and the Hawke name."

At the time Max had just been relieved of his command, a position bought for him by his father, because of the Northford incident. Max had been furious. Wasn't it bad enough he had the bastard Northford breathing down his neck, sending him off to the wilds of North America to fight the bloody French. And all because the general had a tiff with his mistress and came home to find Max asleep in his bed, with the delectable Lady Northford snuggled at his side?

"Who is the lady you've managed to entangle yourself with in the short time you've been in Breslovia?"

Kanakareh sat staring at him, his dark features expressionless and for an instant Max was tempted to tell all. "Oh, only the Queen of this fair land," he could say. Perhaps *that* would get a rise out of his stoic friend. But in the end some shimmer of nearly forgotten chivalry kept him from divulging the lady's identity. He merely shook his head to dislodge the memory of her violet eyes and reached for the decanter of port on the table.

" 'Tis enough to say my position, short-lived as it was, will possibly be terminated."

"What will you do then?"

Max took a drink of port, feeling the liquid slide down his throat. "I don't know, Kanakareh. I don't know." Max set the glass down and turned around. "But for now I've an appointment with Cardinal Sinzen and General Pleshette, head of Breslovia's militia. Perhaps the lady will forget our little dalliance."

Which Kanakareh decided was unlikely an hour later when he opened the door to their rooms to find a short, cloak-garbed woman. Her face was covered by a mask. All he could see were two large green eyes.

"I would speak with Maximilian Hawke," she said after being ushered into the parlor. " 'Tis a matter of great import and I can only speak with him, so do not try to persuade me to give you the message—I can't. And won't. No matter what you say."

A smile nearly curved the brave's wide mouth. "He is not here."

"Not here. But he does reside here, does he not? I went to much trouble to find where he lives. Where can he be? Do you know when he will return? I can't go slinking about like this forever, now can I?"

Kanakareh waited until the woman ran out of breath, then, fighting back a smile, began to answer her array of questions.

"Maximilian Hawke does reside here for the moment. He is at the palace I believe, and I do not know when he will return. Is there a message I can give him?"

"Oh, no." The woman shook her head, causing the linen mask to flutter and a wisp of curly hair the color of fire to spring out. "I must see him and only him."

Kanakareh merely nodded.

"And it is urgent that I speak to him. What am I to do now?" Sophia bit her lip beneath the suffocating mask. Despite her tendency to freckle she'd never been able to wear one of these about as many ladies did. "When do you think he'll return? Soon? What is he doing at the palace?"

Kanakareh shrugged. "You are welcome to wait here. Other than that I can not say." So the object of Max's latest indiscretion hadn't forgotten. She'd come after him.

Sophia glanced about the parlor, then toward the man who spoke. She'd been too nervous when she first arrived to notice more than a few general impressions of him. Tall. Dark. Handsome. Now she leaned forward studying him more thoroughly. He had wide cheekbones, and a straight nose. Thick hair as black as his eyes hung to his shoulders. "Are you . . . ? You are, aren't you?" She circled a stock-still Kanakareh, her cloak flaring out. "I've read about you, of course, but have never seen an actual Indian before. You are an Indian, aren't you?"

"I am Kanakareh of the Seneca Nation."

"Oh, I've hurt your pride, and that was not my intention. It is just that it is so exciting. For me at least. I never thought to—"

"Let me assure you, mistress, my pride is still intact." Kanakareh had to twist around to catch sight of the woman as she continued to circle him.

"Of course it is." Sophia rushed back to face him. "Please, tell me all about yourself." She batted at the troublesome mask finally yanking it from her face and smiling up at him.

All Kanakareh could think as he stared down at her upturned freckled face was that Max's taste in women had certainly improved.

"Your latest conquest was here today."

Max stopped dead still, the door latch held firmly in his hand. "Here? She was *here?*" It seemed inconceivable that the Queen would come to this humble dwelling to seek him out. Especially after she already sent him the message that she wished to see him tonight after the musicale.

But then Kanakareh neither lied nor repeated himself. Slowly Max closed the door and crossed the room, pouring a splash of brandy into each of two glasses. One he offered to the reticent Seneca, the other he gulped down quickly. "Well, what did you think?"

"An interesting woman."

Wasn't it just like Kanakareh to say of the most alluring woman he'd ever met, not to mention the Queen of Breslovia, that she was merely interesting. Though knowing his friend perhaps that was one of the highest compliments Kanakareh could give. Certainly to hold his interest was an accomplishment.

"Well, do not leave me in suspense. What did she say?"

"What did she not say?"

Max paused in pouring himself another drink and lifted his brows in question.

"The lady talks often and fast."

Max shrugged. He had noticed neither. But then the first time they'd met there had been little need for words. And last night . . . there had been little time to say anything of import.

"But she has an inquisitive mind. And a deep interest in the land of my people."

"She does, does she?" Max said, wondering why he felt a surge of annoyance. "But what did she say about me?"

"You?" Kanakareh set his glass down untouched and reached for the knife he was oiling. It was long and bone handled. "Nothing. She spoke only of her need to see you."

"Hmmm." Max settled into the chair across from Kanakareh and propped his long legs onto the fireplace fender. "I have already sent word that I will meet her tonight after the musicale, which by the way you are requested to attend."

"Are you certain you should—" Kanakareh clamped his lips together and rubbed the honed blade more vigorously.

"Should what?"

"It is none of my business what you do."

"But that never stopped you from having an opinion."

"Or you from ignoring it."

Max leveled his gaze. "Out with it, Kanakareh, before you explode."

"I don't know if it's wise to meet with the woman again. And I do not wish to attend a *musicale.*"

"I have no choice. I was summoned. But you needn't concern yourself. I shall simply talk to her, assuring her that we cannot continue our affair. She may find that painful to admit, but I'm certain she will agree with me in the end. At least I hope she will. You can be assured, Kanakareh, I will put an end to it. I have learned my lesson." Max leaned back in the chair and closed his eyes. "And you must attend tonight's festivities. The Grand Duke himself requested your presence."

"How would he even know of my existence?"

"I told him of you. After all, if I am going to suggest you as my second in command I had to at least let him know a bit about you."

By the appointed time to leave for the palace, Max had talked Kanakareh into accepting the invitation, though not the position in Breslovia's Royal Army. The Seneca was quite willing to help Max train soldiers, to even fight alongside those men if necessary, however, he did not wish to be confined by a commission.

Max supposed he understood. At least he tried to. It seemed he'd spent his entire life searching for—and then losing—positions, so it was inconceivable not to accept one when it came along. Which was exactly why he was here and worried about what the Queen had to say to him.

He hadn't lied to Kanakareh . . . exactly.

Max didn't want any liaison with Her Royal Majesty Queen Cassandra of Breslovia. At least he shouldn't. The bad experiences gained from cuckolding one powerful husband were all any man needed in a lifetime.

But damn he couldn't stop thinking of her.

And not just of making love to her. He kept thinking of the way she looked on the daybed with everyone bustling about her. He could have sworn she seemed frightened. Which was ridiculous.

What did the Queen of Breslovia have to be frightened of?

He was the one who should be afraid. Somehow or another Max didn't think the Grand Duke would stop with ruining his military career if he found out about his making love to the Queen. Men had been beheaded for far less.

"By the expression on your face you seem even less excited about this musicale than I do."

Max turned to see Kanakareh garbed in his ceremonial Seneca garb and grinned. "On the contrary, I can't wait to see the reaction at court when you arrive. That is a real scalp dangling from your pole, isn't it?"

"Maximilian Hawke . . . and Kanakareh."

As he announced the two, the footman's voice seemed to vibrate off the painted, domed ceiling of the music room. Though they were late, partly due to Kanakareh's reluctance to ride in the carriage when he could just as easily walk, their arrival caused a general stir. And provoked a few female gasps.

Lifting his hand to cover a grin he couldn't control, Max strode forward, his friend by his side. Most of the guests in the glittering room were already seated on ornately carved gilded chairs, and Max headed toward two in the back corner of the room. True, they were too removed from the small quartet assembling near the front to fully appreciate the music. But then Max didn't think Kanakareh or he cared much.

He didn't expect the woman from this afternoon—the one who'd given him the message from the Queen—to come rushing toward them. Max glanced around to see if anyone noticed, only to find nearly every eye on Kanakareh and him. But though he expected the lady to sweep up to him, she paused . . . beside Kanakakeh.

"Oh, Kanakareh," she breathed. "I may call you that, may I not? You look wonderful. Is this the ceremonial dress you told me about? And the feathers? What fascinating colors. Oh, do tell me these are truly scalps."

Max glanced from the woman to his friend, and back. What in the hell was going on? Lady Sophia Stivelson, he thought her name was, seemed utterly ended by his friend. Which in itself was not too unusual. Kanakareh had his share of female admirers, though admittedly not usually women dripping with diamonds. It was Kanakareh's reaction that caught Max's attention. The Seneca stared down at the woman while she rambled on as if she were the most enticing of females.

Which was surprise enough for one evening without what happened next.

The lady grasped Kanakareh's hand. "Oh, you must come sit with me so I can explain the finer points of tonight's music. You aren't familiar with Handel, are you? I didn't think so. For the most part it can be rather boring, though there are moments. Do come."

Seeing no alternative than to follow in their wake, though he was by no means included in Lady Sophia's invitation, Max found himself headed toward the front of the room. And given a seat beside the Queen.

They shared a single look of dismay before both stared straight ahead, seemingly enthralled with the deep melodic strains of the bassoonist as he warmed up.

"I say there, General Hawke. How are you?"

Turning, trying to avoid looking at Cassandra, Max bowed toward her husband. "Very good, Your Highness."

Thankfully the music began in earnest then, a dazzling performance of Handel's *Music for the Royal Fireworks.* Max had been to enough of these affairs at Salisbury to appreciate the excellence of the musicians. The violinist was superb, nearly making the instrument speak as the bow slid back and forth. Back and forth.

It was hypnotic to watch. Yet Cassandra didn't dare take her eyes off the process for fear she'd end up turning toward the handsome man beside her and demanding what on earth he was doing there. Or worse, lunging across both him and his Indian friend to clutch Sophia and demand what was in her friend's mind.

So she sat perfectly still, trying to fight the crick in her neck—and to ignore the scent of him.

Maximilian Hawke.

Cassandra learned his name from Sophia when she reported that he would meet her after the musicale. So now she knew who he was and that her husband knew him. That he was a general from somewhere, though he appeared too young. And that he had a companion from the New World. Sophia talked of little else but the Seneca warrior named Kanakareh.

Which explained why she ran off to greet him when they arrived.

But explanations didn't help the situation. Cassandra could still think of nothing but the man beside her. Her eyes fanned down and she noticed again the strong curve of his leg. Her squirming in her seat brought Albert's attention. He gave her a sharp look, then busied himself with fingering the gold locket dangling from his neck.

It most likely contained a likeness of Madam Cantrell, Cassandra thought, then decided it mattered naught if it did. The French woman could have her husband's attentions. It spared Cassandra from them.

The last time Albert had come to her private rooms was a disaster. He'd imbibed too much wine and tried to take her quickly only to become angered when, as he said, she simply lay there. He called her names, some of which she didn't understand, and left.

And Cassandra had been relieved.

She only wished that thought hadn't spawned memories of the night she'd spent in Maximilian Hawke's arms.

The music swelled to a stirring crescendo and Cassandra forced herself to breathe slowly. She didn't know how much longer she could stand sitting beside him.

She stared straight ahead and tried to concentrate on the man bent over the cello. He had a raised mole on the end of his nose, and it seemed to sway back and forth as he played like a miniature pendulum keeping time for the musicians.

She watched attentively, trying to focus her energies, but it was the heat from the man beside her that was all consuming.

And then it was over. Echoes of the music faded. A footman announced the serving of dinner and everyone adjourned to the court dining room. Cassandra lost sight of Maximilian for which, she convinced herself she was grateful. She sat at the royal table between her husband, who had managed to ensconce Madam Cantrell on his left, and Cardinal Sinzen.

"I don't believe I've ever heard Handel played more soulfully than tonight," her brother-in-law allowed as he eyed her over the rim of his wineglass.

He'd barely touched his pheasant, which was not unusual when they dined together. Cassandra always wondered how he managed to sustain the rolls of blubber about his middle with the little he ate. And tonight, as on most evenings, he seemed to keep watch over her. Cassandra always found it very uncomfortable to be under his scrutiny. But try as she might to shift the seating arrangements, he always managed to dine at her elbow.

She responded to his remark about the music, and for a few minutes they debated the merits of the musicians. Then as if overcome by concern, Cardinal Sinzen leaned toward her.

"I do hope you are feeling better since your episode last night. You must take better care of yourself. Rest more."

"I am fine. And actually, I am considering becoming more active."

His chin settled further down into his neck. "How so?"

"When my father . . ." Cassandra forced back tears. "When my father and brother first died I was too overcome by grief to spend much time thinking about Breslovia."

"Which is one of the reasons you married my brother. So you need not worry your lovely head over such concerns."

"Perhaps, but—"

"And what of me? I've spent my life studying the affairs of our great nation. When Albert named me Prime Minister it was so I could relieve Your Highness of some of your many responsibilities."

"You've done an exemplary job."

"It is my most profound wish that you think so, Your Highness."

"It still doesn't change the fact that I am the Queen. I feel I've been lax in fulfilling my duties to our country."

"I appreciate your concerns." The cardinal took another sip of wine. "But surely you can see that with your health as it is, you would be doing your subjects no favor if you were to overtax yourself."

"But my health is fine," Cassandra argued, only to have Cardinal Sinzen lay his hand on hers and shake his head till his jowls quivered.

"If everyone doesn't stop insisting I'm unwell, I shall start to think it myself" Cassandra murmured to herself as she examined her face in the cheval mirror. She returned to her private chambers as soon as she could extricate herself from the festivities. The Grand Duke with his penchant for whist had challenged several people to a game.

Maximilian Hawke was not among them.

Actually Cassandra hadn't seen him since the musicale ended. She supposed he stayed for the supper. His friend Kanakareh had. Cassandra had spotted the Seneca Indian, which was not particularly difficult to do, at a table across the room, his head bent toward Sophia as she prattled on about something.

Nervously Cassandra tucked a golden curl behind her ear. She'd removed her wig and the ball gown of gold-embroidered silk, opting instead to wear a simpler gown of blue satin with a stomacher of lace.

She took a deep breath and let her hands drop to her sides when she found herself patting down another errant curl. It didn't matter how she appeared to him. Only that she saw to it that he left Breslovia.

She picked up a candle and slipped behind the tapestry. The tunnel seemed to go on forever, and Cassandra found her knees growing weaker as she neared the rumble of the falls. With practiced ease she inched her way along the ledge, careful not to step into the cascading water.

When she emerged from behind the wall of water Cassandra glanced around. But the mist was rising off the moon-reflecting pool and she could see very little. After taking several steps forward she just stood, wondering what to do. It was not often that she was made to wait. Then from behind her she heard a voice . . . his voice.

"So that's how you seemed to appear from nowhere." She could hear his footsteps coming closer. "As lovely as you are now, I must admit I prefer to see you come through the water."

Four

Cassandra could feel the whisper of his breath on the back of her neck above the lace of her shift. It sent tingles racing down her spine. She swallowed but said nothing. Afraid to turn with him so close. Pride demanding that she not move away.

"If I followed the tunnel through the rocks where would I come out? Her Highness' private rooms?"

"Actually, I imagine you would find yourself in the deepest bowels of the palace. The dungeon."

Was it simply her imagination or did her words have him backing away? At any rate she felt more comfortable . . . more in control. Slowly she moved till she could see him. The light from the candle she held seemed smothered by the mist. And the moon, though nearly full in the clear sky, couldn't penetrate the bower of leaves overhead. He was in shadow yet her memory proved as accurate as her eyes.

"Is that what you plan for me, Your Highness, banishment to the dungeon?" Max tried to keep his tone light, but he couldn't help imagining the worst . . . dark, dank, clammy walls and rats.

"Of course not." Cassandra wondered if her response had come quick because the thought had crossed her mind. In a fit of wishful thinking it may have occurred to her to bury him so she wouldn't be reminded of her moment of weakness. Of course she'd never seriously considered it, though he had no way to know that.

His stance was wary.

"Then I can assume Imperial Guards aren't hiding in the underbrush to pounce and drag me away."

Cassandra laughed. She couldn't help herself. The scene had played in her imagination. Sobering quickly she shook her head. "That isn't why I asked you to meet me here."

"I see." He sighed, then turned and strode toward the pool. He stared into its depths a moment, the mist so heavy near the ground that his boots seemed to disappear. Cassandra watched as he squared his shoulders, then faced her. "It wouldn't work. Oh, don't misjudge me. I wish it could." His tone grew low with longing. "God, how I wish it could. But I've had the harsh tutor of experience to show me it wouldn't. We'd both end up being sorry. With perhaps me the sorrier."

"What *are* you talking about?" Cassandra had listened carefully, but she hadn't a clue of his meaning. It reminded her of instances when she paid close attention to Sophia.

"You are the Queen," Max explained. "When we ended our liaison, you would still be the Queen, and even if your husband didn't find out, my position would be much weaker than yours."

"You think I wanted to—"

"I realize now you might not wish to contemplate the end of our affair, however, passion does dull with time and as I said—"

"You have had experience with this."

"Exactly."

"With another queen?"

"What?"

"Your experience?" Cassandra placed the candle on an outcrop of stone and moved toward a feathering of willow branches. He thought she'd brought him here to continue their tryst of the other night. And he was turning her down, regretfully, but declining just the same.

Cassandra knew she should be insulted, or at least annoyed. But the truth was, she was enjoying herself. *And* it had occurred to her to suggest they continue their meetings. Only briefly. And certainly not seriously. Yet the desire was certainly there. She wondered how deeply the desire ran in him. If his mind could be changed . . . by her. Her fingers trailed along the slender leaves. "Have you had other queens as lovers?" She repeated the question so there could be no mistaking her meaning.

"Nay."

"Then you couldn't know what a queen might do when she . . . when she tired of you." Cassandra worked at keeping the amusement from her voice. Her brother had accused her of being a terrible tease. She'd almost forgotten how to do it since his death.

Maximilian Hawke didn't seem to know how to respond. He folded his arms and though his face was in shadow Cassandra imagined he narrowed those blue eyes.

"I've suffered the consequences of an earl's wrath," he finally said. "I've no desire to trod further."

"Only an earl's. What of his countess, did not you feel the sting of her anger?"

"She hadn't tired of me, Your Highness."

This was said in such a low, silky tone, Cassandra wondered who was teasing whom. She swallowed, realizing how foolish she was to play with someone like him. It mattered not what she'd said to her brother; his revenge was never severe. She didn't know what to expect with General Hawke.

"I see, well . . ." Cassandra stiffened her back, remembering that she was the Queen of Breslovia and this man was . . . She didn't really know who this man was. Nor did she care. "As it happens we won't need to worry about any consequences. For we are in complete agreement." When he said nothing, she continued. "I summoned you this evening to suggest that you leave Breslovia."

The silence, like the mist, seemed to drift around them, its fingers creeping up to enclose them.

"Did you hear what I said?" Cassandra disliked being the first to speak.

"I heard."

"Then you will respect my wishes?"

Again that unnerving silence. "I've been offered a position by the Grand Duke." He paused. "And I've accepted."

He said it with such finality that Cassandra could only stare. "But surely you can understand how awkward, how—"

"Only if we make it so. We both agree that what happened will not be repeated."

"Of course," Cassandra answered quickly.

"Breslovia is not a small country."

"It is hardly large."

"True. However, I believe there is room for both of us. I mean without our being constantly upon one another." Max winced. Bad choice of words.

"That was hardly the case this evening."

Max stepped forward. He couldn't believe he was trying to talk her out of banishing him from Breslovia. If he'd had anywhere else to go he'd have accepted her decree with good nature, and considered the night in her arms worth any punishment. But he wanted to stay. He wanted to command the army and build it, prove what he could do given the opportunity.

"Tonight was . . . an unusual circumstance. I will see that it doesn't happen again. You have my word as a gentleman." Thinking that might not be enough to convince her, he added hastily, "And as an officer in Your Highness' service."

She didn't know what to do. It seemed cruel to punish him when so much of what happened was her fault. He hadn't even realized who she was, she was certain of that. She was the one who should have known better.

"I suppose it could be done." She hurried on. "You must forget this place exists. You must forget everything."

" 'Tis forgotten."

"You could have hesitated a moment to assuage my womanly pride," Cassandra teased, then shook her head. "No. It seems my words offer something else to be forgotten."

He stood there and she felt flustered and foolish. Why could she not simply accept that he was as sorry about what had happened as she? Whatever was done was done. Certainly there was no need for anyone else to know.

"I think you should leave now."

"Your Highness is right." Max hesitated. He should leave—and immediately—before she changed her mind. All and all, things had worked out very well for him. Queen Cassandra seemed a decent sort, fair and not prone to revenge as some women he'd known. He could not ask for more than that their indiscretion of a few nights ago be forgotten by them both.

Then why did he remain? Why did he find himself admiring the way the trickling moonlight caressed her fair skin? And for God's sake why did he have the urge to do the same?

Max retreated a step, his boot sinking into the soft ferns surrounding the pool. He'd lain in those ferns with her, kissing her and touching her . . . loving her. And by damn he wished he could do it again.

Kanakareh was right. He was mad. Perhaps the Seneca never said those exact words, but there were times Max knew he thought it.

Cassandra didn't think she could bear this another moment. The mist, the slivers of moonlight, it was all too reminiscent of the night she'd just sworn to forget. Forgetting queenly pride and protocol she whirled about to leave. She knew he still watched her, and the knowledge made her hand shake as she reached for the candle.

The flame flickered, sending wavery ribbons of light dancing before her eyes.

That was all it took.

God, what was wrong with him? Max mentally shook himself as he turned to leave. He would have to forget this foolishness, as he'd just sworn to do, and remember why he'd come to Breslovia. He would have to—

Max twisted back around when he heard her small cry. The candle fell to the ground, the damp vegetation snuffing out the flame. But though he could make out little more than her form in the eerie darkness he could tell something was wrong.

"Your Highness?" Max took a step toward her, then another. It was as if she no longer knew he was there.

Her arms were wrapped about her waist and she swayed, her skirts sending the mist off in feathery wisps. As if she tried to comfort herself. But her actions offered none. Her cries were more plaintive now, pleading to an unseen being to stop the torment.

Max moved closer, then stopped. She was obviously in mental agony, her face a contortion of distress as she cried for the killing to stop.

But it was just as obvious that there was no killing. Max glanced about, surveying the area for any sign that her garbled admonitions were founded. There were none. The waterfall still splashed into the pristine pool, no sign of the blood she saw.

Was the Queen mad?

Cold fingers of dread slid over Max's skin. And he nearly turned away . . . ran away. She didn't know he was there. He could escape and set about forgetting this as well as the other. No one would know.

To his discomfort, the urge to flee was strong, nigh too strong to fight. Then he noticed the tears. Her face was wet with them. They shone like tiny prisms of light.

Rushing forward Max took her quivering body in his arms. She fought him at first, screaming that he was the one causing the deaths and destruction.

"No, no, let me go," she pleaded. "I must save them. I must save them from you and the soldiers."

"Your Highness . . . Cassie, hush. No, sweetness, let me hold you." His arms tightened and her strength ebbed. "You're safe now. I won't let them harm you."

She glanced up at him, her eyes large. But Max didn't think it was him she saw. "You don't understand," she whimpered. "They are killing them. Shooting them, their horses pounding their bodies into the dirt." She sobbed. "Please, we must stop them."

"We will." Max's hand cupped her head, drawing it toward his shoulder. "Don't worry, Cassie, we will."

She seemed to relax a bit then, as if his words somehow relieved her mind. Her body still shuddered now and then, recoiling against whatever private hell she experienced.

But she allowed herself to be held. And she rested her head on his shoulder.

Max could feel her heartbeat vibrate through his body. She reminded him of a frightened bird, and his arms tightened again. His words made little sense, conveying soothing sounds rather than any rational thoughts. Max imagined they were what someone would say to a frightened child, though he had no experience with such.

But then he'd had little experience calming hysterical women either. He was usually gone by the time they needed that service.

She'd gone perfectly still and Max wasn't certain how long she'd been that way. With his fingers tangled in her golden hair he glanced down. She was looking up at him, her eyes bright with tears, but no longer glazed with the horror only she could see.

If ever there was a moment to let her go this was it. Her body was pressed to his, nearly cocooned by his. Holding her had made sense moments ago when she was tormented by fear. Now he did it only because he couldn't bring himself to let her go.

Her lips parted, to question, to chastise, Max wasn't certain. But then he was certain of nothing but the overwhelming desire to taste her again.

God, he must be as crazed as she.

She was the Queen of Breslovia, and she'd admonished him not thirty minutes hence to stay away from her or face banishment. He didn't want banishment. He wanted to stay and take the position offered him by the Grand Duke. The only position likely to come his way.

All of this rushed through his mind, and just as quickly fled as Max lowered his head. His lips grazed hers and he heard her tiny gasp. She shuddered, but not from fear.

And then he was kissing her. Thoroughly and deeply as he had before. And her arms were wound about his neck, her fingers digging into his silk jacket.

He tasted the salt of her tears, the remnants of her fear, but there was more. Heat and passion. The overwhelming, all-consuming passion of before. It flowed between them, surrounded them like the waters of the pool. Max felt as if he were drowning in her.

The kiss deepened. His tongue plunged, and Cassandra forgot to breathe. She felt swept away and dazed, and so very alive. In the back of her mind she knew the vision had come again, stronger this time than ever, but the touch of his mouth on hers wiped away the pain. Made her forget the killing, the senseless death and destruction. She wanted to drop to the ground with him, touch him everywhere, lose herself in the heat and strength of his body.

But it was that white hot oblivion that she couldn't have. Not again.

"Please, no."

Max fought against the sound of her voice. The hands that pushed against his chest. She turned her head, but his mouth seared a path along the curve of her cheek. Only when he tasted the salt from another tear did he drag himself through the sensual fog enough to tear his mouth away.

Their breathing was hard and raspy. And they stared at each other in disbelief.

How could she have done this after demanding he leave her alone?

How could he jeopardize his position, damn it, his life?

"I should explain," Cassandra began.

"There's no need." Max loosened his hold and she slipped away. He was pleased that her legs seemed shaky.

"Perhaps you're right." What could she say anyway? That she was haunted by visions of death and destruction? That she feared they would drive her mad? No, it was better to say nothing. To hope he would respect her privacy enough to add this to the list of secrets he knew about her.

Cassandra thought to offer him money. An incentive to forget. But as she stared into his eyes she decided against the gesture. A rogue he may be, but she thought he had honor. At least she hoped he did.

"Just a bit lower. Ah, yes, that's perfect." The Grand Duke of Breslovia lay sprawled naked on his bed, the coverlet tangled at his feet, and watched his mistress through hooded eyes. She was all glorious curves and lush mounds, and the sight of her alone was enough to reduce him to a quivery mass.

"Is this what you like, Your Highness?" She glanced up, her amber eyes wide, her tongue, that marvelous tool she used to such perfection, peeking through the slit between her full, red lips.

"Oh, God, yes." Albert could barely catch his breath as she sank, her long silvery hair caressing his stomach and thighs, and worked her magic. "Harder. Faster." Arms flopped to the side, his head rolling from side to side, he screamed out his release.

"That was good for you, yes?" Nicolette slid her body up his till she lay atop him, her breasts heavy on his chest.

"Lord, you know it was." His eyes opened slowly. "You drive me mad."

"I only wish to please you." Her fingernail skimmed across his nubbed nipple, and she smiled slyly as his body trembled. But her eyes narrowed when his next breath rumbled out as a snore. Sleep wasn't what she had in mind for him now.

Nicolette's hand drifted lower, between their bodies. When her fingers fastened about his flaccid sex he mumbled in protest, but she didn't even hesitate. Experience had taught her ways to keep a man hard and panting for more. And awake.

The Duke's eyes slitted open and the snores stopped.

"I can't again. I'm too tired," he complained . . . until she skimmed across the smooth-skinned tip. He sprang to life in her hand.

He fisted his hands in her hair, dragging her mouth down to wetly mate with his. It was long minutes before she was able to separate, but there was no hint that she'd found his kisses less than all consuming.

"But I thought you were tired, my prince," Nicolette purred while he lathed first one, then the other of her pendulous breasts.

"Never too tired," he lied, though at the moment with her fingers feathering between his legs he thought it the truth.

"You are like a mighty stag," she breathed. "Nearly more than I can handle. So strong." She paused, using her tongue to follow the curve of his ear. "So brave. So powerful."

His hands were on her shoulders pushing her down his body, but Nicolette wasn't ready to allow him release quite yet. She wanted him to stay suspended in the sensual haze she wove a while longer. There were things that needed to be said. Erotica was not her only skill.

Gracefully, aware that her every move must be calculated to keep him entranced, Nicolette slid off the Grand Duke. He moaned his displeasure, but the slip of her thigh up his quieted him.

"Oh, Albert, you make it so I can barely think."

"It isn't the time for thinking." The Grand Duke started to roll on top of his mistress. He preferred the French way of making love, but found her body alluring enough to bury himself in her.

Nicolette turned, adeptly thwarting her lover's attempt to mount her. She sat, glancing at him over her shoulder. The look she gave his straining manhood made her sigh, and she reached back to fondle him.

"I shall miss you so." She squeezed her fingers, letting him know what part of him she would miss the most.

"Miss me?" The Grand Duke could barely talk when she

traced the length of him and then twisted her head around to kiss him on the stomach. Her warm breath wafted across his manhood.

"*Oui.* I must return to Paris soon."

"But why?"

The sweep of Nicolette's hair covered the smile his whiny voice elicited. "I can not stay here forever." Her tongue snaked out and he moaned.

"Of course you can." Damn it! She was the first woman who'd really pleased him. Who really cared for him. And she drove him to distraction with her body. He leaned up so he could see her and not the reflection in the mirrors overhead. "I'm the Grand Duke and I demand you remain in Breslovia."

"Oh, Your Highness." She turned large tear-filled eyes on him. "If only it were that simple. But there are those who hate me, and I am but a poor, simple woman." Nicolette arched her back till her breasts caught his attention. Reaching down she clamped on his wrist, bringing his hand up to cover her heart. Swaying toward him when his fingers splayed to caress her nipple.

"Who is it that causes you such discomfort? I shall have their heads."

"What a masterful man you are." Nicolette took him into her mouth, careful to withdraw before he emptied his seed. "And I adore you." She licked her lips and smiled. "But those who would consort against me are too powerful."

"No one is too powerful for me." Albert arched his back, hoping she'd notice how hard his manhood had grown. Not wanting to beg. "Tell me who it is."

"I think you know."

A sinking feeling settled over the Grand Duke and he reached down to touch himself. "My brother."

"He's written letters to Count Duplay, insisting that I return to France, saying that my presence is no longer wanted in Breslovia."

"He what?" Albert pushed off the bed, and marched about

the room unabashed by his nudity. "He won't get away with this. Damn the man. I knew he was jealous of me, but I never thought he'd do this. He knows how happy you make me."

Nicolette left her perch on the side of the bed and hurried to where the Grand Duke now stood, hands on hips, in the center of the palatial room. "Do you mean it, Albert?" She dropped to her knees in front of him, grasping the backs of his thighs. "Do I make you happy? For I could ask no more from life."

"Oh, God, yes." Albert thought his knees might crumble as she worked her wiles on him.

Nicolette suckled, and licked, taking him almost, but not quite over the edge. Then, when he least expected, she let him slip from her mouth and sat back on her heels. "The Queen wants me gone too. Oh, Albert, who can blame her for wanting you for herself, but must it be at my expense?" Her hands flowed around to cup him. "She and your brother will stop at nothing." She rested her head against him. "Nothing."

He didn't know what to do. Albert's mind tried to fix on something—anything. But the sexual fog was hard to penetrate. His brother was a self-important bastard. He'd known that for a long time. But the cardinal had arranged Albert's marriage to Cassandra. He had made Albert the Grand Duke. Still, what good was all this power if he couldn't have the one thing he really wanted?

Albert's fingers tangled in his mistress's silver hair. She was perfect, golden eyes and hair so pale that she didn't need powder to look exquisite. And she adored him.

"I shall do something, do not worry."

Nicolette's mouth skimmed across his sex. "But what, my most powerful man?"

"Something. I'll do something." His fingers tightened. "Take me in your mouth. Now." He would beg if he must.

And she complied as he knew she would. Which made the discreet knock at the bedroom door all the more annoying. Albert tried to ignore the sound, but it continued. Incessant.

Nicolette looked up at him, and he knew he had to answer it.

"What is it?" he growled, and his Lord of the Bedchamber, a short, stoop-shouldered noble who'd seen more shocking things than the Grand Duke standing nude, his mistress on her knees in front of him, opened the door a crack and stuck his head inside.

"I'm sorry to bother you, Your Highness."

"You damn well better be."

"It's just that *she's* insisting upon seeing you and I can't make her go away."

"She?" Albert didn't miss the scathing look his mistress shot him. For God's sake did Nicolette think he needed anyone else when he had her?

"Yes, Your Highness. I assured her you were asleep, but she ordered me to awaken you. Ordered me, sir. What else could I do?"

"Who is it?" Albert asked, though he knew. There was only one woman capable of ordering Lord Gerhard.

"The Queen, Your Highness. Her Majesty demands to see you."

Albert couldn't help thinking what would happen if Cassandra pushed through the door this moment. What a sight would await her eyes. He even let out a small giggle, then tried to cover it by clearing his throat.

"Very well. Tell her I shall be there directly."

"She asked that you hurry."

"Directly, Gerhard."

"Yes, Your Highness," the little man said as he bowed out of the doorway.

Albert took a deep breath. "I wonder what she wants at this time of night?"

"It is probably best if you go find out." Nicolette stood, moving seductively away from the Grand Duke.

"Now?" His head was reeling. His manhood was throbbing. "Come back."

Nicolette trailed her hands up over her hips and breasts. "I can't. Not with your wife in the next room." She reveled in his forlorn expression. Let him blame his unfulfilled erection on his wife. That could only further her goals.

Five

The room was large even by palace standards, lined with mirrors; and Cassandra realized she'd never been there before, though the Grand Duke's quarters were in the new palace. Construction, started by her father, had stopped when he'd died. After she'd married Albert he had begun to oversee the expansion.

Sophia told her Albert had modified the original plans, making the palace larger and more elaborate than her father planned. There were now two state ballrooms, over one hundred guest apartments, a theater that seated four hundred, and a chapel that rivaled Saint Peter's.

"I've heard His Highness has architects studying the palace of Louis at Versailles. 'Tis said it's lovely but truly decadent," Sophia had said, and Cassandra had merely shaken her head and made some inane comment about his being her husband.

So far Cassandra's apartments were in the ancestral castle, a centuries-old structure of stone with towers and walls that had withstood enemy mortars and siege before peace came to the land. Most of the castle had crumbled away over the years, but one section was preserved, as a reminder of the past, a link.

Originally, the new and old were to blend, a marriage of tradition and the future. Her father had planned the castle tower as a living museum where the ancient tapestries could be displayed. It was never thought that Cassandra would live there once the new palace was complete.

Plans for her to move to her new apartments were ongoing.

But as yet she'd resisted. At first she blamed her reluctance on the savage death of her father and brother, telling herself that in her grief she needed the sameness of her surroundings as her world fell apart. After her marriage to Albert . . . Well, she had put off the move again.

Now Cassandra didn't know what strange hold her tower rooms had over her. She only knew she couldn't leave them.

She rose from the gilded chair and began pacing the carpet. She needed to concentrate on what she planned to say to Albert when he joined her . . . if he joined her.

Glancing toward the mirror-paneled door the Lord of the Bedchamber had disappeared through, Cassandra sighed. How long did it take her husband to rouse himself enough to see her?

As if her thoughts were read, the door opened and an unkempt and obviously annoyed Albert pushed through. He glared at her through slitted eyes, then snarled at his valet who was trying to tie the belt of the fur-lined dressing gown the Grand Duke wore.

"You had best have a good reason for interrupting my . . . slumber," Albert said as he waved a hand, dismissing the servant. His brother constantly nagged at him to watch his tone when speaking to the Queen, and Albert could tell by the flash of anger in her eyes that she took offense. But tonight he didn't care.

She wished she hadn't come, wondered now why she had ever thought she should. But it was too late to turn back. Straightening her shoulders, Cassandra stepped toward her husband. "I do apologize for disturbing your sleep. You are rumored to play whist till late into the night so I didn't think you'd have already retired."

"I chose not to play . . . at cards . . . tonight."

"Yes, well, I am sorry; however, there is a matter of great concern to me—"

"That could not wait 'til the morrow?" Sinzen was wrong.

It wasn't necessary to be charming to his wife. He could be any way he chose to her.

Cassandra tried to tamp down the anger his impertinence caused. For some time she'd known there were no warm feelings between Albert and herself. Nothing like the memories she had of the way her father and mother felt about each other. But she hadn't married Albert for love. She had married him for the sake of the kingdom. For Breslovia.

They had that in common. And they had always treated one another with respect if not affection.

Until now.

Cassandra faced her husband. "I have reason to believe Breslovia may become involved in a war," she said and watched as the color drained from his cheeks. "Are you all right? Should I ring for your valet?" Cassandra rushed forward, taking her husband's arm and guiding him toward a settee upholstered in a rich golden material. She should never have told him like that; wouldn't have if not for his annoyed tone.

"No, really. I'm quite all right." Albert sipped the wine Cassandra handed him, then coughed.

"Forgive me. I should have realized how upsetting the news was. I know how much you love Breslovia." That had been the resounding theme of their abbreviated courtship. His love for Breslovia. His family's, the Marinettes', long service to the kingdom.

"Yes, yes, of course I do." Albert tugged at his dressing gown, trying to pull himself together. "War, you say?"

"Yes."

"Where do you come by this information?"

Cassandra opened her mouth to tell him, then clamped it shut again. She'd come here to tell him . . . to tell him everything. Tonight's vision, stronger and more vivid than any before had convinced her that something must be done. And Albert was the Grand Duke of Breslovia, her consort. Her partner in ruling the kingdom.

But she couldn't bring herself to tell him of the visions.

For one thing he would scoff and belittle her for believing in such ancient practices. He hadn't been raised with Simon as a tutor and friend as she had. Hadn't learned to trust in the seers. Cassandra closed her eyes, wishing Simon would return, wishing she had his wisdom to guide her.

But the old man had disappeared when her father and brother were killed. Some even implied Simon had had a hand in their murders. But Cassandra knew better.

"Well, are you going to tell me?" Albert had recovered some of his color and now sat facing her, his expression hard.

"No." Cassandra ignored the widening of his eyes and rushed on. "I can't tell you how I know right now. But I do. And we must do something to stop it." She knelt, grabbing his hands. "You can't imagine what terrible destruction there will be if we don't."

"Who will wage war on us?"

Cassandra's gaze lowered. "I don't know."

Slipping his hands from hers, Albert got to his feet. "You don't know?" Impertinence was back in his tone. "You come in here, interrupting my pleasures, with some wild tale of war with some unknown enemy. And you refuse to even divulge how you know. Surely you understand that I can do nothing unless you tell me where you received your information."

"Actually, I don't understand. Rather than worry about that, we should do everything in our power to make certain Breslovia remains neutral. We should send envoys to the French, the Prussians, the English, making sure that our ancient treaties are still respected."

"And if they aren't? What do you propose we do then?" Albert lifted a jeweled letter opener from his desk and pressed the tip against his thumb.

"I don't know, Albert."

"Perhaps it would be in our interest to expand our army. Arm more of our citizens." He shrugged. "Purely as a defensive measure."

"I'd rather not do that unless . . . well, unless we've no other choice."

"Yes, yes, of course. I understand the problem." He twirled the handle through his fingers. "I shall take care of everything. Do not concern yourself with it again."

"Do not concern myself?" The skirts of her gown swayed as she moved toward him. "How can I not when I fear for my kingdom."

"But you have told *me.* It is naught for you to fret about. *I* am the Grand Duke."

"Yes." Cassandra's voice was low. "You are. However I am the Queen, and ultimately the fate of Breslovia rests with me. I can not merely forget this as if it were a bit of court gossip."

"No, no." Albert set the letter opener down and rounded on his wife. His hands cupped her shoulders. "Of course you cannot. But I fear what may happen if you dwell on this. Your health has not been what it should be of late."

Arguing with him that she wasn't ill seemed useless. Everyone acted as if she were made of blown glass . . . everyone except Maximilian Hawke. Cassandra shoved that thought from her mind.

She was sorry now that she'd come to Albert. She'd hoped for his help and cooperation, instead she received platitudes and references to her health. There was but one way to convince herself that all was well with Breslovia.

They were both uncomfortable with his hands on her shoulders. Cassandra was sure of that. She managed to turn away, not surprised when he allowed it.

"It is late. I hadn't realized." She started toward the door. "Perhaps we can discuss this at some later date."

"Do not worry, Cassandra. I shall take care of everything."

She simply nodded as she stepped into the marble hallway.

"She knows."

Albert pushed past the man at the door of his brother's bedroom. Cardinal Sinzen lay propped on pillows, his bloated form uncorseted and sprawling, his head bald and shiny. He glanced up, waving away the servant then calling him back with the chocolate.

When they were alone, Sinzen took a swig of the rich creamy liquid before fixing his stare on his brother. "I assume whatever it is you're babbling about is important enough to interrupt my morning rituals."

The similarity between his brother's response and his own the previous night was lost on Albert.

"I told you, she knows."

"Knows what? And who is it we are discussing?"

Belatedly Albert glanced toward the door to assure himself they were alone before he said too much. "Cassandra knows about the invasion."

A few drops of chocolate spilled on the pristine white coverlet.

"How do you come by this knowledge?"

"She told me. I don't know who her informant is, but she tells me Breslovia will soon be at war, and that we must do something to prevent it. And yes, before you ask, I did try to get her to tell me how she knows, but she refused."

"Refused her own husband?"

"She let me know that though I might be the Grand Duke, she is the Queen. What did she say? Something about the ultimate welfare of Breslovia being in her hands."

"Which is what I've been telling you all along." Sinzen dabbed at the stain with a lace-trimmed handkerchief. "She was in your rooms last night. Might I hope you performed your husbandly duties?"

"Damn it, Sinzen, she was there blubbering on about war. What was I to do? Besides, how do you know where she was?"

"I have my ways, as I'm sure you know. And I would think when she was 'blubbering away' would be an excellent time to console her."

"You don't know Cassandra."

"No, and you barely do either, much to my chagrin. But I do know that whatever she thinks she knows is too much. She needs to get with child. To focus her energies on producing an heir. After she accomplishes her task for this life"—he paused to sip his chocolate—"then it will matter naught what she knows. She will be expendable."

Albert considered telling his brother that his wife was expendable now. That through Nicolette he'd learned France was willing to support his claim as king in exchange for him declaring war on Prussia. But he decided against it. Let Sinzen believe his younger brother did naught but follow orders. Soon enough the cardinal would realize Albert had his own agenda.

He was a fool, a damn fool.

Max leaned his shoulder against the trunk of a stately chestnut and twirled a grass stem between his fingers. The sun was barely up, the dew still heavy on the forest floor. Birds sang in the leaves overhead, industriously doing whatever in the hell birds did.

While he lounged about.

As if he wasn't supposed to be leaving this morning for a fortnight tour of Breslovia. He'd been charged with reviewing the local militias, and soliciting support from each company's captain for the expansion of the military. Actually the plan was his idea. His Royal Highness, the Grand Duke Albert, whom Max was beginning to think a royal pain in the ass, advocated ignoring the militia captains.

"Let them go back to tilling the fields, or whatever it is they do with their useless lives. We don't need them," he'd said in one of his few contributions to military strategy.

Max had simply glanced from the Grand Duke to his brother, who'd pursed his lips and nodded. "Actually I believe the idea is a good one. It never hurts to have the support of the military, does it, General Hawke?"

"General Hawke." Max said the words under his breath,

deciding he liked the sound of it. He was the commander in chief, in charge of building up Breslovia's military. In charge of the whole damn show.

He briefly wondered what his father would think of that.

"Probably wonder why I'm standing here under a tree when I've a job to do," Max mumbled. "And talking to myself to boot."

He tossed aside the mangled blade of grass in disgust. He was a fool. He'd always been a fool, and damn it he'd always be one if he didn't mount his horse and get the hell away from here.

But he didn't move. Not until he heard hoofbeats coming his way. And then it wasn't to mount and ride away, but to step into the path of the Queen's horse.

She rode every morning, good weather or bad, he'd been told, through the forest adjoining the palace . . . unattended.

Which showed her to be as big a fool as he.

Cassandra saw him as soon as he stepped from the copse of trees. Even though she recognized him immediately, or perhaps because she did, Cassandra's hand slipped beneath the folds of her riding habit.

Galloping by was an option. He wasn't blocking her way. But as she watched him standing, statue-still, the only movement as she approached the play of the breeze in his raven hair, she seemed to have no choice but to pull back on the reins.

He moved then, striding toward her, the sandy soil crunching beneath his high boots, and gave a quick bow before reaching up to pat her mount's neck.

"Your Highness truly should be more careful. These woods could be teeming with outlaws eager to take you hostage."

"You're the only brigand I've ever encountered here, General Hawke." Balough, her favorite mount, usually high spirited and feisty was acting entirely too enthralled by the petting she was receiving at the hand of Maximilian Hawke. That thought led to memories of what those hands had done to Cassandra herself. Uncomfortable and unwanted memories. She shifted in the saddle.

"If you would be so kind as to move, I shall be on my way."

"First, I must beg a moment of Your Majesty's time."

"I'm quite busy today. However, if you will give your name to one of my ministers, no doubt I can give you an interview on the morrow."

" 'Tis about last night."

"I see." She should have known he would not let it be. Her mind raced over what he might want. Blackmail was always a possibility. How much would she pay him to not tell the Grand Duke of her indiscretion? Or would he demand something other than gold? Though he'd seemed eager to end their liaison, perhaps he'd had a change of heart. Perhaps he wanted—

"I beg your pardon?" Cassandra's eyes opened wider.

"I said, at first I thought you mad."

That's what she'd thought she heard. "Well, I assure you I am not." At least not yet.

He shrugged. His long fingers continued to rub Balough. "Surely you can understand why I might think that. One moment you were perfectly fine, the next . . ."

"I'm not mad," Cassandra repeated softly. Though to herself she admitted there were times she wondered.

"I know that." Max couldn't help grinning when she glanced down at him. Her expression was one of relief. "At least I don't think you are. Your eyes, the way they were last night." Max paused. "I've seen it before."

"You have?"

"Aye." The mare took several restless steps, and Max extended his hand toward the Queen. "Wouldn't you be more comfortable standing?"

More comfortable and more easily seduced . . . or more willing to seduce. Cassandra shook her head. "I shall remain mounted."

"As Your Highness wishes. But do you suppose you could

aim that pistol somewhere other than my head. I'm not going to hurt you, you know."

"Oh." She'd nearly forgotten that her palm was clamped around the carved ivory butt of a gun. Her insurance that no harm would come to her while riding. It was a gift from her brother. But she'd never fired it, and wondered if she could ever bring herself to. She slipped the pistol back into its side holster.

"You really should be more careful. If I'd had the mind to I could have disarmed you any of a dozen times."

"Not before I shot you through the heart. I may appear a simple woman, General Hawke, but I assure you I can shoot," she lied. "My father and brother taught me well."

"That's good to know. And let *me* assure Your Highness, I never considered you a simple woman."

"Yes, well . . ." He'd flustered her. There was no other explanation for the way her speech faltered. The way her heart pounded and her stomach fluttered. Of course the intensity of their short acquaintance might be to blame. But Cassandra feared it was more than that. Just looking into his deep blue eyes made her knees weak. "I had best be going," she said, giving the reins a flick.

Again Balough responded to his command over hers.

"Don't you wish to hear where I've seen eyes as entranced as yours were last night?"

"You seem determined to tell me."

"Kanakareh."

"Who?"

"My Seneca friend. He accompanied me to the palace last night."

"Oh, yes, of course." How could she have forgotten? Sophia spoke of nothing else.

"It only happened once that I saw. We were in the mountains of New York, and Kanakareh went off by himself. To converse with the spirits, he told me."

"And did he?" Cassandra was interested despite herself.

"So he says." Max's expression sobered. "I couldn't see

anything, of course . . . except Kanakareh. Then I spotted a small hunting party of Huron and decided Kanakareh could commune some other time. When I found him he had the same haunted look in his eyes that you did last night."

"Ah, so now you think I've been conversing with spirits." Cassandra tried to keep her tone light. But she couldn't remember what had happened last night. Not until she'd found herself in this man's arms, clutching his shoulders.

"Visions, Your Highness. I believe you had a vision. And from what I could gather, not a very pleasant one."

Cassandra's eyes met his and held.

She had told only two people of the terrible spells that came over her. Sophia was sympathetic, but Cassandra wondered if she really understood. Cardinal Sinzen had acted as if she were cavorting with the devil. He'd scolded, and suggested penance. She knew better than to seek any more advice from her spiritual leader.

Her husband didn't even know, unless his brother had defied the sanctity of the confessional.

Yet here was this stranger, who was not really a stranger at all, and she was tempted to tell him. Would he laugh or belittle or merely offer some platitude?

"It wasn't the first time either, I'd wager."

Cassandra took a deep breath. "What makes you say that?"

"The way you . . ." Max lifted his hand in response to the mare's gentle nudging. "The way you seemed to accept what was happening. When it was over you appeared . . . calm. As if you knew you were free of it for a while."

"I'm never free." Cassandra swallowed and turned her head to stare into the forest. A squirrel leaped from one branch to another in a birch. "And I do not accept without a fight."

"Is that the closest to an admission I shall receive?"

Her head jerked around. The mare skittered to the side. "What do you want from me?"

An excellent question and one Max could not answer. Hadn't he been wondering the same thing before she'd arrived.

What in the hell was he doing here, interrogating her about some spell she might have had? No, he knew she had them. He'd witnessed one firsthand.

That still didn't explain his actions.

Certainly not well enough to satisfy anyone who might come along and find them thus. No, he'd be best served by bidding Queen Cassandra a fond but brief farewell and being on his way. To find Kanakareh and travel to Falstave and review the troops and do the things he'd come to Breslovia to do.

But he couldn't seem to look away or make his feet do what his mind knew they should. Her eyes were so lovely and so sad. And he knew the anguish she'd gone through last night while he'd held her.

"Would you believe me if I said I only wish to help you?"

His eyes were so clear. Cassandra wanted nothing more than to sink down into them . . . into him. But she must remember who she was—what she was.

"I would like to be able to trust you."

"Then do it. Tell me. This secret will go no further than the other I've vowed to forget."

That brought a smile to her face, however fleeting. "You're correct. It was a vision last night, and no, Lord help me, 'twas not my first."

"You are a seer, then?" Max reached up, and this time she accepted his help in sliding from the saddle.

"No." She turned on him quickly as she started along the path. "At least I never thought of myself as such. This is a fairly new occurrence and one I mightily wish would cease."

"What do you see?" Max whistled for his horse and, gathering the reins of both mounts, followed behind the Queen.

"Death and destruction," she said so quietly that Max could hardly hear. "Yes, that is the wonder I see. And I cannot seem to stop it."

"If I recall, Kanakareh fasted and chanted to summon the spirits."

"I do neither." Cassandra paused to strip a leaf from a birch bough hanging into the path. "Last night it was but a matter of glancing into the candle flame." She turned to face him. "I am not a heathen, General Hawke. Nor am I possessed by the devil."

"I was fairly certain you weren't." His expression was sober, but his eyes twinkled. "Possessed that is. As far as the heathen part goes . . ." Max shrugged. "I'm not sure Kanakareh's gods aren't as capable as ours."

Cassandra's eyes widened. "I hardly think you can compare the two."

Max grinned. "Ah, spoken like a true queen. You are Breslovia's defender of the faith, I presume."

In light of his teasing, Cassandra felt silly for her outburst. "No, actually that's Cardinal Sinzen's task."

"Good. I should think that would be a weighty job, being responsible for all those souls."

"You, sir, are hardly pious."

"You, Your Highness, are correct."

Her laughter shouldn't make him feel warm inside. But it did. It also made him want to take her in his arms and smother her sweet mouth with kisses. Which he was certainly not going to do.

Max squared his shoulders and started walking again, leading both horses in his wake. Her Majesty fell in beside him. "This death and destruction you see. Is it any more specific than that?"

"It is the invasion of Breslovia." Her eyes met his. "There are mounted troops and large guns, and my subjects falling. Trampled."

"Is that why you sent for me, because of a vision?"

"I don't know what you mean."

"Why you wish Breslovia's army expanded and better trained."

"But I do not wish such a thing . . . at least I did not order it done. Is that why you have come to Breslovia? To join the military?"

Her ignorance concerning him stung his pride. . . . Foolish though it may be, he could not help himself. Making his best bow he introduced himself. "I am General Maximilian Hawke, Commander of the Royal Army of Breslovia, at your service, Your Highness."

The pounding of hooves kept him from hearing her response . . . if indeed she had one. Queen Cassandra seemed struck dumb.

Max turned to see horsemen, at least a half dozen bearing down on them. The queen screamed and Max shoved her behind him. Though it was only a contingent from the Imperial Guard, Max imagined it must have seemed very much like her visions.

The head officer dismounted with a flourish of his plumed bat, bowing deeply as soon as his feet hit the ground. "I beg Your Majesty's pardon." His dark eyes strayed toward Max, then slid back to the Queen. "We were sent to find you."

Cassandra, recovering her composure, stepped forward. "As you can see I am not lost."

"Of course not, Your Highness. It is merely long past your usual time to return to the stables."

"I did not realize I had to be back at a certain time."

Max noticed the captain's cheeks color. The man's name was Paul Debard, if memory served him. And Max had thought him a pompous fool when he'd reviewed the Imperial Guard the previous day. But he took pity upon Debard now.

"Her Highness is grateful for your concern, but as you can see stronger security is needed. I was able to accost the Queen on the pathway with little trouble. We want no one else to try the same. From now on I want a guard to follow Her Highness on her morning ride." Max noticed Cassandra's jaw drop, and added, "at a discreet enough distance to allow her privacy, of course."

Six

There were times she almost forgot the horror of the visions . . . almost. Certainly Cassandra wished she could forget.

But she couldn't. They were too real to ignore. Besides, there was Maximilian Hawke. If he was telling the truth about why he was here, someone else feared a threat to Breslovia's borders. But who? And why?

Her husband had scoffed when she'd told him of her concerns, had acted as if she were a foolish woman. But even if he had believed her contention that the kingdom was at risk of war, that did not explain the presence of Hawke. Obviously Breslovia's newest general was already in the country when she'd spoken to Albert.

She'd confessed her visions to Cardinal Sinzen months ago, when they'd first begun. But he too had paid her no heed, except to lecture her and assign her penitence. "You must purge your heart of the heathen ways, my dear child," he'd said. "Pray, Your Highness. Spend day and night on your knees if necessary. You must fight the devil in you. Fight." He had grasped her hands in his, his knuckles white in the fleshy folds. The ruby ring on his finger twinkling blood red, he implored God to forgive her for her heretical ways.

No. Cardinal Sinzen put no credence in her visions.

Yet someone feared invasion enough to hire a mercenary to train Breslovia's army. And she planned to find out who and why.

However, any attempts she made to discover whether the

terrible images she saw in her head could possibly come true were thwarted. Gently to be sure, diplomatically, but thwarted just the same.

If she only knew what to do . . .

But she had never ruled Breslovia. Not really. Cassandra admitted that to herself now. She never learned how to govern. While her father and brother had lived, there had seemed no need. King Christian had been strong and vibrant, wise and benevolent, a sovereign dearly loved by his subjects. He'd trained his son to succeed him. Trained him well in the art of diplomacy and negotiation, educated him about the needs of Breslovia and her people. Her father had planned carefully, considered all . . . except the possibility that he and his son would be savagely murdered together.

And that his young daughter would come to the throne.

Cassandra tried not to think back to that time when she was but seventeen years of age. To that awful day when the church bells of Breslovia pealed the sad news of the king's death. Of Prince Peter's death.

The king is dead! Long live Queen Cassandra!

Cassandra could still feel the grief . . . the panic. She didn't know what to do then any more than she did now. Yet she had to do something.

Straightening her shoulders, she glanced toward one of the long mirrors gracing the hallway. She had dressed with extra care today. Her gown of emerald green silk sported a jeweled stomacher that matched the diamonds twined in the pompon on her head.

She looked every inch a queen. Now she had but to act like one. Taking a deep breath, she signaled the footman. With a sweep of his scarlet-liveried arm he pushed open the double doors leading into the council room.

"Her Royal Highness, Queen Cassandra," he announced, his voice booming in the large room with gilt trim. Then, stepping to the side with military precision, he allowed her to enter.

Three figures leaped to their feet. Three faces lifted toward her. But she only noted one. His eyes were bluer than she remembered, set in a face more handsome and strong of line. His bow was deep and masculine, without the affected mannerisms of so many of the courtiers.

"Your Highness." Cardinal Sinzen was the first to speak as he waddled forward to take her hand. "This is indeed a surprise."

She was sure it was. Not since the first uncertain days after her father's death, since before her marriage to the Grand Duke, had Cassandra entered the Council Room.

She met the cardinal's eyes. "A pleasant one I hope."

"But, of course. We are all"—his robed arm lifted to indicate those in the room—"honored by your presence. The cardinal breathed heavily. "How lovely you look. Are you on your way to some amusement? A picnic perhaps, or a visit with your ladies?"

"No, actually I have come to join your discussion." Leaving her advisor to puff after her, Cassandra walked farther into the room. The three men, her husband, Cardinal Sinzen, and Maximilian Hawke were seated around an ornately carved circular table when she entered.

She moved toward it now, letting her fingers drift across the maps and charts unrolled on the inlaid surface. One in particular caught her attention. Breslovia, she noticed. The duchies to the South. Prussia to the North. Beyond that, she realized with a sinking feeling, there was little she recognized. Steeling herself for what was to come, Cassandra turned to face the men. "Please, gentlemen, continue."

"Your Highness." Cardinal Sinzen shook his head and smiled. "There is no need for us to bore you. If it is entertainment you wish, we could—"

"What I wish is to be appraised of Mister Hawke's findings." She allowed herself to openly glance toward him now. He wore a dashing uniform of rich, deep blue with gold braid entwined on its sleeves and tight-fitting breeches of purest white.

"General Hawke, if it pleases Your Highness," Max said with a bow.

"Yes, General Hawke, of course." Cassandra thought she detected a touch of amused sarcasm in his voice, but she couldn't be sure, and she certainly had no time to dwell on it as he pulled out a chair for her.

The other two men seemed less eager to join Cassandra and the general at the table. But with a nod from his brother, Albert approached, speaking to his wife for the first time since she'd entered the room. "Though it hardly veils your beauty, my dear, you seem tired. Perhaps you should retire to your room."

"I assure you I am neither tired nor do I intend to leave. Now if you will be seated, I'm sure *General* Hawke will continue his discussion of Breslovia's defenses. That is what you were discussing when I entered, is it not?"

"It is."

"Then shall we continue?"

"It is excessively boring. It seems a pity to waste such a lovely day on—"

"Please continue General Hawke." Cassandra did not look toward Cardinal Sinzen as she interrupted him, but she knew his expression would register disapproval. And she knew later, when she went to him as her confessor, she would pay for her disrespect. But then she'd known before she'd come what his reaction would be.

And she'd come anyway.

Now she would do her best to listen and learn.

Though his father was a diplomat, a man who could sit for hours discussing, analyzing, negotiating, Max had never considered himself adept at any of those skills. He was a soldier, pure and simple, unable to read the subtleties of what was said—and left unsaid. But even Max knew all was not as it should be.

The cardinal was sweating as if he'd just completed a five mile march, and his small eyes continually flicked from face to face. If he caught his brother's bored eyes, Max didn't know. Just as he didn't know what he himself was to do.

The Queen had never been mentioned when he'd been offered his position, or when he'd been ordered to tour the country's militia. And by her own admission she hadn't even known why he'd been summoned to Breslovia. Yet she was certainly here now. From what he'd learned from Kanakareh, she was the ruling monarch of the land.

And she'd asked for his report.

His father might be able to satisfy both Cardinal Sinzen and the Queen. Max could not.

"I spent the last fortnight visiting the many towns and estates of Breslovia." He paused. "It is a lovely country," he said with a smile. Neither the smile nor the compliment seemed to have the slightest effect on her. So much for his attempt at diplomacy.

"How did you find the militia, General?"

"Deficient."

That got a bit of a rise from her. Those violet eyes snapped toward him.

"In what way?"

"They are poorly trained, understaffed and some of the soldiers carried muskets over forty years old."

"I see." Cassandra shifted slightly in her chair. "Then it is a blessing that my subjects need only use their weapons to shoot deer and rabbit."

"It is a blessing deer and rabbit don't shoot back."

Cassandra looked at him a moment in silence. "You are not from Breslovia, and can not be expected to know our ways."

"I have tried to learn since my arrival."

She wished he wouldn't look at her as he did. Cassandra could almost feel the heat from his stare. As if he remembered what she looked like without the trappings of her position. She tried to keep her voice steady. "That is commendable, General. Then I'm sure you've heard of the Edict of Liberstein."

"Aye."

"The treaty guarantees Breslovia's neutrality. We are not a warring nation, and have no need of a large standing army."

"I've studied a bit of history." Though Max was the first to admit he was no scholar, since his youth he had had an interest in armies and warfare. "And it seems treaties and the like are often no more than strips of paper shredded and trod upon by invading armies."

Blood drained from her face. "I can assure you this treaty is not like that. It has been honored for centuries, and will continue to be 'til there's not a breath left in my body."

It was coming again.

Her eye happened to catch the reflected light off the jeweled snuff box her husband snapped open and shut, and her vision blurred. Cassandra grasped the edge of the table, trying to swallow down her panic.

"Your report is very enlightening. However,"—Cassandra pushed to her feet—"it won't be necessary to increase Breslovia's army."

"Your Highness, are you all right?" Max was on his feet and around the table. But she jerked away as he reached for her arm.

"I am fine." Her eyes shot to his in panic. "I must go." Before anyone could say another word Cassandra rushed to the door. She had it open and was crossing the hall before anyone in the room spoke.

The Grand Duke, who'd abandoned his slouched posture when his wife stood, leaned his pink, silk-covered elbows on the table. "What was that about?"

Cardinal Sinzen's eyes narrowed. "I don't know." He snapped his sausagelike fingers at the footman who stood in the still-open doorway. "Send the court physician to the queen's apartments. Then have him report back to me."

When the door was shut again, the cardinal folded his hands and smiled benevolently. "Now, General Hawke, you may proceed with your report."

"I'm not certain I understand."

"Your report." The smile remained. "You were gone a fortnight, surely you have something to show for it."

Max glanced from one brother to the other. The Grand Duke had resumed his annoying habit of fooling with whatever was at hand. Now it was a ribbon on his sleeve. The cardinal, however, was completely focused on Max.

Sliding a parchment across the table, Max pointed to the column at the left. "I've listed the cities and towns and the number of men. A weapon is inscribed by each name."

Cardinal Sinzen's glance was cursory. "Yes, yes. I'm aware the militia is wholly antiquated and unacceptable. What I wish to know is what steps you plan to take to remedy that."

"Steps . . ." Max straightened. "If you'll forgive me Your Grace. I was under the impression Her Majesty ordered there be no change."

This was met by a snort from the Grand Duke, but the cardinal's expression remained the same. "The Queen is . . ." He shook his head. Light reflected off his round cheeks. "Her Majesty Queen Cassandra has not been herself since the unfortunate deaths of her father and brother. She . . . well, you do understood I hope."

"I do, Your Grace. However—"

"There is no 'however' about it. Your position is one I created . . . and thus can eliminate. You report to me." The Grand Duke hesitated before adding, "Or my brother. And you take orders from the same. Do you have any questions, or perhaps reservations?"

"No, Your Highness."

"Albert." The cardinal patted his brother's hand. "There is no need for animosity among us." His gaze shifted to Max. "Is there?"

"No. None." Max felt thoroughly put in his place. Apparently, though Cassandra occupied a figurehead position as queen, it was the Grand Duke and Cardinal Sinzen who ruled Breslovia. He depended upon them for his position. Which was fine with him. Except . . .

"The woman's daft anyway." The Grand Duke toyed with a silver button at his wrist. "How can anyone blame me for my feelings toward her?"

Max felt he should defend her. Hell, he had to shove his hands into the pockets of his jacket to keep from leaning across the table and grabbing the prissy ass by his lace-covered waistcoat. But it wasn't his place to do or say anything. He might not like it, but Max had learned from experience there were some things better left undone. Jumping to Queen Cassandra's defense was one of them.

The Prime Minister didn't say anything either, so her honor went undefended. Instead the cardinal leaned his heavy body toward Max.

"Now, tell me what you propose."

"I met with the cardinal and the Grand Duke, since you asked." Which of course, Kanakareh hadn't. Max sat across from the Seneca warrior, who merely shrugged his wide shoulders at the comment and continued to study the chessboard.

"We are to begin recruiting soldiers immediately, training them." Max watched Kanakareh's dark fingers slowly wrap around the black bishop and move it carefully deliberately to attack the white queen. Max's hand shot out, swiping her up, moving her to safety.

"Artillery has been ordered. . . . From France." Max leaned back, then ran both hands down and over his face. "I know the French have a way with munitions. Hell, they probably manufacture the best in the world. It doesn't really matter where the guns come from, as long as the men are armed. And damn," Max said as he again sat forward, "it isn't as if I'm still wearing the regimentals of the Horse Guards." He referred to the cavalry unit to which he had once belonged. "Why should I care if Breslovia buys munitions from England's enemy?"

"Check."

Max glanced down and scowled, then swiped up the white

knight interposing him between Kanakareh's queen and the black king.

"Queen Cassandra is against the entire concept. She ordered that the army not be enlarged. Cardinal Sinzen countermanded her order." Max watched his friend's dark features as he studied the small carved pieces. "You know it wouldn't hurt you to say something."

"Checkmate."

The grim set of Max's mouth deepened as he noted the untenable situation his king was in. With a growl he knocked the defeated monarch on its back. "One of these days you'll have to explain to me how you so regularly do that."

"It's hardly a secret. I pay attention to the game." Kanakareh began gathering the carved ivory pieces, wrapping each carefully in a bit of cotton before placing them in a leather bag. "Besides, your method wins its share."

"Method?" Max glanced across the table. "I have a method?" He'd learned to play chess when he was a boy. It was a game his father enjoyed.

"You strike quickly, hoping to catch your opponent off guard."

Max's laugh echoed through the parlor of their rooms at the inn. " 'Tis purely by chance if I do."

Kanakareh shrugged. Today, because the air held a chill, he wore a jacket of soft doeskin. "It is your method nonetheless." There was a slight pause. "I would watch my back."

Max's eyes narrowed. "Why do I think you've changed the subject of our conversation from chess?"

When Kanakareh said nothing Max stood. "Are you going to tell me what you know, or think you know?"

"I do not think all is well in that palace."

"That's hardly a surprise. The Grand Duke cares nothing about Breslovia . . . or his wife. That is obvious. Cardinal Sinzen . . . I haven't managed to figure him out yet. He seems pious enough, though obviously he isn't above countering orders. I also think there is more to his wanting a large army than just defending borders."

"And the Queen?"

Max forced himself to lean nonchalantly against the mantel. "What of her?"

"I wondered about your opinion."

"Oh. She seems . . ." Max took a deep breath and strode to the window. "I don't think she has a very easy time of it with those two."

"Her father and brother were murdered."

Max glanced around. "I know, though I've heard no details."

"They went riding as was their morning custom and never returned. When they were found, both were stabbed through the heart."

"Queen Cassandra must have been devastated."

"At first she was unconsolable. She was seventeen and quite close to her father and brother."

Max could imagine her, young, alone, frightened. He glanced around. "When did she marry the Grand Duke?" And why? He wished to add, but didn't.

"Soon after. Lord Albert is of a powerful family, the Martinettes. Centuries ago the Martinettes and Breslovia's ruling family fought over the kingdom. Some think the feud still simmers beneath the surface."

Max's eyes narrowed, and he studied Kanakareh a moment. His taciturn friend was unusually verbose. Not that Max minded. He was grateful for any information he could get. But it certainly was unusual. And as Max continued to stare a touch of color appeared beneath Kanakareh's bronzed complexion.

"Who told you all this?"

"Lady Sophia."

"Ah, from the musicale . . . with the red hair. She talks quite a bit if I recall."

"Yes."

Max grinned and shook his head. It would be interesting to witness a conversation between the redheaded countess and his silent friend. But as soon as the mirth came, it left, leaving him feeling drained. "The Grand Duke says Queen Cassandra is mad."

"Is she?"

Max thought of the time when he wondered the same thing. She'd had another vision today. He was certain of it. "Nay, I don't think so."

Max settled into a chair. Despite what he said to the cardinal and Grand Duke, Max still wasn't certain what he should do. He pulled the chair closer to the cheerfully burning blaze in the hearth. It was late August, and though the days were warm and sunny, the evenings grew chill, a harbinger of the autumn to come.

If he was to do anything with the army this year it must be started immediately. There was no time to waste. Max glanced toward Kanakareh who, now that the chess pieces were stowed away, sat stoically, staring into the fire.

Asking his opinion would be a waste of time. Max knew if the Seneca brave planned to offer his thoughts he would have done it by now. Still, Max tried. "What would you do if you were me?"

"I am not you, Hawke, and glad of it." Kanakareh gave Max one of his rare smiles, an expression that lit up his face, transforming that sober countenance.

Max simply pursed his lips and stretched his legs, hooking his boot heels on the brass fender. There were times he wished he could box his friend's ears. But Kanakareh was right. The decision was not his. It rested squarely on Max's shoulders.

"I was brought here by the Grand Duke and Cardinal Sinzen."

Silence from Kanakareh.

"They offered me the position and sent us about the countryside."

Again, no comment.

"And though you say Cassandra is the reigning monarch, I

see very little indication that she makes any decisions in governing."

"Except the one not to increase the army," Kanakareh said.

Now he had to say something. Max laced his fingers over the smooth, hard lines of his waistcoat. He wanted to stay here. There was no denying it. He liked the idea of training Breslovia's army—of proving himself worthy of command.

And the task needed to be done.

Even if the country were to depend entirely on a volunteer militia, a major renovation was needed. Most of the nobility who served as officers were absent from the districts he'd visited. "Away at court," was the usual response he received when inquiring as to their whereabouts.

Not only were they gone, but the nobles had left no orders to be followed in case the militia needed to muster. No plan in case there was an attack along the borders.

That made him think of Cassandra.

God, she'd looked beautiful when she'd faced her husband and Cardinal Sinzen. Magnificent. He hadn't known those soft, violet eyes were capable of such fire—except in the heat of passion. Max took a deep breath. He had to forget about the night near the waterfall. If not because he'd given his word to put the incident from his mind, then for his own sanity.

Dwelling on the softness of her skin, or the taste of her, headier than the strongest wine, or the way she felt beneath him—all fire and molten desire—only drove him to despair. Max suppressed a moan and pushed himself to his feet.

"I must talk to her."

Kanakareh merely raised a questioning brow, black as a raven's wing.

"Perhaps I can convince her of the need for a larger army." After all, he knew of her visions. Was not that fear of death and destruction reason enough to arm her country?

Yes, that was the solution. He would argue his case to her. Convincing her would be relatively simple once she understood the politics of military force. Then there would be no need to defy her order. Cardinal Sinzen would no doubt commend him for a job well done. Feeling better already, Max splashed Madeira into a goblet.

He smiled as he sipped and then stared out the window. And he refused to dwell on the fact that the thought of seeing her again warmed him more than the wine.

"There you are. Do you realize everyone is searching for you? Well, perhaps not everyone, but surely a large number of servants, not to mention Doctor Williamson and his staff. I have only just heard of your disappearance. Naturally I went to your apartments first. But then I thought of here. Of how we used to come here and stare out the windows and pretend that a knight on a white steed was riding toward the castle to claim our hearts. And I thought, perhaps . . ." Sophia paused in the doorway to catch her breath. It was a hard climb up the winding steps to the top of the ancient turret above Cassandra's rooms.

Sophia's eyes fixed on her friend. "Are you quite well, Cassandra?"

Turning back to stare through the narrow window that overlooked the forest below, Cassandra nodded. "I am now, yes."

"You shouldn't be up here, you know." Sophia walked cautiously into the octagonal room. Old tapestries, threadbare and heavy with dust, hung upon the stone walls. "Cardinal Sinzen says 'tisn't safe. What if it crumbled to the ground while we were here? Let's go down to your apartments, or outside to the gardens. 'Tis a lovely day, warm, and the sun is shining. We could—"

"This part of the castle has stood for centuries. I don't think it shall collapse today."

Sophia stepped farther into the room, looking about her as if she expected the fortress might do just that. "What happened to you? The gossips are abuzz."

Cassandra glanced over her shoulder and smiled. "I imagine

they are." With a sigh she continued. "There was another vision."

"Oh, Your Highness." Sophia rushed forward, stopping just short of embracing the Queen. "I thought they'd stopped."

"No. I simply stopped speaking of them." Because she could not bear the pity she saw in Sophia's wide green eyes, Cassandra twisted back to stare out the window. She'd come here to escape the prying eyes of people, the vision itself.

But once here in this tower that her ancestors had used to defend their land, she wondered if her choice of retreat might be more than mere chance.

Standing atop the turret, looking down on the fields where so many lost their lives before peace came to this kingdom—to her kingdom—empowered her. She squared her shoulders. "Today, I was not alone when the vision came to me." This was not a first of course. She'd been overcome the night she'd met with Maximilian Hawke. But she'd never told Sophia of that night, or the one on which she first met the handsome general.

Cassandra forced her thoughts from him to catch a few of the many words Sophia hurled her way. "Cardinal Sinzen and my husband and General Hawke," she replied to one of her friend's questions. "They were in the Council Room when it began. I rushed out, so I can't be sure if they noticed anything. But yes, I did run into someone, quite literally, when my gaze was unfocused."

Cassandra paused and Sophia, apparently anxious to hear who, did not fill in the silence.

"Madam Cantrell."

"No." Sophia breathed the word as she sank onto a carved wooden stool. "That one will keep no secret for you. Why she may smile sweetly to your face, but her heart is black, Your Highness, believe me. She flaunts the Grand Duke's affections, talking openly about how she uses her tongue to—"

"Sophia!"

"Oh, Your Highness, I am so sorry." Sophia leaped to her feet. "I didn't mean to say that, you must believe me. You know how my own tongue wags. Sometimes I wish I would simply be struck mute, for I do not seem able to curb this excessive talking."

Laughing, Cassandra moved to embrace the redheaded woman. "Poor Sophia, do not despair so. And please do not wish for silence. Especially not now," Cassandra teased, "for I have something to ask of you."

"Anything, Your Highness, you know that." Sophia gave the queen a squeeze. "It is so good to see you smile. You have grown so somber. Oh, I know you have reasons. Why, these visions alone would cause most to lose all patience. But we used to have so much fun. Do you remember the day we caught all those frogs and sneaked into Peter's bedchamber to let them loose?"

"Aye, and he was . . . entertaining Lady Judith," Cassandra said with a grimace.

"Well, that was a bit of misfortune."

"Especially when Papa heard of it."

"His Majesty King Christian thought it funny. You know he did. Why he barely did more than send us to our separate rooms to ponder our actions. And I still swear there was a smile on his face as we left him. And you know Peter would have laughed . . . if not for that woman."

"She did her share of screaming, for certain."

"She did at that." Sophia giggled. "I never did like her, you know. I don't think she is at all lovely. There's a wart on her cheek, and her voice, so low and breathy one can barely hear what she says. 'Tis a wonder her husband, the Earl of Snedron, listens to her at all."

The wart was a mole. Most considered Lady Judith's voice pleasing. And Cassandra wasn't surprised by Sophia's reaction to her. Since she could remember Sophia had been in love with Prince Peter. Eight years older than the two girls who bedeviled him, Peter had been strikingly handsome. He'd had Cassandra's blond hair, though his hung with nary a wave, and his eyes were a truer blue. He was fun loving, with a temperament that encouraged laughter.

So like his father.

There were still times when Cassandra could not believe they were both dead.

She shook her head. She refused to dwell upon that or she truly would go mad.

"Sophia," she said, interrupting yet another anecdote from the past. "You have become friends with the man Kanakareh, have you not?"

A rose blush camouflaged the freckles across Sophia's pert nose. "I know him, yes. We have talked. But I do not know if you would call it a friendship. I admire him, of course. He knows so much and—"

"I would like to speak with him."

"You would?"

"Yes. Do you think you could ask him to come to me? Here?"

"Now? You wish it to be now? But I am not certain where he can be found at this moment or—"

"I realize I am asking much of you, Sophia. But I must see him. And I am afraid to wait any longer."

There were more questions. Sophia always asked questions. But in the end the petite redhead turned with a resigned sigh to do her sovereign's bidding. And Cassandra was left alone in the turret. Hoping the Indian could help her.

Seven

"I do not understand what you wish of me." Kanakareh stood before the young queen, his strong body straight. To honor Her Majesty he'd donned a headdress of silver and feathers.

"I'm not certain I know myself." Cassandra sank onto a marble bench. Her sigh mingled with the tinkling sound of the water that fountained from the statue to her right into the pool below. They were in her private gardens, alone except for Lady Sophia who walked among the flowers near the gate, far enough away to hear nothing of their conversation.

"Lady Sophia said it was a matter of great importance . . . of life and death."

Cassandra glanced up and smiled at that statement. It was so like her friend.

"Perhaps not that." Cassandra sighed again. "Although I am not sure."

He did not ask what she meant by that, or indeed why she had summoned him. The silence spread between them like a mantle of snow, with only Cassandra to trudge through it.

"General Hawke speaks of you fondly."

"And I him," Kanakareh responded.

"Yes, of course." Cassandra didn't know for sure how she felt about Maximilian Hawke, but he was not her concern at the moment. She stood, then sat again, her gown of pale blue silk swaying softly. Taking a deep breath she spoke, her voice low. "I am haunted by visions. Terrible visions of death and suffering."

"Perhaps it is a sign."

"Yes. 'Tis what I fear." Her hands twisted in her lap.

"Visions are not to be feared, but acknowledged and learned from."

"Oh, I did try that." Cassandra's fingers were pressed to her lips. "When they started I did." Her eyes met his. "They frighten me. And I cannot escape them." She turned her head toward the fountain, her chin lifted in defiance. "I hardly dare look this way, so afraid am I that the sparkle of sun on the water will bring on another . . . episode."

"They have taken control from you."

"Yes, they have." Her eyes were back on him now. "I'm at the mercy of this haunting destruction only I can see." Cassandra leaned forward. "If Simon were here I would go to him."

Kanakareh raised a dark brow, and Cassandra explained. "Simon is a man wise beyond his years, though he is very old. A seer, who often counciled my father, King Christian. He tutored my brother and sometimes myself." She stood once again, picking a petal from a boxwood and tossing it to the ground. "Simon is gone, though. He disappeared the day my father and brother were killed." Cassandra shook her head, trying to clear her mind of the sorrow, attempting to face the reality of her life.

"General Hawke mentioned that you, too, have visions." The Seneca merely nodded, showing no sign that he wondered when she and his friend discussed such a thing. "I thought perhaps you could tell me . . . could help me understand."

"First, you must not show fear. The spirits do not respect it."

"But how can I not? Yesterday one started when I was with the Grand Duke and Cardinal Sinzen." She did not mention Maximilian Hawke, and she wasn't sure why. "They must have thought I was mad as I ran from the Council Room."

"They should admire you as a chosen one."

Cassandra's snort wasn't very queenly. "I can assure you they don't. Cardinal Sinzen feels 'tis the devil who possessed me."

"Do you feel as he does? For I cannot help you stop the spirits."

"Nay." Cassandra grasped his hands. " 'Tis not evil, though the visions show horrors beyond words." Her eyes were beseeching. "I must understand. I must."

She hadn't eaten in three days. The hunger pains which tempted her to seek another course had stopped yesterday. Now all Cassandra felt was elation that the night was finally here. She was dressed as Kanakareh advised in a loose-fitting gown. Her hair was unbound, curling to her waist.

Sophia, obviously nervous, chattered even more than usual, but Cassandra seemed unable to focus on anything her friend said. Not until Cassandra moved to the tapestry and pulled the hidden lever did Sophia quiet. When the secret door groaned open Cassandra glanced back at the redhead, smiling when she saw her astonished expression.

"It has been here since the old stronghold was built in ancient times."

"Where does it go? Oh, Your Highness, are you certain we should go into that dark . . . ? Cassandra, wait for me. Oh, goodness, I can't see a thing."

"Here, take my hand and follow closely."

"What of spiders? Oh, or bats? Are there bats here? Why didn't we at least bring a candle?" Her fingers tightened around Cassandra's.

"I don't know yet how to control my visions, and the flickering flame oftimes brings them upon me. Do not fear. I know the way."

"What's that noise? It sounds like thunder."

" 'Tis only the waterfall. And you needn't worry; there is a way so you won't dampen your gown. I noticed you wore your emerald green. The one you said was your favorite."

"I like it, yes." Sophia was oddly silent.

But she didn't need to speak. As Cassandra hurried along the uneven path she found herself almost euphoric. Understanding flowed through her like warmed honey. She glanced back at her friend, but of course could see nothing. Not even a dim outline gave any indication she was not alone. The only link was their clasped hands.

"You are fond of Kanakareh?"

"Of course I am." Again there was unnatural silence followed by an abrupt explanation. "He is all the rage at court, you know."

Which was true. The tall dark Indian with his straight black hair and clothing made of animal skins was near the top of all invitations. His popularity was only surpassed by that of his friend, General Hawke.

Cassandra's step faltered, and she only continued after Sophia bumped into her with an "Oof."

"What is it? Are we lost? Oh, Cassandra, you do not know the way after all. We shall be swallowed up here beneath the earth."

"Do hush, Sophia. We are not lost. Look ahead. Can you not see the light?"

Through the wavering flow of the waterfall there was an unexpected brilliance. As they stepped from the tunnel, Cassandra could make out a bonfire burning in the clearing near the pool.

On the ground, to the side, sat Kanakareh. He was naked to the waist, and his skin shone with a coppery glow.

Maximilian Hawke stood near the fringe of willow trees. Looking much as she'd seen him that first night. Cassandra's breath caught as she remembered. She didn't want him here. She said as much to Kanakareh. But all the warrior would say was, "Hawke insisted upon coming."

Max stepped forward now, taking Cassandra's hand, then Sophia's, to help them off the slippery rock ledge.

"Are you all right?" His voice was low as he turned back to Cassandra.

"Yes." Hers was even lower. "I think so anyway." She forced her gaze away from him to stare at the Seneca warrior. "Is he?"

Kanakareh did not appear to know she and Sophia had arrived. He sat on the ground, legs crossed, and stared into the fire.

Hawke nodded toward him. "I think he's calling on his guardian spirit." Reluctantly, Max took both of Cassandra's bands and pulled her toward the shadows. "Are you certain you wish to do this? I didn't know until this morning what was planned or I might have protested."

"Protested?" Cassandra slipped her hands from his, though she immediately felt the lack of warmth. "I hardly think it is your place to question anything I do."

"You are, of course, correct," Max said with a bow. "I simply thought you might wish to reconsider."

"I don't."

"Very well then, Your Highness." Max started to turn away only to have a royal hand on his sleeve stop him.

"Please. I did not mean to be abrupt." Cassandra tried to smile when he glanced around. But her heart was pounding, and all she could do was stare.

"The fault is all mine, Your Highness." His aloof tone softened. "It's only that I've seen you under the spell of these visions and I question whether you should purposely bring one on."

"They come regardless." Letting her fingers slip from his sleeve, Cassandra walked toward the fire. Before Sophia could spread a scarf on the ground, Cassandra sat. Through the flames that licked into the night sky, she could see Kanakareh's face, all dark angles and hard planes.

When he began to chant, a low steady sound that seemed to vibrate through her body, Cassandra shut her eyes and waited.

The Seneca warrior had told her what to expect. How she would feel.

The vision would come . . . because he summoned the spirits for her. And she must remain calm. She must maintain control and let them tell her what they would.

A breeze trickled down through the trees, fanning a lock of curly, golden hair, and still she waited. The fire warmed her face, and crackled, burning so brightly she could sense the light through her eyelids. And still she waited.

This was not going to work. Perhaps because she was not of Kanakareh's tribe. Cassandra could feel Max watching her, waiting for any sign that the vision was upon her. Knowing there was none.

Behind her, Sophia asked a question, then another, talking quietly but steadily, and Cassandra wondered if she should rise, go back into the castle. Cloister herself in her rooms. She felt foolish, and the dampness of the evening soaked through her skirts.

She would get to her feet and thank Kanakareh for his efforts. Then she would—"No." The word was out of her mouth before she knew there was a reason to protest. Despite Kanakareh's admonition to the contrary, Cassandra resisted, fighting to keep her mind focused, her world from tilting.

But it was no use. It was never any use. No matter what she did the images came, wrapped in mist and swirling lights that made her stomach knot and threaten to revolt.

Max stepped from the shadows. The soft keening sound came from her, and he was certain she didn't know she made it. Tears rolled down her cheeks unchecked as her body rocked to and fro.

He couldn't stop himself. Max reached down, ready to wrap his arms around her . . . to comfort her. 'Twas only the firm grip of Kanakareh's hand on his shoulder that kept him from doing just that.

"I will take care of her. Have no fear."

"Damn it, Kanakareh, can't you tell she's in pain?" Max jerked his head toward her lady-in-waiting, hoping for some support. But Sophia merely stood there, blissfully silent for the moment, staring.

"The discomfort is not of her body," the Seneca said before kneeling beside Cassandra. "What do you see?"

"Stop them. We must stop them."

"Who? Tell me what you see."

When her only response was a strangled sob, Kanakareh settled down beside her, pulling her hands toward him. "You must remember what we said. Do not be frightened. Stay calm. Stay in control. Now breathe. I want you to breathe."

She tried. His voice was like a beacon of sanity in a world gone mad. Summoning her strength, Cassandra took a deep breath, feeling foolishly happy when he praised her.

"More. Breathe more. And deeply." When she obeyed, Kanakareh leaned toward her. "Now tell me what you see."

"Awful." The sob was back in her voice. "Blood. Blood everywhere and killing. They are all being killed."

"Who?"

"I don't know. They live in the villages, the countryside."

"How are they dying?"

"Can't you see? We must do something. Something now." Impatiently she batted at the warrior's hands.

"You alone can see this vision. You must tell us more. So we can help you."

Those words calmed her. Cassandra took a deep breath. "Soldiers are riding through the snow-covered fields, tossing spears. Shooting guns. I can smell the sulphur." Her nose wrinkled and she twisted her head to the side.

"What do the soldiers look like?" This from Max who was now kneeling beside her in the dirt. "Their uniforms, can you see them?"

"No, no. They've killed a young man, a child really. Run him through as if for sport. His mother is wailing in the doorway of their hut, crying as only a mother can. Oh! They've seen her." Cassandra's eyes were open, unfocused. "They always see her and drag her inside. I want to warn her. Tell her to hide, but it's always the same." She tried to get to her feet. "I can't bear to watch."

"Stay." Kanakareh's hands clamped over her shoulders. He didn't even glance around as Lady Sophia voiced her protest.

"Please, let me go." Cassandra wanted to flee and hide, to try to forget as she always did. But someone held her down, made retreat impossible, made any attempt to block the carnage from her mind impossible.

"Stop this!" Sophia pleaded. "Can't you see how frantic she is? Why are you doing this? I thought you would be gentle with her. I trusted you."

Kanakareh simply shrugged the arm where Sophia grabbed in trying to make him let go of her friend. A mere lift of his eyes and Max was beside the woman, pulling her firmly away from the Seneca warrior.

"Kanakareh knows what he's doing," Max said as he guided Sophia some feet away from the fire.

"Tell me what is happening now." Kanakareh's voice was commanding, Cassandra's flat as she answered.

"They raped her. Tore her clothes away and raped her, one after the other. Why won't they stop?"

"Do not watch. You can not help her. Look outside. Look at the soldiers. Tell me what they wear."

"Green. They're wearing green coats and breeches." Cassandra let out her breath. "Green."

"That is good. Are you watching a soldier?"

"Yes. He is sitting on his horse. Talking." Her eyes squinted shut. "I cannot hear what he says." Her voice grew weary. "And now I can barely see him."

Cassandra opened her eyes and stared into the fire. The flames burned lower now. She felt dizzy and disoriented. And weak, so very weak. As if all she wished to do was lie back in the grass and sleep.

"Cassandra, are you all right? Oh, you look dreadful. Here, take my handkerchief. See what you've done to her." Sophia's gaze took in both men.

"Don't." Reaching out, Cassandra touched her friend. "They did not do it. This is what I have been suffering for months. But I did control it . . . just a little. Didn't I?" Her eyes locked with Kanakareh's.

"Yes."

"Then will they stop?"

Her expression was so hopeful Max glanced away as Kanakareh stared at her, his dark eyes solemn. "I do not know. No one can predict what the spirits will do."

She knew as much before she'd asked him. Cassandra nodded, then lifted her chin. "But I can have some control over what they tell me."

"Over what you choose to focus on, yes."

Where before he'd held her down, now Kanakareh helped the Queen to her feet. Sophia seemed more concerned with the leaves and twigs littering her overskirt, but Cassandra stood still while her lady-in-waiting brushed at the silk.

She was tired and a bit disoriented as always after the visions left her. But her mood was brighter than usual in the aftermath. True she'd seen the death, the evil. But she'd been able to divert her attention. The feeling of empowerment that gave her was exhilarating.

"General Hawke," Cassandra said as she moved past him toward the waterfall. "I want to see you on the morrow."

"As you wish, Your Highness." He was scheduled to leave early the next day for Nelse, a city near the French border, where recruiting was brisk. "Shall I wait on you sometime in the morning?"

"No, actually the afternoon will be better."

Better for whom? Max wondered as he watched the Queen and Countess Sophia disappear behind the cascading waterfall. Certainly not him.

But Max couldn't deny that he wanted to see her. Wanted to be near her again. Something about her seemed to twist at his insides, and it wasn't simply the fact that his body stirred whenever he thought of her.

It pained him to watch her suffer in the throes of her vision. Though he knew it foolish, he'd wanted to knock Kanakareh away and take her in his arms. To soothe and calm, wipe the terrible scenes from her mind. To make love to her as he had before.

Which was about the most foolhardy thing he'd ever considered.

It was one thing, though hardly brilliant, to cuckold the Grand Duke when he had no idea what he was about. But to even consider repeating the deed, now that he knew who was who in this kingdom, was . . . Max couldn't think of words strong enough to describe it.

"Her Highness will see you now."

Max glanced up as the footman made his announcement. He sat in the small anteroom outside the Queen's apartments. Compared to her husband's, this appeared to be in an older section of the palace. The walls were of stone, thick by the look of them, with narrow windows, and tapestries to soften the effect.

The council room was the same, though larger, and Max couldn't help glancing about as he was ushered inside.

"This is part of the original castle, dating back centuries," Cassandra commented from her seat near a large rectangular table.

"It appears as though it could hold off a small army," Max said before remembering himself and bowing low. But as soon as she swished her hand for him to rise Max walked over to the wall. He rubbed his hand across the old stone.

"You are interested in old castles, General Hawke?"

"I enjoy military history." It was one of the few academic areas in which he excelled, according to his tutor.

"Most people find the new section of the palace more intriguing."

"Obviously you don't."

"No . . . yes." She could not explain to General Hawke as she could not explain to herself why she stayed here. There were rooms for her in the new palace. Beautiful rooms with large windows that looked out on her private gardens. Yet she found excuse after excuse to stay here. "I shall move to my new apartments soon," she finally said with more conviction than she really felt.

Cassandra stood and circled the table, busying herself sorting through maps and books piled on one end. She was watching him too closely, the way his strong, tanned fingers caressed the age-old stone. Her pulse quickened as if it were her own flesh he touched. She swallowed, hoping her voice wouldn't betray any of her silly imaginings. "I feel more at home in these rooms. But they're old . . . the stonework crumbling in some places."

"It could be dangerous."

Cassandra glanced up from a volume on Breslovia's history. For a moment when he spoke she thought he meant something other than the castle. She thought he meant . . . Cassandra mentally shook herself. She was becoming too fanciful.

"Cardinal Sinzen pesters me to move."

"Yet you stay." Max left the window and moved toward her. She seemed more beautiful each time he saw her, though he would swear that impossible.

"Yes. This part of the castle reminds me of . . ." She shook her head.

"What, Cassie? What does it remind you of?"

"Of when my father was alive, and my brother. Before I became queen."

She seemed sad and a bit overwhelmed. And who wouldn't be with Cardinal Sinzen acting as if she didn't have an opinion worth repeating. The urge to put his arms around her was strong. If only to offer a bit of empathy. But Max wasn't stupid. He knew where that would lead.

He took a deep breath. It was too easy for him to lose himself in the depths of her violet eyes. To want to know her. All of her. To forget who her husband was. Lifting one of the maps on the table and giving it a cursory glance, Max offered what he could . . . or thought he should. "Perhaps Cardinal Sinzen is right about this. It does no good to live in the past."

She said nothing, only stared at him a minute before sitting. "Last night," she began, "you asked me what the soldiers looked like." Her gaze found his. "Why?"

Max forced himself to shrug. "You see soldiers marching on Breslovia. I am the commander in chief of the army."

"But you don't think . . . ? Could I be seeing the future? What of the Edict of Liberstein? We have always been a peaceful country."

"Not always." Max nodded toward the window slits. "You said yourself this keep protected your country from invaders."

"Yes, but centuries ago." Agitated she pushed up out of her chair, moving about the room restlessly. "I remember nothing but peace and happiness. It was always such. A magical kingdom Simon called it."

She noted his quizzically raised brow and explained. "Simon was my father's advisor. A wizard some said." Her smile was self-effacing. "Though I know you'll tell me none exist."

"Where's this Simon now?"

"He disappeared the very day my father and brother were killed. When I needed him most." Cassandra folded her hands. "But I can't think of that now. Last night I saw the color of the soldiers' uniforms. Green. You know more of armies than I. Does that tell you anything?"

"Aye. The invaders you see could come from anywhere. Prussia, France, England—more than likely even Breslovia has militia units with green jackets."

"Oh." Cassandra let out her breath. "I was hoping—"

"I think you're making a mistake in refusing to expand your army." Most likely he was making one by bringing up the subject. She'd already stated her views. And Cardinal Sinzen had overruled her. To stir up the pot again could be a serious error in judgment, but certainly not his first.

"It only makes sense to have the capacity to defend your land. Peace comes from strength."

"And, of course, it's in your best interest for Breslovia to have a large army."

"Perhaps, Your Majesty. But 'tis in your best interest as well."

* * *

Well, he'd tried. Max stood in the hallway that led toward the newer section of the palace. Behind him in the corner, looking old and outdated, was the tower. "And inside the beautiful queen hides," Max mumbled to himself.

Living in the past. Afraid to face the future. Terrified, really. Not that he could blame her. If he had only Cardinal Sinzen and the pompous Grand Duke to depend upon, he'd be wondering what to do himself.

She didn't seem to understand how they undermined her. Her words meant nothing. It was the cardinal who ruled the country. The cardinal who ordered him to disobey the Queen.

For which he should be exceedingly grateful, Max reminded himself. If it were up to the lovely Cassandra, he'd be packed and headed . . . Where in the hell would he go?

Luckily that wasn't an issue. For he was staying right here and training a new army, whether Queen Cassandra wished it or not.

Still, there was a part of him that wished he didn't have to disobey her.

"And how are our plans proceeding?"

"Exceedingly well, monsieur." Cardinal Sinzen's step faltered only a little as the man stepped from behind a statue of Aphrodite.

"The king will be glad to hear that." They walked along through the gardens, the short, stout cleric and the tall dignified diplomat. Anyone who saw them would think nothing of the meeting, for Count de Mignard was a regular at court, a handsome gentleman whose presence was required at all functions, revered for his wit and charm.

"Your General Hawke appears to be doing well. Sir Blanderz tells me recruits are standing in line to enlist in the provinces."

"I'm glad you are pleased. I did mention that our general's father is Lord Belmead, did I not?"

"Ah, yes. He has the ear of the English king I'm told."

"A trusted advisor, to be sure." The cardinal's laugh showed how breathless the walk had made him. He was only too happy to make use of the bench that the count motioned him toward.

"And how does our sweet Cassandra fare?" The count wiped the marble with a lace-trimmed handkerchief before settling down beside the wide girth of the cardinal. "I have not seen her for days."

"She's a bit under the weather, or so her ladies tell me."

"Perhaps she is enceinte."

Though the cardinal knew this to be impossible, he laughed and joked with de Mignard. "It is a joyous day for Breslovia if what you say is true."

"For Breslovia, my dear Cardinal Sinzen, or for your esteemed family?"

"Soon, Count, it will be one and the same."

Eight

"You are angry with me."

Lady Sophia opened her mouth to answer the question, to deny it for courtesy's sake, when she realized it wasn't a question at all. Kanakareh had simply stated a fact. She pressed her lips together and she feigned interest in the passing landscape.

Not that pretending to enjoy the scene spread before her was necessary. The royal barge floated down the River Breze. All around her early autumn's splendor was reflected in the tranquil waters, the scarlet-tinged leaves of the maples lining the waterway, the spirals of St. Peter's looming in the background.

The sky was so blue and crisp she could see the snow-crowned mountains in the distance. Yes, she was very happy and content to drink in the beauty of her country . . . except for the man who stood silently beside her.

She would not allow him to ruin her day.

Sophia didn't even know what he was doing here on the barge. The outing had been planned days ago by Count Wenzel. "We must take one last journey down the river before the weather turns frightful," he'd said to Sophia as they'd wended their way through the maze of boxwood in the south garden. "I do so enjoy the picnics." He'd taken her hand and had brought it unerringly to his lips. "And your charming company."

So it was decided. And left to her to arrange the guest list.

She hadn't included the Seneca warrior.

Not that she wouldn't have wished to, several days ago. But he was not at court then. And after last night near the waterfall . . . Well, she didn't wish to think about it.

But of course she couldn't help it. Poor Cassandra. Sophia wouldn't have left her friend today, except she had arranged this expedition and the Queen insisted she go.

Well, she would not spend her time pressed against the rail. Turning abruptly, Sophia rushed toward a group of her friends huddled near the stern. Talk was of the upcoming Festival of the Pax. The three-day event celebrated the signing of the Edict of Liberstein. The peace that prevailed, wrapping itself about this beautiful kingdom like a down comforter.

It was an annual time of joy and celebration, much anticipated throughout the country.

And this year there was speculation.

"Do you think Her Majesty will lead the processional to St. Peter's?"

"Of course she will. Why would you think otherwise? She rode in front last year and the year before. The year before that as well. When King Christian lived, he led the masses. It has always been so."

"No one can deny that," Lady Diana agreed. "However rumors do fly about, whether we wish them to or not." She shrugged a delicate shoulder, showing off a beauty patch stuck daringly low on her breast. " 'Tis said the Queen is not well."

"She's perfectly fine."

"Now, Lady Sophia, there is no need to sharpen your tongue on me. *I* am not the one saying such things. But you must admit she is acting very strange. Her fainting spell at the ball, and then she barely goes about the palace anymore, choosing instead to stay in that awful tower. Why now that I think on it, I haven't seen her in days. And I'm one of her ladies-in-waiting."

Chosen by the Grand Duke, if Sophia recalled correctly. But that was neither here nor there. What was a problem was that everything Lady Diana said was true . . . or at least had a thread of truth in it. Cassandra didn't seem well. Those dreams or visions interfered with her sleep.

And the ceremony—or whatever it was—the other night hadn't helped. Sophia's gaze slid toward the tall straight figure of Kanakareh before she returned her focus to the group of nobles.

A smile lighting her pixie face, Sophia fluttered her fingers along one row of Breslovian lace that trimmed her sleeve. "Don't tell me you are out of favor again, Diana. What did you do this time to garner the Queen's wrath?" Sophia kept talking and laughing, improvising as she went, while a red-faced Diana did her best to deny she had done anything to Cassandra.

"I'm certain if she apologizes Her Highness will forgive her," Sophia told the group of noble ladies and gentlemen after Lady Diana excused herself to admire the view. Sophia couldn't be certain her performance had helped, but at least the talk was not now of Cassandra's ill health.

When the barge docked at the elaborately canopied quay, the guests disembarked for an afternoon of communing with nature. Of course the lawn was freshly shorn, smooth and thick as the finest rug, and the walkways were well trimmed. Still, the ladies and their beaus enjoyed the chance to promenade about in a setting other than the palace gardens before the liveried servants served the exquisitely prepared meal.

Sophia usually enjoyed these outings. But today her natural good humor and pleasant outlook were sorely pushed. She was worried and angry, and she couldn't really pinpoint where to focus her wrath. While the others promenaded about, chatting about an unusual bird they sighted, or the masquerade ball, Sophia wandered toward the river.

Though he moved on quiet feet, it did not surprise Sophia when she glanced around to see Kanakareh behind her. "Are you not afraid you will miss some fun? I believe the ladies have challenged the gentlemen to a bit of archery. I imagine you are expert in that. I do believe that is a Seneca's preferred weapon, is it not?" Sophia tilted her head. "Why are you smiling?" And why did the sight of him, his fine dark features softened in mirth, cause her skin to heat?

"You are not angry with me any longer." He seemed as certain of this as when he'd told her earlier, on the barge, that she was.

"Whatever makes you say that? I've told you neither that I was or was not angry, yet you insist upon deciding for yourself. Why now have you decided I am not?"

His grin was even wider, and when he reached out to hook a strand of flame red hair behind her ear Sophia's knees grew weak. "You are talking to me."

"I always talk. Ask anyone. That is what I do best," she said as she slapped his hand away. But she didn't want to. She wanted to take his long, dark fingers and bring them to her lips. The thought shocked her.

"Perhaps," Kanakareh said. "But you were not talking to me earlier."

"That's ridiculous. I was talking, wasn't I? Besides, I have every right to be annoyed with you after last night."

When he said nothing, Sophia continued. "Well, shouldn't I? Poor Cassandra trusted you, and you could see the pain she suffered. The agony you made her endure."

"It was as she wished."

"She didn't know what would happen. You knew and you had her do it anyway."

"How is she today? Angry with me as she is with Lady Diana?"

Sophia's head jerked up. She would have sworn he hadn't heard a word anyone said from where he stood on the side of the barge. She studied him a moment wondering if he seriously believed what she'd told the others. His expression was sober, but she detected a bit of humor in his dark eyes. "Oh, you know she isn't upset with you or Diana. I simply couldn't let her"—Sophia glanced toward a group that contained Diana—"spread rumors about Her Majesty. Even if they are true."

"Oh, Kanakareh, I am so worried about her. She hardly sleeps. And—blast her—Diana was right about the tower. It's almost as if Cassandra is drawn to the place. As if she's possessed." Her green eyes widened. "You don't think that could be true, do you? Kanakareh, tell me it isn't possible."

The Seneca warrior looked down at her mitted hands where they grasped his, then his gaze traveled up to meet hers. He could tell she wanted to let go of him, but refused to now that they were both aware of her touch. He would not embarrass her further. Kanakareh shrugged and turned so that he too faced the meandering current of the river.

"I do not know all the spirits can do."

Sophia took a deep breath and nodded. But she did not look at him even though he stood shoulder to shoulder with her. But that did not help. She could feel him, his heat, his power. Though his words did not answer her question, somehow just having him here, beside her, made Sophia feel better.

"Did you know that Breslovia exports hundreds of pounds of lace a year? All painstakingly made by the women in the northern provinces?"

"No, I didn't. Why aren't you ready? You knew I was returning late. Oh, Your Highness." Sophia yanked on the brocaded bell pull moments before Emma, one of the Queen's maids, knocked at the door. "Bring the royal hairdresser and see that there's water in the tub."

"And cheese. Breslovia's cheese is known the world over," Cassandra continued.

"That is wonderful. Hand me that book." Sophia glanced at the leather spine, then up at her queen. "Whatever are you reading?"

"I'm learning about Breslovia." Cassandra's voice was muffled as her lady-in-waiting pulled her afternoon gown over her queenly head and then tossed it toward the bed. It landed on the floor.

"Whatever for? You've lived here all your life. You are the Queen, for goodness' sake. What more is there to know?" Sophia led her into the dressing room. "Here, step into the tub."

"But there's so much I don't know, Sophia. And I must learn." Cassandra blinked as her friend poured water over her head. "What are you doing?"

"Washing your hair. You." Sophia pointed toward one of a bevy of maids who stood nearby. "The perfumed soaps."

Later as Cassandra sat before the dressing table, the royal hairdresser, braiding and twisting her hair atop her head, she caught Sophia's eye in the mirror. "Now will you tell me what this is about?"

"There's a ball tonight," Sophia answered with uncharacteristic simplicity.

A delicately shaped golden brow arched. "There's a ball or some fete nigh every night."

"Which you have taken to not attending. And if you must know your absence is noted and speculated upon. There is much talk—"

"I don't care about court gossip." She twisted her head to the side. "Thank you, Henry," she said, as he patted the last curl into place. He bowed deeply and backed from the room, followed by the maids Sophia shooed in his wake. When they were alone Cassandra stood, her arms crossed.

"I think the royal rubies," Sophia began. "They will set off the deep blue and give you color. You do appear a bit pale, perhaps we should call Henry back to powder your hair. What do you think?"

"I think you should tell me why I've been scrubbed and polished till I nearly shine when I've no desire to attend tonight's festivities."

"We took the royal barge on the River Breze today. It was lovely, Your Highness. You really should have gone. The trees are beginning to color, and the sky was so blue. Though the air was a bit chill. Yet once we stopped near the summer palace it was warm enough. I barely needed my—"

"Sophia." Cassandra's voice was tinged with exasperation. "I am pleased you had an enjoyable time. However I do not see what your afternoon has to do with my attending tonight's ball."

"There is talk you are ill."

"Ill?" The wide silk skirt swished softly as Cassandra settled back in the chair. After a moment she glanced up. "But I am not. Except for the visions, I feel very fit. Why I ride every morning and—"

"No one sees you. There was even speculation as to whether you would lead the procession at the Festival of the Pax."

"But of course I shall. It is the duty and privilege of the monarch." Cassandra let the last word drift off. She sat silently a moment before standing and leading the way from her dressing room, signaling for Sophia to follow. She picked up a book from the cluttered table and handed it to her friend.

"I was reading it when you entered this evening. It contains information about Breslovia, a lot of which I did not know. And this one." She pointed to a tome that appeared too heavy to lift. "It chronicles our kingdom's history." She sighed. "When I was younger and spent my days in frivolous pursuits, I used to tease Peter about the time he spent with his tutors. Now I wish I had done the same."

"There seemed no need. And you excelled with your dance lessons. And French. Latin. I was always impressed with your ability to speak those languages."

"If only I could read them as well," Cassandra said. "But I shall learn because I fear I have not done a very good job as Queen."

"That's ridiculous. You are a wonderful queen. The people love you and—"

"If they do love me 'tis because of my father, for I have done naught to earn their love or respect. Something is wrong in Breslovia. I feel it. Perhaps 'tis the visions." She shook her head. "I don't know, but I have decided I must find out."

"By reading books? Your Highness, I do not understand how that will help. What can you possibly learn from all these old words written on parchment?"

"History. But I need tutors also. I do wish Simon were here, though I shall have to make do without him." Cassandra signaled for Sophia to pull the bell. "And you are correct about attending the ball . . . and the jewels. I need to assure my nobles that their queen is well." She just hoped a vision didn't descend upon her while she was doing that.

The scores of crystal chandeliers sparkled, glittering above the throng of jeweled ladies and gentlemen in the ballroom. But none shone quite like Cassandra.

Max stood near one of the many doors leading out to the illuminated gardens and watched as she arrived. With a flourish of trumpets Her Highness was announced and the music stopped. The Grand Duke, looking particularly foppish in a gold jacket, left his mistress to saunter toward his wife. He greeted her with a bow, then escorted her down the row of nobles.

Last night she seemed vulnerable and hauntingly beautiful. Tonight she sparkled brighter than the rubies caressing her delicate throat. Her golden hair, curled and twisted about her head, caught and reflected the candlelight. Her skin, the skin he knew to be soft and sweet smelling, was white as the finest ivory, and her eyes were the color of rain-washed violets.

Max felt his mouth go dry just looking at her. The lady on his arm, a delectable young thing with a reputation as a gifted courtesan, was forced to repeat some trite witticism thrice before he even heard her.

But for all Cassandra's royal grace, Max detected shadows in those large, lash-framed eyes. She was frightened. And given what he knew of her, of the circumstances at court, he could hardly blame her. Despite the presence of the Grand Duke, she seemed very much alone. It was all Max could do not to step forward and offer his hand to her.

Which would be a frightfully stupid gesture.

The ball room was crowded, the lofty frescoed ceilings echoing with the strains of a lively country tune and laughing voices. Max caught glimpses of the Queen as she and the Grand Duke led the first set, then later as she danced with Count-What's-His-Name. He'd been introduced to so many over the last fortnight he couldn't remember their names.

He did know that this nobleman had no country seat and thus no militia. He was merely one of the multitude of young men who passed their lives at court. Doing nothing more worthwhile than dancing and playing loo.

Which wasn't an entirely fair assessment for him to make. Max wasn't sure he wouldn't have relished existing as a rich and spoiled aristocrat. It certainly seemed preferable to his role as a poor one.

But, he reminded himself, he wasn't destitute now. Thanks to Grand Duke Albert and Cardinal Sinzen his pockets were full, his wardrobe stocked with splendid uniforms and his future . . . well, if not secure, at least he had a future to concern himself with.

Max took a deep breath and smiled down at Lady Katrina. She was fluttering her fan and whispering some tidbit of gossip his way. His gaze was drawn to her bountiful bosom, then back up to meet her eyes. 'Twas rumored her current lover was enamored of a young actress and wished to set the beauty up as his mistress. Which left Lady Katrina looking for a new patron.

Finding one shouldn't be difficult for her, Max decided. Her charms were numerous. She'd been companion to the Grand Duke before the Frenchwoman Madam Cantrell arrived at court. Yes, most men would be flattered by her attentions, and for the chance to have the Grand Duke's former mistress as their own.

Max just didn't think he would.

His eyes scanned the crowd until he saw her. She stood near one of the many arched doorways leading to the covered walkway overlooking the gardens. Beside her, Cardinal Sinzen appeared to be pontificating about something or another. Max excused himself from Lady Katrina, leaving her in the capable hands of Sir Frederick, who happened to pass by at that moment.

With a firm step, but not without questioning his sanity, Max moved toward the Queen. She glanced up, caught his eye, and immediately dropped hers. The light from the hundreds of candles lighting the ballroom showed the pale blush that colored her cheeks.

"Your Highness," Max said with a bow before turning to the cardinal and greeting him.

"General Hawke, how nice that you could join the festivities tonight."

Of course he wasn't supposed to be within miles of here, but on his way to the province of Nelshire. Max could almost see the unasked question forming behind Cardinal Sinzen's eyes. Well, any annoyance the cardinal might experience would evaporate when Max told him of the Queen's change of heart concerning the expansion of the army.

Limited change of heart, to be sure, but she had sent him a message late this afternoon stating that she wished him to recruit more militia and train them. "I am taking your advice," she'd stated simply.

But Max wasn't interested in vindicating himself to the cardinal at the moment . . . though perhaps he should. It was Cassandra who drew him here. And, Lord help him, he wanted to touch her.

She should refuse him, politely to be sure. Dancing with him was a mistake, Cassandra knew that; yet when he asked permission to escort her in a quadrille, she couldn't force her lips to refuse. Cardinal Sinzen didn't seem pleased by her acceptance, but then Cassandra didn't feel he was happy with her anyway.

"Was the good cardinal sucking lemons?" Max asked as soon as he and the Queen were out of earshot.

"That's hardly an appropriate question," she countered, though her smile showed she did find it amusing. "He finds my conduct inappropriate."

Max ushered Cassandra to the head of the line of dancers before taking a position opposite hers. "What terrible thing have you done?"

Their eyes met and Cassandra's breath caught. He did not mean on the night they met. He couldn't mean that. His question was innocent enough, even if he wasn't.

"Cardinal Sinzen thinks I am foolish to concern myself with politics and wars. He berated me for asking for his tutelage."

The music began, a swell of horns and strings. General Hawke bowed, and Cassandra curtseyed, then they both stepped forward.

"Perhaps he felt a ball was no place to discuss such matters," Max said with a smile.

"Do not patronize me, *General.* For one thing I did not make the request this evening. And for the other, I shall discuss whatever I please, whenever."

"Spoken like the Queen." The intricate steps of the dance separated them momentarily and gave Cassandra time to reflect. Her eyes were narrowed when they faced each other again.

"I *am* the Queen, you know."

"That was made quite clear to me . . . the morning after I arrived in Breslovia."

Cassandra had the good sense to look away. "I should have told you immediately, 'tis true. But that is not the issue. I wish to understand more so I may govern with knowledge."

"Perhaps Cardinal Sinzen doesn't wish you to rule at all."

"Of all the silly things to say. Of course he does. He has helped me immensely since my father's death. He only has my best interests at heart."

She was right about one thing. It was silly, nay stupid, of him to say anything against the cardinal. It was obvious Cassandra held him in high regard . . . certainly higher regard than she held Max himself.

She seemed to prove his assessment by keeping her eyes averted for the remainder of the set. For some perverse reason this made Max all the more determined to get her attention.

As the last strains of the music faded he took the Queen's hand in his own. "I could tell you of the world situation."

"Are you a diplomat then?"

"Merely a soldier, as you well know. But where the diplomats of the world plan the wars and break the treaties, 'tis the soldiers who risk their lives."

She stared at him a moment from beneath her lashes. He was handsome, of that there was no doubt, and confident. But he also seemed truthful and forthright. And though she wished otherwise, he could not be blamed for her indiscretion with him. "I think perhaps you *are* the one to teach me."

Max hadn't thought she meant now, but it appeared the Queen was nearly as impetuous as he.

With little more than a lift of her royal finger, she led him from the ballroom, through several small anterooms to a library, where thousands of books lined the walls.

Cassandra stood in the center of the room, hands on her wide panniers and turned slowly about. Her silk skirt, embroidered with gold and silver threads, swayed and glimmered. "Do you suppose anyone ever reads all these?"

"You mean you haven't?" Max said with a lift of his brow.

She simply mimicked his stare before moving to one of the glass-fronted bookcases. "My father read . . ." Her fingers traced the leather-bound spines. "And my brother as well. Their library was quite extensive really."

"This isn't it?"

"Oh no." Cassandra turned, her hand sweeping out to indicate the library . . . and lost her train of thought. He was staring at her with that look that made her stomach quiver and her mind go blank. His blue eyes seemed to draw her to a vortex of passion, where memories only fueled the desire. Cassandra tried to swallow, to break the spell of his gaze. She was mad to dance with him tonight, let alone bring him here. Alone.

As if he took pity on her predicament, it was General Hawke who glanced away. He turned with military precision and showed great interest in the wall of books opposite her. Cassandra forced herself not to collapse against the shelves.

"Perhaps we should return to the ball."

"I thought you wished to discuss world affairs." Max felt more in control with the width of the cavernous library between them. Damn, he had to remember who she was! Who he was. What in the hell could happen to him if he gave into his baser needs? Unfortunately, when he watched the way tiny tendrils of golden hair curled behind her perfect ears, when he recalled how soft and sweet her skin was there, it didn't seem like a baser need at all. It seemed as fundamental, as important, as taking his next breath.

And when she'd turned and caught him remembering, when she stared at him, all dreamy violet eyes, as if she too were lost in that other time, it was difficult to choose discretion.

Max pulled out a volume of Voltaire to give his hands something to do other than fist in his pockets. His bark of laughter vibrated off the marble busts of Socrates and Plato that stared down from the ledge above the bookcases.

"What amuses you so?" Cassandra skirted the large circular table.

"The Grand Duke commissioned this library, I take it." Max's laugh had settled into a chuckle.

"Yes, of course. What do you have there?" She was beside him now, trying to see over his wide shoulders, when he shifted, holding out to her the strangest "book" she'd ever seen. "Why there's naught but a spine. The book has no pages."

"Precisely."

Cassandra's gaze swept about the room as her smile broadened. "Are they all like that?"

Max moved about, fingering book after book, finding nothing substantial behind any. "I wouldn't count on learning much in this library."

"Most certainly not." Cassandra also examined a score of volumes, finding them all only false fronts. "Why do you think Albert built such a room as this?"

Max shrugged. "I've no idea. He's your husband." The words were no sooner out of his mouth than he regretted them. Max glanced over his shoulder in time to see her face flush. He hadn't meant to sound accusing, yet knew he had. She was married. To a man who pretended to love books . . . to a man she'd cuckolded.

All that and more was evident in her expression. And Max could not bear it.

"Cassandra . . . Cassie," he whispered as his legs ate up the space between them.

"Please. No, please." Her plea muffled against the braided front of his uniform, Cassandra seemed to have no choice but to lean into his strength as Max's arms circled her shoulders. It felt so wonderful to be held again—to be held by him.

Slowly she raised her face. His mouth, mere inches from hers, was grim as if he was in pain. Her lashes lifted further, her gaze tracing the narrow blade of his nose, then on to his eyes. There was no humor in them now. Only a hunger that Cassandra could feel in the pit of her stomach.

But this hunger had naught to do with food, and everything to do with the man who held her. His head lowered till she could feel his breath, hot and eager on her flesh. A caress she could not resist.

When his lips . . . finally . . . touched hers it was like a spark shooting forth from flint. Cassandra moaned deep in her throat. His mouth was hard, commanding, as he kissed her. Eagerly she opened for him, accepting his tongue, capturing it with her own.

Heat speared through her. Cassandra tried to think, but couldn't. Especially when his hand moved round to cover her breast. Her knees grew weak, her breathing labored. Her hands reached for his shoulders, those broad shoulders she dreamed of and held on to as he backed her against the wall.

Books that held no pages braced her body. And the kiss deepened, deepened until Cassandra thought she might explode from need. His hands dug behind her, cupping and lifting till she was pressed against him, woman to man. Her petticoats were many, the gown thick with jewels, yet she could feel him, hard and hot. And she knew the magic he could work.

Remembered . . . and knew . . . and wanted.

He could not get enough of her. His lips tore from hers to burn a path across her jaw and down the slender stem of her throat. The feel of her, the taste, he craved.

Her fingers were in his hair, her body molten. And he was so hard he hurt. Max arched, pressing his hips against hers. His chin nudged, then scraped at her bodice, his frantic mouth clamping over her nipple as soon as it was exposed.

She called his name as his hands clutched at her skirts, shimmying them up till he touched the hot flesh above her stockings. She was wet, nearly sizzling, and the first aggressive stroke of his finger sent her into uncontrolled spasms, Max looking for somewhere, anywhere, to finish this coupling.

His eyes snagged on the polished table and he jerked around, clasping her to him. Blood pumped through his body, pooling in his manhood so that it throbbed. Her frame quivered and her movements were frantic as she covered his face with kisses and clutched at his jacket.

Max lunged toward the table, falling over it, pressing her down onto the polished wood. He would have her. Have her again. Squelch this frantic desire that strummed through him night and day.

Half rising, he fumbled for the front of his breeches, groaning when she reached to help. Now. He needed her now. He needed—

Max didn't mean to catch sight of the royal seal over the door.

It was gold, depicting a unicorn under a fanciful crown. He had seen it many times since he'd been in Breslovia, decorating wall and sofa, porcelain and fountains. So common was it in the palace that he often did not notice the circular emblem.

But now he did.

He jerked up, his rasping breaths loud in his ears. So loud he barely heard Cassandra's muffled cry of protest.

"My God," he said, as he pushed off the table. He looked down at the Queen. She appeared radiantly debauched, one lovely nipple, strawberry red and glistening, peeking from above her gown. Her hair tumbled around her creamy shoulders like molten gold, and her clocked stockings were askew beneath a rumpled skirt.

But it was her face that Max watched. Her expression faded from passion to disbelief. "My God," she whispered, echoing his words. She raised onto her elbows, then refusing Max's assistance slid off the table. Max did grab her arm when her knees buckled, but she recovered quickly and yanked herself free.

"My God," she repeated, pushing rumpled curls off her face. "What have I done?"

"Cassie," Max began, but the heat of her stare had him retreating a step. "Your Highness, this was all my fault." What in the hell was he saying? Heads had been served up on a platter for admitting less.

"No. No," she insisted, though Max had the impression she wished to accept his guilt. "It was me. I . . ." Her head whipped around. "I can't even remember how it started." She stared at him through startled eyes. "It just did." She must have noted the way his gaze kept drifting down. With a gasp of outrage, she jerked her bodice up.

"I think you should leave."

"Your Highness is right, of course. As soon as I straighten my clothes I'll be out of your royal presence."

She didn't like his impertinence, and Max decided he must have a death wish for speaking to her like that, but—damn it!—he was the one who'd stopped before it was too late. Him. If not for his clear-headedness, or stupidity—he wasn't sure which—she would be sprawled beneath him right now and he'd be emptying himself into her luscious royal body.

Lord knows she wasn't going to stop him.

She knew it too. Which was probably why she couldn't look

him in the eye. "You must go further. Away from the palace," Cassandra insisted. "Away from Breslovia."

Hell and damnation!

This was exactly why he should not have come within ten rods of her. What was he going to do?

"I have sworn to raise an army for Your Majesty."

"I don't—" Care. She wanted to tell him she didn't care if there was an army or not, as long as he disappeared from her life. But what kind of queen would say that? What kind of queen would send away the best man to do her country's bidding because she couldn't control her own lust? An immature one. A selfish one. A queen who cared more for herself than her country.

And Cassandra would not be that kind of queen ever again.

"Then go do your duty." Cassandra raised her chin. "But stay away from me. You may report to . . . to Cardinal Sinzen, or . . . or my husband."

"As Your Highness wishes." Max scooped the ribbon from his queue off the floor, a gesture that doubled as a bow and headed for the closed door. He glanced back only once before leaving and that was to see her stiff back.

Minutes later Cassandra rushed from the room, lifting her gown and heading for the tower. Her eyes were too blurred with tears to see the man straining to hide his wide girth behind a marble column.

But he saw her, and a feral smile curled his lips.

"What are you doing here?" Cassandra looked up in shock as General Hawke seated himself beside her on the marble bench. Just last night she had banished him from her sight. And here he was as brazen as ever.

"I will not be long, Your Highness. And as you can see, we are well chaperoned." Max motioned toward the bevy of lords and ladies enjoying the garden.

"We hardly need to be chaperoned . . . I mean . . . That is hardly the point. I do not wish—"

"You wanted a lesson in world affairs," Max interrupted her to say. "If you will listen, I shall give you one." He didn't wait for her reply before continuing.

"Understanding all the causes of the present conflict that rages through Europe and the New World is difficult . . . perhaps too difficult for my simple soldier's mind to comprehend." His eyes met hers and she flushed. "But it involves pride and lost territory and balancing the power of nations."

"But Breslovia has little power."

"I am not speaking of Breslovia now." Max lifted a dark brow. "Do you wish to hear this?" Coming here was another of his foolish, impetuous acts. But he couldn't seem to help himself. She'd asked for his assistance. Regardless of what happened afterward, he intended to give it to her—or try.

Cassandra took a deep breath, forcing herself to ignore the way his nearness made her feel. "Yes. Tell me."

"During the War of the Austrian Succession, Frederick of Prussia invaded and annexed Silesia. Austria's empress, Maria Theresa, wants her province back." Max paused. "Alliances were made. Elizabeth of Russia fears Frederick, so her treaty with Maria Theresa is natural. Unlike the alliance between Austria and France, who have a long history of conflict between them. But then expediency, and a British-Prussian agreement, call for desperate measures."

"So there you have the chessboard of players, major players anyway." She opened her mouth to speak, but Max lifted his hand, stopping her. "You wish to know how Breslovia fits into this." His mouth thinned. "I do not know. Perhaps not at all. However, there are often pawns in games such as these."

"I do not consider war a game, General."

"Nor do I."

She could tell from his expression he spoke the truth, and was sorry she'd questioned his semantics. "We share borders with France and Prussia."

"That you do," Max agreed. "At the present time there seems no winner, though I would wager money on Frederick's eventual victory."

"Because your country is Prussia's ally?"

"I am loyal to Breslovia, Your Highness . . . and to you." Max stood, awaiting her permission to do so no more than he did when he sat beside her. "Now I shall leave to train your militia."

He turned, his movements precise, and Cassandra reached out, touching his sleeve. "General Hawke." She waited till he glanced over his shoulder. "Max. Thank you."

He nodded and strode away.

Cassandra watched his straight back as he walked from her life, and she tried to ignore the tightening about her heart.

Nine

Life was perfect.

Or nearly so, Max decided as he gazed down over the valley. A gently sloping basin of meadows and woods, bisected by a ribbon of crystalline water, the spot was the training grounds for the Breslovian army.

From his vantage point Max could see the neat rows of winter barracks, the parade grounds, the men. To the left, nestled near a bend in the stream was the village of Bordgarten. Usually a sleepy little community of less than fifty farmers and shopkeepers, Bordgarten now bustled with newfound prosperity brought by the army.

His army.

The horse beneath him shifted, prancing about, anxious to complete the journey and savor a bag of oats. But Max, content to savor the well-organized scene below, calmed his mount with a pat.

He had done this.

Not alone. Kanakareh was a considerable help. Still, Max had recruited an army and in a little less than two months had trained it, pulling the soldiers together into a true fighting unit. Untested to be sure. Small by European standards, granted. But an accomplishment all the same.

And, damn it, he was proud.

Especially considering how things might have turned out. Max shook his head as the memory of Cassandra threatened to shatter his elation. Damnation, when would he cease this obsession with her? Stop thinking of that night in the bookless library. Of how she tasted, of the sweet scent of her skin. Of how damn much he wanted her.

Hell, just the thought of her kept him from partaking of the charms of any of the camp followers. Even Isobella, renowned for her skills and obviously willing to use them on him, held little appeal. He'd lived the life of a damn monk since leaving Liberstein. Hell, he hadn't had a woman since his encounter with the Queen by the waterfall.

Max kicked his mount into motion. Perhaps his life wasn't so damn perfect.

Kanakareh awaited him when he reached the farmhouse that served as their headquarters. The building was squat despite a second story, made of the native limestone, and sturdy as a fort.

"Colonel Marquart is here."

Max dismounted, handing the reins to a private who led the spirited horse away. Sweeping off his hat, he used it to bat at the dust clinging to his breeches. "Colonel Marquart? Of the Imperial Guard?" When the Seneca warrior nodded, Max stepped toward the doorway. Another soldier opened the door then saluted smartly.

The colonel stood in all his colorful splendor, staring out the front window in Max's office. He didn't turn until Max shut the door behind him, and even then he appeared reluctant. His salute bordered on insolence, and contrasted sharply with the military precision of his stance.

"Colonel Marquart, 'tis a surprise to see you here." Max had met the commander of the Imperial Guard in Liberstein and both men seemed to take an immediate dislike for the other. On Max's part the colonel reminded him of Lord Northford his commanding officer in the Horse Guards. He imagined Colonel Marquart's complaint was a bit more fundamental. As commander of the Imperial Guard the man was the highest-ranking military leader in Breslovia . . . until Max's arrival.

"Surprise?" The colonel arched a gray brow before placing his gold-braided riding gloves on Max's desk. "Did you expect

I would disobey an order . . . even if I do find it not only useless but offensive?"

Moving into the room, Max paused only long enough to pick up the gloves and return them to their owner before settling into the leather chair behind his desk. Then he folded his hands atop the polished wood. "Orders? What orders are we discussing, Colonel?"

The blotches on the older man's face were nearly as red as his elaborately decorated jacket. "I was ordered to bring all but the most essential men of my corps here for training . . . as you well know, General Hawke."

Max leaned back, studying the colonel through narrowed eyes. What in the hell was the man talking about? Max had given no such order. Though all military troops in Breslovia were under his command, he'd done nothing to interfere with the Imperial Guard.

Despite his personal feelings for Marquart, and the old man's obvious contempt for him, Max considered the colonel a good soldier. After briefly examining the Guard's history, he'd decided to give them free rein unless a national emergency required he do otherwise.

Max rose to his feet. "Do you have this *order* on your person?"

"Your orders were conveyed to me verbally."

"By whom?"

The intensity of Max's voice, booming off the painted walls, seemed to offend the colonel. "His Highness Grand Duke Albert."

Max studied the colonel again, looking for any indication the man was lying. He found none. The Grand Duke? What in the hell was that twit doing? Albert had no interest in military matters, or anything else except the perfection of his toilette and perhaps what mysteries abounded beneath Madam Cantrell's skirts.

"You're certain it was the Grand Duke?"

The colonel's chest puffed out. "I assure you I know my own sovereign, General Hawke."

Hands clasped behind his back, Max strode toward the window. When he jerked around, the colonel took a retreating step. "He gave you this order personally?"

"He did."

Max shook his head. Apparently Colonel Marquart did know his sovereign. And just as likely, Max did not. He would never have guessed the Grand Duke would bother himself with giving orders . . . idiotic though they may be. Cardinal Sinzen, perhaps, but not Albert. But the man was the Grand Duke, and as such Max's superior.

"Very well then, report to the quartermaster. He'll see to lodging your men." When the colonel simply stood before him, his face registering surprise, Max turned toward the window. "You are dismissed, Colonel."

But before the older man could salute and reach the door, Max called out, stopping him. "How many men did you leave to protect the palace, Colonel?"

"As you ordered, General, twenty-five."

"Pompous old bastard," Max mumbled under his breath as soon as the door clicked shut.

"He does not appear to have too high an opinion of you either."

Max whirled around to see Kanakareh standing in the room. "Sometimes I wish to tie a bell around your neck. God damn, you could sneak up on Satan himself."

"If his mind were on other things perhaps."

"Do you know why Colonel Marquart is here?" Max hurried on before the Seneca could answer, if indeed he intended to. "Because I ordered it. Yes, me. Through the Grand Duke of all people. At least that's what Marquart thinks."

"And you didn't?"

"Hell no." Max blew air out in exasperation. "I've no desire to step on his toes any more than I must. Besides, I'm not sure it's a good idea to leave so few soldiers in Liberstein."

"Send them back."

Max fingered the corner of his mouth. "I could . . . possibly should. But for some unknown reason the Grand Duke decided to play soldier. I doubt he'd appreciate my interference in his little game." He glanced out the window again. The one that faced south toward the capital. "I'll let them stay a bit. Give them a taste of a real soldier's life then send them packing back to Liberstein. She should be safe enough until then."

He meant "them." Them, for God's sake, not just her. Max settled into his chair that night, a bottle of Breslovia's best cognac by his side, a cozy fire in the hearth. When he'd made his slip of the tongue earlier in the day, he'd glanced around to see if Kanakareh had noticed. The Indian's expression had told him nothing.

Max slid further down in the winged chair, resting his boots on the brass fender. She was the Queen. It was only natural that he would think of her first where the Imperial Guard was concerned.

"Hell," Max mumbled. He thought of her first, last, and always. And it had to stop.

But his resolve was already faltering when the knock sounded at his door. For a moment he considered saying nothing, hoping she would think him asleep and go away. Max sighed. "Enter."

Isobella did, in a flourish of bright-colored silk. She was descended from Gypsies, she'd told him the first day she arrived in camp. "Hot-blooded, passionate Gypsies." Looking at her now, Max did not doubt it. She smiled, her red lips spreading wide, her dark eyes smoldering.

"You sent for me, General Hawke?"

"Aye." Max let his eyes trace the enticing swell of her voluptuous breasts. She wore no restraining corset, only a loose-fitting shirt that promised easy access to the treasures beneath. "Come here, Isobella."

She moved slowly, her eyes never leaving his till she stood with her thighs pressed between the V of his. Here too she'd forgone the usual array of feminine underclothes. Max could feel the heat of her body through her skirt.

"What can I do for you, General?"

"I think you know."

"Oh, yes, I do." With one fluid motion she straddled him, pressing her mound against him as she wriggled closer. "I have known all along you would want me." She let her hand drift down his shirt till she cupped his manhood. "And I have looked forward to this with much relish." Her tongue flicked out to wet lips that already seemed moist and inviting.

When she leaned forward to bite his lower lip, his fingers dug firmly into her hips. He was hard and aching, and she laughed, low and throatily, when he jerked her closer.

"I knew you'd be like this," she whispered huskily in his ear as he tore at the skirts flowing around her thighs. "Such a big, handsome brute you are." She was shifting her shoulders, tugging the silk bodice down over her breasts. Her nipples where dark and elongated, and Max didn't have to move before one rested against his mouth.

He suckled and she screamed, clasping his head and shoving herself farther into his mouth. And all the time she wriggled about, skimming her softness over his manhood, till he thought there'd be no need to even enter her before he exploded.

"Some don't like the army, but not me." Her tongue traveled down his neck. "I don't care if the taxes are raised." She chuckled as her teeth bit into his shoulder. "You won't see me taking to the streets against the likes of you."

What was she taking about? Max tried to concentrate on the way her fingers deftly unfastened his breeches. He didn't care what the woman had to say. At this moment he didn't care about anything else. Or anyone else. Damn it, he didn't.

But she kept talking, jabbering on about riots in the streets and what she planned to do to him in graphic detail, and he should have liked it. Hell, he did like it! Except he couldn't quite understand what she meant. Not about her mouth massaging his manhood. He understood that very well.

It was the other.

"What in the hell are you talking about?" His hands clasped firmly on her hips, pushing her away this time. His breathing was as harsh as his words, and it was obvious she didn't know what to make of his sudden actions. She laughed, then snapped her mouth shut.

"What is it you want, General? The bed? With this big bull of a rod in your pants, I imagine—" She fell silent again when his hands clamped over hers, effectively stilling her fingers.

"I want to know what you were saying. Something about riots in the streets."

Her almond-shaped eyes narrowed. " 'Tis nothing for you to worry about. I don't imagine they'll amount to much. We Breslovians are lovers, not fighters." This time when she leaned into him Max turned his head away.

"Tell me all."

With a screech that reminded Max of a squawking crow, she leaped from his lap. "What do I look like, some simple country gossip?" She flung back her mane of black hair. "I only know what I hear. Perhaps if you spent less time riding that fancy horse of yours about, you would know what's going on."

"I said tell me." Max was on his feet, his hand whipping out to slam the door shut, the moment she opened it.

Now there was fear in her eyes, but she tried to camouflage it as she turned to face him. Her chin shot up, and for that instant Max saw the attractive woman she was. But he didn't care about that now.

For some reason there was a nagging worry he couldn't formulate in words. But she could. Max would wager his commission, this sensual camp follower knew everything that went on.

She seemed to weigh her options carefully before speaking.

"I've heard, though I've no proof mind you, that there's to be some sort of demonstration in Liberstein against the new taxes."

"When?"

She lifted her shoulders seductively, then apparently thought better of it. "During the Festival of the Pax. In two days."

For an instant Max stood stock-still, then his hand slid from the door. "Get out" was all he said, even when her remarks concerning his manhood, or lack thereof, became graphic.

Max was already headed down the hall and barely noticed. He pounded on Kanakareh's door, bursting in before the Seneca warrior could rise from the floor. Max didn't even take the time to chastise him for eschewing the bed and its soft mattress. "We're leaving for Liberstein within the hour. Make ready."

There were no time-wasting questions from Kanakareh; Max knew Colonel Marquart would not behave as well. But then, he didn't much care. Bordgarten was three days from Liberstein. Three damn days.

And Cassandra was there. With only twenty-five guards to protect her from a potential riot. Twenty-five guards.

Max didn't even knock before breaking in on the sleeping colonel.

Cassandra sat alone in the gilded carriage.

She leaned back against the soft leather squabs. She and Albert had had a row, and he'd refused to accompany her when she led the procession for the Festival of the Pax.

It had been partly her fault. She'd discovered just how much gold he'd spent on the palace and had questioned his authority. At the time she'd been indignant and had felt justified in her accusations. But now . . . Today was one of celebration, and Breslovia's Grand Duke would not be a part of it.

But there was more to it than that. Cassandra sighed. Perhaps she should do something to reconcile with Albert. They barely spoke, and when they did the words were rarely pleasant.

He was supposed to be her helpmate, someone who could

guide her as she ruled Breslovia. At least that's what Cardinal Sinzen had said when he'd proposed the marriage. It was possible she hadn't tried hard enough. At first she'd been so filled with grief for her slain father and brother she could do naught but keep herself secluded and mourn.

But now . . . now . . . Perhaps if she went to him. If they talked openly and freely. He was not perfect, but then neither was she. He loved Breslovia, surely. What difference did it make if he adored his mistress? Except to produce an heir, she had no desire for him to visit her bed. Cassandra swallowed, ruthlessly pushing back a memory of broad shoulders and eyes the color of the autumn sky.

She would not think of him. She would not.

Cassandra forced her mind back to thoughts of Albert. What was the harm if he wished to build a magnificent palace? She inwardly cringed recalling the exact amount of gold the Master of the Palace told her had been spent to date. Perhaps he would need to curb his desire for luxury just a bit.

However, as long as she could count on his help to establish new schools in the provinces, they were better off friends. Was that not what Cardinal Sinzen had told her?

With a royal blast of trumpets the carriage lurched forward. Ahead the gates with their fanciful carved unicorns opened, and a cheer drifted back to her on the clear, crisp air.

The citizens of Breslovia awaited her. Her people. Cassandra sat straighter, filled with pride. Today, as her ancestors before her had done, she celebrated her country's most solemn national holiday. She rode to the Cathedral of St. Peter to symbolically present the Edict of Breslovia to a prince of the church.

The ceremony marked three hundred years of peace and prosperity for the kingdom, and for Cassandra a renewed sense of dedication.

She smiled, remembering those years when she and Peter had sat across the coach, on the seat now vacant, and had watched as their father acknowledged the salutes of his happy subjects. "Oh, Papa, it is so exciting," she had whispered before raising a hand to wave.

It still was. All along the route bright banners of purple and green hung from roofs and windows, flapping in the breeze. Cassandra leaned from the coach, laughing and waving as a man held his infant high in his arms. The future of Breslovia.

Slowly, the Imperial Guard led the way through the crowded streets. The hooves of horses clattered on cobbled paving, crushing the flower petals strewn in their way. The fragrance of those petals mingled with the pungent smell of woodsmoke as fires smoldered in the town square under hundreds of roasting pigs that would later feed the masses.

Pealing throughout the city, church bells rang in celebration. Gaiety and happiness enfolded Cassandra like an ermine cloak. It wasn't until the coach drew to a stop by the cathedral's wide stone steps that another sound niggled into her consciousness.

This one struck a dissonant tone.

She glanced to her left as she stepped from the carriage and saw the faces of those pushing toward her. But these faces were not wreathed in smiles.

Still, the first jostling shove caught her by surprise. Cassandra glanced round to tell someone, the officer of the guard. But the fresh-faced young man already knew. He pressed forward, trying to insinuate himself between the crowd and his queen, only to be knocked to the ground.

Cassandra screamed. Men surged toward her and she caught the glint of sun on steel when a sword was brandished.

"No." Someone tore at her jewel-encrusted skirt but Cassandra hardly noticed. Her hands flew to her face, covering her eyes. "No, not now, please."

But the vision would not be refused. Blackness surrounded her and she whirled forward, her arms reaching out to steady her path.

"Don't fight what the spirits give you." Cassandra could hear Kanakareh's words as if he were beside her. She tried—oh, how she tried—to follow his command. But someone jarred her and all around she could hear yelling. A man shouted that she should get back into the carriage, but she couldn't move.

Cassandra concentrated on the vision as it cleared. Above her the sun shone bright and the birds flew, their feathers vivid as they circled. But she couldn't hear them for the commotion. Bells rang and people screamed, though the sounds were but an echo in her mind.

"Follow the vision," he'd told her, and she tried. Her gaze lowered till she could see the angry faces. Cassandra shook her head. They were shrieking at her, but she couldn't understand what they said. And then from the crowd a man appeared.

His hair was gray and limp, greasy, and his eyes were red rimmed. He growled, spittle spraying from his mouth as he shouldered his way toward her. When she saw the knife he pointed at her, Cassandra's blood ran cold. This was like no other vision. This was . . .

The image disappeared, and Cassandra's eyes flew open.

Her vision had shown her this scene. Had she seen the future?

My God!

She swallowed and jerked her head around. Her coronet now tilted over one brow, and her hair, so carefully coiffed by the Royal Hairdresser, hung freely about her shoulders. All around her people fought. She tried to back up, to reach the open door to the coach, but her way was blocked.

It wasn't till she looked back toward the cathedral that panic set in.

He was there, staring at her, his eyes burning into her skin. The man from her vision.

Cassandra screamed as he started toward her. She looked about frantically for an Imperial Guard, but there were so few and the closest one had his back to her, protecting her from the crowd to her right.

And all the while the man surged closer. With the knife she could not yet see . . . but knew was there.

She turned to flee, but it was impossible. There was nowhere to go.

When she heard the thunder, Cassandra feared it was another vision for there was not a cloud in the sky.

But the sound roared nearer, pounding, making the very road beneath her feet tremble. There were more screams, and then the crowd split as if a giant hand had willed it so.

The horse appeared as from nowhere, followed by what seemed like hundreds more. Yet it was the first, the black stallion, that captured her attention. And when the rider swooped toward her she lifted her arms in welcome.

"Make way for your queen," he commanded as he held her tight against his side.

And she clung to him.

His uniform was sweat streaked and caked with dirt, his helmet askew, yet she couldn't get enough of breathing his fragrance and the solid feel of him.

Beneath them, his horse pranced nervously, and Max chanced one glance toward Cassandra before urging the mount forward, up the cathedral stairs. The horse's shoes clattered on the stone steps, but the horse took them to the top with little trouble.

After letting her slip down to the top step Max dismounted, grabbing her arm before pounding on the door. It wasn't until he yelled to Cardinal Sinzen to "open for the Queen" that the carved wooden portal came ajar. Pushing his way inside, past the startled cardinal, Max pulled Cassandra with him.

"My God, what goes on out there?" Sinzen wrung his bejeweled fingers.

Inside the noise sounded far away. The dark, cool interior, with the sweet scent of burning candles and the muted colors cast by the stained-glass windows, was far removed from the chaos beyond the door.

A sanctuary.

Max cupped the Queen's shoulders, forcing her to meet his eyes. "Are you hurt? Did they hurt you?" he repeated when she only stared at him, her wide violet eyes dazed.

"No." She shook her head, further dislodging the crown. "No. There was a man . . . with a knife." She reached up and clasped his elbows. "He was going to kill me. But you came. I saw it. I saw what was going to happen."

He couldn't help himself. For just a moment Max dragged her against his chest. "You're safe now." His eyes strayed to meet those of Cardinal Sinzen over her bowed head.

"Yes, yes, child, come with me," the red-robed cardinal said as he came forward.

Cassandra reluctantly loosened her hold on Max. Then she straightened, refusing to lean into Cardinal Sinzen as he led her toward a private alcove.

"Where was he, this man?"

"In the crowd. I don't know exactly. He was small, with little eyes, and I really can't remember more."

Max stared at her a moment longer, then turned on his heel. "Stay in here till I come back for you." With his hand on the gold door latch, he paused, unholstered a pistol, then turned and laid it on the table beside Cassandra.

"There's no need of that. This is the Lord's house."

Making no reply, but also not retrieving his gun, Max pushed open the door. "Bolt this," was all he said before leaving. Once outside, he was pleased to see the chaos that he had met on his arrival was nearly quelled. Members of the Imperial Guard, mounted on horses that had carried them since before dawn, patrolled the square, dissipating the crowd.

Max spotted Colonel Marquart near the entrance to the Court Buildings. The man, for all his age and dignity, seemed unperturbed by the ragged appearance of his uniform. Or the dirty smudges across his cheek. Max tried not to grin as he approached. The colonel's salute was smart.

"Is Her Highness all right?" He seemed genuinely concerned.

"Aye. A bit shaken." Max turned to survey the near-empty square. The few people left hurried by as if afraid to linger.

"We've cleared out most of the rabble, though I can't for

the life of me understand what happened here. The old king, God rest his soul, would turn over in his grave if he knew how his daughter was treated today."

With a nod, Max handed his mount's reins over to a nearby guard and set out to find Kanakareh.

Ten

"As your closest advisor, I must insist that you leave Liberstein."

Cassandra sat in an ornately carved straight-back chair and watched as Cardinal Sinzen paraded his considerable girth back and forth across the polished marble floor. Each time he paused to turn, he swept the skirts of his robes out in a blur of scarlet. Hardly something she should notice, when the discussion was one of such importance, but she did nonetheless.

"Are you listening to me, Your Highness?"

"Yes, yes, of course I am. However, as I said before"—repeatedly—"I do not wish to leave the capital."

A flash of annoyance sprang to the cardinal's eyes before he masked his emotions. "My dear Cassandra," he began, sinking with a huff into the chair opposite hers. "I promised King Christian to watch over you." He took her hand, enveloping it in ten sausage like fingers. "It would be your father's primary wish that you be safe."

He'd used this argument before—repeatedly. And it was the one most likely to sway Cassandra.

"Perhaps the Grand Duke can accompany you to the palace at Saint de Verde. Yes, that is what should happen." Cardinal Sinzen's fleshy face wrinkled in a smile. "You and your husband need some time alone after this terrible ordeal."

In contrast, this argument held little weight. Cassandra wondered if the cardinal truly assumed it did.

He stood, then settled behind a large rosewood desk. "I shall see to all the arrangements at once. The less time you spend here, the less threat to your safety. Do not concern yourself, I shall take care of everything."

"There's naught to see to. I'm not leaving."

The slam of his fists on the hard wood jolted Cassandra, but she met his stare defiantly.

"You are being a selfish child, Cassandra. Selfish and stubborn."

"I am not a child." She rose to her feet. "I am your queen, and I shall not—"

Without so much as a knock, the door to the office burst open. Startled, Cassandra lunged for the pistol General Hawke had left. Before she could aim it toward the intruder, the general himself pried it from her hand.

" 'Twas never meant to be used against my person," he said before holstering the weapon.

"Then perhaps you should take care lest you startle someone into shooting you."

A grin creased his face, a gleam of white against sun-bronzed skin. "I see you have recovered some of your wit. Put this on." The "this" was a cape, long and black, of coarse material.

Cassandra had no choice but to take the garment he thrust toward her. She did not, however, have to follow his orders. "I will not wear this."

Ignoring her argument and the cardinal's questions about where he'd been, Max wrapped the cloak around the Queen's shoulders. She had the good sense not to fight him. "Come with me," he commanded, after lifting the hood to cover her golden hair and the cockeyed crown.

"Wait! Where are you taking me?"

"General Hawke, I must demand that you cease pulling Her Highness about."

Max stopped, let go of Cassandra's arm, and wiped a weary hand down over his face. Two days' worth of stubble darkened his visage as he stared toward the Queen and her advisor. "I beg your royal pardon," he said with a mocking bow. "For not explaining myself satisfactorily. I'm a bit fatigued after my mad dash across the country to come to your aid."

"I do appreciate your—"

"However," Max interrupted. "After learning more about the nature of this little foray, it is my opinion that you should be taken to safety. And I suggest you travel there incognito."

Cassandra opened her mouth to dress him down for his impertinence. How dare he not only push her about but interrupt her recognition of gratitude. Then she looked at him, really looked at him, and it was all she could do not to reach out toward him. To draw his head down to rest on her breast. To brush the wayward lock of raven hair from his brow.

She didn't, of course. She only stared at him and he at her. And then without another word, he took her arm and led her toward the door.

"Where are you taking her? I demand to—"

The remainder of Cardinal Sinzen's words were cut off as Max slammed the door. Half pulling, half dragging her, Max managed to cross the chapel and escape the cathedral through a door behind the nave that opened onto a side street.

After the dusky light inside the cathedral, the sun was blinding. Cassandra yanked the hood down further over her face. The fabric smelled of unwashed bodies, and she would have protested her treatment, had she thought General Hawke would pay her any heed. As it was all her energy was needed to keep up with him.

She thought she knew Liberstein well. Though she'd never been allowed the freedom to roam the streets, she had ridden about in her coach.

But nothing about the narrow alley they hurried along seemed in the least familiar. The buildings were small and cramped, huddled together as if for comfort. Most of them seemed to list toward the street, making the already narrow byway appear more so.

Doors were open, as were windows, and Cassandra could

hear babies crying and children playing. The smells were strange, too. Cabbage, she guessed, and onions . . . sweat and rotting garbage. She wanted to ask where they were, but realized General Hawke wouldn't answer her.

They turned a corner and she saw Kanakareh and, beside him, two horses. Without a word of greeting he bent over, offering his cupped hands as a mounting block. Knowing nothing else to do Cassandra accepted his assistance. When they were mounted, Max looked to her.

"Are you doing all right?"

"Yes, but—" The rest of her words were lost as he twisted his mount around and headed toward the outskirts of the city. Cassandra followed.

Now she knew where they were heading.

The clumps of trees thickened till they were in the forest to the west of town. They rode side by side on the leaf-strewn road, Cassandra's borrowed cloak billowing behind her. Overhead she could hear geese winging their way south.

When they reached the stone bridge Max led the way down the embankment, turning in the saddle to watch as Cassandra followed. Then they rode alongside the stream till they could hear the roar of the waterfall. At the pool, Max dismounted, then reached up for Cassandra.

The sun was setting, throwing jewel-like sparkles across the water. The air seemed charged with memories, and Cassandra's mouth went dry when his hands clasped her waist.

Why had he brought her here?

Why had she allowed it?

"Does anyone else know of this place?"

"I'm not sure. Perhaps." He stepped away as soon as her feet touched the soft ground. "I can not say if someone else has stumbled across the pool." Her voice grew husky. "You did."

"Aye." He glanced her way quickly, then returned to his study of the waterfall. "But I meant the tunnel to the castle."

"Well, yes. Sophia knows and Kanakareh was here."

"Anyone else? I'd like to know if I should have a weapon handy."

"A weapon?" Sensual memories of their first meeting gave way to hard-edged reality. "What are you talking about?"

"I'll explain once we're inside. Just tell me if there's a chance we'll meet anyone along the way."

"No. My father ad brother knew. Simon told us all, but . . ." Cassandra took a deep breath. "No one is likely to be lying in wait."

"Now if you could only assure me there would be no rats," Max mumbled.

"What did you say?"

"Never mind." With a flourish of his arm, Max merely waved her forward. He took her hand to help her with her footing, but let her lead the way.

Darkness enveloped them.

Cassandra knew her way as surely as she knew her own face, had traveled this tunnel since she was a child. Yet she'd never experienced such a journey as this one with Max. She could feel his every move, hear his breathing, so very close to her; imagined she could hear the steady beat of his heart.

The climb had never left her breathless before, yet now she wondered if she would make it. But she did, covering the last stairway slowly, feeling for the lever that opened the secret panel.

As she slid through the doorway and around the unicorn tapestry, she glanced about the room, glad to see it empty. "Now," she said, turning on the general, "will you tell me why I must sneak into my own rooms wrapped in . . . in this?" Her hands flared out the cape, then dropped.

Stepping forward Max reached beneath her chin, untying the hood, letting the cape fall from her shoulders. It landed on the floor, surrounding her like a giant thundercloud. But his fingers still lingered, the backs, where tiny hairs curled, just touching the tip of her chin.

Cassandra could barely breathe.

"I came as soon as I knew, though truthfully I didn't realize the danger you were in."

She was drowning in his eyes. So blue. She could stand like this forever and not complain. It was he who cut the moment short. Taking a deep breath he brushed his knuckles across her chin in a parody of a punch, then turned to flop into a chair near the hearth. "Good God, I could sleep for a fortnight."

"Oh, no you don't." Hands on hips, Cassandra marched forward. "Not until you tell me what this is all about."

She was magnificent. There was no other word for her, Max decided. All thick golden hair and fiery violet eyes. She didn't look like a modern-day queen but something out of Greek mythology. He wondered why she wasn't set off by lightning spears.

But that was just his sleep-deprived mind taking a fanciful bent.

Max dragged both hands down across his face and sighed. "We found the man with the knife . . . well, actually Kanakareh found him."

"He did?" Cassandra took a step forward. "I wasn't certain until just now that there really was someone. I thought perhaps it was part of my . . ." Her eyes sought his.

"There was a knife all right. And a damn scoundrel ready to use it." It still made him weak to think what might have happened had he been minutes later in arriving at the square.

"But why?" Cassandra sank into the chair across from him. Absently she pulled the crown from her head. "I don't understand what happened today."

"There was a riot, Your Highness. Perhaps a unique phenomenon in Breslovia, but not unheard of elsewhere."

"It was frightening."

"Most civil disobedience is. But as it happens this time it

seems very localized. Actually, Kanakareh could find no more than a dozen men who took part."

"It seemed like so many more than that."

Max shrugged. "Toss twelve loud angry men into a crowd and you have chaos. Add to that the lack of Imperial Guards and there could have been disaster."

As she spoke Cassandra fingered the jeweled tips of the coronet. "What about the man with the knife? Why was he angry? And why, if you've captured him, did we have to sneak into the castle like thieves in the night?"

"I have no idea why he was angry, though some of the others we questioned ranted on about you dissolving the Diaz."

"I didn't dissolve it. Breslovia's Parliament is very important to me." When Max said nothing, Cassandra continued. "I think Albert and Cardinal Sinzen decided to disband the Diaz for the time being." Which was another way of saying they dissolved it, Cassandra decided.

"In any case, I don't believe our assailant cared one way or the other. He admitted to being paid to attack you."

The blood drained from her face, but Cassandra tried to keep her voice calm. "Did you discover who paid him to kill me?"

"No. The scoundrel doesn't know who hired him, which is why I bundled you in here like I did." Pausing, Max eyed the large tester bed. It looked like half a regiment could sleep beneath the brocaded canopy. "Whoever wanted to hurt you might not give up so easily."

"Hmm." Cassandra stood. Then she paced, from the hearth to the high windows looking out on the river below. "Cardinal Sinzen wants me to go to the country."

"That might not be a bad idea." Max glanced over his shoulder. "Do you mind if I try this?"

Already listing the reasons why she didn't wish to run off to the palace at Saint de Verde, Cassandra paid him no more heed than a flip of her hand. "I've only begun to actually take over some of the power left me by my father. When he died it was so easy for me to turn over the government to advisors and . . . and Albert. But now I plan to— What did you say?"

When there was no reply, just a loud unmistakable snore, Cassandra whirled around. The general lay sprawled on her bed, his large form spread over the purple counterpane. He still wore his muddy boots and dirt-tarnished uniform. Only now the dirt and grime was also on her bed.

Cassandra moved forward, full of indignation, then stopped abruptly as another snore reverberated through the room. How dare he fall asleep when she had so many more questions. Reaching out, she touched his shoulder, but stopped short of rousing him.

As he lay there on his back, with the last rays of filtered sunlight splayed across his body, there was nothing to stop her from looking her fill. As if she were starved for the sight of him, her eyes devoured him.

He was disheveled and dirt streaked, hardly at his best, yet Cassandra found herself strongly attracted to his gritty appearance. She studied his face, from the wide forehead with its wayward lock of dark hair to the nose she found so fascinating. The heavy shadow of beard didn't hide the bold bones and valleys or the strong determined chin.

He looked like a dark knight . . . if a bit tarnished.

But the days of knights were gone. With a sigh Cassandra watched as his chest rose and fell. She would have to wake him. But when her hand moved again it was to gently swipe the hair from his forehead.

His beard abraded her skin, and his warm breath sent shivers down her spine. She swallowed, leaning closer when he mumbled.

"What?" she whispered, not certain if he were asleep or not.

"Beautiful," came his murmured reply. "My beautiful queen." His words were followed by a muffled snore and Cassandra's heart melted.

* * *

"Leave us!"

"You . . . you have no right to burst in—"

"Tell her to get out!" Cardinal Sinzen's face was nearly as red as his robes. He swept back and forth in front of the door he'd just entered, glancing up often to see if his order was being followed. He didn't miss the looks passing between his brother and that French whore, his mistress. Her look attempted to infuse a spine down Albert's back. Sinzen was just as determined to snap it.

"Whatever you must say can be said in front of—"

Patience gone the way of his piety, the cardinal rushed forward, shocking both by leaning across the table on which their cards were scattered. "If she isn't gone in two minutes I'll see that she is expelled from Breslovia."

"Perhaps . . . perhaps you should go." Albert's eyes skittered from one to the other. "Only to rest. Yes, you need your rest for tonight."

He had to give the woman credit, Sinzen thought. She didn't argue or put up any resistance, though her expression spoke volumes as she gracefully rose. Without a backward glance, she exited the room, leaving the door open.

A door the cardinal quickly slammed.

"Now," he said, resuming his pacing, huffing and puffing as he went, "just explain to me what was in your mind."

"I don't know what you mean, and I really must protest your treatment of Nico—"

"You should feel fortunate I don't have the woman expelled from Breslovia."

"You can't—"

"Oh, but I can, little brother." The pacing stopped. "I can do anything I wish. Was this fiasco her idea?"

Albert snapped open his snuff box. "I don't know what you mean," he repeated, his voice nearly an octave higher than normal.

"Did you think I wouldn't find out. Did you? Don't you realize I have eyes and ears everywhere in Breslovia. That scourge of humanity you hired was not to be trusted with your secret. Not when I had my way with him."

"We don't need her." Albert spread his hands wide and the jewel-encrusted box flew to the floor, fine tobacco dust littering the rug.

"Albert." The cardinal's rage was concentrated in that one word. "Knowing you even as I do, I am disappointed. I can only surmise it is that woman who corrupts you."

"Leave Nicolette out of this. She didn't— You won't send her away, will you?"

"Stop your whining." Sinzen settled onto the chair recently vacated by the Frenchwoman, his bulk spilling over the sides. "Tell me everything and I shall consider what should be done." He leaned across the table, scattering the playing cards. "And I mean everything."

Once he'd started, Albert confessed his deed with relish and no small amount of pride. His glazed expression actually brightened. "So I sent the Imperial Guard to General Hawke . . . for training. And to insure there was no interference in my scheme."

"Hawke is back." Sinzen relished the sight of blood draining from his brother's face. How dare Albert assume to do more than follow instructions—his instructions.

"Back? But . . . but we sent him to Bordgarten."

"And he returned—with the Imperial Guard in tow—in time to squelch your little uprising."

"Does he know?"

"That you're behind the assassination attempt on the Queen? No."

"Then she still lives."

"Yes, thank God." The cardinal lifted his hands in supplication. "Did you not even have the courage to discover how your plan fared? Were you so unconcerned that you spent your time frivolously playing whist?"

"There was nothing I could do," Albert mumbled.

"Except nearly ruin all that we've worked for." Exasperation set in and the cardinal hefted himself from his seat. "Do you realize what would have happened had your stupid plot succeeded?"

Albert's chin rose. "I would have been named ruler of Breslovia."

Sinzen's nostrils pinched as he sucked air into his lungs. "You are an idiot. The Diaz would not appoint you. If they or Cassandra wished that, they would have named you king rather than Grand Duke. The throne would have passed to one of the Queen's cousins, most likely that babbler, Sophia. Or perhaps Frederick of Prussia would step in and decide he must declare himself ruler to save Breslovia from unrest."

"I'm the Grand Duke—I'm married to the Queen."

"Which is exactly where your power lies." Albert flinched as his brother approached, but it was only a squeeze on the shoulder the cardinal delivered. "I have explained this to you before. The only way Cassandra is expendable is if she bears your child."

"But Nicolette said—"

The fingers clawed, digging into Albert's shoulder. "You must forget what that one tells you. She doesn't know. Who has always looked after you, Albert? When mother went into one of her rages, who hid you in the chapel?"

"You did?"

"And when she threatened you with the knife, swearing she would sever your cock and toss it to the wolves, who stood up to her rantings and protected you?"

"You, but—"

"There can be no buts, Albert. We are in this as one. We have been since that night in Lansing Forest."

"Perhaps we never should have killed them." Albert cringed.

"Strange talk coming from a man who just tried to murder his wife."

"What if someone else finds out?" His voice quivered. "Hawke. What if General Hawke discovers my involvement?"

"He won't. By now he should be learning that the plot was

contrived by Count Wenzel. At least that's what the assailant told the guards."

"Count Wenzel?" Albert's brow wrinkled in consternation. "Why would he tell them that?"

"Because I paid him to, you idiot. God, I had to think of everything."

"But Count Wenzel will—"

"Deny everything, of course. I believe he already has—vehemently." Sinzen's face wrinkled in a smile. "But then, who will believe him?"

"But what if my man changes his mind and tells the truth?"

"He won't."

"How can you be so sure? Perhaps Hawke will convince him."

"That will be difficult to do Albert." The fingers tightened once more before Sinzen turned and walked toward the door. "From beyond the grave." As his pudgy hand latched onto the gold knob the cardinal glanced over his shoulder. "Find your wife. Be prostrate with grief over her ordeal. Take the wench to bed. Ram that cock I saved from mutilation into her. Impregnate her, by God, or I'll take up where Mother left off."

Albert pushed himself to his feet. "Where . . . where is she?"

"I don't know. Hawke took her!"

Paradise.

Max moaned as the sensation flowed over him. Like the waters that splashed over the rocks. Consuming. Overpowering.

Like his reaction to her.

He could see her in the mist, her lithe body shrouded in a white gossamer gown, nearly transparent from the water droplets. Her rose-tipped breasts, the beckoning shadow between her long legs. Beautiful and sensual with her hair streaming about alabaster shoulders. Her lips in a smile.

She watched him watching her, those eyes sparkling in the moonlight. Her gaze stroked his body and she knew, knew how much he wanted her. She called to him, a siren's song of desire, and he tried to move.

Frustration coursed through him. He was stuck, unable to lift a foot or budge, as if buried alive in warm, smooth mud. The more he struggled, the deeper he was enveloped by the smothering mess.

He looked up and she was still there; still looking at him, but now others surrounded her. Max couldn't see their faces as they pulled at her, till she acquiesced and let them take her away.

"No. Come back. Don't leave me."

The sound of his own voice woke him with a start. Max's eyes tore open . . . and stared into a pair of equally shocked violet eyes. It took him a moment to realize he'd been dreaming, and to remember where he was.

But nowhere in his memory did he recall lying on the royal bed with the Queen. And unless he was mistaken that was what he was doing.

"Are you all right? You were yelling."

"I do that at times. Talk in my sleep. It drives Kanakareh mad." If she could act nonchalant about their sharing a pillow so could he. Except that she wasn't acting so accepting of it anymore.

"I must have fallen asleep," Cassandra murmured as she tried to shrink away from the general. How could she have been so careless? It had seemed innocent enough while he slept to crawl onto the edge of her bed. And she was so very tired. But who would have guessed that while sleeping she would nearly crawl on top him?

Her arm lay draped across his chest. Her nose nearly touched his. And the warm bulge beneath her leg felt too hard to be the mattress.

So *this* was why her dreams had been filled with erotic images instead of men with knives.

"Where are you going?"

The query seemed innocuous enough, but it was accompanied by the touch of his hand on her shoulder.

Cassandra stopped breathing. Memories flooded her mind. And, oh, she wanted to make them real again.

But real was the crown that she could see on the table beside his head. Real was the people of Breslovia. The whisper of his lips as he moved toward her.

"Please," she breathed as his mouth caressed hers.

And neither of them knew whether she begged him to stop or continue.

Eleven

The kiss seemed to go on forever, first slow and sensual, then hot and wet. Deep, so that he could feel the mind-drugging thrust to the tip of his toes.

It consumed him. Made him want more. What he had before. What he'd dreamed of since.

Yet for some reason he couldn't seem to take the next step. The next logical step. Her body, warm and pliant from sleep, pressed against his, wriggling closer every time his tongue touched hers. But his hand only cupped the silk-covered curve of her shoulder almost as if trying to hold her at bay.

God, what was wrong with him? He was in her bed, damn it, sprawled beneath the royal tester. With the woman he desired more than any other, willing, nay eager, and lying beside him. What difference did it make that she was the Queen of Breslovia? After all, he just saved her life. And did it really matter that she called another "husband"? He certainly was no innocent where married women were concerned.

"Max." His name was little more than a breath of air that tickled his lips as he pulled away enough to see her face in the faint candlelight.

He swallowed, wondering if he had the strength to roll off the bed when she reached up clamping her hand over his and dragging his palm slowly over the smooth skin of her throat and lower. He took control before his fingers encountered the plush swell of a breast, making her moan as he delved lower, beneath the layers of bone and jewel-encrusted silk.

The hell with the consequences.

He wanted her. He was mad from wanting her, and she was willing. There was no mistaking that.

In his frenzy to find the opening to her gown Max didn't hear the tapping on the door, or even the startled feminine gasp. It wasn't until Cassandra stiffened, then shoved his hand aside as she pushed herself up, that he realized anything was amiss.

And then his passion-drunk brain could only wonder at the surprise of seeing Lady Sophia with her mouth shut. Actually, it wasn't, though. A troop of cavalry could ride through the opening, but no sound came out.

Cassandra was the one babbling away. Something about things not being as they appeared and that she'd just lain down for a moment because she was so tired and then when she woke . . .

Despite himself Max had an inkling of interest in just how she planned to explain why he was groping the front of her gown. Why her hands were clutching his shoulders. But before she reached that part of the scenario, she paused and stuck her chin in the air, though Max could detect a slight quiver in it. "What is it you wished, Lady Sophia?"

It was as if the redheaded woman were struck dumb. She continued to stare, wide-eyed, and Max did imagine they made quite a spectacle there on the bed. He with his two days' worth of traveling dirt and grime and the queen, disheveled but still splendidly attired in the royal jewels.

"Sophia."

The word seemed to shake the lady-in-waiting from her stupor. Her mouth snapped shut with such force Max could hear the clink of her teeth from across the room.

"Tell me what you want."

"Oh my, Your Majesty." Sophia started toward the bed, ignoring as best she could the general's presence. "I am so glad you're safe. You are, aren't you? Safe, I mean. There have been such awful rumors spreading about the palace. I've been so worried. I wanted to leave and look for you myself, but the

Grand Duke would not allow it. He is searching for you everywhere. But some said you were dead, murdered at the hands of a fanatic. And they say Count Wenzel is behind the whole thing."

By the time Sophia paused for breath she was being comforted by Cassandra who slid off the bed and wrapped her arms around her friend.

"As you can see, I'm neither dead, nor injured," the Queen began. "And for that, I have General Hawke to thank."

Sophia's eyes skittered, snagging on Max for the minutest of moments before returning to Cassandra. "Pray tell, what happened? Albert was vague, though he does seem in a state over your whereabouts. No one thought to look for you here because you didn't return to the palace through the gates. It wasn't till moments ago that I myself remembered the secret passage and wondered if perhaps you'd come back that way."

"You told no one of the passage, did you?" This from Max who received only an indignant look in response. Sophia kept her eyes locked on his as she pulled Cassandra to the side. Max pretended not to notice they talked about him.

"What is he doing here . . . in your bed?" Sophia's loud whisper cut right through the brocade hangings on the side of the bed. "I apologize for asking, but I simply can't believe . . ." She shook her head, sending red curls flying. "Not that an affair of sorts might not be an idea—a grand idea, considering the Grand Duke—but, Cassandra, I can't imagine you . . ."

Cassandra took a deep breath and studiously avoided glancing toward the bed. Sophia was right. Affairs and peccadillos were commonplace at court. *She* simply didn't participate in them—at least she hadn't until Maximilian Hawke. "As your queen I could order you to stop questioning my behavior." Her shoulders drooped forward and her eyes pleaded. "But as your friend I am asking you to trust me."

"Oh, Cassandra, you know I do." Sophia's arms shot around the Queen. Her hug was quick and sincere. "I am so glad you're all right. From now on you must take me with you wherever you go, though since Count Wenzel has been captured, I doubt there's any further need to worry, but—"

"Wait a moment." Arms linked, both women looked over at him and Max felt strangely out of place. At least he wasn't still sprawled on the rumpled bed. Before Sophia could start talking again Max combed ten fingers back through his hair. "What makes you so sure Wenzel had anything to do with this?" He'd met the young noble once or twice and found him boring, content with court life and hardly the type to mount a revolution.

"He confessed," Sophia answered with uncharacteristic brevity.

"Just like that?" Max snapped his fingers.

"I don't know for sure. But Lady Diana did say that she'd heard from Sir Winston there was an awful man who shot at you, and Cardinal Sinzen rushed down the cathedral steps and captured the culprit who was struck by the enormity of the sin he'd nearly committed and confessed on the spot that it was Count Wenzel who'd paid him ten thousand rubles to kill you."

"Ten . . . ten thousand rubles," Cassandra said with a laugh. "Didn't that strike you as rather a large amount?"

"I can't understand how you can find this amusing. I certainly don't. And by the looks of him General Hawke doesn't either."

"I am sorry." Cassandra gave her friend's shoulders a squeeze before stepping away. "It just amazes me how inaccurate gossip can be." She looked around to see Max running his palms along the wall beside the unicorn tapestry. "Where are you going?"

He glanced over his shoulder, briefly, before resuming his search. "To find Kanakareh. Where in the hell is the lever?"

"To your right. But why? I wished to talk with you further." Cassandra crossed the room toward him. "There are things we need to discuss, but you fell asleep."

"For which I beg your forgiveness. Ah, there it is," he said, as the secret panel opened.

"What about me? You were to protect me?" Which was a

ploy on her part to get him to stay, she knew, and from his expression, so did he.

"You heard what Lady Sophia said. Count Wenzel was captured." He reached out and, grabbing her hand, pulled her toward him. Her eyes widened, but she came, soft smells and warm woman. "I'll send Imperial Guardsmen to watch over you. Just stay in your apartments till I get back."

"But—"

The kiss he used to stop her argument lasted longer than he'd planned. He headed into the dark chasm with the taste of her on his lips and the echo of Lady Sophia's startled gasp in his ears.

"How in the hell could he be dead?"

Max didn't expect an answer, and received none. He and Kanakareh stood in an anteroom of the palace waiting to see Cardinal Sinzen. They'd been waiting for near an hour, and for a large portion of that time Max had been asking the same question.

Tiring of striding the perimeter of the room, Max now flopped into a chair. "Tell me again what he said. Just humor me," Max replied to the Seneca's grunt of exasperation.

"He said nothing."

"No mention of Count Wenzel?"

"Not when I questioned him."

"And you were thorough?" Max winced. "Yes, of course you were. I simply don't understand."

"What is it you don't understand, General Hawke?"

Max stood, bowing toward the doorway where the cardinal stood. "Your Grace. It's the untimely death of the prisoner, that I've trouble comprehending."

"Yes," Cardinal Sinzen shook his head. "A tragedy to be sure. Do come in."

Once inside the gilded and mirrored room where Max had

first met with the Grand Duke and Cardinal, Max continued. "Do you have any information about how he died?"

"Trying to escape, I'm told. Please." Sinzen motioned toward a pair of seats. "Luckily he chose to indicate his employer before a guard was forced to kill him."

"Yes, luckily." Max leaned forward. "Count Wenzel is in custody then?"

"Of course."

"I'd like to see him."

"At the moment I'm afraid that is impossible."

Max paused a moment to control a temper that was beginning to seethe. He had to remember who had just spoken. Cardinal Sinzen, the man responsible for his present lofty position as commander in chief of Breslovia, stood, smiling benevolently. But there was steel behind that warmth, razor-sharp steel. Max kept annoyance out of his tone—at least he tried.

"I don't understand why I cannot speak with the prisoner. Kanakareh is very adept at gathering information. Certainly you—"

"General Hawke,"—the smile never wavered—"have I told you how pleased the Grand Duke and I are with your work? From all the reports you send it appears that the army is shaping up nicely. I'm certain you wish to return to your duties as soon as possible."

The fragile threads of Max's composure were breaking. Beside him Kanakareh shifted, a reminder, perhaps. Max settled back in his chair. "Thank you for your confidence. Kanakareh and I, and all the officers and men, have worked very hard."

The cardinal nodded, smiling.

"However," Max continued, ignoring the Seneca's sharp grunt, "I did ride day and night for two days, bringing back the Imperial Guard to help stave off a tragedy."

"Breslovia is in your debt."

Now Max smiled. "I am pleased to offer my services wherever this great kingdom needs me." He paused just a moment.

"Which is why I would like to interrogate the prisoner. Perhaps I can—"

"Officially, this incident is not under your jurisdiction." The shiny cheeks were less puffed out now.

"I was under the impression I was in charge—"

"Of the army General Hawke. The army. This is a police matter. Certainly you see the difference. But as I said before we are very pleased with your innovative ideas concerning the military." The cardinal settled his porcine frame in a chair. "Now there is the matter of the Queen."

"She is safe."

"Of course she is, yet no one seems to know where she is."

It occurred to Max to use Cassandra as a trade. A visit with Count Wenzel in exchange for Her Highness' whereabouts. And he might have suggested it if the door to the council room hadn't opened that moment for a liveried footman to announce the very woman under discussion.

Cassandra floated into the room, her bearing regal, her chin held high. She hardly deigned to glance his way, which was a good thing because Max was wondering what the hell she thought she was doing. Hadn't he given her explicit instructions to stay in her apartments?

"Your Majesty, I cannot express how pleased I am to see you looking so well."

"Thank you, Cardinal Sinzen. I am just as pleased to be well and safe."

"But I don't understand. How did you get here? I had guards at the palace entrance to escort you to your rooms."

"That wasn't necessary. General Hawke accompanied me," Cassandra replied, without really answering his question. "I've come to speak with you about plans for another Festival of the Pax."

"It seems a bit early to worry about next year, Your Highness. And then, I'm not certain we should have a ceremony such as today's."

"Breslovia has celebrated the treaty of peace for centuries.

We shall not change tradition because of a few misguided rowdies. However, it was not of next year that I spoke. I wish to reschedule the ceremony for a week from now. I want to show the citizens of Breslovia that their queen is well and—"

"A fool." The tenuous restraint Max had on his emotions snapped. "Are you mad?" he said, leaping to his feet. "Don't you understand what could have happened to you today?"

He paused then, and Cassandra, who hadn't flinched even when he'd advanced on her, lifted her brows. "Are you finished, General Hawke?" She didn't give him time to answer. "For I assure you I am neither a fool nor mad. I simply plan to do what is best for Breslovia. The citizens need a sovereign they can depend upon. And I"—her focus widened to include the cardinal—"intend to be such a queen." She turned, her lilac silk overskirt sweeping the marble floor. When she reached the door, Cassandra glanced over her shoulder. "Please do what you must to arrange the ceremony, Cardinal Sinzen."

"But, Your Highness, what of your trip to the country?"

The cardinal's question remained suspended in the air, for the Queen had already exited the room. When the door closed Max rolled his eyes toward Kanakareh who nodded and stood.

"If you will excuse us," Max began. "It appears that you have business to attend to. We shall not keep you."

"Uh, yes, it would seem so." The cardinal's eyes finally strayed from the spot where Cassandra last stood. "Yes, I do," he said more firmly. "As do you. I shall expect an updated report from you on the progress of the army's training soon."

"And you shall have it. I just thought it might be a good idea for us to stay until after the ceremony."

"Can you believe him? He as much as ordered us to leave before Queen Cassandra's ride through the streets," Max said later as he and Kanakareh strolled through one of the many boxwood-lined paths outside the palace. The tinkling splash of a fountain depicting Diana, goddess of the hunt, filled the

NEW YORK TIMES BESTSELLING AUTHOR
JANELLE TAYLOR
DESTINY MINE
SHANNON DRAKE
BLUE HEAVEN, BLACK NIGHT
BESTSELLING, AWARD-WINNING AUTHOR
GEORGINA GENTRY
SONG OF THE WARRIOR
BETINA KRAHN
MIDNIGHT MAGIC

air. "That man's smiles are beginning to grate on my nerves. No one *smiles* that much."

"You do."

Max's head snapped around. "I do not smile. Grin perhaps." He paused. "Hell, the ladies seem to like it." Max walked along silently for several steps, his expression sober, his hands clasped behind his back. His next words came without a break in stride. "Do you know where they're holding Count Wenzel?"

"The dungeon beneath the old castle."

Max knew of one way to get there, if Cassandra wasn't jesting that first night, but he thought a more direct route better. Making an about-face, he headed toward the palace, Kanakareh by his side.

"You have thought this through?"

"I know what you're thinking," Max said, as he walked even faster. "But I'm not being impetuous. The Queen's life may be in jeopardy, and I believe it my duty to do what I can."

"Cardinal Sinzen doesn't agree."

"And he can end my military career as effectively as Lord Northford did. I know. And I've given it a great deal of consideration." Max glanced toward his friend. "I have. And I still want to talk with Count Wenzel, to find out why he would wish to kill the Queen."

Dressed in the regimental uniform of a general, Max had no trouble passing through two stations of guards. As he and Kanakareh left the opulence of the palace, he again had the feeling that he was crossing not only a stone walkway but stepping back in time. He could almost understand the pull Cassandra felt for the old castle.

Not that there was anything pleasant about the dungeon. There was a spine-chilling slam of iron against iron as the last guard closed heavy gates. Now, lantern in hand, they walked along a narrow passage with heavy wooden doors to either side. Occasionally a tunnel gaped off to the left or right, but they ignored these.

"Stick to the straight and narrow," the last guard had said, "and you'll be seeing the jailor standing watch. He'll let you in, if he hasn't fallen asleep or run off." The man's laugh revealed the absence of all his front teeth.

"There are not many prisoners," Kanakareh said, lifting his lantern toward the barred opening in one of the doors.

"Either that or they're all taking an afternoon nap. It's so quiet down here, except for . . ." Max winced at the unmistakable squeals and the skittering of tiny feet. "God, I hate rats."

But even that was forgotten as they caught a glimmer of light ahead. Then the jailor, a squat, thick-necked man with skin as dark and greasy looking as the sweating stone walls, lunged forward, his pike thrust toward them.

"Who goes there, and what be your business?"

"Jailor Smoots, is it?" Max backhanded the pointed steel aside. "General Hawke here, and my aide the Seneca warrior, Kanakareh. We've come to interrogate your prisoner. This is where Count Wenzel is confined, is it not?"

"Aye, 'tis." Even in the dim light Max could see the skeptical lift of the man's bushy brows. "But I don't know 'bout lettin' ye in. My orders were—"

"Changed." Max pushed passed him toward the door. "Perhaps spending all your time down here you do not know who I am." He cast a questioning glance over his shoulder.

"Well, aye, sir. I know."

"Then I wonder at your insolence." Max nearly smiled at his own tone. Perhaps he *had* learned something from his father.

And just as with his father the arrogance paid dividends. Though obviously reluctant to do so, Jailor Smoots produced a rusty ring of iron keys from the pocket of his stone gray jacket. With a clanging that echoed down the corridor he unlocked the door. A strange keening sound came from deeper in the dungeon but Jailor Smoots merely shrugged it off.

"Damn prisoners won't keep quiet," he said before adding, "You'll be having to leave your weapons out here."

"I'd have reported you if you hadn't demanded as much," Max said as he unbuckled his sword. Kanakareh handed over the tomahawk hanging from his belt. But neither removed or mentioned the knives tucked into their boots.

Max winced as the door slammed shut, then raised his lantern. The cell was small, perhaps three yards square, windowless and damp. The air was so fouled by human excrement Max longed for one of the Grand Duke's perfumed handkerchiefs.

Nearly devoid of furniture, the cell contained a small table holding a bowl of thin stew, a tankard, and a pallet on the straw-littered floor. Max didn't see Count Wenzel at first. Gone was the court dandy with his polished manners and curled wigs. This man huddled in a corner, his arm thrown over his head to ward off the light or a blow, and he didn't move until Max spoke his name. Then he sprang up, stopping short of throwing himself into Max's arms.

"Thank God. You've come to tell me this is some awful mistake." Max's expression must have dampened that hope, for Wenzel backed up, his dirt-streaked face a study in horror. "What is it? What do you people want from me?" he screamed, the last words ending on a sob.

"The truth."

"Ha." A bit of Count Wenzel's old personality surfaced through the grime with that one syllable. "Not one of you are interested in that or I'd not be here and forced to rot in my own filth."

Max almost felt sorry for him until he remembered the man coming at Cassandra with the knife. The horrified expression on her lovely face. "What did you hope to gain from this Wenzel?"

"Gain?" His laugh bordered on maniacal. "There is the thrust. What could I possibly gain from hurting the Queen?" His head dropped back till greasy hair skimmed along the torn collar of his jacket. "There is nothing. Nothing. And I did nothing. Why won't anyone believe me?" The last words were no more than a whisper.

"The man you hired to kill Her Highness gave your name."

"He lied."

"Tell us what he would gain from for doing so?" This from Kanakareh.

Count Wenzel made no reply at first, only walked to the table and lifted the tankard to his lips. "I've wondered that myself." After drinking, he glanced toward Max. "Sorry I can't offer you some refreshment, but they give me precious little to drink." He glanced toward the stew. "The food isn't fit for a dog." He took another sip, scowling at the taste.

"The truth is, I don't know why he lied. I never hired anyone. I never planned to hurt the Queen. Hell, until yesterday my main concern in life was having a pleasant time of it." He shook his head slowly.

"I'll see about having you moved." Certainly there were more humane quarters that could house Wenzel while Max searched for the truth. And he was beginning to wonder if he wasn't hearing it now. He nodded toward Kanakareh who knocked on the door. Minutes later the portal creaked open.

But before it closed again behind Max and the Seneca warrior a strangled choking sound came from the cell.

"Takes 'em a while to get used to it down here," the jailor said when Max looked his way. "He's just in there puking his guts out. Nothing to concern yourself over."

It did indeed sound as though Count Wenzel was vomiting. Max decided he'd probably be doing the same if he were in the other man's place. He and Kanakareh made their way back toward the palace, their pace quickening as they climbed toward the light.

"Did he seem to be lying to you?" Max paused to brush the sleeve of his uniform when they reentered the wide hall of mirrors.

"Men are capable of great deceit when their lives hang in the balance."

"True enough, but something about him rings true. I never cared for the man, don't get me wrong, but he just doesn't seem like a revolutionary, or even a fanatic to me."

"Are you going to speak to the cardinal about moving him?"

This was tantamount to admitting he'd disobeyed Sinzen. "Hell, I suppose I have to. I said I would." Max slanted his friend a look of disgust. "You could have stopped me from saying it."

Max expected a sharp rebuke about thinking before he spoke, but Kanakareh was too busy staring down the long gallery. He'd slowed his step till he hardly moved and Max glanced around to see what held the Seneca's rapt attention.

Sophia hurried across the marble floor. She'd found Kanakareh and the general, for that she was grateful, but she didn't relish the idea of facing Maximilian Hawke. Not so soon after finding him in Cassandra's bed. Still, some things had to be done, and she'd promised the Queen. . . .

Besides, she couldn't deny, at least to herself, a wish to see Kanakareh one more time. Her eyes never left him as she approached. And she could feel his on her.

"Lady Sophia," Max said with a bow. She barely glanced his way. Which suited Max for he wasn't anxious to answer the plethora of questions she might toss his way.

"Her Majesty wishes to see you," Sophia finally managed to say. For some reason as she looked into Kanakareh's dark, dark eyes her mouth felt as if it were filled with wool. Sophia took a deep breath, straining the laces of her corset. "Can you come with me now?"

"It would be my honor, Lady Sophia," the Seneca answered in a tone Max had never heard before. He looked from one to the other, wondering what the hell was going on. They'd started along the corridor, taking several steps, before either remembered Max's presence.

A red head bobbed around, though her gaze did not meet his. "You are to come too" was all she said.

He was to come too. Well it was a good thing, for he had a few choice words for Queen Cassandra . . . which was ridiculous. He didn't tell her what to do, she told him. But—damn it all!—he didn't want her risking her life again.

Max's eyes narrowed as he studied the two walking several

paces ahead. Lady Sophia chattered away like the magpie she was, and Kanakareh smiled down at her fondly.

But Max forgot them when he entered Cassandra's apartments. She was in the small anteroom, sitting at a desk stacked high with books. One large volume lay open on her lap, and she used her finger to mark her place when they entered. Her gaze seemed to skitter away from Max.

"I've brought them both as you can see, Your Highness," Lady Sophia began. "Though I did have a difficult time locating them. Sir Winston said he saw them in the gardens, but when I sent several servants to look, they were nowhere to be found. Then—"

"Thank you, Sophia. And I do appreciate your coming." The words were for both men, yet Cassandra still managed to avoid eye contact with Max. "I wished to speak with you about my visions. They've changed."

"Very often what the spirits wish us to see changes."

"Yes." Cassandra stood, leaving the book open on the chair. "That may be what happened. I saw the man with the knife in a vision."

"When?"

Cassandra glanced toward Max, who asked the question. "Moments before he appeared in person. It was the strangest thing. In the vision I'd just alighted from the coach. There was yelling. I could hear it, but as if it happened far away. Then the man came at me. I screamed. The vision faltered only in reality."

She had mentioned something of the sort to him in the cathedral, but Max hadn't given it much thought. Now he turned toward Kanakareh. "What do you make of it?"

"All visions are different. It appears you no longer fight with the spirits."

"No. I try to do as you taught me."

The Seneca nodded. "That is good, for it seems there is a spirit watching out for you. My guardian spirit is the hawk of my clan. He came to me in my vision and he protects me."

"A bird? Do you think 'tis a bird that watches over me?"

"I do not know, Your Highness. Perhaps one day your spirit will reveal himself to you."

"Perhaps," Cassandra sighed.

"But in the meanwhile you need a more *human* protector," Max said.

Kanakareh rolled his dark eyes. "Hawke does not always believe in the spirits, though they brought us together."

"That's not true. I trust everything Queen Cassandra tells us she sees. I simply don't think we should take chances that this . . . this spirit will always keep her safe."

"I don't either," Sophia added. "What happened yesterday was frightening. I can't bear to think of it. I become quite faint knowing a man with a knife was after my dear friend. It just is too much for words."

"Which is exactly why I want you to stay in your apartments and allow the Imperial Guard to do their job. Forget this foolishness about riding through the streets again."

"It isn't foolishness, and I shall do it." Cassandra lifted her chin. "Please, may I speak with General Hawke for a moment?"

"Alone?" Sophia asked.

Cassandra simply lifted a queenly brow and her lady-in-waiting bowed, backing out of the room. When Kanakareh and Sophia closed the door behind them, Cassandra began pacing the width of the room.

She set her chin high, kept her eyes straight ahead. "I am grateful to you for your assistance, possibly even for my life."

"It is my honor to serve you, Your Highness."

Cassandra's head whirled to the side. Did she detect a note of sarcasm? Deciding she wasn't certain, she continued. "However, I will do what I must." She held up her palm to stop his interruption. "The people of Breslovia need me, and I shall be their queen—in every way." Cassandra shut her eyes for a moment, realizing all that entailed.

Her voice was lower, but no less firm as she continued. "I

have studied and learned. Will begin meeting with ambassadors tomorrow. And the Grand Duke and I have reconciled."

She knew he was watching her. Cassandra found it hard to look at him and continue to speak. She had to. "Albert and I are in complete agreement that Breslovia needs an heir." She swallowed. The room had gone suddenly still. She could hear the pounding of her heart. "Cardinal Sinzen lauds your work with the army, and I join him in that. It is time for you to return to your soldiers."

"In other words you want me away from you."

Her skin hurt from holding herself so rigid, but Cassandra feared if she let down her guard she would shatter like a glass vase. "If that is how you choose to view this, then yes, I—"

"I don't choose to view this at all, Cassandra. Damn it, will you look at me? Do you think I wished to entangle myself with you? Hell, I didn't," he answered before she could. He had her by the shoulders now and his fingers itched to climb higher, to touch her flesh, the curve of her chin. "You are the last woman on earth I want to want. But damn it"—his voice broke—"you're the only one I do want."

Twelve

She couldn't breathe.

It was as though all the air in the room vanished leaving in its place the sharp tingle of desire. Cassandra wanted to look away, to break the spell of his blue eyes, eyes that saw to the very core of her soul. That knew her secret needs. But she couldn't.

Time seemed to stand still, frozen like one of her visions. But thanks to Kanakareh she could now control the visions. There was no controlling this.

They stood, touching only where his hands gripped her shoulders, saying nothing . . . feeling everything.

Cassandra was the first to move—later she tried to tell herself it was Max, but knew better. She couldn't resist the pull. She wanted the hard maleness of him against her. One step was all it took, one simple step and his hands traveled across her shoulders till they touched bare skin.

Cassandra moaned as his fingers opened, his thumbs moving up to bracket her jaw. She could taste his kiss before their lips touched. Yet anticipation didn't compare to the bone melting way his mouth made her feel. He tilted her head, deepening the caress, his tongue wetting the seam of her mouth before pressing inside.

Her hands clutched his waist, knocking aside the scrolled sword hilt with a clatter. But she didn't care. Cassandra was beyond thinking of anything but him.

What started slowly, like smoldering tinder, suddenly sprang to life. His arms enveloped her, dragging her against him, holding her as if he would never let her go.

But reality was as hard edged as desire. Max straightened, brushing her lips with his once more before letting his head fall back against the door. He still held her, relishing the way the pulse at the base of her throat fluttered. He'd done that to her. He'd sent her blood racing—made her want him as badly as he wanted her.

Her chin trembled.

Max squeezed his eyes shut. "I'm a bastard."

When she said nothing, he shifted, slitting one lid open. "You could disagree. . . . No, don't." Max let out a shaky breath. "I . . . Jokes are not appropriate here."

Tightening his arms quickly before letting her go, Max strode toward the desk piled high with books. "Of course, not much of this is appropriate." He glanced around. Her shoulders were slumped, her head bowed. Seeing her like that tore at his heart.

"You were right, you know. 'Tis best, this reconciliation with the Grand Duke. Heirs . . ." He shook his head, brushing at a wrinkle on his blue wool jacket. "All kingdoms need heirs. It gives continuity. Makes the world go round." Hell and damnation. He was babbling away as badly as Lady Sophia. But it was either that or take her back in his arms and ravish her on the spot.

Or leave.

"Well . . . I have a duty also. To my men. And I'd better return before they all decide enlisting wasn't the fantastic idea I told them it was."

"Max." Her lashes lifted as he walked by.

"No need to say anything, Your Highness." He couldn't quite keep himself from touching her. Her cheek dropped to press against the back of his hand as it lay on her shoulder. And then he was gone.

* * *

"Kanakareh!" Max snapped the name out as he shut the door behind him. The Seneca warrior was nowhere to be seen, and probably was in no mood to talk with Max anyway. Max left a message with the first servant he saw and made his way out of the palace and to his rooms off the Boulevard de Pax.

He was still awake, staring at the moonlight-splashed designs on the ceiling when Kanakareh came in, but he gave no sign of it. Max heard the Seneca warrior go to his room and shut the door. And he wondered again why he couldn't treat the Queen as he had all the other women from his past.

He had fond memories of a few. Some could elicit a smile. A few a frown. But no one—not one—had ever consumed him as Cassandra did.

The kiss, her scent, came floating back to him, and Max groaned. Turning over, he fisted the pillow then flopped back down. God, he was going to have to forget about her. It was good he was leaving Liberstein. There was no other way.

But though Cardinal Sinzen ordered it, and Max desired it, he did not exit the city for over a week. Kanakareh only shook his head as Max delayed the date of their departure until finally, seeing no other choice, he admitted the truth.

"I won't return to the army till after this idiotic ceremony."

"It is not idiotic to the people of Breslovia."

Max only snorted. "I forgot how immersed you are in tradition and the like. Please excuse my affront to all Breslovians and peace-loving individuals everywhere. But you can't tell me you don't think Cassandra's . . . Queen Cassandra's . . . idea a dangerous one. You saw the chaos when we reached the city. And my God, a knife-wielding lunatic nearly killed her." The thought still made his skin crawl.

"Perhaps you are not seeing through the eyes of a soldier."

"What in the hell is that supposed to mean?" Max paused, the fork inches from his mouth. He and Kanakareh were in a tavern near their inn, eating a late repast.

Kanakareh's stare didn't waver. "Sovereigns are always at risk. Precautions must be made to protect them."

"My point exactly." Max motioned with the fork holding a bite of pork, then stuck the morsel in his mouth.

"It is the Imperial Guard's duty."

Max stopped chewing. Kanakareh was right. Colonel Marquart and his guards were doing an excellent job. If the chaos in the streets and the attempt on the Queen's life did nothing else, it rallied them to action. Reminded them their job was more than wearing large plumed hats and shiny gorgets.

Swallowing, Max slapped the fork down. "I'm staying," he said, and didn't care what Kanakareh thought of the situation.

Hell, he probably already knew all there was to know about his dalliance with Cassandra. The Seneca had a way of absorbing information. Lord knew Kanakareh was chummy enough with the babbling Lady Sophia. And Cassandra's lady-in-waiting had seen enough when she'd walked in on them to assume the rest.

Which led him to wonder if anyone else knew. If the Grand Duke knew.

He gathered not, on the day of the rescheduled Festival of the Pax. The weather was perfect, autumn at its most glorious, with a hint of frost in the air. The brilliant shades of the maple leaves backdropped the green and purple banners streaming from every window. It was as if the populace, feeling accountable for the last debacle, decided to spare no effort to make this festival perfect.

Standing on the corner of the Boulevard and Breze Street, Max couldn't help getting caught up in the enthusiasm of the crowd. Beside him a small child tugged at her mother's skirts, begging to see the Imperial Guard clattering by.

The young mother, infant in arms, tried to hush the child, then looked at Max beguilingly. She was pretty, with soft brown eyes in a heart-shaped face. Max glanced down toward the child. "Allow me," he said before lifting the clapping girl to his shoulder.

"I do thank you, kind sir," the woman told him. "My husband is away in the north with the army, or he would lift his daughter."

" 'Tis nothing," Max responded, guessing the woman had no idea she addressed her husband's commanding officer. Having decided it was best not to draw attention to himself, Max wore civilian clothes. He stood on the brick walkway like any other citizen of Breslovia, waiting to see his queen.

Across the way, blending into the crowd with a bit less success, stood Kanakareh.

Max still wasn't sure why he was here, in the shadow of the great cathedral. If trouble began, there was little he could do, even without a child squirming about on his shoulder.

At the back of his mind was a plan to rush forward and save Cassandra. But he didn't know how he'd accomplish that. And as the royal coach approached and the crowd began cheering in earnest, it didn't appear his services would be needed.

The woman beside him, Laura Mulgrade she'd told him, pressed against his arm. "Isn't it thrilling!" she said, her cheeks bright from the wind and excitement. "The Queen is so beautiful."

Max did little more than grunt his agreement as the eight matched white horses pulled abreast. He was taller than most and able to see without difficulty. The golden coach. The beautiful queen.

He recognized the crown from the last ceremony. Then it had sat cockeyed on her head. Now it rested, twinkling, among her golden curls, a reminder of ancient times and long traditions. She smiled, waving her gloved hand at the cheering crowd, completely in her element.

Across from her, a man leaned forward, making a comment that only she could hear, and she laughed. Max tore his gaze away from Cassandra to momentarily glance at the Grand Duke. He, too, wore a crown, smaller and less grand than

Cassandra's. He appeared the dandy he was, but the woman beside Max seemed to find him fascinating.

"Oh, Grand Duke Albert is so handsome," she crooned, shifting the sleeping babe from one arm to the other. " 'Tis said he and the Queen are like a fairy tale, so much in love. She was crushed, poor thing, when her father and brother were killed, as we all were. But it's heartwarming to know she's found true happiness."

"Yes, heartwarming," Max agreed in a grumble. How could anyone think she loved that prissy bastard, he wondered. But then he had to admit, it didn't appear such a farfetched notion.

The carriage drew to a stop beneath St. Peter's wide steps and the Grand Duke alighted, his ceremonial sword gleaming, a prince who turned back for his queen.

The Grand Duke smiled, offering his hand to her, and Max wanted to leap over the wooden barrier and knock him aside, child on his shoulders or no. Of course, he didn't. He, like everyone else, stood and watched as Queen Cassandra, splendid in a gown of pristine white, shining more than all the silver and gold that encompassed her, accepted her husband's help.

Max didn't realize he moaned until Laura Mulgrade leaned her full breasts into him and inquired what he'd said. "Nothing . . . only that you're correct. The Queen does seem happy."

"Oh, she does," Laura exclaimed as Cassandra started up the stairs toward Cardinal Sinzen. Behind her a page dressed in purple carried a gold box. Then came Grand Duke Albert. "The Edict of Liberstein," Laura explained when Max asked about the box. "The Queen is delivering the sacred document to the head of the church, as her father did, as his father did before him."

"Tradition."

"Yes, the monarchy is an old and grand one, and will go on for many years to come. When Liza is a mother she will bring her children to see Queen Cassandra, or perhaps her heir, deliver the edict."

Nothing—no one—would come between the Queen and her

destiny, Max knew. Until she turned her head and above the crowd their eyes met. She stopped, the young page nearly tripping on her skirts. And Max nearly stepped toward her, the pull was so strong.

Her smile disappeared then, and a sad longing filled her violet eyes, Max thought of rain-washed flowers and how it felt to hold her.

At that moment the yelling crowds disappeared. There were only the two of them. At least that was how Max felt. Then Cardinal Sinzen stepped forward and the Grand Duke took Cassandra's arm. She turned back to her task.

"I wonder what could be the matter with Her Highness," Laura said, staring up at Max, her brow wrinkled. "Perhaps the rumors are right then."

"What rumors?" Max still felt dazed.

"That she's carrying the heir to the throne right now."

Cassandra pregnant? Max tried to catch another look at her, but she was out of sight behind one of the cathedral's large pillars. He shook his head. The idea of her making love to Albert almost made him ill. So he tried not to think on it. Kanakareh was right. He should return to the army.

Immediately.

Tomorrow.

For tonight he would keep the lovely Laura Mulgrade company, Max told himself. There was no question in his mind she would have him. Since he'd settled beside her in the crowd she'd given him signs, signs that were becoming more blatant as the afternoon wore on.

After the Queen and Grand Duke left the cathedral, Cassandra making every effort not to glance his way, the people began to drift from the corner. Max lifted Liza from his shoulder, though the child wordlessly placed her hand in his.

"Come with us to the park," Laura said. "Unless you have other obligations, that is."

He had nothing else to do that day. Cassandra was safe, ensconced back in the palace with her husband. "We have reconciled," she'd told him. What in the hell did that mean? Max pushed the thought from his mind. It was a beautiful day, celebration was in the air, and there was a willing woman on his arm. She was married to be sure, but perhaps he was destined to spend his time pursuing the species. Just as Cassandra was destined to be queen and to reconcile with the Grand Duke and give birth to a royal heir.

"The park sounds perfect." Max's words brought a smile to Laura's lips. Her teeth were crooked, but he convinced himself that added a certain charm to her appearance as they walked along the wide, mansion-lined avenue. He carried the baby now, a robust boy named Christian for the late king, and found he actually enjoyed himself.

Laura was sweet, if not entirely loyal to her vows, and the children were so excited about the celebration that almost anything made them squeal with delight.

Max bought Liza a purple hair ribbon from a street vendor, and her mother some flowers. Christian laughed and drooled over a carved horse that an old man with one leg sold from the curb. They all ate roast pork and potatoes baked in the huge pit dug at the north end of the park, and drank wine made in Breslovia and given to the citizens by Queen Cassandra.

Laura talked, of her family, her husband, and her fears. Max listened and grew to like her. By the time the sun tinged the western sky mauve and he'd escorted Adam Mulgrade's small family back to their rented rooms, Max hardly thought of Cassandra at all.

Laura put the children to bed in their small nursery while Max watched the fireworks from the parlor window. When she returned it seemed natural to drape his arm around her narrow shoulders as the last of the celebration lit the sky.

She was clean and pretty enough, and willing. Lonely. Max took a deep breath, then pressed his lips to her soft brown hair. Lord knew he was lonely. And randy. Why the hell didn't he take her simple gown off and spend the night in Adam Mulgrade's bed?

The absent soldier would never know. And if he did find out, *he* posed no threat to Max.

Which made it all the more difficult to understand why Max brushed his lips across Laura's and bid her a fond good night. She was as shocked as he, gaining her voice only as he was about out the door. He didn't know whether her whispered "Thank you" was for the presents he'd bought or the fact that he'd left her virtue intact.

Whichever, her words warded off the evening chill as he made his way through the town. Merrymakers still crowded the wide, open squares, reluctant to call an end to a day so full of promise and hope. Which had nothing to do with the reason Max wandered toward the palace.

He was restless; anxious for the morrow when he could quit Liberstein and the memories here, yet oddly disinclined to leave.

The palace was alight with what seemed like thousands of candles; a fairyland for a fairy queen. Max stopped at the gate where two elite members of the Imperial Guard stood watch. It occurred to him that with a few words he could pass through, could join whatever celebration went on inside. He'd have the devil of a time explaining to Cardinal Sinzen, of course. The man thought him miles away in Bordgarten. But wouldn't it be worth the risk to see her once more?

Shaking his head, Max walked along the fence till he could see the old castle tower, a dark, unlit shape looming in the night sky. Cassandra's rooms were there and he could reach them without anyone knowing. He was pretty certain he could find his way through the tunnel.

He imagined her asleep, envisioned the kiss that would wake her from slumber. Felt her arms around him, the softness of her bed, the sweet smell of her skin. Acknowledged the possibility that her husband was with her.

Turning on his heel, Max walked back to his rooms and packed his campaign trunk.

* * *

She had the nerves of a bride with none of the joyful anticipation.

Cassandra lay in her wide bed her head turned, staring at the unicorn tapestry. Albert was coming to her tonight. He'd sent word through his Lord of the Bedchamber who'd told Cassandra's lady-in-waiting. Sophia had been too surprised to do more than repeat the message to her queen.

"Good," Cassandra had said at the time. Simply good. And it was a good thing. She had to keep reminding herself of that. Albert was her husband. The Grand Duke of Breslovia. The man who must sire her children. Her heirs.

Cassandra sighed, wishing Albert would come, glad he hadn't. This waiting was torture. Pushing aside the blankets that Sophia had sprinkled with lavender water, Cassandra slid off the high mattress. Her fingers traced the silken threads of the unicorn's horn, and she fought the urge to flee through the hidden passage.

More and more that was all she wished to do. Harder and harder, she battled the desire. And it wasn't simply to escape. That she could understand. No, now she felt compelled to wend her way through the catacombs, for no other reason than to be in them.

After wrapping the ermine-lined dressing gown about her shoulders Cassandra settled down in front of her dressing table. Ignoring the styled disarray of her curls, she leaned forward, digging ten fingers back through her hair. She glanced up, frowning at her reflection in the mirror, squinting to eliminate any glare. She didn't want to have a vision now.

Cassandra twisted around on the padded stool. Wouldn't Albert be shocked if he came upon her in the throes of one of her spells. He really would think her mad then. She could just imagine his face. The chuckle died in Cassandra's throat.

What if she were mad?

The thought wouldn't leave her in peace. Perhaps she could control the visions now, but they still came upon her. And what of her compelling desire to roam the underground passages? At times it seemed unseen fingers wrapped around her arms, tugging her toward the tapestry. If that wasn't madness, what was?

Her obsession with a man she could not have.

Cassandra shut her eyes and let her head fall back. She could still see the image of him as he'd watched her when she was atop the cathedral steps. She hadn't known he was in Liberstein, for she'd not seen him at court for a sennight.

Yet she could have sworn she felt his presence. And when she'd looked, there he was. Tall and handsome and staring at her with eyes the color of the sky. With the same longing that clawed at her soul.

"I expected you to be in bed, ready for me."

Cassandra's head snapped forward and she blinked. Albert stood in the doorway, a branch of candles created a shimmering aura about him. Cassandra lowered her lashes.

" 'Tis no wonder I never come here," he said, his voice dripping with disdain as he entered the chamber. Lifting the candles he examined the arch of a window, the centuries-old chest. " 'Tis like a mausoleum in here."

What he said was true. Compared to the rest of the palace, to the new part that shone with light and gold, the tower paled. Many a day she woke with the notion to vacate her apartments and move to the new wing set aside for her. Yet something kept her from giving the order. A magnetic force that bid her stay close.

Cassandra rose to her feet, not wishing to think on the subject. "It is good of you to come, my Lord."

Her words brought Albert's attention from the tapestry, and he studied his wife. "Yes, well, let us get on with it, then."

With a nod, Cassandra padded back toward the bed. She approached from the left, he from the right, and she didn't look as he jerked the cord holding his dressing gown closed. The candles were on the table beside the bed; she wished he would extinguish them, but hadn't the courage to ask. What did it really matter?

She lay on the bed and took a deep breath. Perhaps she would conceive a child on this night and they would both be spared further embarrassment. She could only hope.

"Well, you are going to have to do something other than just lie there."

Cassandra twisted her head, to see her husband doing just what he'd admonished her not to do. She considered saying as much, then decided arguments would not help this end quickly. Ignoring the sting of pride, Cassandra inched across the expanse of mattress, reaching out with tentative fingers to touch his chest.

He wore a nightshirt, ruffled and short enough that she could see his dark legs and feet sticking out from the bottom. She was looking at them when he grabbed her wrist. "Come, come, Your Highness," he said, dragging her hand down his stomach. "You are not some shy virgin sacrifice. Or do you forget that I am your husband and have had you before?"

"No." Cassandra tried to keep her voice steady as he pressed her palm against his flaccid manhood. "I haven't forgotten." There was little she could do but acquiesce as he forced her to rub back and forth. She squeezed her eyes shut and wished this were over, wished for some response from him.

He wished it too, she could tell. As minutes passed and his male part remained soft, Albert's movement grew more frenzied. Her wrist hurt where his fingers dug into its tender flesh and her arm ached from being stretched, still there was no sign of arousal.

"Damnation, can't you do anything right?" The question spewed from his mouth as he flung her hand aside.

Startled, Cassandra squealed when he grasped her head, forcing her lower. "Stop it. You're hurting me." Tears stung her eyes, and she blinked them back.

Then his hand curved behind her neck, squeezing with enough pressure to make Cassandra lightheaded. She wasn't certain what he was about till he wriggled and squirmed, using his free hand to jerk up his nightshirt.

Cassandra groaned, her breath coming in sobs now as he shoved her face into his hip. She could smell the sickeningly sweet perfume he used. Nausea rose in her throat.

"No, stop, please." His forefinger and thumb pinched her neck and Cassandra cried out, using her own hands to shove away from him. But he was strong; while she, doubled over as she was, was weak.

And he *was* her husband.

Surely whatever he did to her—forced her to do to him—was as it should be. Surely this was part of the marriage act.

Her thoughts flew to another time . . . another man. How could there be so much difference?

"You're pathetic." Now it was Albert shoving her away, sitting up and twisting so that his legs were over the side of the bed. Cassandra rose onto her elbows just as he turned his head back around. "You shouldn't even call yourself a woman. Look at me." His hand swept down toward his limp manhood. "You can't elicit a modicum of desire in me."

Then, before she knew what he was about, he slapped her. Hard enough to knock her back, and for tears to spring to her eyes.

Cassandra's fingers flew to her cheek. Then rage rushed through her veins as he yanked the nightshirt over his head. "Now we shall try again," he said. "I will show you what Nicolette—"

"Leave my room."

To Cassandra's surprise he seemed honestly amazed by her words. Then anger took over as she repeated them.

"I'm staying until this deed is done." His reach just missed her as she scurried off the bed. "Get back here, Cassandra." A whiny edge entered his voice. "I didn't mean to hit you. I'm just upset. Surely you can understand how it is for a man. Cassandra . . ."

But she was no longer listening. Driven by a desire to be rid of him, she hurried through the rooms, from her bedroom to the dressing room, to the anteroom. Outside the door stood two Imperial Guards, put there at General Hawke's insistence.

"The Grand Duke needs an escort back to his apartments," she said, as both men turned toward her. "Please see to it."

Cassandra didn't follow them back so she had no idea what they thought when they saw Albert sprawled out nude on her bed . . . or if he still was by the time they arrived. All she saw was Albert jerking his arm out of one guard's grasp and insisting that he was perfectly capable of walking by himself.

At the door, he wrenched free, pulling his robe over the nightshirt and glaring at her. "This isn't going to change anything, Cassandra. You are still my wife."

At a nod of her head the guards ushered him through the door. She shut it with a slam that took a bit of the sting from her cheek. But she didn't have long to be thankful he was gone. As she turned to walk back into her room her gaze snagged on the reflection of dancing candle flames in the mirror.

Darkness surrounded her, and the air screamed with the sound of exploding artillery shells.

Thirteen

"I can assume you've come to report success?" Sinzen didn't take his attention from the crusty roll he slathered with butter when his brother entered the room. He was breaking his fast, a ritual he considered all important.

Albert's expression soured. "Must you always pose questions to me, as if I don't know my duty?"

The cardinal focused briefly on his brother before devouring the greasy morsel. "You do not have the look of a satisfied man."

Albert flopped into a chair across the table from his brother and toyed with a small crystal jelly pot. There were probably a dozen arranged in a semicircle around the cardinal, catching the morning sun and throwing off a rainbow of brilliant colors.

"You *are* a satisfied man, aren't you?"

"If you mean by that, did I visit the Queen last night, the answer is yes. Though I fail to understand how *you* can gauge a man's satisfaction."

Sinzen made no comment, only began tearing apart a crisp roasted pheasant, licking the grease from his fingers as he did.

Unable to watch the gluttony any longer, Albert pulled out the miniature of his mistress and traced the gold filigree frame with his thumb.

Thank God he had Nicolette. She was a woman to fuel a man's passions, not leave them withered and dying. Albert sighed. If not for her vigorous sex last night he might think himself as dried up and useless as his brother. A sweat broke out on his upper lip as he remembered how it was with his wife. Straining, trying by the force of his will to become aroused.

Despite his session with Nicolette, the sour taste of defeat still fouled his mouth. "She is a woman more suited for a nunnery than a bedroom," Albert blurted out with enough venom that Sinzen lowered a succulent breast from his teeth.

The cardinal's beady eyes narrowed and studied his brother for so long that Albert dabbed at his face with a perfumed handkerchief. "Let us hope, then, that you impregnated the Queen quickly so you will not have to suffer the ordeal many more times."

"Perhaps last night was enough."

Sinzen's bald head shot up. "We won't take that chance." He pressed greasy fingertips together. "The fate of an empire rests on your ability to sire a child, Albert. See that you take that responsibility seriously."

The door had barely closed behind the pouting Grand Duke before the French ambassador meandered from behind the screen depicting Christ's triumphant entry into Jerusalem. Count de Mignard took a deep breath and pursed his lips before striding toward the cardinal's side. The Frenchman's sneer of distaste as he glanced at the abundance of food spread over the table went unnoticed by Sinzen who gouged a ripe round orange with his thumb. The sweet tang of sunshine perfumed the air, but it was no match for the overpowering fragrance left behind by Albert.

"What do you make of it?" Sinzen popped a section of fruit into his mouth.

"Curious to be sure." The ambassador ignored the cardinal's gesturing that he sit, preferring to keep as much distance as possible between himself and the gorging cleric. "Do you believe him?"

The cardinal's smile revealed a bit of grape skin caught between his teeth. "I had him followed. He went to the Queen last night."

Count de Mignard's lips curved and he rubbed the tip of one long finger down his equally long nose. "Then perhaps your spies told you Albert was escorted under guard from Cassandra's chambers less than an hour later."

Sinzen's jaws dropped. "Under guard? There must be an explanation." He managed to get to his feet. "Perhaps your sources are wrong. Cassandra is a biddable woman. I have counseled her at length on the duties of a wife."

"Cassandra may not be as *biddable* as you think. She has requested several ambassadors to wait upon her within a sennight."

"She is playing at being a monarch." Sinzen fluttered his hand. "She will forget such foolishness once she carries a child."

"We no longer have the luxury of awaiting your brother's pleasure to impregnate his wife. Affairs outside Breslovia are moving more quickly than anticipated. His Royal Highness, Louis, needs Breslovia's declaration of war against Prussia soon."

"Soon . . . But we aren't ready. Surely you don't think we can attack Prussia without a proper army? Without the support of the ruling monarch? Frederick would overrun us in a matter of days."

"Nonetheless—"

"You promised me time, Mignard, and support." Sinzen pushed away from the table.

"Time I have given you. Three years to be exact. Certainly long enough to put your plan into effect."

"And I have. Albert is married to the Queen."

"Yes, and merely a Grand Duke. If your Diaz had seen fit to appoint him king . . ." Mignard shrugged. "As it is, he has little power and seems disinclined to seize more."

"As soon as a child is born we—"

"You don't seem to understand Sinzen. There has been no child for three years, and time is running out. His Royal Highness, Louis, has armies that are . . . well, shall we say they are not having as much success in the new world as hoped. And our ally Austria has suffered defeats."

"Nothing disastrous, surely."

The count examined his long aristocratic fingers and sighed. "When we first discussed this . . . venture, you assured me there would be no problems."

"I have kept my end of the bargain." Cardinal Sinzen rose and shuffled forward. "Certainly you must be impressed with Breslovia's army, transformed into a fighting force, and in such a short time."

"Your General Hawke has done well. But even he flounders, concerned more for Queen Cassandra's safety than the military he was commissioned to serve."

"An unfortunate turn of events, but one quickly remedied."

"He did not follow your orders to return to his troops at once."

"I know." Sinzen gave one last longing look toward his half-finished breakfast, regretting he couldn't take the time to finish. With a sigh he turned back toward the French ambassador. "But now he is back where he belongs, and from all reports the army should be ready soon."

"To attack Prussia."

It was not a question but a statement of fact, and Sinzen feared what might happen if he argued the point. Somehow he had to make certain Breslovia would be ready. Count de Mignard's offer of three regiments of French Dragoons helped, as did the promise of heavy artillery and muskets.

Still, the cardinal could not help blanching when the count turned steely eyes on him. "We shall need this accomplished before snow flies."

"But . . . but Your Excellency that might be only a matter of weeks. Surely you mean the spring? How much better it would be to start a campaign as the weather warms. By May, June at the latest." Sinzen's mind clicked off the months. With luck and prayers, Cassandra might be delivered of a child by then.

But luck and prayers were not to work this time. "Before

the snow flies," Mignard repeated before marching toward the door. He paused, glancing back over his shoulder and smiled. "Or I shall have to assume Cassandra is the power and deal directly with her."

"But you do still hold the Edict of Liberstein as your sacred bond?"

Cassandra leaned forward, to better hear the Prussian ambassador's reply. He was elderly, with straggly white hair and sunken cheeks. Neither his hearing nor his voice were strong. But after nearly an hour of conversing with him, she found his mind alert, his judgment keen.

"Of course, Your Highness. Frederick considers the peace between our two nations of utmost importance."

The words were welcome, and she believed him . . . almost.

Would have believed him completely if not for the latest of her visions. She had closed her eyes and flowed with the spirits, as Kanakareh had taught her to do. Perhaps she had been so eager, so willing to give herself over to the experience because she'd wished to forget Albert's visit.

Whatever the case, she hadn't tried to stop what was shown her. On the contrary she'd used her seer's eyes to notice all she could. The uniforms, the destruction; listening, tuning her ears to ignore the whine of bullets and pick up the subtle words spoken.

She heard a mother's dying profession of love to her child . . . who was dead too by this time. The officer's anger that the cannon were aimed too high. "We are not trying to kill the treetops," he shouted.

Cassandra stayed with him, though she found him repugnant, only to realize fear was a knot deep in the pit of his stomach as well. For it was not merely the village he fought, but the army beyond.

Her army. General Hawke's army.

The realization almost made her fling herself from the bed

where she lay, but she remembered the Seneca's words and she took a calming breath.

And that's when she realized the officer was Prussian. The army invading her homeland was Prussian.

Cassandra forced herself to smile at the Prussian ambassador. She wanted to believe him. He was her father's friend, a man who mourned the king's passing nearly as much as she.

"Your Highness seems worried and upset," Hubert said, placing his gnarled hand over hers. "I assure you Prussia will not start a war with Breslovia" He shifted, then moved his head toward hers. "But my sovereign cannot help but be perturbed by the buildup of troops along our shared border."

"There are soldiers along the frontier, of course. We've always maintained a few guards at several remote outposts near . . . Why are you looking at me that way? I tell you—"

"My dear highness," he said patting the hand in his grasp. "I feel I can call you that because of our long history." His eyes crinkled in a smile. "I remember when you were born, you know. But that is neither here nor there." He sat back and, despite his years, assumed the persona of a diplomat. "It is my misfortune to inform you that there are large numbers of soldiers, and that Emperor Frederick is very upset by their presence."

Cassandra swallowed, folding her hands to allow time to think of a proper response. Her father would have known what to say to this representative of Prussia, as would her brother. But she had never been included in discussions of diplomacy. She wasted moments wishing Simon were still with her and wondering if she should send for Cardinal Sinzen. He'd met with ambassadors of foreign countries after King Christian died.

Cassandra thought at the time the comment was of little import. There were never any major disagreements; relationships had been harmonious as far as she knew.

But Count de Glasman, the Prussian ambassador, did not seem to be in good humor. What had begun as a pleasant conversation now seemed to require more diplomacy than Cassandra possessed.

She swallowed again. "You understand I must look into this matter myself. Not that I doubt your honesty," she hurriedly added. "Quite the contrary. Had anyone less trusted told me this I would have dismissed his words immediately. 'Tis because you are a friend that I question my own military leaders. However, rest assured I shall discover the truth, and if there are troops, I shall see them dispersed."

"That is all His Highness asks. You know how much he values Breslovia."

Perhaps too much, Cassandra mused after the count hobbled from the Council Room, leaning heavily on a gold-knobbed cane. Memories of her last vision flooded her mind. Prussian soldiers sacking Breslovian villages.

The past fortnight of studying had taught Cassandra many things. Not the least was how wealthy a kingdom she ruled. Prussia was a relatively new military power, testing its wings like a baby bird, attacking weaker states, annexing them.

Max had told her that the war now raging through Europe and the New World owed its roots to Prussia's forced takeover of Silesia from Maria Theresa of Austria. And to the fact that she wanted it back.

It was possible Frederick of Prussia merely wanted an excuse to plunder Breslovia. And what better ploy than to claim self-defense?

Rising. Cassandra moved to the door. She had several options. Discussing the situation with Albert she dismissed. She hadn't seen her husband for several days, not since the night he'd visited. And she wasn't the least bit sorry.

She had attributed her bruised cheek to a fall from her bed. It was a story many people were quick to accept due to her supposedly weakened state. Yet she wished to give Albert no further opportunity to repeat his abuse. How they would produce an heir was a subject she had contemplated and for which she had found no answer.

As much as she wished for a child, that was not her main concern at the moment. She had advisors, of course, men who studied situations and devised logical solutions. Her father had depended upon these learned counselors, as well as on Simon. Yet weeks ago, when Cassandra had decided to begin asserting herself as queen, she'd discovered most of her father's advisors gone, replaced by men she did not know. Had she signed documents approving this? Cassandra couldn't recall. However, she was aware that most of the new advisors made her uncomfortable. When she spoke, it was Cardinal Sinzen they looked to for a subtle nod of approval.

Yet she was queen. And the fate of her country, of Breslovia, depended upon her. Lifting her skirts, Cassandra swept through the door toward her private apartments.

"We are doing what? Your Highness, have you lost your mind? Do you know how far it is to the frontier, and just the two of us. Well, I never heard the like. What if we're accosted by . . ." Sophia couldn't imagine who might accost them, but that didn't keep her from rambling on. "It is very dangerous, and everyone will wonder where we've gone. I simply—"

"It is not my plan to go riding off toward the frontier without guards. We shall take servants with us—and Colonel Marquart—and we'll be perfectly safe."

"Yes, but why are we going? The season is upon us. The Imperial Opera House is opening this week, and you know how—"

"Sophia."

"Oh my, I do apologize. Of course we must go. But why is it we must? No, there is no need to tell me. I am but your lady-in-waiting and I—"

Cassandra held up her hand and laughed. "Please, do not tell me you are my lowly servant, or I shall be consumed by giggles." Her countenance sobered. "I am sorry to take you away from all the fun. But you know you are my friend as well as my lady." Cassandra paused. "And more important, I think you are the only one I can trust."

Which was a silly thing to say, Cassandra thought later. In truth she hadn't meant to utter these words that left Sophia speechless. It took a bit of time to convince the redhead that she was only jesting, but Cassandra finally did it.

Now if she could only convince herself.

Certainly circumstances were not ideal. Her father and brother were dead, and her husband was . . . Well, she did not wish to think of him at the moment. But there was no reason to suspect a conspiracy, she told herself, though that thought wouldn't leave her mind. It was as if a spell were cast upon her, making her doubt those around her . . . making her doubt her own sanity.

Cardinal Sinzen was her confessor and chief advisor—the Prime Minister. He loved Breslovia as much as she, yet a small voice within whispered that she should stay clear of him. A small voice very much like the one that kept her from leaving the ancient tower for the opulence of the palace.

This voice made her sigh when the cardinal was announced by the footman.

"Ah, there you are, Your Highness." He waddled into the room, bowing his head slightly and smiling, his face shining with sweat. "I've heard the news and I'm delighted."

Cassandra only lifted her brows.

"You are taking my advice and retiring to the country for a holiday."

Torn between wondering how he knew she was leaving and having to explain that her trip couldn't be termed a holiday, Cassandra said nothing. But her lack of a response went unnoticed.

"I can't tell you how much better I'll feel with you out of harm's way for a while. I know you tried not to seem upset by the incident with the knife-wielding maniac, but I can tell it took its toll."

"I'm perfectly fine, Your Grace. And of course, Count Wenzel is no longer a threat. You did have him moved to the city jail as I requested?" As Max had requested of her.

The cardinal's smile slipped a bit. "I did. But it's most unfortunate."

"What is?"

"Count Wenzel." Sinzen's wig slipped a bit as he shook his head. "He's dead." The cardinal's fat shoulders lifted. "A fever contracted at the jail."

"I see." Despite what the young count had nearly done to her, Cassandra didn't wish him dead.

Cardinal Sinzen beamed at her, his fat fingers braided over his stomach. "Do not let that spoil your holiday. I'm certain Albert is pleased to leave the palace for a while, too."

"Albert isn't going."

The smile faded.

"Are you certain that's wise, Your Highness?" His arms spread. "The Lord put us on this earth to go forth and multiply. 'Tis our Christian duty, not to mention your supreme duty as queen of Breslovia to produce an heir."

"I am quite aware of my duty, Your Grace." This was not the first time he'd spoken to her thus, but it was the first time Cassandra questioned his motive. Which was ridiculous. Every citizen of Breslovia wished for the birth of an heir to the throne.

"Your Highness." Sinzen's tone turned conciliatory. "I only wish what is best for you."

"How very kind. I do appreciate your concern, and it is true the stress of recent weeks is affecting my health. But a fortnight in the country should make me stronger."

He agreed wholeheartedly, though he did suggest again that Albert's company might be beneficial as well. Cassandra only smiled and wished she didn't feel the necessity to lie about why she was going to her father's hunting lodge.

The Royal Hunting Lodge sprawled over three hundred acres of woodland and meadows near Breslovia's border with Prussia. When King Christian was alive it had been used extensively, for Cassandra's father had loved to hunt, and her brother had excelled at the sport as well.

Cassandra ofttimes had accompanied them, especially after her mother had died. Though she'd never understood their fascination with bringing down a large buck, she was an excellent rider and had enjoyed the freedom allowed her at the Lodge to roam about.

Which doubtless had something to do with the exhilaration she felt as her entourage approached the main compound. A large château of native stone and half-timbers, the building, built by her father, afforded the rustic appeal of a hunting cabin while providing the luxury Cassandra's mother had enjoyed.

The rooms were light and airy, with windows lit by the southern sun and finely crafted furnishings nestled beneath impressive racks of deer antlers.

Three years had passed since Cassandra had last visited, and as she approached, riding astride her favorite mare, she couldn't imagine why she'd stayed away so long. She took a deep breath and marveled at the freedom she felt. She could almost imagine the visions gone, evaporating like mist over the valley.

She hadn't had one since she'd left the palace three days ago. Not since the spirits had led her through a labyrinth of tunnels and shafts, surrounded by darkness and punctuated only by faint calls of distress. It was a strange vision, like none she'd had before. And though she'd tried to follow Kanakareh's advice and learn what she could from the experience, Cassandra had found herself fighting the images. She had been able to bring herself to see what horrors lurked at the end of the tunnel. She hadn't wanted to know.

But now the sun was shining, the trees were splendid in their autumn cloaks, and Cassandra could almost forget why she'd come to the Lodge.

The staff was skeletal, supplemented by the few attendants Cassandra had sent ahead with her belongings, but they managed to have the Lodge in order when she and Sophia arrived.

Her rooms were clean, as cozy as she remembered, with a cheery fire roaring in the large stone fireplace.

"I doubt my bottom will ever be the same," Sophia said with a laugh as she gingerly settled onto a large sofa. "Are there any roads here or did we travel upon a washed-out river bottom?"

"You should have been on horseback rather than in the coach," Cassandra said. She still wore her crimson velvet riding attire as she stared out the window. It offered a perfect view of the plain and the forest beyond, of the meandering road that followed the river's bends.

"You know I have no love of horses. Not after Lady Diana's dogs spooked that beast I rode to the hunt five years ago. If you recall I kept my seat quite admirably at first, but with the barking and screaming—granted it was my screaming—the creature couldn't be calmed. Not even when two of the Imperial Guards leaped to the ground and tried to assist me. It was a harrowing experience to be sure. One I never wish to repeat. And certainly not one I—"

Sophia pushed herself to a standing position with less than ladylike grace. "What do you find so fascinating outside? You are staring so intently I'm certain you haven't heard a word—Oh!" Sophia clamped her hands together, then realizing she probably shouldn't be so excited to see him, forced her arms down to her sides. "I did not know General Hawke and Kanakareh were to be here. Why didn't you tell me?"

Cassandra pulled her attention away from the window. "I did not know myself."

The moment he saw the purple and green banner whipping in the wind, Max felt the blood quicken in his veins.

The Queen was in residence.

But what in hell was she doing here? The question, which he voiced to Kanakereh, went unanswered as they galloped toward the Lodge.

At least he didn't have long to wait before discovering why she was miles away from the safety of the palace. As soon as he dismounted, handing the reins to a stable boy, a liveried servant rushed forward announcing the Queen would receive him in the petit salon. And the tone of the messenger seemed to indicate Her Highness meant *now.*

Following the bewigged footman, Max barely had time to shrug his shoulders at Kanakareh before being led through the ornately carved door. After more doors and long halls, Max was ushered into a large room with mounted deer heads lining the walls, their eyes seeming to stare down at him.

But it was Cassandra who drew his attention, standing in a puddle of sunlight streaming through the tall casement window. The instant the door shut behind him she whirled about.

"What are you doing here?" Her voice sounded strained.

"I might ask you the same. I see very few Imperial Guards about."

She seemed taken aback by his inquiry. Her chin lifted. "I don't believe it is required that I answer to you."

Max grinned. "You have a point there." God, it was good to see her, regardless of the turmoil looking at her caused his senses.

"Most assuredly. And furthermore I *do* require an answer from you." Cassandra tried not to look into those blue eyes. There was no need to muddle her thinking.

"Kanakareh and I are on a reconnoitering expedition."

"Reconnoitering what?"

"Rumors most likely." Max gave in to a devilish impulse and took a few steps toward her. She tried to back up, but the window sill only crushed her overskirt of red velvet.

"Are you going to tell me why you've come?" he asked.

Cassandra fidgeted with the tassels on the drapes, realized what she did and pushed by him, her sleeve brushing his as she passed. "I'm on a holiday." She didn't know what to think of his presence. Perhaps Count de Glasman was right. What if

General Hawke was massing soldiers near the border with Prussia?

Glancing back over her shoulder Cassandra took a deep breath. She would not allow him to unnerve her. She was the Queen, after all. *She* had a perfect right to be here for whatever reason she chose. It was her Hunting Lodge.

He, on the other hand was an uninvited—and regardless of the way he made her pulse flutter—unwelcome guest.

"You mentioned rumors." She lifted a winged brow. "What did you mean?"

Max tore his attention from the way wispy golden curls strayed in the hollow behind her ear. He needed his wits about him, and he already knew the Queen had a way of scattering them.

He wasn't certain of what to tell her. Hell, he wasn't sure himself why he was here. A recruit's questionable ramblings about large numbers of fighting men massing in the area. As far as he knew, Max was the commander of Breslovia's army, and he had sent no divisions north toward Prussia.

There was always the possibility that Frederick might decide to abandon the peace treaty and make a small foray into Breslovia. Except according to the recruit's description, the soldiers didn't sound Prussian.

Which was why Max was here. To find out for himself if a phantom army, that sounded suspiciously French, was roaming the northern frontier of Breslovia.

But he hadn't planned on encountering Cassandra. Or answering questions. And he didn't intend to—not until he discovered for himself what was going on.

With a smile, Max moved toward her. "I've come looking for soldiers," he answered honestly. " 'Tis my job."

Cassandra refused to retreat. "I was under the impression men came to you for training."

"At times I have to weed them out. Are you frightened of me, Your Highness?"

"No, of course not." Cassandra swallowed. "Whyever would you think that?"

"Perhaps the fact that you are backing up as I approach."

"I'm not." Cassandra rooted her feet to the carpet despite the fact that he was mere inches from her and consumed her entire focus.

Max stared down at her and realized he was going insane. What was he thinking, to press himself so close to her? Resisting temptation was never his forte, and he'd never been so tempted.

Fourteen

"I'm curious, Your Highness. Did the Grand Duke accompany you on your holiday." Max grinned when her chin shot up.

"I don't think that's any of your concern."

"He didn't come."

Cassandra's eyes widened. "I did not say that."

"You didn't have to." Reason edged lust aside and Max stepped back, giving them both a modicum of breathing room. "If he were here you'd be only too pleased to tell me." He shrugged. "As it is, I assume you're pretty much on your own."

"Lady Sophia is attending me."

"Ah, the little chatterbox."

"How dare you insult one of my ladies."

"You misunderstood. I personally find Lady Sophia delightful."

"You do?" The sudden twinge she felt bore all the earmarks of jealousy.

"Of course." Max sprawled on a sofa beneath the watchful glass eye of a stuffed lynx. "I have wondered what she had to say about walking in on us in your bed." He thought then he'd gone too far. Sitting in Her Royal Majesty's presence was one thing, reminding her of things she most likely wished to forget, another.

She stared at him openmouthed for a moment, her face turning nearly as red as her riding attire. "We were *not* in bed together. I simply lay down to rest and you were there, and then—" Cassandra's teeth snapped shut. "I assume you will not be staying long, General Hawke."

"A day or two."

She wanted to tell him to leave. There were other places to stay in the area, inns. . . . At least she thought there were. But forcing him away from the Lodge would prove nothing. Having him nearby and showing that she could resist him was the best course. If only she were sure she could resist.

"You, of course, are welcome to stay here. Your friend, Kanakareh, also."

"How gracious of you."

She was sorting through a stack of papers on the desk, papers that looked to be years old, but her eyes snapped up to meet his when she heard the sarcasm in his voice.

Again Max wondered if he had pushed her too far . . . and why in the hell he was doing it in the first place. True, he enjoyed the way those violet eyes lit up when he annoyed her, but that didn't seem worth the risk.

Besides, he really didn't wish to offend her. It wasn't her fault she was married to the prig Albert. Or that Max couldn't think of another woman but her. Or that seeing her here like this, her hair in wild disarray, her face soft and pretty, made him wish he could take her in his arms and love her as thoroughly as he had that first time.

When they were simply Cassie and Max.

"You look well." Max wasn't certain what provoked the comment, and he could tell by the lift of her brows she wasn't either. Except that it was true. The last time he'd seen her at the palace, her face had seemed taut and mauve crescents had shadowed her eyes. Not that she hadn't been beautiful even then. But now that haunted expression was gone. "Have the visions stopped?"

"Yes." Cassandra paused. "And I don't know whether to be thankful or not."

Pushing himself to his feet and moving forward before she could back away, Max touched her cheek. "Be thankful," he said. For a moment he allowed his fingers to drift down her skin's softness. Then he reached down to chuck her aristocratic chin. "Have a good holiday, Your Highness."

He turned on his heel and was gone—without her permission—before she said another word.

And she was glad . . . truly.

She had too much to do to be bothered with him. And he did bother her. Even now her skin tingled where he'd touched her. Cassandra pressed her hand to her cheek and smiled.

She was still smiling when Lady Sophia burst into the room. "Well, what did he say? You did talk with him, didn't you? Why are they here? Did you speak with Kanakareh also?"

"I don't know why they're here." Cassandra motioned for Sophia to close the door. "General Hawke mentioned something about seeking soldiers for the army, but I question that. And no, I did not see Kanakareh, though the general did speak of him."

"If he isn't telling the truth, why do you think he came? Oh, no." Sophia's hand flew to cover her mouth. "You don't think he followed you here, do you?"

"Certainly not. Why would he do such a thing?" Cassandra turned away when she saw the expression on Sophia's face. They never discussed the time Sophia walked in to find Max and Cassandra lying on the bed, but that didn't mean it wasn't remembered. Sophia had had the good grace not to mention it, and Cassandra certainly wasn't going to bring it up.

Which meant that the room was quiet for several minutes. Until Sophia, apparently reaching the limits of her endurance, sighed.

"I don't like the idea of your going riding tomorrow by yourself. What if something happens? I should go with you. Or take one of the guards—better yet, take several. You can't be too safe after what happened near the cathedral during the celebration."

"I shall be fine."

"What if you do find soldiers? What will you do then?"

"Tell them I am their queen and order them home."

"You're teasing me, and I'm perfectly serious about this. I should never have agreed to come. What of General Hawke? Surely he can tell you everything you need to know without your riding out over the countryside. Or he could go with you. I daresay the general could protect you from anything."

Other than my own desires, Cassandra thought. But she said nothing, and by the time she and Sophia retired for the night, the lady-in-waiting seemed to think the question was settled.

Which it was.

Cassandra would go alone. She had ridden here often as a child, sometimes with her brother, ofttimes alone. She knew the area; didn't even have to consult one of the many maps she'd recently studied to know the few places where an army could be. Most of the short border between Prussia and Breslovia was mountainous. But there were passes leading into highland meadows and fields.

Cassandra was up before dawn, breathing deeply of the country air and fumbling with her corset and petticoats. She finally despaired of dressing herself, summoning a lady's maid but ordering her not to wake Lady Sophia. Cassandra was in no mood to argue anew the advisability of her solitary trek.

She rode astride from the stable yard, sending her mount into a trot as soon as they had crossed the wooden bridge over the River Keln. Mist curled about the mare's withers, shrouding the countryside with a gray cloak that became tinged mauve as the sun rose.

All around her warblers sang as the sky lightened with the peaceful blessing of dawn. Cassandra sighed. The countryside was as she remembered . . . as it had always been. There was no ugly threat of war or scourge of armies. Breslovia was peaceful and quiet, a haven in the troubled world.

It wasn't till midmorning that she discovered someone was following her. She'd stopped on a rise, giving her mount a rest and herself a chance to use the shiny brass spyglass she'd brought. Looking first north toward Prussia, she swept the landscape and smiled. Then she gazed east toward the valley and west toward the mountains. Nothing. All was as it should be.

Except that as she turned to place the instrument back in her saddlebag a movement caught her eye. Lifting the glass she mumbled a curse. Remounted, Cassandra headed down the valley at a gallop, determined to outdistance the rider. But her horse was tired, and though her heart was strong, a glance over Cassandra's shoulder confirmed that she was losing ground.

Guiding her mount with the reins, Cassandra headed up a slope toward the woods looming to the east. She'd lose him there and then ride south. Her plan was excellent and would have worked if her mount hadn't jolted to a stop.

The move was so unexpected Cassandra flew over her horse's neck and the ground raced up to meet her, knocking the air from her lungs and leaving her dazed.

Past the ringing in her ears, she heard pounding hooves. When she glanced up, shielding her eyes from the sunlight glimmering through the leaves, she saw General Hawke running toward her.

His face was in shadow, but she could see his hand, see him reach for his sword.

"What . . . ?" Cassandra could barely formulate the question as he raced toward her. Her heart stopped and her mind frantically searched for a reason for his actions.

And then she heard the snort.

Her head whipped around and a silent scream died on her lips. "Be still," she thought she heard Max say, though it was a useless command. She couldn't move if she tried. She could only stare at the wild boar as he stared at her.

There was only the general between her and the frightening beast, and he had nothing but a sword he'd unsheathed and now held in his right hand. Compared to the boar's tusks the gleaming steel seemed fragile.

The animal snorted, steam gurgling from its snout, and Cassandra watched in awe as the general waved his arms, taunting the boar. As he did, he inched to the side. The beast followed the movement with his beady eyes, twisting his head, then his thick shouldered body to square himself with his tormentor.

Cassandra's relief at escaping the boar's attention was short-lived. "Max." He ignored her, continuing to shout and step about, entrancing the boar who seemed confused by his behavior.

But not for long.

Obviously deciding he'd had enough entertainment for the day, the boar pawed the soft ground. Snorting again, he started forward. Cassandra saw Max slam his sword against the nearest tree trunk, but didn't have time to wonder why as she leaped to her feet.

The general's horse skittered to the side as she grabbed for the musket, sliding it from its casing. She whirled round hoisting the gun to her shoulder just as the boar charged toward Max. Who sidestepped, two-handing the broken sword into the creature's neck as Cassandra pulled the trigger. She didn't have time to pray that the musket was primed. She'd barely had time to aim.

She didn't even have time to view her handiwork, for the force of her shot landed her smack on her royal bottom, jarring her to the bone and knocking her head against an exposed root. Then all was dark.

Cold water dripping on her forehead made her open her eyes. At first she thought she had seen a vision. But this one so real she could still smell the fear. Then the general's face came into view and she remembered.

"No, I think you should stay down." Strong hands clamped over her shoulders. "You have a nasty lump on your head."

Now that he mentioned it, her head did ache. "What happened to the boar?" Obviously the beast hadn't killed either of them, but the general was blocking her view.

Max twisted about. "Dead," he announced, "Though whether from a stab wound to the neck or a musketball in the rump, I'm not sure."

"You mean I hit him?" Cassandra brushed aside his hands and sat, trying to look around him. "I never shot a musket before."

Settling down beside her, Max rested an arm on his raised knee. "Speaking for myself I'm glad you decided to try it today. Though you should have mounted and ridden away when you had the chance. Lord knows, if I'd known you could move that fast, I'd have suggested it."

"It wouldn't have done any good." Cassandra slanted him a look. "My God you're covered with blood." She twisted to her knees, wincing at the pain in her head. "Are you hurt?"

"Not as badly as you, I'd wager." Max cupped her shoulders and turned her, settling her down on the bed of soft pine needles. "This isn't my blood, thank God." Jerking at the buttons Max unfastened his jacket. He took it off, tossing it aside. "How does your head feel?"

"As if I had knocked it against a tree." Cassandra gingerly fingered the lump. She felt better lying down, and she had to admit, after the scare with the boar, lying safe beside Max had its appeal. But it must be getting late. She had no idea how long she'd been unconscious. Returning to the Royal Lodge had to be her first priority. "I can ride," she said with what she considered stoic grace.

"Actually, Your Highness, you can't."

"What are you saying?" She turned her head toward him. "I may be a bit groggy, but I can sit a horse."

Max lifted a brow. "Your horse ran off frightened by the boar, I assume."

"Then we'll ride double."

"Mine bolted when you fired the musket."

Cassandra pushed up on her elbows. "You mean we've no horses?" He shook his head. "Or food?"

"We've the boar."

"The boar?"

"Aye. Haven't you ever had roast boar, Your Highness?"

"Of course I have. Oh . . ." she groaned, slowly lowering her head, surprised when he cushioned it with his shoulder.

"You probably should rest."

"I suppose you're right. But *you* aren't hurt. You could go after our horses. Surely they haven't gone far."

"That might be a good idea." Max shifted. " 'Tis doubtful another boar will happen along while I'm gone." His smile broadened when she grabbed the arm pillowing her head.

"Perhaps you shouldn't leave. You must be tired. After all, you did ride all day and then risked your life fighting the boar."

"That was strenuous," Max agreed, tightening his arm around her shoulder.

"Of course it was." Cassandra yawned. "I think you should stay here and rest, too."

"Whatever you say, Your Highness." Max scrunched farther down the tree trunk, keeping his arm around her. He wished he could make her more comfortable, but before he could wonder what else to do, her eyes closed.

Max leaned over, brushing his lips along her hairline, smiling when curly tendrils tickled his nose. She smelled warm and sweet and alive. He let out a shaky breath, remembering that moment of panic when he'd turned and seen the boar coming toward her.

"Max." Her voice was whisper soft.

"Yes."

"You won't leave me, will you?"

"Nay, Cassie, I'll not leave you, he said, and wished that it were true. For he wanted nothing more than to spend his life near her, protecting her. Forgetting that she was the Queen of Breslovia.

The smell of roasted meat dragged her from the depths of sleep. Cassandra stretched, opening her eyes to find that night had fallen. It wasn't completely dark, though, for a fire crackled nearby. And spitted above that fire, a joint of meat—wild boar if she wasn't mistaken—sizzled.

"I see you were serious about eating the boar."

Tossing the last few twigs into the fire, Max stood and brushed his hands together. "No sense to waste a perfectly good boar," he said before hunching down beside her. "How are you feeling now? Better?"

"I must be, for all I can think of is that meat."

"Hungry, eh? 'Tis no wonder. You barely stopped for a midday meal. Let me see if it's ready." Max rose.

"How do you know?"

"I've done my share of cooking in the field."

"No." Cassandra sat up, brushing aside the pine needles falling from her hair. "How did you know I didn't stop to eat today?"

"I was following you," he stated simply. When he sliced through the crisp outer skin of the boar with his broken sword, grease sizzled into the fire, making it hiss and sputter. Fanning away the smoke Max cut off a chunk of meat, placing it on a slab of bark that served as a platter.

"So you admit it then?"

"What? That I followed you?" He glanced around and shrugged. "Of course."

"Why?"

"I should think that obvious." His gaze swept over her. "Given the circumstances."

Cassandra leaned forward, hugging her knees. "You're contending you did it to save me from a wild boar?"

Walking toward her he offered the steaming meat. She took it, setting the bark on the ground beside her and tearing off a piece of pork. "Ouch."

"It's hot," he tossed over his shoulder as he cut his own piece from the spit.

"Your warning"—Cassandra paused to suck on her burned finger—"came a little late. Somewhat like your protection."

Settling down beside her in the pine needles, Max looked hurt. "I saved you, didn't I?"

"Yes," Cassandra admitted. "But I wonder if there'd have been a need if you hadn't chased me into the woods."

"I hardly chased you."

She sighed, too hungry to argue. "I probably shouldn't have ridden off by myself." Especially since it seemed there was no need. There was obviously no large army in the area. Count de Glasman and the Prussians must be mistaken.

Cassandra was certainly pleased, but the knowledge didn't help her at the moment. The last person she should be alone with was Maximilian Hawke. It seemed they proved that at every opportunity. Yet here they were, stranded . . . alone.

And now that the danger was passed and her head didn't hurt, that was all she could think about. The fire threw light and shadows across his big body. The body he'd placed between hers and the boar. He wore only his weskit and shirt leeves, having tossed the blood-soaked jacket aside. Despite the grime and dust smearing his breeches, he looked dashing.

"Is there something wrong with the pork?" Max had finished his and returned to the fire for more.

"No. Actually, it's amazingly delicious." Cassandra tried to keep herself from following his movements with her eyes. She was the Queen . . . the married queen, she reminded herself. Even if she wished . . . Cassandra could not put what she longed for into words. "I'm surprised a general has a skill," she blurted out. Most of the generals she knew were old and pampered . . . wart covered and gray haired.

"I wasn't always a general."

"No, of course not." She felt foolish again.

"When I was in the English colonies I learned a lot about surviving in the wilderness."

"That's where you met Kanakareh?"

"Aye." Max returned her smile. "You should taste his roasted venison. Though with his penchant for planning ahead, he usually dries his deer meat and pounds it with berries."

"Oh." Such a silly reply, but she could think of nothing else. It was back. The longing she felt for him. Stronger.

"Is your head hurting again?"

"Nay." Cassandra lifted her fingers to brush the lump on the side of her head. Her hair was down around her shoulders, curling wildly, and she hastily twisted it. Had all the pins fallen out when she'd fallen?

"It looked uncomfortable," Max said nodding toward her. "Your hair was tangled and knotted under your head. I smoothed it out a bit while you slept." Reaching into his pocket he retrieved several silver pins, holding them out toward her in his open palm.

He sat close, close enough for her to feel his heat, the near magnetic tug of his body. But she couldn't reach the pins without leaning toward him . . . erasing the small distance that separated them. And she couldn't bring herself to do that. So she simply stared at his hand, so wide and dark, so capable of bringing her ecstasy.

Cassandra turned her head away. "Tell me of Kanakareh," she said letting her breath out. "How is it that he travels with you?"

Max closed his fingers over the pins. "He has some fool notion that I saved his life."

"Did you?"

"Possibly." Max slipped the hairpins back in his pocket. "But no more often than he saved mine." Leaning back, he studied her. "There's also the vision."

"Vision?"

"According to Kanakareh he was told by his guardian spirit to follow the hawk."

"You?"

Max shrugged. "That's how Kanakareh interpreted the message. But the truth is, we're friends. When I left the New World, he did as well."

"Do you want more pork?" Standing, Max strode toward the fire.

Cassandra shook her head. "No," she answered quickly when he glanced around. "What are we going to do?" He was tossing more wood on the fire. By this time the stars were twinkling through the branches overhead. "What time is it, do you think?"

Extracting his pocket watch, one of the few things he had left from his life at Salisbury, Max told her the hour.

"It's so late. Sophia will be worried."

"Kanakareh will tell her."

"Tell her what?"

"That I followed you."

"Mmmm." Cassandra remembered her friend's suggestion that she take the general with her. "That should ease her mind." Except if Sophia also recalled the time she'd walked into Cassandra's private bedchamber to see Max and her queen on the bed, their arms intertwined, their lips sealed. The thought kept tickling at Cassandra's mind, especially when Max sat back down, closer than ever.

"What are you doing?"

"I thought I'd try to sleep." Though how he could manage that with her lying next to him and the night like a soft cocoon surrounding them, he didn't know.

Cassandra still sat, her back straighter than ever, but she wanted to sink down beside him. She wanted to do all manner of things. She glanced down toward him. He lay on his back, arms folded. His eyes open and on her. Her breath caught.

It was so much like that other night by the waterfall. Just the two of them, as if no other human existed. The temptation to believe that overwhelmed her.

"Are you cold?" she asked because the night was chilly, and even with her heavy velvet riding habit gooseflesh prickled her skin. And because she could think of nothing else to say. He still looked at her. She swallowed.

"Are you?" he asked, reaching up to pull her down beside him.

"Yes. No. I mean, you have only shirt sleeves." Cassandra

gave in to his gentle tug and wriggled herself down. She lay beside him, facing him as he now faced her. Their breath mingled, and Cassandra clenched her fingers into fists. She could see his blue, blue eyes, the fan of thick dark lashes.

"Cassie."

The whisper of her name sent chills up and down her spine, but it wasn't like being cold. As a matter of fact, hot was how she'd describe herself now. And flustered.

What was she to do?

She was the Queen, reason warned. Married to Grand Duke Albert. Responsible for thousands of Breslovians who looked to her for leadership.

His fingers caressed her cheek.

Moral leadership.

His lips touched hers.

And all her arguments evaporated like mist in the sun. Cassandra's eyes drifted shut. "Max . . ."

It was all the invitation he needed.

Fifteen

"I should never have let her go. It's my fault for sleeping late this morning, but I blame the country air. It always has this effect on me. I eat more. Sleep more. Oh, I wish we were back in the city. Why did I allow her to go by herself?"

Kanakareh waited for Lady Sophia to take a breath. "It was not your decision."

"Oh, you're right, of course." Sophia let the heavy velvet drapes fall over a window that showed her nothing but black sky and twinkling stars. "Yet, I do feel I could have done something. I did warn her, you know. And begged her to take General Hawke with her, though I hesitated, knowing what I do about them."

This time there was no need to await a chance to leap into the conversation—such as it was. Kanakareh's eyes narrowed and he stared at Sophia with unabashed curiosity. She stood by the window in the library, beneath a stuffed deer head. Her green eyes were enormous above the hand she clamped over her mouth.

"I didn't mean to say that," she began. "Sometimes I just blabber away. Surely you've noticed. But that was a secret I meant to keep. To take to my grave." She quickly crossed herself. "Though I suppose if I had to blurt it out in front of anyone, it had best be you. I'm certain you must know already."

"Know what?"

"Oh, my." Again the delicate, freckled hand clamped over

her lower face. But this time it didn't stop her from talking. "Mnplphd. Wtbmdtpqut."

"What are you saying?" Kanakareh stepped forward, taking Sophia's round shoulders in his hands. She was so soft. And short. Straight black hair swung against Kanakareh's cheek as he bent toward her.

"I thought you knew." Her eyes were pleading. "Really I did. I gossip, yes. I am fully aware that I do . . . and that I shouldn't. Cardinal Sinzen is forever meting out penitence to me, but though I pray for forgiveness, it seems I cannot stop. Still, never have I revealed anything about Cassandra. She is my dearest friend. And I certainly did not mean to walk into the room and find her in bed with General Hawke, it just—"

His bark of laughter cut Sophia's words off. She blinked, burnished lashes lifting in surprise. "Why, Kanakareh, I don't believe I ever heard you laugh before. It is a most intriguing sound, much like a giant waterfall or thunder. Though I don't mean to imply it's an ominous sound. Quite the contrary, I—"

"Sophia." His fingers tightened on the warm silk. "Are you telling me that Hawke and the Queen are lovers?" It sounded unbelievable, yet it would explain so much.

"Lovers?" Sophia bit her bottom lip as if the idea was simply too overwhelming for her to comprehend. "Oh, I can't believe they actually . . . Do you think?" But she hurried on before Kanakareh could answer. "When I say they were in bed I don't mean exactly . . . I mean I didn't see anything but kissing, and they stopped that as soon as they saw me—or perhaps heard me. I know I gasped. But I was so surprised. They were both fully dressed," she added as an afterthought, and her face blossomed with color.

He should have known. Kanakareh shook his head. The Queen! Had Hawke lost what was left of his mind? What did his friend think the Grand Duke would do when he found out? What could possibly induce a man to lose his head so completely over a woman?

Of their own volition Kanakareh's eyes met Sophia's.

She was talking again, lamenting the fact that Cassandra was off in the night somewhere alone with General Hawke, then agonizing bitterly about the fact that the Queen might also be off in the night by herself. "Or worse. She may have been captured. By outlaws and thieves who have her tied up and are torturing her at this very moment. Or perhaps she's—"

The pressure of Kanakareh's lips on hers silenced her.

They were warm and firm, moving ever so slightly in a rhythm much like the beating of her heart. Eyes open, Sophia stared as his blunt black lashes drifted down. Then, leaving her dizzy enough to be glad his hands still steadied her shoulders, Kanakareh pulled away.

"What?" Sophia sucked in a breath that tasted wild and free. "Why did you do that?"

Kanakareh's grin was wry. "I am not sure. It seemed a likely way to quiet you."

"Well, yes." Sophia nodded, wondering why her voice sounded quavery. "It did that."

"Should I apologize?"

"Yes! No." Sophia shook her head, spilling fire-colored curls over her shoulder. When she glanced back up her eyes sparkled. "Actually I feel another fit of babbling coming upon me." She smiled. "I wonder if you would be so kind as to shush me again."

A task Kanakareh was only to glad to undertake.

Her mouth opened under his, and before he could begin to discipline the wild surge of lust shooting through him, she was kissing him back and it was a lost cause. His hands left her shoulders, traveling down and around her back, pulling her as close as her hoops and petticoats would allow.

She murmured, uttering some nonsensical words even as he deepened the kiss, mating his tongue with hers. Lifting her up till her toes in the fancy silk slippers barely grazed the rug. Her arms reached up, locking about his neck, her fingers tangling in his hair.

"My. Oh, my," Sophia breathed when his mouth left hers

to trail a string of kisses along her cheek. Chills raced down her spine as his teeth clamped over her earlobe.

When he finally put her down, letting her body slide along the hard muscled length of his, Sophia could barely hold a rational thought in her head. It wasn't until he led her to the small crimson settee, that she remembered her friend.

"Poor Cassandra," she said, her head resting comfortably on Kanakareh's shoulder. "I hate to think of her out there somewhere . . . miserable."

Could heaven be so splendid? Cassandra wondered, then banished that blasphemous thought from her mind. Still, she couldn't help believing that kissing Maximilian Hawke the most glorious thing imaginable. At least she would have thought that had she not known about much more wondrous things he could do.

She felt hot and cold at the same time and as if every bone in her body had turned to water. And still his mouth caressed hers.

She clutched at his sleeves, pressing herself against him, longing to feel the hardness of his body. Wanting him to prove her memory a poor substitute for the ecstasy of their joining.

Wanting him now.

But what she wanted and what she got were quite different.

With a groan that seemed to echo through the woods, Max jerked away. Rolling onto his back he threw an arm over his eyes and sucked in huge, shaky gulps of air. Cassandra wouldn't have been more surprised if he'd sprouted wings and soared into the sky.

"What is it? What's wrong?"

He wished he knew. He peeked out from beneath his forearm, feeling foolishly at a loss for words. She was looking at him, her beautiful face a study in bewilderment. And why shouldn't she be surprised by his actions? He desired her—a fact she could ascertain for herself if she allowed her focus to drift beneath his belt. He'd never been so hard.

Max took another deep breath, filling his lungs and trying to stifle the desire to crush her beneath him and take her. "A few more minutes of that," Max said, his voice unsteady, "and I would break my promise to you." Break? It's a wonder he hadn't smashed it to smithereens.

"Promise? What promise?" Cassandra flipped frizzled curls behind her shoulder. She did know what he was talking about, and truthfully didn't much care.

"By the waterfall," Max moaned. "I gave you my word as a gentleman—and an officer in your service—to keep my distance from you."

"And almost immediately set about to break your vow." Cassandra's voice rose. "At nigh every chance you found."

She was angry, and Max couldn't blame her. "Cassie," he cajoled, only to wince when she flopped back on her rump and stuck her chin in the air.

"It's Your Highness, if you please."

Letting out his breath on a sigh, Max sat up too, facing her in the light of the flickering fire. "I know I've been a bit of a—"

"Rogue," she offered readily.

"Aye," Max admitted. "But that was before I . . ." Max searched for the right word. The word "loved" nearly came out, but that was ridiculous. He didn't love her. How could he? She was the bleeding queen, for God's sake. And he . . . he was the disowned son of a duke, who owed his present position to her husband and brother-in-law.

"That was before I knew you," he settled on. "Well, actually I *knew* you before we met. In the Biblical sense." Max shook his head. "Pray forget I said that. My mind doesn't seem to be working in conjunction with my mouth. What I mean to say is"—Max's gaze caught hers and held—"I've grown to admire you. And I don't want to break my word to you." He lifted his hands in supplication. His explanation sounded as ridiculous as the thought that he might actually be in love with her, but there it was. He was being as honest as he could.

Possibly as honest as he'd ever been.

Cassandra's eyes narrowed and she gingerly fingered the bruise on the side of her head.

"Does that hurt?"

"No. I was just thinking about what you said."

"And . . . there is an end to this, isn't there?"

"Your reasoning seems a bit flawed." Cassandra's head tilted to the side. "You could make love to me before you admired me. But now you can't."

"Not can't," Max insisted. "Never think that." He rested an elbow on one bent knee. "I simply don't wish to force you into something you'll regret in the morning."

"And you fear I shall . . . regret this?"

"You did the last time."

Cassandra traced the edge of a leaf that fell onto her lap. It was true what he said. She had rued the day she'd first seen Maximilian Hawke. But she'd also remembered his embrace fondly. The sweet oblivion of his kiss. Her lashes lifted. In the shimmering shadows she saw him watching her. His eyes, that intense blue that always made her heart flutter, seemed to bore through her.

"I don't want you despising me . . . or yourself," he said, his voice low.

"The decision is mine, then."

"Aye, I suppose it is." Honesty forced him to add, "Though I'd recommend for your sake that you hold me to my word." His smile was crooked. And Max wondered what strange new sense of chivalry guided his tongue. It was as if he argued against what he wanted most in the world—and could not stop himself. "I fear I won't be as gallant in the future."

Her chin rose a fraction, though her eyes never left his. "What makes you think there will be a future time?"

He simply lifted a brow. But it was enough to make Cassandra feel foolish for her question. This was not the end they were discussing but the beginning. If they made love this time there would be no turning back.

They both knew what they were about to do, and thanks to Max they were discussing the possibility of an affair in a clearheaded way . . . or at least as clearheaded as she could be when he was near.

She would be taking a lover.

And she knew, despite the fact that she was the Queen and he her general, Max would be demanding. He would complicate her life—his actions now proved it. He could have taken her earlier with nothing from her but total cooperation. But he hadn't. And now the choice was hers.

But there really was no choice.

Cassandra leaned forward till there was barely an inch between his lips and hers. He let out his breath and she smiled. "You are my liege, General," she whispered. "And I release you from your pledge to me."

She feared he might argue or question her decision. But he did neither. His hands snaked out to tangle in her hair. Yet instead of pulling her to him as she desired, he just held her a moment, his gaze caressing her face.

Cassandra thought she might die from the tenderness of his expression; then desire flamed in his eyes and his lips crushed hers. All else fled her mind.

He wanted to be gentle, but feared it beyond him. The feel of her, the taste of her, coursed through his body like the strongest of wines.

Her lips, forced open by his, drove him wild. His tongue plunged, dueling with hers, as he pushed her down on the carpet of pine needles.

He was so hungry for her, he could barely stand it. "You drive me mad," he said, as his fingers worked feverishly on the row of buttons marching down the center of her chest. God, he never knew such a simple task could be so difficult. Losing patience he cupped her breast, kneading the mound through the thick velvet, eliciting a long, low moan from her that sent his hands on another mission.

Her skirts were as much a hindrance as her bodice, layer upon layer of lace and ruffle. He wanted her out of the trappings of civilized society—of Queen Cassandra—and deliciously naked. As before when they were simply Cassie and Max.

But he didn't think he could wait. She wriggled beneath him, clutching at his arms, splaying her hands over his back and lower, till he thought he might burst.

"Now, Max, please."

His mouth covered hers, his tongue plunging deep. A poor substitute for what they both desperately wanted. It was as if their discussion—the possibility that they would, that they could, stifle this passion—sent them both teetering on the edge of ecstasy.

He wanted to go slowly, to caress her body and run his tongue along the dimpled curve of her knee. But could manage no more than a rough squeeze of her thigh when his hand encountered warm flesh.

Propped on an elbow, his face buried in the silken curls behind Cassandra's ears, Max struggled along with her to release his pulsing manhood from his breeches. He surged forward, sliding his finger along her slick heat, muffling her scream with his mouth.

And then he was inside her.

His thrusts there not gentle. Max could feel her knees pressed into his hips, the tight glove of her body urging him on. When she shuddered, calling out his name, Max felt a oneness with her such as he'd known with no one else.

Meant to be. Meant to be.

The words echoed through his mind as his seed emptied, hot and strong into her. He tried to think what that could mean, but rational thought was beyond him. And anyway it couldn't possibly be more than a silly fantasy.

Nothing about this was meant to be. She was the Queen of Breslovia; he a lowly soldier. Yet he couldn't stop thinking of her. Couldn't care about any other woman. And now he'd taken her on the ground, her skirts rouched up, his breeches still slung to his hips.

And he felt like a king.

Propping himself on his elbows, Max looked down at her, surprised but pleased to see her staring up at him. Her wild hair spilled over the pine needle-covered ground, a golden nimbus. Her face seemed pale in the feeble light, all large shining eyes and a smile that matched his own.

Bending down Max kissed the end of her nose.

"It was not my intent to be so rough. It's just . . ." He didn't think it wise to tell her there'd been no other woman since he'd taken her by the waterfall. Besides, Max didn't consider his abstinence the cause for his explosive desire. "God, you're beautiful," he finished, brushing curling tendrils from her forehead.

She could say the same of him, though she doubted he would appreciate the compliment. He was beautiful in a strong, masculine way. She lifted an arm that felt weighted with lead and touched his cheek, happier than she could say when he turned his head to press a kiss to her palm.

"How long have you been a soldier?"

They were lying on the ground on the frothy white bed of petticoats Max had fashioned from her undergarments. The pallet itself was simple, and only took so long to construct because Max had insisted upon stripping every layer from her body himself. They'd lost track of the reason they were undressing. Discomfort seemed a minor inconvenience when passion called.

And it seemed to call continually. Max no sooner sprawled on top of her, spent from a second overwhelming climax, when he felt the stirrings of his body again.

So they made love three times before the mattress was complete, before they lay side by side, gloriously naked beneath the blanket of Cassandra's velvet riding skirt.

Max propped himself on one elbow and considered her

question while his finger traced the delicate line of her collarbone. "It seems all my life, but in reality it's only been ten years, since I was eighteen."

"That seems so young." His hand drifted lower, and Cassandra sucked in her breath as his palm covered her breast. "Yet you were queen at seventeen."

"I thought we were just Cassie and Max," Cassandra said, her voice breathless. His hand spread over her stomach now, making her skin quiver.

"We are." It was an agreement they'd reached after making love the second time. They were to forget that she was Queen Cassandra of Breslovia and he her commander in chief. "As if we were at a masked ball," she'd said. "Only instead of wearing costumes we shall strip away everything and simply be ourselves."

It had sounded easy enough, and Max had laughed and agreed that stripping everything from her was his primary goal. But actually forgetting who she was, who he was, proved difficult.

"I understand," she said, as if she could read his thoughts. "We are what we are." Cassandra giggled. "I sound like Simon. The old seer I told you of," she explained when he lifted a brow. "He was always saying things like, 'Truth is the light feared by evil' or 'Question not what is meant to be.' "

Max fingers stilled. "What was that last thing he said?"

"Simon spoke often of what was meant to be. There are legends that the ancient ones handed down through the ages. Cardinal Sinzen thinks them heathen and refuses to acknowledge they could be true." Cassandra sighed. "I wish Simon would return. He left Breslovia the day my father and brother were murdered. Cardinal Sinzen saw him last, and couldn't persuade him to stay."

"It seems strange he even tried, knowing how he feels about the legends."

"That's true, except the cardinal knew how much I loved Simon. He begged him to stay for my sake."

" 'Tis difficult to understand how anyone could deny you"—Max's lips pressed down on a rosy nipple—"anything."

A curtain of lacy golden curls draped out the light from the smoldering fire, completing Max's notion that they were the only two people in the world. She straddled his hips, moving slowly, with an expertise that belied her inexperience. But then she was an eager and apt student in every way. Despite the fact that she seemed quite innocent and virginal for a woman married nearly three years.

Another topic they did not discuss, though on this one they each had come to the same conclusion independently, and without any verbal understanding. They simply did not mention Grand Duke Albert, and for his part, Max tried not to think of him.

His hands spanned the tapered waist, fingers flaring over hips that straddled his. She arched and the tension swelling inside him nearly erupted.

"God," he moaned, using all his strength to hold back his climax. His throat was dry from hoarse grating breaths that matched hers. She leaned forward, her breasts grazing the curling hair on his chest, setting his nerves on fire. His tongue sought hers, dueling smoothly before their lips met.

Her movements no longer needed his tutelage. His hands drifted lower, cupping the rounded mounds of her buttocks, spreading and exploring between her thighs.

Her body convulsed, surging, plunging; her fingers tore into the thick mane of midnight black hair, tripping the explosion that ripped through them both. Tearing at his senses and leaving him strangely off balance.

She collapsed in a heap on his chest and Max wrapped about her arms that felt weak from release, yet were strong in resolve. He would not let her go. He could not.

Still, nothing had really changed.

Reaching down, careful not to disturb her for he could tell

by her breathing she slept, Max pulled up the emerald velvet to cover them. She snuggled closer and her moist lips pressed the hollow beneath his ear. His hand combed long tangles of pale hair from her face. He lay there, softly caressing, trying not to think of what would happen on the morrow and the day after that.

Yet he could focus on nothing else.

He spoke the truth when saying this was a beginning. Neither of them could turn from what fate had in store for them now. But was it a true beginning . . . or the beginning of the end?

The pounding of horse's hooves. The rattle and clang of spurs and sabers. The sounds began as if far away and echoed into the netherlands of sleep.

Cassandra moaned. Days had passed since her last vision. Since she had left the castle behind. She hoped—prayed—she was rid of the power to see what was not there. Yet here it was again. The voices, the—

Cassandra's eyes flew open as something tightened around her. For a moment relief flooded her senses as quickly as the erotic memories of the past night. She was there, in the woods, her naked body pressed to his. Her skin tingled as his hair-roughened flesh abraded hers.

Her lashes lifted, her gaze caught the square angle of his stubbled jaw. She raised a hand to touch, surprised when his grip manacled her wrist. "What—"

"Shhh." His breath stirred the hair curling on her temple as he shifted, setting her down none too gently in the cradle of wrinkled petticoats.

Bent low Max went toward the fire, relieved to discover nothing but burned-out ashes. Then, keeping low, he scurried back to Cassandra.

"What is it?" Her voice was a whisper now. Who is making all that noise?" It was not a dream or a vision. The entire valley seemed alive with the sounds of men and horses, rumbling wagons and shouted commands. Twisting about, Cassandra tried to stand. But his hand caught her again before she could see what was happening.

"I don't know." He stopped, yanking a shirt over his head and tossing her her shift. "Get dressed," was all he said.

Which was easier said than done. Though she hadn't had the assistance of a lady's maid yesterday morning when she'd donned her riding habit, at least she had been able to stand. Now, forced to stay low to the ground, she could only wriggle and squirm into her skirt and jacket, leaving the voluminous petticoats and bone-stiffened corset behind. Even so, she took longer than Max, who dressed quickly and then crawled to the edge of the rise, where the thicket of trees formed a barrier of sorts.

Within moments he was back, hunched low, gathering up her remaining clothing and his bloodied jacket before she'd pulled on her second boot. "Tell me," she whispered. The noises seemed to have multiplied and were all the more ominous because she could not see what caused them.

"Soldiers," Max answered succinctly as he buried the frilly white ruffles beneath layers of fallen leaves. "French by the look of them."

"French. Count de Glasman was right."

His gaze cut to hers, his eyes searing. But he asked no questions, only scattered the rocks and ashes and knocked aside the spit he'd erected to roast the boar. The animal itself he'd already dragged away from their camp.

Taking one last look, assuring himself a cursory glance wouldn't reveal their presence, Max grabbed Cassandra's hand. Keeping bent over, he pulled her farther into the woods, ignoring her protests.

Ignoring them, that is, until they grew too loud.

"For God's sake, be quiet," he hissed, yanking her behind a thick-trunked sycamore.

"Why should I?" Her chin rose, though she was breathless.

"And why should I run? I'm the Queen of Breslovia, and those soldiers are on Breslovian soil."

"And just what does Your Royal Highness plan to do about it? Request that they leave?"

She hadn't really thought too far ahead, despite her teasing words to Sophia. And this morning, awakening as she had and rushing so, there had hardly been time for serious thought. But what he said had promise. "Yes," Cassandra said with a nod. "That is exactly what I should do."

His snort of derision had her chin notching higher. "I command you to move aside," she ordered in her most queenly voice. But instead of allowing a path for her he moved closer, blocking off any movements, pressing her back against the rough bark.

"Listen to me, Your Highness." His arms were hard bands of steel, his eyes devoid of any tenderness from the night before. "If they believed you were Queen Cassandra—"

"What do you mean *if?"* No one had ever doubted her before. But then she never found herself in like circumstances before. The rake of Max's stare as it traveled from her wild hair littered with leaves and twigs down the front of her wrongly buttoned tunic to her wrinkled and dirty skirt told her as much. She was grateful when he made no comment about her appearance, or about what the soldiers would assume if they saw her with Max. Instead he went on as if she hadn't interrupted him.

"If they believed you, what makes you think they would obey? They obviously don't belong here. And I'd be willing to bet they haven't come to enjoy the autumn climate."

"Yes, but—"

"Whatever their reason, I don't intend to hand you over to them, or let you hand yourself over to become a hostage."

"A hostage?" Cassandra's eyes widened. "But they can't do that. Breslovia is neutral. What of the Edict?"

Max only shook his head. "Come on," he growled, grabbing her hand again and running toward the east. Unfortunately he didn't know how abruptly the shelter of the trees ended, or that the French regiment had a foraging party on its flank.

He shoved Cassandra behind him as several musket snouts pointed his way. "Let me do the talking," he managed, but for the life of him he didn't know if she heard. Or if she would obey.

Sixteen

"What is it?" The general set his fork aside, with a sigh as the sergeant entered the tent. "Can I not even enjoy my meal in peace?"

He listened dispassionately to his aide, then waved a hand. "Bring them in." Resigned to eating his stuffed pheasant cold, General Henri Valliere pushed his chair away from the starched white linen table cover. He eyed the two people escorted into his presence, his lips curving in a smile when his gaze settled on Cassandra.

He stood, thrusting out a leg and inclined his head. "Mademoiselle." His greeting to Max was curt. "My men tell me you were caught running through the forest." He brushed a piece of lint from his immaculate white jacket. "Can you tell me what you were doing there?"

"Perhaps you should tell us—"

"Cassie, sweetheart." Max stepped close to her, his arm circling her shoulders. The soldiers who'd captured them had kept them separated until this moment, or he would have regaled her with the reasons she should keep her own counsel. As it was she glared up at him. "You must forgive my darling, General. She is frightened." He shrugged. "It appears our little indiscretion is discovered."

Though his French was less than perfect Max made it even more so. He slouched, and forced Cassandra by the weight of his arm to do the same.

"What indiscretion would that be?" Again the general's eyes feasted on Cassandra.

"A small matter of a husband," Max said with a self-effacing grin. "My darling and I met last night to . . . admire the stars, and, well, we seem to have fallen asleep. We were understandably in a hurry to return to her husband's farmhouse when your soldiers came."

"Is this true?"

Cassandra swallowed. "Yes." Color crept into her cheeks. It made her words more persuasive, but her blush came from the way the French general stared at her bodice. She was uncomfortably aware, as was he, that she wore no undergarment beneath the jacket. "My husband will have my head if he discovers me gone."

He came closer, bending at the waist to examine her, touching a lock of wildly curling hair. Cassandra felt Max stiffen, as she stepped from his embrace. She tilted her head and smiled at the general, eliciting a similar response from him.

He lifted a finger and slowly rubbed it across his upper lip, his gray eyes never leaving her face. "Perhaps you should be more careful whom you choose for your trysts, madam."

"Perhaps I should."

"Where is this farm of yours?" The general circled Cassandra, pausing only for Max to step out of his way.

"To the north, sir, by the River Web."

"Ah." The finger slid down over his chin. "Perhaps I shall visit you there."

Cassandra merely inclined her head. "Does that mean we are free to go?"

"Oui. By all means run along to your husband." He fluttered his hand in dismissal. "And allow me to return to my food."

"What in the hell was that about?" Max kept his voice low as they walked through the rows of tents.

"What?"

"Don't play innocent with me. You know exactly what I mean. You practically invited that bastard to become your lover." Max kept his head bent, but his eyes scoured the area. There were more soldiers than he'd first thought. An artillery regiment. He'd counted three four-pounders and one nine-pounder. Enough firepower to wage a spirited assault.

"I only did as you suggested. Max?"

"Stand still so I have to come back for you."

"What?"

"Just do it, Cassie. Pretend you're angry with me." Max's voice was low.

"That shouldn't be difficult." She folded her arms, and held her ground, shaking her head when he turned toward her. "What are you doing?"

"Counting." Satisfied, Max grabbed her elbow. "Now let's get the hell out of here."

"I don't know why you're so worried," Cassandra said later as they hurried along a path that led through a meadow. "They let us go."

"Which is exactly what does worry me. Taking nothing from your performance for the general." Max slanted her a look. "It was a performance, wasn't it? What the hell am I saying?" Max shook his head. "Anyway, the general didn't seem concerned that we knew of his army or that he was on Breslovian soil."

"Which means?" Cassandra lifted her skirts and ran a few steps to catch up with him. Though the air was crisp, the sun shining, the unaccustomed exercise of walking over the countryside was taking its toll on her. She longed to stop and rest.

"Which means, Your Highness, that he was invited here."

"That's impossible. I'm the Queen for goodness sakes. I would know such a thing."

"Or he considers Breslovia no threat."

"Are we?" Cassandra grabbed at his arm, causing Max to pause.

One look at her face and Max pulled her down beside him. "We'll rest for a moment."

"You heard my question."

"Can Breslovia's army ward off an attack from France?" Max leaned back against the stone fence and shut his eyes. "I think you know the answer to that as well as I. That regiment back there has over twice the number of cannon we can muster."

Cassandra swallowed. Was this it then? The reason for her visions. Had she been wrong about the Prussian soldiers? Was it really the French who would override her country, slaying Breslovia's people?

Except that the French soldiers didn't appear ready to make war on her country. The tents they had set up seemed more like a small city with merchants and cooks and enough women so that General Valliere certainly didn't have need of her.

And the general, for all his lecherous looks, didn't possess the steely-eyed determination of the leader in her visions. Still, she was the Queen, and the safety of Breslovia and of her citizens rested on her shoulders.

"I need to return to Liberstein." Cassandra stood, giving her skirts a determined tug.

But her bravado waned as the afternoon progressed. She was tired and hungry, despite the apples Max found. So she was delighted when they spotted a farmer on a cart ahead of them. Progress was still slow—Max and the farmer walked near the sway-backed horse's head—but at least she could ride.

"Oh, Your Highness, are you all right?" Sophia hurried down the torchlit path from the Lodge, following Kanakareh. "I was so worried. I know Kanakareh said all would be well, but I just couldn't help thinking of you out there, all alone. Goodness, what happened to your clothes? And your poor hair? Do come along."

Almost without breaking the thread of her conversation with Cassandra, Sophia tossed out orders to the bevy of maids fluttering about. Hot water was ordered, as well as a meal of chicken and pastries. "Oh, and mulled wine," Sophia called out.

Cassandra barely had time to call back her thanks to the farmer for the use of his cart and to exchange a glance with Max before she was bundled away. Not that she was complaining. It was heaven to have her soiled riding habit removed and to sink into warm, rose-scented water. And she could blame fatigue for her inability to answer Sophia's questions about missing undergarments.

Her meal was brought to her room. When Cassandra insisted she was well enough to join the others in the dining room, she was told there were no others. Kanakareh and Sophia had already eaten, as had the general.

Cassandra wanted to see Max.

She was ensconced in the royal bed, propped up by a mountain of pillows, washed, fed, and pampered till she glowed. But she was willing to trade it all for one of Maximilian Hawke's crooked grins.

Which was ridiculous and quite silly of her.

Her country was in peril. The French had invaded the quiet countryside. Yet she dreamed of broad shoulders and blue eyes and arms that made her feel safe.

And someone to talk with concerning what she must do.

Cassandra held her tongue with Sophia for fear of worrying her friend. Besides, her lady-in-waiting's counsel was not usually sought on national issues. During a lull, when Sophia stopped to catch her breath, Cassandra considered asking her to send for General Hawke. But she remembered the expression on Sophia's face when she'd opened the bedroom door to see Max upon her bed, the frown when her friend had discovered the lack of petticoats and corset.

Perhaps tomorrow would be soon enough to see Max.

Except that when she woke Cassandra found her general gone.

The Lodge was bustling with activity. Before succumbing to sleep the previous night Cassandra had given the order that the household would return to Liberstein on the morrow. Coaches were being packed, and Cassandra's trunks, barely aired from the journey made but days before were crammed with her belongings. Maids dressed her and her fast was broken. But she had to summon Kanakareh before she could find an answer to her most pressing question.

"He left last night, Your Highness."

"Last night?" With a wave of her hand, Cassandra dismissed the servant who'd brought chocolate in a gleaming silver pot. "But we only arrived here at nine o'clock. Surely he took time to rest."

"He did eat, though barely. He felt it urgent that he return to the army to await Your Highness' orders."

"I see." To give herself something to do, Cassandra poured herself some chocolate and a cup for the Seneca brave. She wanted to ask if Max had left a message for her, but she feared she knew the answer. Kanakareh would already have given it to her if he had. "I see," she repeated, for she could think of nothing else to say.

"I am at your service to escort Your Highness to the capital. And Colonel Marquart has assembled the Imperial Guard."

So there was nothing left for her but to leave. Which, Cassandra reminded herself harshly, was what she should do with all haste. A queen had no time to ponder strained love affairs when her country was in jeopardy. Affairs of state must be uppermost in her mind.

Yet she couldn't help a twinge of sadness as the royal carriage rolled away from the Lodge.

"He's been waiting to see you for three days, sir."

"Who?" Max had ridden hard, covering the miles from the Royal Lodge to Bordgarten in two days. Trail dirt covered his clothes, his eyes felt gritty from lack of sleep, and he needed to summon his officers and put Breslovia's army on alert.

But all his aide-de-camp did was prattle on about some envoy wishing to see him.

"Count de Plausy," the lieutenant responded, which meant nothing to Max. He dropped onto the seat behind his camp desk, spent valuable time trimming the quill point, then penned several sets of orders. It wasn't till he pressed his seal into the soft red wax that he glanced up to see his aide still standing in the doorway.

"Who is this count? A local noble? Tell him I haven't time to spare for him unless he is coming to enlist." He gathered up the folded parchment.

"Sir, I don't think he plans to do that. He's already in the army. The French army."

Max stilled, his knees still bent from rising from the chair. "What did you say?"

Lieutenant Robert Lowell seemed not to know how to answer his general. He swallowed, his prominent Adam's apple bobbing above his tunic's collar. "He's with the French army, sir. At least that's what he said."

"Where is he?"

"In the town I believe, sir. He and his entourage are staying with the mayor, though I'm not certain His Honor is too—"

"Get him and bring him here." Max dropped the sealed orders on his desk. "Now," he barked when the young soldier only stared at him.

He thought there was no time for a proper bath, though in truth by the time Count de Plausy arrived with a dozen or so aides, Max could have been shriveled like a prune had he been in a tub. Instead he managed to wash with pitcher and bowl, to shave and change into a proper uniform and then eat. He still had time to pace his office and wonder why the hell a French envoy wanted to see him.

The Count de Plausy sported enough gold braid on his scarlet uniform to weigh him down. His wig was freshly powdered and elaborately curled beneath a fur-trimmed hat he removed with a sweeping bow. His jowls were loose, his face pleasant, and his manner effusive as he entered the tent.

"I am so glad you have returned, Monsieur General. I have been anxious to deliver my gift to you . . . on behalf of my sovereign, His Highness Louis the Fifteenth, of course."

Max offered the count a seat and a glass of port, both of which the Frenchman accepted with smiles.

"What gift are you talking about?" Max asked after the count tasted the wine, declaring it to be magnificent.

"Why the cannons, of course. Artillery."

Max's jaw dropped.

"Not a sennight away in the valley of the River Web, there is a regiment of grenadiers and several nine- and four-pounders. They are at your disposal. Two more regiments will follow."

Max snapped his mouth shut. "Why?"

"Why are they still en route? Surely you can understand how difficult it is to transport cannon of such size. We were barely making six miles a day, and I was anxious, on my sovereign's part, to convey his profound best wishes and prayers."

"And soldiers."

"Oui." The Count de Plausy smiled broadly. "And soldiers."

Max rubbed his chin. "Please do not misunderstand me. I am certain the regiments you bring are greatly appreciated. It is only that I do not have the authority to accept such a gift. My sovereign, Queen Cassandra, may not wish—"

"Ah, but of course Her Highness knows of His Majesty's generosity. Her husband, the Grand Duke Albert requested they be sent."

"The weapons. I know we ordered muskets and cannon."

"Oui, and the soldiers. Three regiments of Louis' finest fighting men. For your assault on Melena."

Max tried to keep his confusion from showing. Why in the hell would Albert ask the French king to send troops to Breslovia? And what of Melena?

"How long can we expect the pleasure of your company, Count de Plausy?"

"I must return immediately to the regiment, but I shall be back with the artillery. Unless, of course, you can accompany me to the frontier?" His round face lit up at the prospect.

"I must apologize, but I cannot. Pressing duties here, you understand."

"But of course." De Plausy stood with as much flourish as he'd sat. "I must be on my way, I have tarried too long."

Max felt the same. As soon as the French count took his leave, he bade an aide to see that a horse be saddled and provisions packed. The orders to his officers he had hand delivered, explaining the situation as best he could and omitting any reference to the Queen's visit to the frontier.

"What would you have us do?" Colonel Clark of the Horse Guards asked.

"Exactly what you've been doing. Drills, firing exercises, precision marches. All I ask is that you remain with your troops and stay alert. Colonel Klausman will be in charge during my absence, which will not be long."

"But where are you going?"

"It is obvious I cannot learn the truth from the French."

"You are going to Liberstein?"

"I am."

Cassandra stifled a yawn behind her fan.

Around her the sweep of richly clothed dancers blurred, and at first she feared another vision was upon her. But no. She blinked and the ladies and gentlemen of the court came into focus. It was merely lack of sleep causing her dizziness.

This lack, however, was caused by the visions that, since her return to the palace, would not cease. It was almost as if, granted the brief respite on her journey, she was now to pay for the lull threefold.

What her mind's eye saw rarely stayed the same. At one time she was in the highlands, at another in Liberstein itself. The only common threads were the death and destruction.

They never seemed to cease.

Nor did the evasions and excuses Cassandra received from her ministers and envoys. Cardinal Sinzen was convinced she was mistaken about the French soldiers. He intimated she was having delusions.

"But I saw them myself. General Hawke saw them as well. There were tents and cannon. We were even captured by some pickets."

"Captured. Your Highness," he said, his belly quivering, "that is unforgivable. We must demand an apology from Louis immediately."

"They didn't know who I was," Cassandra said with a sigh. "General Hawke thought it better not to tell them, under the circumstances." Remembering exactly what those circumstances were, Cassandra snapped her mouth shut. "Their general released us unharmed, which is not the point. What are French soldiers doing on Breslovian soil?"

"We must petition the French ambassador."

"Yes, we must," Cassandra had agreed, though it was what she'd demanded when Cardinal Sinzen had entered the council chamber.

"As soon as he returns from the country, we shall."

Cassandra shut her eyes and prayed for patience. When she opened her eyes she spied Count de Glasman, the Prussian ambassador, wending his way toward her. He was understandably uncomfortable with what he considered a French-Breslovian alliance against his country.

No amount of cajoling on her part would convince him that his fears were unfounded.

"Your Majesty I must speak with you."

Cassandra pasted a smile on her face and prepared herself for another harangue. Her greeting was barely acknowledged by the Prussian ambassador before he drew her toward a windowed alcove. Tiny lights sparkling in the trees made the garden below appear a fairyland. But de Glasman had not led Cassandra aside to enjoy the view. Nor did he care overmuch for privacy. He nearly shouted. "I have just received word the French regiment is on the march."

"Back to their native soil perhaps?"

"To the contrary, Your Highness, toward Bordgarten, to meet up with the main body of your army."

Meet or attack? Cassandra tried to keep her composure as de Glasman continued. "I have tolerated your refusal to do something about this situation because you are the daughter of my dear, departed friend—and because of what Breslovia and Prussia have meant to each other in the past. But I am afraid it is the past of which we speak. Your government—"

"No, Count, you are wrong. I am as committed to peace between our nations as my father was, as his father before him. Neutrality—"

"Is a word I fear Breslovia now uses to lull her neighbors into a false sense of security. It is a word you used while building up your army."

"For defense purposes only," Cassandra interjected though she didn't think he heard—or cared—what she said.

"And now you have invited the French, our enemy, to enter your land, to cross the buffer between our two countries, and you expect us to sit quietly by and let this happen."

"I have sent envoys to France asking, nay, demanding that all foreign soldiers remove themselves from Breslovian soil immediately." Three days ago she had dictated the message, her words and resolve firm, to Cardinal Sinzen. He had assured her it would travel to Versailles by fastest courier. "Please, Count de Glasman." Cassandra took his hands, her eyes holding his. "You must believe me. No one wants peace between our nations more than I." For she had seen the death and misery if it should fail. If she should fail.

"Your Highness"—the old man's gaze faltered; then he quickly pulled his hands from hers—"you ask too much from me. Too much in the name of friendship. I can do no more. I can wait no longer."

"No, please." Cassandra followed him from the alcove, conscious of but ignoring the sea of faces staring her way. "What will you do?"

"I've no recourse but to apprise His Majesty Emperor Frederick of the situation—and of your refusal to act."

"She's called an emergency meeting of her ministers. I'm expected to be there of course," Albert said with a sigh. "It is all so tiresome. Especially when I know what she will say."

"But there is nothing she can do."

"You are right, my sweet." Albert trailed a finger along the wickedly low décolletage of his mistress. They were in the south gardens, outside the petit château Albert had built for such rendezvous. In the distance could be seen the palace, his palace, ablaze with thousands of candles. "All is in motion. Once war is declared, France will send her forces in in greater numbers. With victory will come my coronation as king."

"And mine as queen," Nicolette reminded him.

Albert closed his eyes as his mistress dipped her hand, fondling the front of his silver-threaded breeches. He sighed. "There is naught Cassandra can do to stop destiny."

It seemed Albert's words were true, though Cassandra had no way of knowing he'd uttered them. The hour was late, the ministers a grumbling lot as she stood before them. She spoke of the French, of the Prussian threat, and of her own quandary as to what to do.

Sir Winston and Albert suggested a strongly worded protest to the French court, even though she'd specifically mentioned that had already been done. Another advisor was in favor of war, with whom he wasn't concerned. As long as Breslovia's honor was not trod upon.

"What of her citizens?" Cassandra demanded. "The innocent women and children, the men who will die if such action is taken!"

To his credit Lord Drake settled back in his chair, a sheepish expression beneath his crooked wig. He had no other suggestion.

"Breslovia is not prepared for war."

"That is not entirely true, Your Highness." It was Cardinal Sinzen, his face wreathed in condescending smiles. "Of course we all want peace." His pudgy hands lifted as if he were giving a benediction. "And the Edict of Liberstein is a sacred document. However, as you requested, our military has been improved, our army increased."

As she had requested? Cassandra looked from the cardinal to her husband in disbelief. She may have agreed to expand the militia, but it was not her suggestion. Sinzen stared back, his expression benign. Albert simply let his eyes drift to the layers of gold lace at his wrist.

What did it matter who had suggested the buildup of the army? Breslovia was still not strong enough to wage war. Either with France or Prussia . . . or England or Russia or any other country now engaged in mortal combat.

Cassandra took a deep breath. "I have sent messengers into the countryside to assemble the Diaz."

"Your Highness, I appreciate your concern, but that hardly seems necessary. It will take months for the parliament to convene. By then the snow will fly and the crisis will be over. If there ever was a crisis," he added, tilting his head and nodding toward the other ministers.

"Let there be no mistake. There is a crisis." Cassandra could feel the ministers' attention slipping away. "Prussia is ready to take measures against us." Her voice was rising and her control was slipping. She could almost read her ministers' minds. Her majesty is hysterical, they were thinking.

She'd heard the rumors in court that she was ill, that her mind could not handle the rigors of being queen. The visions interrupting her sleep and haunting her days gave the gossip validity. But it wasn't true. She was strong of mind and capable of leading.

Squaring her shoulders, Cassandra dismissed the ministers—all but Sinzen. When they were alone her eyes hardened. "Do not do that to me again, Cardinal Sinzen."

"Do what, Your Majesty?" His distress seemed genuine. His robes flowing, he approached, dropping to his knees with difficulty. "If I have done something to offend you, Your Majesty, please accept my most humble apology."

"You undermined my authority, Cardinal Sinzen." Anger coursed through her. But when she looked down at the shiny bald head bowed before her she could not summon the cruelty to chastise him further.

As he had said, he had always been her staunchest ally and friend.

With a wave of her hand, Cassandra dismissed him, even leaning down to help him rise.

"Do not trouble yourself, Your Highness. I shall take care of everything. Leave this problem to me and soon it will be finished."

When he was gone Cassandra stood alone in the Council Room beneath the great unicorn seal of her kingdom. She tried to think, but her mind felt numb. What was she to do?

Her body craved sleep, and she nearly decided to stay in one of the rooms set aside for her in the palace. She'd noted a link between her visions and the pull she felt toward the old castle. Tonight she needed respite from the spirits. Tonight she needed rest.

But the urge to return to her rooms was too great. Grabbing a branch of candles, Cassandra moved through the shimmering hallways, past the frescoed walls and domed ceilings trimmed in gold. Back to the stark stone tower.

Her maid was asleep on a cot in the anteroom, and despite the fact that she wore a shimmering evening gown of jewel-encrusted silk, Cassandra did not wake her. Somehow she would remove the skirts and bodice. It would be difficult, but she preferred that to listening to her maid's prattle.

Tonight she wished to speak with no one . . . no one except . . . "Max."

Though she whispered his name, the sound of her voice pulled him from slumber. Pushing up onto his elbows, Max stared at her across the expanse of her bed. She stood in the doorway, the candles she held reflecting off the shimmer of her gown, shining in her upswept curls. She seemed a vision, like the first time he'd seen her, and the tension in his body drove any thought of sleep from his mind.

He lifted a hand toward her, smiling when she closed the door behind her and walked toward the bed. She placed the candles on the table beneath the window, then moved from the pool of light. When she was nearly to the bed she paused and blinked once.

"What are you doing here?" she asked before adding, "You are real, aren't you?"

"Very." Max leaped from the bed, turning her, pressing her body back across the mattress with his own. "And as for what I am doing." His hand slid beneath her skirts. "I should think that is obvious."

Seventeen

"God, I missed you."

Max hadn't meant to say that. The words startled him so, he lifted his head, staring down at her in disbelief. Not that he'd never mumbled such inane niceties before. The sweet seduction, the harmless lie—they were part of the game. They meant little coming from a rogue.

Except this wasn't a lie.

Something tightened in his chest as Max looked down into her rain-washed violet eyes. He'd meant it. He'd missed her and longed for her since the morning he'd ridden off, leaving her in Kanakareh's care. Max realized now why he'd left as he did. He couldn't face her to say good-bye, feared he might not be able to make himself leave.

And it wasn't just the sex, though Lord knew he grew hard just thinking of her. It was her. Her smile. The way her voice sometimes quivered when she was angry. Even her damned Stivelson chin that tended to lift into the air more often than not.

His fingers cupped her there now, and his grin was a bit shaky. "I did," he said, taking a deep breath before going on. "I can't stop thinking about you."

"I think about you, too."

The grin broadened. His fingers spread to gently brush aside a silken curl. "You do?" God, how could the knowledge that she thought about him affect him so? Women thought about him all the time.

His lips brushed across hers, lightly . . . a tender counterpoint to the passion firing his lower body. He was right when he'd told her this wouldn't end. It couldn't. Not for him. But the sad truth was, it had to. Sooner or later, this woman who was coming to mean everything to him would be taken away.

And it would break his damn heart.

Max blinked. He was ahead of himself . . . way ahead. The future wasn't something on which he normally enjoyed dwelling. His kiss, her response, brought him reeling back to the present.

His mouth trailed lower, skimming the edge of her squared bodice, feasting on delicately plumped skin. He wet the dusky cleft between her breasts, frustrated with the stiff pearl- and diamond-covered stomacher that blocked his progress.

"How?" he growled, barely able to catch his breath, "do I get you out of this?"

Golden curls spilled over the red velvet spread as Cassandra's head turned from side to side. "I don't . . . Ah." He'd stopped his assault on her breasts and slid toward the side of the mattress. With all the determination of a man seeking gold, he attacked the billowing splendor of her skirts.

"I know you're in here somewhere," he said, his voice muffled by layer upon layer of ruffles and silk.

"What are you doing?" Cassandra raised onto her elbows. Her skirts hid him from view. All she could see was the mad rustling. A giggle erupted in her throat, but changed to a moan before it escaped.

His hands had found her. In triumph he pulled his head from beneath her skirts to report, a wicked grin creasing his face. Cassandra wondered how anyone could look so sexy with a wisp of lace stuck to the unshaved whiskers on his chin.

Then he disappeared again beneath the bountiful skirts and Cassandra lost her hold on reality. All she could do was feel. The callused palms that spread her legs. The warmth of his breath as it fanned the tight curls guarding her womanhood.

His whiskered cheeks abraded the tender insides of her

thighs and her fingers flexed, bunching handfuls of air. Anticipation . . . Memory stirred her senses, poising her body on the brink of some wonderfully erotic chasm.

His tongue seared, and she cried out, certain that she could stand no more of the sweet torture. Yet he persisted, using his mouth, his lips, nibbling and plunging till there was nothing left of her but a white hot flame. Languidly her legs spread beneath the petticoats, offering more—more of her body, more of her soul.

Then she arched, stiffening, unable to control the wild, wondrous spasms that raged through her. Lost and dizzy, her world spun till there was naught but sweet oblivion. And Max.

And then he was in her arms, his hair unfettered, midnight dark and curling, catching the candle's glow. "I want you naked." His mouth melded with hers.

It was all he could do to breathe. He had never been so crazed, so wild with desire. The very act of loving her had driven him nearly to the edge.

She had his breeches unbuttoned and pushed below his hips. With frantic fingers she traced the long, hard length of him, skimming the rounded tip, pushing to his root.

Max tried again to unfasten her bodice, or the billowing skirts. Desperation clumsied his efforts. If she didn't stop, if he didn't find a way to bury himself inside her, he would embarrass himself, spilling his seed like an inexperienced youth.

He was off the bed before she could protest, finding her ankles and pulling her toward the edge—toward him. He stood between her open legs, grabbing her buttocks and plunging forward. He drove deep, filling her, driving them both over the edge.

"How do you manage to dress yourself?" Max sat in the center of the giant bed, Cassandra in front of him, her back wedged between his legs. His bottom lip was caught between his teeth and he squinted as he tried to unravel a knot in her corset laces.

"I don't." Cassandra twisted around to catch a glimpse of him. "I have maids who do that. They undress me, too."

"Perhaps we should call one in."

"If that's what you wish." Cassandra wriggled her bottom more firmly into the V between his thighs.

"Stop it." Max dropped the ribbon and clutched her shoulders, giving her neck a playful bite. "I'm having a hard enough time as it is."

She wiggled again. "So I feel."

"God, you've become a shameless hussy," he said with a laugh. "But I'm determined to have you naked before we make love again so you had better be still."

Cassandra sighed and decided it was in her best interest to comply. She didn't think it too distracting if she traced lazy circles on his hair-roughened thigh, though.

"Devil," he whispered, returning the favor, tracing his fingertip along the swell of her breast, before pulling himself together and reattacking the ribbon.

"Max."

"Hmmm? I almost have it."

"I'm glad you're here." Cassandra felt his fingers still, his body stiffen. "What is it?" This time she turned her body, draping her legs over his thigh. "What's wrong?"

She was sitting in his lap, staring at him, and Max leaned back against the headboard. "I was going to wait until morning. Actually, the way I felt after wending my way through the tunnel . . . you know, it's full of rats." Max shook his head. "Anyway, I thought I'd probably sleep till morning."

"Wait till morning for what?"

"Cassie, I have something to tell you. About the French soldiers we saw—the artillery."

"The Prussians are truly upset, and I can't seem to get an answer from Louis no matter how many envoys I send requesting he withdraw his troops. I just don't—"

"Albert invited them."

"What?" Cassandra pressed her hands to his chest, leaning back so she could see his face.

"I don't know why but—"

"That can't be true." Cassandra looked down to where black hair curled around her fingers, then back to meet his eyes. "I've discussed the problem with the Grand Duke. He's as concerned as I." It was an exaggeration yet she felt obliged to defend him. Whatever her husband was, treason seemed beyond him. "I don't know how you came by this infor—"

"A colonel with the French regiment told me."

"But how—"

"He awaited me when I returned to Bordgarten. Apparently he was sent ahead to inform me of the French arrival." Max hesitated. "I knew of the cannon and small arms." Max hurried on even though her expression registered surprise. "They were ordered soon after I arrived in Breslovia."

"From France? But why? We have a munitions factory in Glester."

"Hell, Cassandra, that place can barely keep up with the orders it receives from those Breslovians too stupid to order their sporting weapons abroad." He could tell he insulted her. Before he could stop her she scurried off his lap. Still garbed in chemise and corset she paced to the unicorn tapestry and back, not looking at him while he continued.

"The militias were armed with museum pieces. And the recruits . . . well, mostly with nothing at all."

"So you took it upon yourself to elicit help from the French."

"No." Max leaped off the bed. Grabbing his shirt he yanked it over his head, suddenly feeling very naked. This wasn't the way he wished to spend what was left of the night. Damn the Grand Duke and the French, and hell, damn Her Royal Highness Queen Cassandra while he was at it.

"*I* didn't order the weaponry. Your husband took care of that."

"Don't be ridiculous. Albert isn't capable of knowing what to do about anything, let alone equipping an army."

Her hair curled wildly about her bare shoulders and Max thought fleetingly about wrapping her in his arms and coaxing her out of this mood. Then he thought about what she said. It seemed to him that she was defending her ass of a husband at his expense. Never mind that her arguments made Albert out to be a boob, she had as much as called Max a liar.

Max faced her, hands on hips, linen shirt barely covering the essentials. "Don't complain to me about his incapacities. He's your spouse, not mine. I assume you knew how inadequate he was before marrying him. Hell, that's probably *why* you married him."

Her pose was as belligerent as his. "Are you finished?"

"Yes." Max decided he could jut his chin out as far as she could. "Except perhaps Albert had help . . . Cardinal Sinzen, for instance."

"Ah, now you add my minister and confessor to the list of maligned. Who shall it be next." Cassandra threw up her hands before turning away from him. "Countess Sophia?"

"I doubt she could stop chattering long enough to conspire with the French." As soon as the words left his mouth, Max knew he'd made a mistake—another mistake. Cassandra whirled around, her hair floating out like a golden nimbus. Her eyes sparked lightning.

"It was a jest," he said quickly. "A jest. I admire Countess Sophia, really I do. And Kanakareh—"

"I think you should leave."

Max wasn't sure whether she meant the room, the palace, or the whole damn country. And at this moment he didn't much care. Except that he'd known something like this would happen, had known it from the beginning. Why in the hell couldn't he keep his mouth shut and his breeches buttoned.

He was—or had been—the commander in chief of Breslovia's army. He could have dallied with any woman he chose, or nearly so. But no. He had to pick the Queen to fall in love with.

Max stopped, one leg partway in his breeches. My God! Love. He was in love with her. He glanced up to see her standing, her stiff back toward him, and another wave of questions flooded over him. Why him? Why her? What in the hell was he going to do?

His bare foot pushed through to the floor. She had made him angry. But she was alone and frightened, and carried a hell of a lot of responsibility. And he had a feeling things were only going to get worse. He thought about her visions and quickly fastened his pants.

She didn't move when he stepped up behind her, barely flinched when his hand brushed aside a tangle of disheveled curls. "Cassie."

It was all she could do not to turn into his arms. She bit her bottom lip and blinked back the tears threatening to seep through her lashes. What was she to do? She'd thought she could trust Max, but now she wasn't sure her desire for him didn't cloud her thinking. From the beginning—the moment he'd arrived in Breslovia—he had worked toward enlarging the army, turning the tiny kingdom into a country preparing for war.

And now he'd come to her blaming Albert.

"Count de Plausy, the French colonel, told me the Grand Duke invited the French soldiers to join our army. He was proud to be in Breslovia, proud to bolster our attempts to force the Prussians from Melena." Max kept talking as she turned to stare at him wide-eyed. "Like you, he thought I was a part of this scheme."

Cassandra couldn't meet his eyes, afraid of the power he had over her. She might sink into those blue depths and forget all else. And she had to keep her wits about her—to think. "Why would Breslovia attack Melena? It makes no sense. The province has belonged to"—Cassandra tried to remember her recently learned history—"Prussia for centuries."

"I don't know, Cassie." It was a mistake to call her that

now, Max realized as her chin notched up. Despite her provocative state of undress she was still the Queen, thinking like the Queen. And she apparently didn't want to be reminded of her liaison with a common soldier.

Indeed it seemed she wanted nothing to do with this particular soldier, for she turned her back again, repeating her request that he leave. She neither glanced around nor said good-bye when he pushed the lever behind the unicorn tapestry.

As soon as the door shut behind him, Cassandra wished she could call him back. But no. She needed to be alone, to sort out her thoughts. By the time the faint fingers of dawn lit the sky outside her window, she had come to only one undeniable conclusion.

Unless something was done, Breslovia was hurtling toward the horror of her visions.

"He's sleeping with the Queen, under your very nose."

Albert twisted about so he could see in the mirror how the long powdered curls lay on his pink silk waistcoat. He was feeling especially fine this morning, thanks to Nicolette's good temper of the previous night. "It will not be long now, my prince," she'd said, looking up at him across the expanse of his chest. "Soon French soldiers will march into Liberstein and declare you king."

Albert liked remembering the sound of that word from her luscious lips, and he found his brother's interruption annoying. Especially when Sinzen rambled on about some foolishness. Cassandra having a lover. The very idea. She was as cold as a wind off the Alps.

Albert told the cardinal as much.

"Well, apparently General Hawke does not find her so."

"Hawke?" This was incredible. Albert still harbored a twinge or two of jealousy caused by his mistress' first reaction to the raven-haired general. Jealousy, only partly assuaged when Nicolette denied her initial reaction to General Hawke, saying she didn't find his tall form attractive or his shoulders broad, and adding that a bit of padding could fill out anyone's jacket and breeches. Albert had readily agreed, though in truth he'd doubted the man had need of such artifice.

Still . . . Albert shook his head, spraying a fine fog of powder. He leaned toward the gilt-framed mirror, deciding his cheeks needed no more rouge. "It is not possible."

"They were together at the Royal Lodge."

"Ridiculous."

"He slept in her room last night."

Albert straightened. "Hawke is in Bordgarten."

"Wrong again, little brother. He is in Liberstein. He has requested an audience with me this very day, as has the Queen."

"Together?"

"No." Sinzen settled into a chair with a huff. "Though I imagine the topics will be similar."

"The French."

"That and Prussia's reaction."

"So far you've managed to defuse Cassandra's concerns. Or at least kept her from upsetting our plans." Albert gave a snort of laughter. "How many of her couriers have you waylaid?"

Sinzen's smile lacked its usual pretense of warmth. "There has been no need to waylay anyone. I simply do not send the urgent messages she relays to me." His mouth straightened. "I can perhaps keep up this hoax for some time, especially with the French envoy's assistance. It is not Cassandra that concerns me, for I have her trust." He heaved himself out of the chair. " 'Tis Hawke that I worry about."

"Because of this silly affair you insist he carries on with Cassandra?"

"Because he knows the French forces were invited by you—"

"But how?"

"Count de Plausy told him, thinking him in on the scheme. I discovered this yesterday from one of my spies. Upon hearing the news, Hawke left immediately for the capital. For a rendezvous with the Queen."

Albert walked about his dressing room, touching first one crystal bottle, then another. "What harm can Maximilian Hawke cause? You said he was loyal to us, that because we gave him his position he owes us allegiance. You said—"

"Would you stop tossing back my words as if they were alms to the poor! That was before. Before Hawke aligned himself with the Queen. Before you allowed her to be lonely and vulnerable."

The Grand Duke was tired of hearing his brother's harangues about Cassandra's lonely bed. Especially now that it appeared not to be lonely at all. "She is a slut, and as soon as the French arrive—" Albert cut himself off, thankful his brother didn't seem to notice. The cardinal still insisted Cassandra needed an heir. That the two brothers would be co-regents when the Queen met her unfortunate accident.

But Albert had different plans. Plans which Sinzen would find out . . . in time. But not now. When the French entered Breslovia in sufficient force and declared him king, there would be no need for Sinzen or Cassandra.

"I still don't understand why Hawke is a problem." Albert pulled himself back to the present.

"He is popular with the troops. Men he recruited and trained." Sinzen folded his hands. "He controls the army."

"But the French—"

"Do not wish to fight us as well as the Prussians." The cardinal's robes swayed as he moved toward the door. "However, I have a plan to eliminate the general, so that you can claim his bastard son as your own."

Walking through the open door, Sinzen resisted the urge to look back and see his brother's reaction. True, Sinzen was only speculating, due to Cassandra's ill health and the whispers of her maids. But it gave Albert something to think on.

* * *

"What you tell me is very disturbing." Cardinal Sinzen steepled his pudgy fingers. "And he said the Grand Duke invited France to send soldiers to invade Breslovia?"

"He didn't say invade, Your Grace. Nor did I."

"No, no, of course not. I apologize, General Hawke. As you can see I am simply at a loss for what to say . . . my own brother." He paused a moment, his expression reflective. "You have spoken with Her Highness?"

"Yes." Max wasn't about to tell the Prime Minister Cassandra's reaction.

"Good." He settled his hands onto his knees, pushing his bulk up. "Then we shall get to the bottom of this quickly. The French ambassador is due back from his holiday soon." He smiled sadly. "Perhaps this is all a misunderstanding."

"I pray so." Max stood. He had the distinct impression he was being dismissed. "In the meantime I have a regiment of French infantry heading toward Bordgarten."

"And they have artillery?"

"More than we have."

The cardinal shook his head. "Yes, I see the dilemma. I think until Her Majesty and I work this out it would be best if you did nothing. You say the officers are friendly?"

"Yes, but frankly, Your Grace, it isn't the French that concern me."

"Oh?"

Max pushed on, despite the warring voices of reason and experience that suggested he hold his tongue. "I understand from Queen Cassandra that the Prussians are disturbed by our willingness to allow their enemies freedom to roam Breslovian soil."

"I see."

"I think we should let the Prussians know immediately that we plan to force the French to leave."

"An interesting concept." The cardinal smiled, and Max wondered why he'd never noticed how much like a snarl the expression was. "I didn't realize you were both a master of military strategy *and* diplomacy."

"It is precisely my ability as a soldier that urges me to state my views. We are no match for Prussia on the battlefield."

"As you, General Hawke, are no match for experienced diplomats." Sinzen leaned forward. "Thank you for your input, but you must excuse me. I have important negotiations to attend."

All of which showed Maximilian Hawke where he stood with the good cardinal.

Anger simmered in Max's veins, had done so since Sinzen dismissed him. It was the worst kind of rage. Impotent. He wanted to do something—anything. But there was the crux of the problem.

"I might as well be under damn house arrest," Max groused, staring out the window at the golden elm leaves drifting off the tree in front of the inn. The flat of his palm connected with the sill as he turned toward Kanakareh. "What did Lady Sophia say?"

"She would take the message to Her Highness."

Max plopped down onto a chair. He had to hand it to the Seneca warrior. Kanakareh showed considerable restraint in his answer, though it was at least the third time Max had requested one.

Max had sent a letter to Cassandra through her lady-in-waiting, requesting an audience. He had to talk with her about the French and Cardinal Sinzen. Hell, he needed to see her.

He needed a lot of things. To be with his troops, for one. But he'd been ordered by Cardinal Sinzen—ordered—to stay in Liberstein. He'd been there for four days.

Yesterday he'd decided to contact Cassandra. His first thought was to follow the tunnel to her rooms. He'd take her in his arms, they'd make love, and then they could talk.

With a flash of guilt Max had remembered all those French

soldiers. Perhaps they should talk first, then . . . Oh, the hell with it. The last time he'd seen her she'd thrown him out with about as much finesse as Cardinal Sinzen. So he'd sent a message, and he waited.

It was late afternoon when a servant wearing the royal livery knocked on the door. But the summons he brought was not from Cassandra, but from her husband.

The Grand Duke requested, though he might as well have demanded, that General Hawke attend him immediately.

Max barely had time to give Kanakareh a questioning look before being escorted to the palace by the two guards standing outside the door.

For all the rush, the Grand Duke made him wait for over an hour. Each time Max considered rising and stalking out, he thought of Cassandra or of his troops. As yet he hadn't been relieved of command. He'd only been ordered to stay in the capital and wait. But what did the Grand Duke want with him?

Max grimaced, afraid he already knew.

People such as he shouldn't go around accusing the Queen's husband of treason. All right, maybe he hadn't actually said Albert was risking the lives of his countrymen with his little French intrigue. But he'd sure as hell implied it. To his damn brother. To his wife.

When he was finally escorted into the Council Room it didn't take long for Max to realize he was right. The Grand Duke was livid, his complexion, always prone toward red, now almost purple. He didn't even wait for the servant to shut the door before he began yelling.

"How dare you!" He pranced around Max on his gold-plated heels. "You, a mere general, have the audacity to do this to me!"

"I simply repeated what I was told," Max countered, but he didn't think the Grand Duke heard. Albert was pacing now, even in his anger unable to appear more than a fop. But Max had to remember this man was more.

"You have insulted me and all the citizens of Breslovia with your actions. Your affront cannot go unanswered."

"Your Highness, I still believe—"

"I . . . the Crown does not care what you believe. From this instant consider yourself relieved of your commission."

Max sucked in his breath. "Your Highness I—"

"You shall pay for what you have done to the monarchy, Mr. Hawke. You shall pay dearly."

Max was already paying. Damn. Why had he come riding to Liberstein? Why had he told Cardinal Sinzen about the Grand Duke—the man's brother.

For a second it occurred to Max that perhaps it was Cassandra who'd told her husband. But he dismissed that notion . . . until the Grand Duke mentioned his wife's name.

Max took a deep breath. No. Cassandra wouldn't do that. She may have been angry but she—

"What did you say?" Max asked.

Anger bulged Albert's eyes and tightened the skin over his cheeks. "How dare you!" he repeated. "Did you think I would overlook the fact you are my wife's lover?"

"Her . . . ?" The blood drained from Max's face. He swallowed, then met the Grand Duke's narrowed gaze. Damn, this wasn't about the French or Albert's treasonous ways.

"Cassandra told me everything," the Grand Duke continued. "Of how you forced yourself upon her. Of your blackmail."

The expression on Max's face registered none of the emotions warring within his mind. He refused to dwell on any of them—on Cassandra.

The Grand Duke had accused Max of cuckolding him. And it was an accusation Max could not even deny.

The heels of Cassandra's shoes *tap-tap-tapped* on the marble floor as she hurried down the hallway. Her skirts were lifted past her ankles, and her rush caused several ladies to titter behind their fans. But Cassandra didn't care.

She needed to reach Albert's apartments before it was too late. She swerved around a corner, nearly bumping into the Prussian ambassador. He stared at her openmouthed when she simply excused herself and hurried on.

Sophia had come to her this morning, telling her General Hawke wished to see her. Which wasn't the cause of this reaction. It was the rest of what Sophia had told her. The court gossip that linked her with Breslovia's commander in chief. The whispered innuendos that the Grand Duke knew of her liaison with the handsome general and was furious.

Cassandra had pressed a hand to her brow and shut her eyes, wondering what she could possibly do. That was when a message from Kanakareh had arrived for Sophia.

Her friend had read it, then glanced up, her freckles standing out in bold relief against her pale skin. "Kanakareh says the Grand Duke sent for General Hawke."

What was he going to do? Cassandra hurried her step. Albert didn't care for her. But she'd stung his pride and now—

Without waiting for the servant who stood outside her husband's rooms, Cassandra grabbed hold of the handle. She hurled herself through the entry so quickly she nearly bounced off Max's broad chest.

His face was hard, his blue eyes disdainful as they glared down at her.

"What . . . ? What happened?"

Without even the slightest of bows, Max stepped around her. "I suggest you ask your husband that, *Your Highness.*" Max shrugged off the hand on his arm and strode out of the room.

Cassandra watched him go, then pivoted around to face her husband. Albert stood in the doorway between the Council Room and the anteroom, a smug smile on his lips. "Tell me," was all she said, all she could say.

"What should I say?" Albert played with the lace at his wrist. "I have challenged your lover to a duel."

Eighteen

What in hell was he going to do?

Max cupped the goblet, running his fingers along the smooth glass as he stared into the dying flames in the hearth. Kanakareh would no doubt think him drunk if he woke and entered the spacious parlor. Max wore only his breeches, boots, and a shirt soiled from the day and open at the throat. His hair was unfettered, his posture slouched.

But Max was not so stupid as to drink himself senseless hours before facing a man on the field of honor.

"Just stupid enough to get myself into the situation," he mumbled.

Tired of trying to find a resolution to this tangle, Max let his mind drift back over how he'd managed to get to this point. His bark of laughter was sharp and self-directed.

"You can't seem to keep yourself out of other men's beds," he said with a mock toast.

Max shut his eyes without sipping the warm liquid. There was more, much more. This web tightening about him had little to do with sex, though Lord knew there was that. Even now Max wanted Cassandra with an intensity that made him finally gulp down the wine.

Yet there was more. He loved her.

Max wiped his mouth with the back of his hand and set the empty glass on the floor beside his chair. How in the hell had it become so complicated?

He could kill Albert.

There was no doubt in Max's mind that if dawn saw them facing each other, pistols in hand, Max would prevail. It had happened before with better shots, more accomplished men than the foppish duke.

Max let his mind travel the pleasant path of fantasy. With the duke dead, Cassandra would be a widow. He could step in, marry her, be with her every day, father her children. Rising from the chair, Max called himself a fool.

She was the Queen of Breslovia. He might be good enough to take as lover. But marry him? The man who killed her husband? What in the hell was he thinking?

So, if he didn't kill the Grand Duke, should he allow the bastard to kill him? Max dug ten fingers back through his hair. He might feel half-dead now, but he didn't want to take the necessary steps to complete the process.

Leaving was an option. Simply waking Kanakareh, packing a few belongings, and heading for the border. The notion had some appeal. Cassandra would be spared mourning either her husband or him. And he could go wandering off to . . . where? Max crossed to the window, staring out into the blackness of night. Perhaps there *was* no place for him. Perhaps his father was right.

Cassandra took a deep breath and tried to relax, tried to follow Kanakareh's instructions. "Control the vision," he'd told her. "Do not allow it to control you."

But all she could see was mist.

Swirling.

Smothering.

And though she allowed herself to wander down the paths that appeared through the eddying haze, they led nowhere. Each step she took only blanketed her deeper in the gray nothingness of her vision.

Then her focus began to clear and her limbs felt weak. And Cassandra knew it was over. Though at any other time she would have welcomed the bland, almost benign sights, that was not the case this morning.

She hadn't asked for the vision. It had simply come upon her as they all did. But as the sick feeling swallowed her up, she'd thought, hoped . . . feared she might catch a glimpse of what the day would bring.

Despite the nausea, Cassandra pushed back the blankets and summoned her maid. She would not lie abed and do nothing.

Pleading had done no good. Nor had reason. Albert had insisted upon going ahead with this duel. He saw no hypocrisy where his mistress and Max were concerned. It mattered not that he rarely visited Cassandra's rooms himself or that he didn't love her. He didn't even seem to care that Max was a trained marksman and would no doubt lodge a bullet in his heart.

And her order that he call off the duel had only sent him into a twitter of giggles. He'd still been laughing when he'd walked out on her.

Cardinal Sinzen offered nothing but prayers and an admonition to look into her heart and beg forgiveness for her transgressions. The reproof stung, too close to her own thinking for comfort. For Cassandra knew the fault was hers. As much as Max's arms comforted and pleased her, as much as thoughts of him filled her mind and heart, it was wrong. But she would not let others suffer for her mistake.

Garbed simply in a deep blue riding habit, her hair unbound and hidden beneath the hood of a black cape, Cassandra rushed from her bedroom. She ordered the Imperial Guard outside her apartments to remain. His expression, though it changed little, said he wavered, not knowing what to do. He was sworn to protect her, yet she was his sovereign, and he, at least, obeyed her commands.

When she arrived at the side entrance Cassandra saw by the light of lanterns illuminating the drive that the carriage she had requested was not outside the door. Impatient, she glanced about for a servant to send to the stables with a message to hurry.

That was when she saw Cardinal Sinzen lumbering toward

her down the long mirror-lined hall. The buttons of the scarlet robe billowing in his wake were fastened askew, and his cap sat awry on his smooth white head. Cassandra whirled back toward the entrance, hoping to hear the clatter and jingle of an approaching carriage.

There was none. Nothing but an empty cobbled courtyard.

"Whatever are you doing at this hour, Your Highness?" Sinzen puffed as he neared her.

Letting out a breath, Cassandra turned to face him. "One might wonder the same of you."

"I have come on an errand of mercy," he countered evenly, his expression as pious as the painting of St. Peter in the cathedral.

"Your guidance is not needed this morn, Your Grace." Cassandra glanced toward the outside. Surely the carriage would arrive at any moment. She had sent Emma with her request nearly an hour ago, long enough to harness seven coaches.

"My guidance is always needed, Your Highness, at some times even more than others."

Cassandra shut her eyes momentarily, though when she turned back toward him they were open and focused. She pushed down the ermine-lined hood so he could see her face, know her resolve. "Seek your bed, Cardinal Sinzen. For you shall not stop me."

"And you shall not stop them. The Grand Duke, your *husband,* has every right to demand satisfaction from General Hawke."

"What of the commandment against killing?" A bit of the panic Cassandra was beginning to feel crept into her voice. Was it her imagination or was the eastern sky paler?

"There is a matter of honor." Sinzen moved to block her view of the courtyard. "And Your Highness, I'm certain, does not wish to enter a discussion on broken commandments."

Cassandra notched her chin higher, biting the inside of her lower lip to keep it from trembling. "I do not face you as confessor now, Cardinal Sinzen." She didn't know how she faced him or how he happened to be here, at this exit, at this time.

Realization came slowly, for her mind was cluttered with fear and worry and annoyance over the absent coach. Her jaw dropped. "Emma came to you. I sent her for a coach and she went to you." Cassandra glanced once again toward the empty, silent courtyard. "Did you counter my order?"

"Your Highness." Sinzen moved closer, reaching for a hand that Cassandra immediately withdrew. He accepted the rebuff with a resigned shake of his bald head. "You are in a fragile state. I . . . we all fear for your health. Surely you realize there have been episodes—"

"There is nothing wrong with me."

"Of course you would deny it, but those who see you, those who love you, cannot."

"I shall go for the carriage myself."

Cassandra's progress toward the doorway was stopped by a surprisingly strong grip on her arm. Her gasp as she whirled toward him only elicited a sad smile.

"No one blames you, Cassandra. Not God . . . not your husband. General Hawke is a handsome, virile man. You are not the only lady of this court to fall from Grace beneath the spell of his manly charms."

Cassandra's eyes narrowed. "Unhand me."

"You doubt my veracity, Your Highness? I who have lived only to serve God and you?"

"At this point the truth matters naught. I must stop the duel."

"Truth always matters, Your Highness. The truth that Maximilian Hawke enjoys the attentions of women, married women. Did you know he lost his position in England because of an affair with his commander's wife?"

She hadn't. And the knowledge caused a quiver in the pit of her stomach. Cassandra swallowed. "His indiscretions mean nothing to me," she lied. "I need the general's assistance. He knows of the French. He—"

"Also knows of the British. France's enemy. Prussia's ally."

"Of course he does. He—"

"Did he tell you, Your Highness, of his father when you lay in each other's arms?"

"Let go of me!" Cassandra tried to jerk her arm free. Why had she dismissed the guard?

"Did he mention that his father is one of King George of England's most distinguished diplomats? Did he whisper to you in the throes of passion that he was sent to pull Breslovia into the war on the side of his motherland and Prussia?" His fingers loosened their grip. "I thought not," the cardinal said as she faced him, her eyes wide.

Damn, why did these duels of honor have to be held so early in the morning? And why was it always foggy?

Max dismounted, his boots sinking into the damp soil, and waited for Kanakareh to do the same. The Seneca complied, with a stoic expression on his handsome face. "I would not ride for just anyone, Hawke."

Max simply shook his head. "You must get over your distaste of horses. It is not as if you were forced to bear its weight." They had exchanged barbs and quips since leaving the inn. Max had started the sallies, deciding it better than speaking what was really on their minds.

Kanakareh had not questioned why the Grand Duke had challenged his friend to a duel, not even when Max asked him to act as second. If he'd heard the gossip at court—if there was gossip at court—the warrior made no reference to it.

They were in a clearing on the north side of the park, an area perhaps seven rods by four. Small, but not too small for two men to face each other by eight paces, and for the few who came to watch.

The referee was there, along with the royal surgeon. Max nodded acknowledgment of their greeting, then stepped back to await the Grand Duke's arrival. Water from last night's rain dripped off the trees and plopped intermittently, an accompaniment for the early songbirds.

"Perhaps he won't show up." Max didn't realize he spoke aloud until Kanakareh grunted his agreement. Max flexed his shoulders, trying to loosen their tightness and wondered if he could be so lucky. What a perfect solution for Albert to simply stay abed this morning.

His stay in Breslovia, at least as commander in chief, was at an end, Max had no doubt of that. But Albert's absence would make things easier for Cassandra. And it would relieve Max of deciding whether to put a bullet through the bastard's heart or not.

As the first rays of sun began streaming through the bare tree limbs, the referee pulled a watch from his pocket and Max began to think the Fates were being kind. Then the muffled sound of clomping hooves reverberated through the woods.

Max caught Kanakareh's eye, shook his head. But he still hadn't decided what he would do, even when the Grand Duke's party came into view. The half-dozen horses in Albert's entourage were followed by a carriage, carrying Cardinal Sinzen. The group crowded the small clearing.

When the assemblage of nobles dismounted, Max sent his second to discuss terms with Lord Winston. The tall Seneca, dressed in simple buckskin, contrasted sharply with the host of dandies in brightly colored waistcoats and breeches. The Grand Duke acted more as if he were on his way to a picnic than a duel. His wig was long and elaborately curled, his jacket struck through with silver and gold thread.

Albert didn't seem much like a man prepared to meet his God.

Which was enough to make Max question the Grand Duke's sanity. There were those who considered Max an expert marksman. Those who would not give the duke much chance of walking away from this encounter. But if Albert were concerned by the prospect of feeling the hot sting of lead slam into his body, he showed no sign as he laughed and joked with his friends.

By comparison, Max seemed downright sober. After stripping off his black cape, he wore only dark breeches and a white shirt. His hair was unpowdered and pulled back to a neat queue. Eyes narrowed he studied the man facing him confidently across the clearing, and the question that had savaged him through the night persisted. What in the hell was he going to do?

Weapons were chosen, examined by the seconds, and Max and the Grand Duke walked to the center of the dew-covered lawn. Back to back they stood, pistol snouts aimed toward the heavens. Kill or be killed. Disgrace Cassandra or end your life. There didn't seem to be much choice. They were close enough to hear each other breathe, to smell the fear. Except the only fear Max sensed was his own.

He waited for the count to begin. Wished he could see her one last time. To explain. He'd never meant to hurt her. To apologize. He wasn't angry. He no longer believed she'd told Albert . . . didn't think he even cared if she did.

"One. Two . . ." Each clipped word from the referee was accompanied by a crunching of leaves as the men measured out each pace.

". . . Four. Five." Three more steps. Three more heartbeats left. Kill or be killed. Kill his lover's husband or be killed.

Six. Seven. Max took a deep breath, his hand gripping the sweat-damp pistol butt. His ear, attuned to the next called number, recoiled at the sound of the shot.

Max whirled around. Albert stood, the smoking pistol aimed at Max, an incredulous expression on his face. He had fired before the appointed count. The bastard had tried to shoot him in the back. Thank God Albert's aim was no better than his sense of honor.

"You are entitled to your shot."

Max's gaze speared toward the referee, who'd just spoken,

then toward Cardinal Sinzen. Both men returned his stare without flinching. Time seemed to hang in the misty air.

Slowly Max returned his eyes to his opponent. With the steady precision taught him in the military, he lowered the brass-trimmed pistol, taking aim at the Grand Duke's heart. The desire to squeeze back on the trigger was strong. Max's finger flinched. One eye squinted shut and he held his breath.

The Grand Duke was a scoundrel who aimed at unguarded backs. He no doubt deserved to die. But not by Max's hand. With one quick motion he raised the gun, firing into the sky and sending a bevy of quail flying.

He had just enough time to turn and see the Queen, her mount's nostrils spewing steam, before another report sounded.

"Max!" Cassandra's scream was the last thing he heard before oblivion deadened the fiery pain.

Kanakareh's dark eyes flew to Max, then toward the bank of holly trees. A thin swirl of white smoke and the flash of sun on metal marked the spot where the shot came from. With a fluid motion Kanakareh slid the knife from his leggings and whipped it end over end through the air. He heard a thud and a gasp of shock and agony from the assailant before rushing to kneel beside his friend. He didn't wait to see the man fall into view, a knife buried in his chest.

"Max, oh Max." Cassandra tried to turn him over but he was so heavy. There was blood everywhere. His blood. On her hands. But she couldn't think of that now or of how this was her fault. She had to think of Max, of helping him. Of stopping the bleeding. But he was so heavy and she couldn't turn him and the blood trickled out between her fingers when she tried to staunch the flow. What was she—

"Your majesty."

Kanakareh's deep voice snapped Cassandra from her hysteria. He grasped her shoulders, moving her aside, then gently rolled Max onto his back.

Cassandra fell to her knees and cradled Max's head. With her fingertips, she brushed the dirt and leaves from his pale cheek, from the tangle of wavy hair. His dark lashes fluttered open and Cassandra sobbed. His slitted eyes were nearly black with only a thin rim of the deep blue that had so entranced her from the moment they'd met.

He looked at her leaning over him, and a hint of a smile stole over his lips. "Don't cry, Cassie." His voice, rusty and barely audible, tore at her heart. "I didn't kill him. I didn't kill your husband."

"Hush." Cassandra leaned forward. Tears streamed unchecked down her cheeks as she pressed her lips to his forehead. Somewhere in the crowd the Grand Duke stood. But she didn't care about that. "I saw what happened, Max. I saw," she whispered, though in truth she had not seen it all. Later she would learn of the cowardly deed of her husband. For now, she knew only that Max had fired into the air and someone, undoubtedly the man lying facedown by the edge of the clearing, had shot Max. Her Max.

He swallowed and Cassandra watched the muscles of his strong neck contract and relax. Watched as his eyes drifted shut.

"Max. *Max.*" Her gaze flew from his ashen face to Kanakareh who knelt beside her. He and Doctor Williamson were doing something to the wound. Something that would help Max, Cassandra prayed. But there was so much blood.

"We need to take him someplace," Doctor Williamson said, pushing up from his knees.

Kanakareh nodded his agreement as Cassandra wiped a hand over her streaming eyes. "The palace," she said. "We can take him there. 'Tis close."

"For God's sake Cassandra." This from Albert who up to this moment she would have hoped had disappeared from the earth. "The rogue is going to die. You can't take him back to the palace. It simply isn't done. He must have rooms someplace."

Without glancing around, Cassandra gave her order. "We shall go to the palace."

Kanakareh commandeered Cardinal Sinzen's coach. Cassandra climbed in, followed by Doctor Williamson after Kanakareh. Then Lord Winston lifted an unconscious Max across the seat. Cassandra was never so aware of every bump and rut in the road as the coach started back toward the palace. She held Max's hand, squeezing his fingers, trying to ignore the blood that seeped scarlet through the makeshift bandage.

When they reached the entrance she ordered that Max be taken to her private rooms. She did step into the anteroom when the doctor insisted, but only long enough to decide that wasn't where she should be. Williamson glanced up, his long face taut with annoyance when she reentered the bedroom.

"The ball went through his shoulder, but he's lost too much blood."

Cassandra glanced from the doctor to Kanakareh, who had refused to leave the room as well, then back. "What should we do?"

"I would summon Cardinal Sinzen."

"No." Ice seemed to form about her heart as realization of what the doctor meant hit her. "No, he's not going to die." Cassandra walked past the doctor toward the bed, stopping only when Kanakareh touched her shoulder.

"There are herbs, medicines my people use."

Again her stare shifted from one man to the other before going back to her bed where Max lay. "Do what you will, Kanakareh."

"Surely, Your Highness, you do not plan to use this heathen's medicines."

"If it would save General Hawke's life I would barter with the devil himself." An exaggeration perhaps, but certainly enough to make Doctor Williamson blanch and quickly exit the room.

Cassandra turned to Kanakareh before the door closed. "Tell me what you need and I shall see that you have it."

As it turned out, the Seneca warrior required only that the fire be built up and kept roaring. The room became warm, then hot as more logs were thrown on the flames.

"This will sweat out the poisons," Kanakareh said when he

returned from his room at the inn. Cassandra sat in a chair she'd pulled close to the bed. Her own skin was moist from the heat, but she refused to leave.

The application of leaves Kanakareh soaked in water stopped the bleeding and seemed to keep the wound free of infection. Even Williamson, who did return to the queen's rooms after several hours of pouting, acknowledged the improvement.

"I still contend that he's lost too much blood," he said after suggesting Cassandra lie down in another chamber.

She waved him away with a sigh and continued to watch Max. Some color had returned to his face. She leaned forward to touch his cheek, smiling when his eyes opened.

"Cassie."

"Shhh. Don't talk. You must rest and save your strength."

He slept then, and Cassandra, though she hated to leave him felt she must. She called a meeting of her ministers and asked for the French ambassador to attend her.

"He is not at court, Your Highness."

"Still?" Cassandra turned on Cardinal Sinzen, seated to her right at the huge oval table. "Has there been any reply to the messages I sent Louis?"

"I am confident he will send an envoy soon, Your Highness. We must be patient and all will—"

"I grow tired of waiting while French soldiers roam my kingdom at will."

"Surely Your Highness must see that there is nothing to do but wait. If you were not so tired—"

"I am *not* tired." Though of course she was. Cassandra lifted her chin. She had to be strong. Breslovia's future might be at stake. This was no time to let her problems overwhelm her. Yet she felt like weeping.

The only thing she could be thankful for was that her visions seemed to have stopped. At least they weren't troubling her now.

Cassandra sat listening to her advisors, most of whom sided with Cardinal Sinzen preaching patience, and acting as if she were made of porcelain. She'd heard them whispering as she entered the Council Room. If the duel and her insistence that General Hawke stay in her rooms wasn't the main court gossip, she'd be very surprised.

"Gentlemen." Cassandra was pleased by the firmness of her voice. "I can wait no longer to insure the safety and sovereignty of Breslovia." She turned toward Cardinal Sinzen. "As my Prime Minister, I order you to send an envoy to Paris immediately. The message must be couched in the strongest terms possible. We shall tolerate no further delay in the removal of French troops from Breslovian soil."

That said, Cassandra swept from the room. Her exit would have been more dramatic if not for the swoon that overcame her as she stepped into the hallway. She landed on the tiled floor in a puddle of silk and petticoats before a footman could catch her.

Cassandra's eyes opened slowly to the bustle about her. She was lying on a bed, though not her own. Max was there. Yes, she remembered that well enough, it was just the last few moments that escaped her. She tried to sit up, but firm hands gripped her shoulders. Before she could look around to see who held her Doctor Williamson came into view.

"Well, I see you are awake." He leaned down to stare into first one eye, then the other. Then he signaled for the Imperial Guard to unhand the queen. "I would remain prone if I were you. It is a lucky thing you did not hurt yourself or the child when you fell."

It took a moment for his words to register. When they did her expression must have revealed her shock.

"You did know you were enceinte, did you not? No, I can see you did not," the doctor continued. "Then it is with pleasure I inform Your Highness of the impending birth of an heir to Breslovia's throne. The Grand Duke will be overjoyed."

A child. Cassandra closed her eyes and savored the thought,

wondering how she could not have known. She could only conclude that the visions had so upset her and consumed her that she hadn't noted the time since her last monthly flow. And she had nearly given up the notion of conceiving.

With Albert.

As it was, Cassandra doubted her husband would find much about the news pleasing.

The heir-to-be was not his child.

What would Albert do when he learned of her condition? After the events of the last few days she believed him capable of anything.

"The bastard. I should have killed him when I had the chance."

Cardinal Sinzen's small eyes flicked up to meet his brother's. "As I recall you tried *your* best."

Alfred clamped the gold locket shut with a snap. "He moved."

"Still General Hawke's back seems a broad enough target."

"What you had planned for him, after all, was a musketball in the back."

"I did have a plan, though not to shoot him in the back. My tactic had a chance of success. But, of course, it lacked the advantage of showing you to be the stupid coward you are."

Anger sparked in Albert's eyes, but he said nothing as his brother continued. "Whatever made you decide to turn and fire before the count? You knew I had a sharpshooter hiding in the bushes. All you needed to do was aim and hold your fire and he would be dead by now."

"And so perhaps *would* I. You were so anxious for me to challenge him to a duel, but it was not you who had to stare down the snout of a loaded pistol."

Sinzen dismissed his brother's words with a wave of his sausagelike beringed fingers. "You are her husband. It is for you to defend her honor."

"The bitch has no honor. She has her lover ensconced in her apartments."

"Where he will no doubt die."

"I thought Doctor Williamson said he was greatly improved."

The cardinal smiled. "There is more than one way for our dear general to meet his death."

Rising suddenly, Albert began pacing the Council Room. "Dead or not she carries his child."

"A minor inconvenience."

The Grand Duke turned, his face distorted by righteous indignation. "I shall renounce the Queen and the bastard she whelps, before the kingdom." His open palm slammed upon the gilded tabletop, punctuating his words.

Sinzen waited for the echo to fade before speaking, though his expression, as he sat, head buried on thick neck folds, was grim. "You will accept the child as your own." The cardinal ignored his brother's gasp. "You will announce the impending birth with a blare of trumpets and the ringing of bells, and you will stop trying to think when it is so clearly beyond your capability." His voice rose with each word.

"I have seen you flaunt your mistress. I have watched you try to assassinate Cassandra. Try to shoot her lover in the back, and commit Lord knows what other thickwitted acts," Sinzen continued. "But I shall not allow you to ruin what fate has thrown in our laps."

"But . . . but the child will be a bastard."

"The child will be heir to the throne. A Godsend." Taking a wheezy breath Sinzen spread his hands on the table. "We should be thanking General Hawke. He may not be what we wished for as commander in chief, but he did manage to impregnate the Queen. Something you obviously could not do."

"She—"

"Yes, yes, we know all about how cold she is and unresponsive," Sinzen recited with a shake of his head. "The point is, Cassandra is expecting a child, and no one will gainsay it is yours. When the babe is born, the mother is expendable." A benevolent smile wreathed his broad face. "And we shall become regents."

"But what of Mother's dream—of our dream, to place a Martinette on the throne? The bastard will not be of our blood."

"And will live only long enough to secure our position. Then . . ." Again a hand was waved in the air. "The Diaz will vote you King, and whatever heir you sire on your new queen will someday rule the kingdom."

Albert stood still, his fingers frozen on the curlicues atop the golden clock on the desk. "Cassandra will not allow it. She knows the child is not mine. What if she denounces my claim?"

"And swears the child was fathered by her dead lover?" Sinzen snorted. "She would not do such a thing. Her devotion to Breslovia runs too deep. No, Cassandra may fear you and your wrath, but we need not fear hers."

Nineteen

"They smile at each other as if there were no one else on earth. As if the Grand Duke isn't likely to come marching into the Queen's bedroom at any moment, and the Prussians aren't complaining loudly enough for even me to notice." Sophia caught her breath. "She sits by his bed, plays chess, and smiles."

"They are in love," Kanakareh stated simply. He and Sophia walked in the Queen's private gardens. The day was warm for autumn, clear, with a wind brisk enough to send spirals of fire-colored hair swirling about Sophia's face.

Sophia sighed deeply. "It would take a dunce not to notice. Yet, truthfully what good can come of it? She is wed to another, and though goodness knows I've never cared for Albert, he is the Grand Duke. His family is highborn and— Oh, never mind that," she said, brushing curls off her cheek.

"And she's the Queen," Sophia continued as if she needed to remind Kanakareh. "Whatever will they do? I mean, I know he is nearly healed—"

"Thank you for your help."

Sophia's smile was as bright as his. " 'Twas the least I could do." As soon as she'd heard of the general's wound and of the Seneca's ministrations to him, Sophia had offered her assistance. She'd stayed with Kanakareh all day, every day, for near a sennight, returning to her rooms only to sleep.

As she had said, Sophia felt it was the least she could do to help General Hawke . . . and Kanakareh. She might know nothing about caring for a wounded man, but she could hand leather pouches to the warrior. And she could watch him, shirtless and glistening with sweat as he called on his spirits to save his friend.

For now, as well, she could simply stare up at him as he stared down at her. Smiling. As if no one else in the world existed.

"Checkmate."

Max stared at the board, a frown deepening the lines around his eyes. "Damnation, Cassie . . . again." He flexed his bandaged shoulder. "I didn't think it was in you to take advantage of a convalescing man."

"Oh my." Cassandra feigned sympathy as she adroitly knocked over his king. "Is your wound hurting you, General Hawke? Keeping you from making the moves your mind commands perhaps?"

Max's lips thinned. "I shall see that you pay for your insolence, Your Highness."

Her laugh was infectious and within seconds Max had joined in. "Where did you learn to play so well? God's truth you could beat Kanakareh."

"My brother showed me. My father taught him, and he needed someone to practice on."

"I'll wager you beat them both soundly."

"I never played with Papa, but I did occasionally checkmate Peter."

Max leaned against the chair back, his eyes on the Queen. "Tell me about their deaths." As color drained from her cheeks, he admonished himself for hurting her.

Still, he didn't let his inquiry drop when she asked, "What do you wish to know?"

"Who killed them?"

"Brigands, I assume." Cassandra stood. "No one knows for certain. Their bodies were found in the riding park. Both were stabbed several times."

"Were there no Imperial Guards about?"

"They rode alone."

"Like you."

"Like I used to before you ordered guards to stay with me at all times," Cassandra reminded him. She walked to the tapestry, glancing over her shoulder as her fingers traced the golden-horned unicorn. "Why do you wish to know?"

"I'm not sure. I've simply wondered. You told me of the man Simon."

"The seer. Yes, he was the king's advisor. Papa relied on Simon's wisdom."

"And his visions?"

"At times, yes." Her brow furrowed. "Why do you ask this now?"

He was damned if he knew, and told her as much. But as he'd lain in Cassandra's bed, stayed in her rooms, questions had kept coming into his mind. And though he wished to ask Cassandra about the French troops or Prussia's reaction—or to simply drink in her beauty—it was the past that seemed to occupy him most. Shaking his head, Max got to his feet, wincing only slightly when the movement jarred his shoulder.

"You really shouldn't move about so much."

"Cassie," he said with wry grin. "I am nearly healed." He lifted his arm as proof.

"But it was not so long ago . . ." It still bothered her to think how close Max had come to dying. "Never mind. You will do as you please anyway."

Not as he pleased, but as he should. "I think it time I moved from the castle—from your rooms."

"But why?" Before he could answer, Cassandra shook her head. "It is too soon. What if the wound begins bleeding again, or the fever returns? Kanakareh feared it might, and Doctor Williamson said it was a miracle it hadn't."

"Cassie." Max lowered himself onto the carved bench near the window. When she continued listing reasons why he couldn't leave, he simply lifted his hand in a signal to cease.

Cassandra moved toward him, stopping only when her gown swayed against his knees. "I order you to stay here." She tried the gambit, her voice small.

"You know I would if things were different." His blue eyes bored into her. "As it is, I can imagine how tongues must be wagging."

"I don't care about that."

"You should." Max lifted a hand to caress her soft cheek. "You will need all the support Breslovians can offer in the coming weeks."

"You think war will come." She lifted gold-tipped lashes. "I fear it, too. But nothing I do seems to have any effect. I've ordered Cardinal Sinzen to send envoys to the French court. Frederick of Prussia grows tired of my excuses."

"The Breslovian army is headed for Liberstein."

"What?" Cassandra's skirts swayed as she backed away enough to see his face.

"I sent orders the day of the duel."

"But I don't understand. Why?" And why didn't you inform me?" The unasked question sizzled in the air between them.

"With your army here it will be easier for you to command. Easier to protect the capital. And I thought it better for the French and Breslovian armies not to meet . . . at least for a while."

"I see." Cassandra swallowed and moved beyond his reach.

"Do you have concerns?"

"No," she insisted. His explanation made sense. Then, "Yes." Curls escaped from the amethyst and feather pompon as she shook her head. "I don't know. I simply wish you would have discussed this with me first."

"There was little time. And then I was unconscious."

"True." Cassandra grabbed hold of the bedpost. "But you haven't been for a while. And—"

"And what?" Max stood.

"I just wondered why you never mentioned that your father was Lord Hawke, Duke of Belmead?"

Max took two steps in her direction. "Perhaps because I didn't consider it important."

"Oh." Cassandra took a deep breath. Since the day Cardinal Sinzen had told her of this she'd wanted to ask Max about his father. Now she wasn't so certain. But she'd already started. "I suppose you didn't consider it important that he is one of England's most influential nobles?"

"No, I didn't." Max wasn't sure where she was going with this, but he didn't like her tone. Or the way her damned Stivelson chin was sticking up in the air.

"I have received word from him. On behalf of King George of England, he wishes to inform me that His Majesty is perturbed by the French presence in Breslovia."

"So? Hell, Cassie, that is hardly news. Frederick of Prussia is perturbed, too."

"Yes, but he didn't send his son to be the commander in chief of my army." There, she'd said it. What had been bothering her since Cardinal Sinzen had first told her.

"That's what you think? That I came here to build up your army so I could keep your soldiers from siding with the French?"

"No." When he said it like that it didn't make sense.

"No?" A dark brow quirked. "You don't sound convincing, Your Highness." Max took another step toward her. "Perhaps you think there's more. Since I'm obviously a spy or plant of some kind, then maybe I was instructed to become the Queen's lover as well. I was ordered to wait outside her secret tunnel until she came. To watch as she stepped through the falls, her clothing transparent, then take her in my—"

"Stop it!" Cassandra turned on him. "I didn't say that and you know it. I didn't accuse you of anything. Is it too much to ask for an explanation?" This time it was Cassandra who moved closer. But that didn't stop him from seeming distant.

"No, Your Highness. It isn't too much to ask. You should have complete devotion from your subjects. And you should be able to trust your generals without reservation."

"I do trust you Max. It's just that—"

"My father is a duke and a diplomat. You are correct about his being very powerful in England, though I didn't realize he was one of the king's negotiators. You see I haven't seen or heard from my father since I left the New World."

"Max—"

"No. You deserve to know this. I thought you did. But then, I think I presumed too much. I am the second son of the Duke of Belmead. Naturally my older brother Stephen would inherit which never caused me any great amount of distress.

"Unfortunately distress is what I seemed most capable of causing my father." His dark lashes lifted, blue eyes boring into hers. "My duel with your husband was not my first."

Cassandra swallowed. "Who . . . ?"

"Were the others?" Max lifted a brow. "There were two." He forced out air. "Irate husbands." He looked away. "I seem to have a penchant for married women."

Cassandra wondered how many of them had fallen in love with him, but she didn't ask. It would be too close to admitting her own feelings.

"I'm a rogue, Cassie. My father knew it from the first, and I've finally come to admit it to myself."

"Max." He stepped aside when she would have reached for him.

"At any rate, my father bought me a commission in the cavalry, which pleased me greatly. Military history was another passion of mine, and I'd always pictured myself the romantic hero," he said, a wry grin on his face. "But, of course, it didn't take me long to find I couldn't resist Lady Northford's charms."

"Or she yours."

Max glanced over his shoulder, chuckling despite himself. "Or she mine," he admitted. "Too bad she was married to the Earl of Northford . . . my commanding officer. He didn't go in much for duels, being nearly old enough to be my grandfather." His expression sobered. "No doubt part of the reason for the young Lady Northford's attraction to me."

Cassandra questioned that, but said nothing.

"Anyway, Lord Northford saw to it that I was demoted and sent to fight the French in America. My father, rather disgusted with my escapades, as he called them, sent me a letter through his solicitor expressing his feelings."

"And that's the last you heard from him?"

"No." Max unconsciously pressed a hand to his bandaged shoulder. "America wasn't as bad as I'd expected. Actually I rather enjoyed working with and training some of our Indian allies."

"And I imagine even that faroff land has its share of married women."

Max whipped around to face her, but he couldn't tell by her expression how she'd meant the remark. He decided to answer honestly. "I've never pretended to be a saint, Cassie. But I didn't involve myself in any scandal in America." He paused. "I was, however, accused of treason." His eyes met hers. "Aren't you going to ask me?"

She didn't say anything, simply stared at him, her eyes large.

"I didn't sell secrets to the French. And as it turned out there was not enough evidence for a court-martial. But that didn't stop my father from believing the worst. I received another letter just before I left America. And that *was* the last I heard from him."

"I'm sorry," Cassandra said, though she knew how ineffectual the words were. She also wasn't certain what she apologized for. Was it the Duke of Belmead's behavior toward his son . . . or her own?

Questioning him about his loyalty to her had started this explanation of his past. Did he think her like his father? Cassandra hoped not. She'd never truly doubted him.

"I'm sorry too, Your Highness."

Cassandra wanted to ask him what he apologized for. And why he didn't call her Cassie. But before she could, the door to her private rooms opened and Sophia entered, Kanakareh close behind.

Max assured his friend he was strong enough to move back to his rooms. Since Kanakareh agreed, it was decided, with Cassandra having no say in the matter. She did insist that he leave through the palace, however.

"It is hardly a secret that you are here," she reminded him when he shook his head. "I am not ashamed of anything."

Including the child she carried, Cassandra reminded herself. She was even tempted to tell him, but didn't. Her son or daughter would be heir to the throne of Breslovia. She would have to claim the Grand Duke as the father.

But she would have something of Maximilian Hawke when he left her . . . and she knew that was what he planned. She watched him leave, her head held high, her heart breaking.

When the door closed behind him, when she was alone, she turned toward her bed. A glint of sunshine caught her eye and her world tilted off center. "No," she whispered as the vision grabbed her, hurtling her forward through a maze of swirling lights. She'd hoped this torture over. But now it was back—worse than ever.

Cassandra tried to remember Kanakareh's advice. She tried to breathe slowly and deeply. To control what the vision—the spirits—told her, but she couldn't.

It happened so quickly. The mist swirled then disappeared, taking with it all the light till she was surrounded by darkness, utter and complete.

She could see nothing, but knew she roamed through the labyrinth of tunnels beneath the castle. The air was foul from disuse. Her hands, when they reached out to steady her, slipped on the damp, chiseled stone. Scurrying feet and sharp rodent squeals told her she wasn't alone.

Somewhere in the background Cassandra could hear her name being called; could swear it was Sophia. But what was her lady-in-waiting doing in her vision?

Lower and lower she went, down the carved stairs, along the

spiraling tunnels. Deeper. Following the twisting maze away from the waterfall into the very bowels of the ancient castle.

Cassandra wasn't certain when the vision ended and reality began. She just knew that suddenly she felt ill and confused and the images before her melded with the ones she'd seen in her head. Leaning back against the uneven stone, Cassandra brought a hand to her forehead. It did no good. She still felt dizzy, as if her head were spinning. And voices, faraway voices, still seemed to echo through the turmoil in her brain.

She tried to think. Where was she and how had she gotten here? Perhaps more importantly, how was she to find her way out?

The visions had never done this before—brought her into the scene so completely. And Cassandra was at a loss as to what to do. But she did know standing still would accomplish nothing. Taking a deep breath of the musty air, Cassandra decided to move toward the voices.

She stepped out, tentatively at first. Then, as she grew certain that this was what she should do, a force she didn't understand, but could nonetheless feel, drew her on. Cassandra's pace quickened.

Her scream sounded hollow when her feet slipped out from under her into nothingness and she landed hard at the bottom of the steps she hadn't seen—or known—were there.

Sobbing brought little comfort, as she sat up slowly, feeling her arms and legs for any sign of damage. Finding none she scrambled to her feet, wiped the muck from her hands onto the side panels of her gown and began again to go on. This time she inched forward, feeling her way, till she rounded a corner and saw a glimmer of light.

The voices were louder now, and so was the pull; the feeling that someone drew her forward. That Simon drew her on.

Cassandra didn't stop to think what that might mean. She simply headed toward the light, stumbling toward two men who sat, their booted feet propped on a rickety table. When she spoke they both started, falling as one from their perches on the edge of the bench.

The one with a nest of grizzled hair and a thick neck forced himself up first. He grabbed for the pike resting against the wall and squinted into the darkness. "Who goes there?"

"I told ye I heard something before. What is it?" The younger one said as he scrambled to regain his footing.

"It is I, Cassandra." She stepped farther into the puddle of light thrown off by the lantern swinging overhead. "Your queen," she added when neither guard seemed impressed by her introduction.

"What ye doing back there?" The pike's point hadn't budged an inch. It was still angled toward her heart.

"Did you not hear what I said?" Cassandra's chin notched up. She would certainly speak to someone about the impertinence of these men. "I am Queen Cassandra."

"Aye, and I be the pope," the old man said, drawing a loud guffaw from his mate.

"I insist that you show me the way out of here. Is this the—"

"Cassandra. Your Highness."

Cassandra's head snapped around. "Who is that?" Someone was calling her from behind one of the thick wooden doors. "Is that you, Simon?" She whirled around and rushed toward the voice. She stood on tiptoe, trying to see through the small barred window into the cell.

"Your Highness, I knew you would come."

"Get away from there, old man."

Cassandra jumped back when the pike shaft banged against the portal, near her head. "How dare you?" Indignation colored her voice. "Free him—this moment." She glanced around when both men continued to stand still. A large ring of keys hung from a rusty hook. Yanking up her skirts she lurched toward them, her hand just closing over the metal when the gray-haired guard clamped bony fingers around her upper arm.

"That will be enough of that, wench."

"I'm the Queen, I tell you." Cassandra jerked her arm free.

"Let me go." But neither her words nor her actions had any effect.

"Will," her tormentor called toward the other man.

"Aye."

"I think we should be finding out what to do here."

"There is no question what should be done." Perhaps she did not look like a queen in her torn and dirt-smeared dress, but she could still sound like one. "Release your prisoner and escort both of us to the palace."

But her orders were dismissed as so much babbling. Though she fought, scratching and kicking as best her skirts would allow, Cassandra found herself slammed into the cell with Simon.

Indignation made her pound the splintery wood once with her fists before turning toward the old man. What she saw made her gasp.

Leaving the palace grounds was like stepping from calm to chaos. Inside the tall, iron-gated fence, there was no indication of the turmoil below in the streets except a muted rumble of noise.

Max guided his borrowed mount by the reins and stared across at Kanakareh. No words passed between the two, but their message was the same. What in the hell is going on?

From their vantage point on the palace's hill above Liberstein they could see that the streets and squares were clogged with wagons and horses. Twisting in the saddle, Max glanced back at the Imperial Guards. A dozen of them stood sentinel still, their tall, fur hats set above faces that showed no expression, no reaction to the masses of humanity in the streets.

With a kick of his heel, Max sent his horse galloping down toward the melee. Panic sizzled through the chill air, as much a reality as the rumble of cartwheels, the neighing of horses, the excited voices of frightened people.

Max's yelled questions had little effect. Those addressed simply ignored him, more concerned with negotiating the clogged roadways. It wasn't till Max leaped from his horse and grabbed the jacket of the fifth person who tried to evade him that he received any response.

"What in the hell is going on? What's happened?" Pain shot through his shoulder as he jerked the frightened man toward him.

"Let go of me! Are you crazy? I have to get my family out of the city."

That much was obvious. Max tore his gaze from the man's terrified face, his focus broadening to take in hundreds of like expressions. "Why?" he demanded as the man tried to break free. "What are you afraid of?"

"The French." The words were screamed at him as if he were daft. "And the Prussians."

"But—"

"For God's sake, let me go before their armies get here. My wife . . ."

Max didn't hear the rest of the man's plea for he'd loosened his grip, allowing him to return to a cart piled high with chairs and tables, trunks and bedding.

Maneuvering his horse through the mass of humanity that surged about him wasn't easy. By the time Max reached the palace gates he was tired and his wound hurt like hell, but he was determined.

Unfortunately the Imperial Guards were as well.

Two stepped forward, muskets crossed, blocking his way when he would have passed through the gate.

Max drew himself up. "Let us pass."

The soldiers said nothing, only continued to block the entrance, looking as much like statues as the marble creatures gracing the parks on the palace's grounds. "As your commanding officer, I demand—"

"Your demanding days are over, Mister Hawke."

Max glanced up to see a captain striding from the guard house to the right. He recognized the uniform, but not the man. But obviously the news that he'd been relieved of command by the Grand Duke was known.

"You will have to leave, Mister Hawke."

"I must see the Queen."

"That won't be possible."

"She must be informed of what's going on." Impotent anger strained through his voice. "Goddamn it, let me in."

But though he hurled himself toward the guards blocking the gate, all he received for his trouble was a fiery pain shooting from his wound and the captain's clipped assurance that the Queen was fully apprised of the situation.

"Like hell she is," Max hissed at Kanakareh as he wrenched free of the Seneca's grasp. Kanakareh, coming up behind Max had tried to calm his friend, then had yanked him away from the palace gate.

"That is not the way." Kanakareh's dark eyes passed from the entrance to Max's scowl.

"She's in there and she doesn't know what's happening." Max squared his shoulders, ignoring the pain.

"Then you must tell her."

Reason replaced rage and, taking a deep breath, Max nodded. Then he hurried back to his horse, mounting in a fluid motion. "I don't know any of those guards." He motioned toward the men standing silent a mere rod or two away. "See if you can find Colonel Marquart. He may be with the army. I ordered them to camp near the Breze, west of the city. If they . . ." Max paused, trying to calm his excited mount. "If they are still loyal to me, bring them to the palace." His voice lowered. "Through the tunnels. I fear Her Highness may need protection."

"Oh, my goodness, General Hawke." Sophia's hand fluttered to her throat. "You startled me. I thought it was Her Majesty.

At least I hoped it was. What's happening? I was in the hallway and there is talk of—"

"Where is she?" Max rushed into Cassandra's bedroom, grabbing her lady-in-waiting by the shoulders. Sophia stared up at him with green eyes as big as gold coins. But for once her mouth seemed locked shut. Max gave her a shake. He turned his head, following the direction in which she'd pointed as she'd slowly lifted her arm.

"The tunnels?" Max questioned. "She's in the tunnels?" He'd just come up through them, was still damp from the water's spray. And he hadn't seen Cassandra.

"After I walked with you and Kanakareh toward the palace, I came back to see if Cassandra needed anything. She'd seemed so sad and"—Sophia clamped her lips shut and took a deep breath—"as I opened the door she was slipping through the opening. I called to her, but she didn't stop. She never even looked back."

Max let his hands drop. Where in the hell had she gone? He would have seen her if she'd left the tunnel through the waterfall. Wouldn't he? It had been barely more than an hour since he'd left her. Unless she had wandered away from Liberstein he would have passed her on the road. Or maybe not. Hell, she could be anywhere.

But for some reason he couldn't explain, Max didn't think she'd left the castle. "Where else do the tunnels lead?"

"I . . . I don't know. Oh, I should never have let her leave. But she just kept going and I was afraid." Sophia wrung her hands.

"The dungeon. She told me once I could end up in the dungeon if I followed the tunnel." Max prompted.

"Yes." Sophia followed him back to the unicorn tapestry. "There is an old dungeon under the castle. But why would she go there?"

Max didn't know. But he couldn't fight the strong pull to find out. "Hand me that candle." He pulled the lever while Sophia rushed to follow his order. When she gave him the taper, his fingers folded over hers. "I'll find her," he said. "Kanakareh should be coming soon, with some soldiers. Tell him where I've gone." With that he plunged into the darkness.

Twenty

"Well, if it isn't Her Royal Highness."

Cassandra sprang through the door as soon as it creaked open, leaping at the man standing before her. Cardinal Sinzen squealed, jerking back, his foot catching on the hem of his robe. He landed hard against the stone wall. "Get her off me." He almost choked on the words.

Albert reached for his wife, hesitated, then motioned for the guards. Her hands were latched around rolls of fat on his brother's neck. But Cassandra was no match for two men. They pulled at her and she was dragged away, twisting and kicking. The fire in her eyes was more than Albert could face. He busied himself wiping at the dirt on his hands.

"You evil bastard," Cassandra screamed, venom and anger hardening her voice. "How could you?"

"Do you think she knows?" Albert couldn't hide the smirk that came to his face.

Cassandra's sudden move caught the jailers off guard. She slipped through their hands, lurching this time toward her husband. His high yelp would have been amusing if she hadn't been so intent on cutting out his liver.

"For God's sake, keep the woman subdued." Sinzen lifted a hand to straighten his robes; used it instead to point toward the grizzled guard. "Don't hurt her," he ordered. "We don't wish to bring any harm to the child she carries."

"How can you pretend to show consideration for my well

being when you killed my father and brother?" Cassandra blew golden curls from her face.

"Do not fool yourself into believing I care what happens to you, Cassandra." Sinzen waddled toward her, flinching only slightly when she tried to break free of the men holding her arms behind her back. "Your babe is my only concern."

"You shall never have my child."

"Unfortunately for you, my dear, after you give birth you shall have no say in the matter. For you shall be dead."

"The Queen will not die."

Everyone turned, their eyes drawn to the small man wrapped in dirty brown robes. His gray hair hung limply around a face grown gaunt with age and malnourishment. An ineffectual figure until you noticed his eyes. Dark, though of no easily perceived color, they glowed like simmering coals. The fire in them also permeated his voice. " 'Tis not Cassandra who will meet her doom this day."

The words hung on the old, musty air, freezing all who stood in the dungeon.

It was Albert who spoke first. Taking a shuffling step forward, he held out his hand, palm up. "Who is it that will die? It's not me, is it?"

"Shut up," Sinzen snapped. "You act as if what that old man says his any bearing on what shall happen."

"You're the one who feared taking his life. Who shut him up in this dungeon because you thought him some sort of wizard who would haunt you from the grave," Albert whined.

"As well you should have," Cassandra said. "How do you think I found him? 'Twas no accident that I wandered down to the very cell where he's been imprisoned. He called to me through spirits and visions."

"Spirits?"

"For God's sake can't you see what she's trying to do? Get control of yourself Albert."

"But it is me, isn't it?" Albert hunched toward Simon. "Tell me. It was me you spoke of when you said someone was doomed."

"You'll wish that to be the only fate awaiting you if you don't desist in this rubbish instantly. You!" Sinzen motioned toward one of the guards. "Put the old man back in his cell."

"You won't get away with this." Cassandra began struggling as soon as there was but one man clamping her arms. "I shall see you both hanged for your murdering and treasonous ways. I shall—"

"Stick her in there as well. Perhaps we'll keep her here until the babe is born."

"You can not. I will—"

Bootsteps pounding on the age-old stone made Cassandra's head jerk around toward the tunnel in time to see him explode into the light. "Max!"

He held a sputtering candle in one hand, a drawn sword in the other. He looked like a conquering hero of old.

"Unhand her." It took a moment for his eyes to adjust to the light after traveling through the near dark tunnels. But Max could tell that someone was roughly handling Cassandra. He aimed the point of his sword toward that man.

"Do something." This from Sinzen who backed up as he spoke.

"They killed my father and brother," Cassandra cried. "Albert and the cardinal murdered them."

In the commotion the younger guard hefted the pike. With a savage yell he rushed toward Max, who flung the candle, scattering hot wax across the jailor and ducking and dodging in time to miss the sharpened steel point. Catching his attacker off balance, Max brought his sword down, leaving a crimson strip in its wake. The guard bellowed his pain, then tumbled onto the rocky floor.

Cassandra let out a breath she didn't realize she'd held, then drove her elbow back. Her captor's grunt and the momentary loosening of his hold told her she'd caught him by surprise.

She turned in his grasp, raking her nails across his face. He screamed, releasing her to bring his hands up for protection.

He didn't see Max's fist fly toward his jaw. His head snapped back, and he crashed to the floor to join his fellow jailor.

"Where are they?" Cassandra whirled around, but found only empty space where Sinzen and Albert had once stood.

Max started forward, stopped, and turned back. "Are you all right?" At Cassandra's nod, he flashed her a grin. "Stay here. Kanakareh's coming," he told her. Then he plunged along the passageway that led to the castle.

Unlike the back tunnel, this one was lit. Tin lanterns hanging from iron hooks threw oscillating patches of light along the ancient passageway as Max raced after Sinzen and the Grand Duke. Up ahead, the tunnel curved. They couldn't be far ahead of him. Sinzen certainly couldn't maneuver through the tunnels quickly and Albert—

Whack!

The force of the blow sent Max slamming back against the carved rock wall. Pain radiated from his shoulder, sending a wave of nausea to his stomach. He shook his head, catching a glimpse of steel headed his way. Shifting aside along the craggy wall Max just missed the thrust aimed at his heart.

He lifted his sword, pushing away from the solid stone as a form rounded the corner stepping into view. Max arched a brow. "So we meet again. You surprise me, Albert, stopping to face me, so unlike the time you shot me in the back." Max twisted the sword, eyeing his opponent down the long, sharp blade. "I expected to run you down like the cur you are."

Steel clashed against steel in response. "I knew bringing you here was a mistake." The Grand Duke feinted right.

"It will be your last." Max's thrust drew blood. "Where is your fiendish brother? Did he send you back so he could escape?"

"He sent me back to kill you," Albert said as he lunged forward.

Max sidestepped and the Grand Duke sailed past him to

slam into the wall. The maneuver gave Max the advantage. He whipped around to follow through—and saw the Grand Duke grab Cassandra as she came running along the tunnel. The blood drained from Max's face when Albert brought his sword blade up beneath her breasts.

"Let her go, Albert. You've already proven yourself a coward once. Don't do it again." Max started forward when Cassandra gasped. The razor-sharp blade nudging higher.

"Unlike the last time we met, Hawke, there will be no one to question my bravery or lack of it now. For I shall kill you both. My pregnant wife . . . and her lover."

Blue eyes met lavender.

"Ah, did you think I didn't know? That you could cuckold me, then plant your seed in my wife." Albert's arm tightened, forcing air from Cassandra's body.

But Max felt as if air were being forced from *his* body. His eyes found hers again. The answer to his unspoken question as clear as if she'd said the words. A son . . . or daughter. His son or daughter. "Let her go, Albert. She's no use to you dead. What do you expect to do? You're only the Grand Duke, after all. Keep Cassandra alive." Max's sword clattered to the rocky floor. "Take me."

"No . . ." Cassandra strained against her husband's binding arm, against the blade pressed beneath her breast.

"Touching to be sure. But the truth is, I shall kill you both and be done with it. I— Aughhhh!"

Albert's fingers slipped from the sword hilt and the blade tilted toward the floor. Max leaped forward, grabbing Cassandra, shoving her behind him as he scooped his own weapon from the rocks. But though he angled the point toward the Grand Duke's chest, there was no need to thrust.

Crimson blossomed on the front of Albert's puce and gold waistcoat, beneath the lace cravat. And amid all the blood could be seen a silvery tip. Albert's expression showed bewilderment as he fell to his knees. When he collapsed onto his stomach Max and Cassandra could see the pike sticking at an obscene angle from his back . . . and Simon.

His eyes gleamed in his besmudged pinched face. "He was right to worry," the ancient seer said. "It was his time to die."

Cassandra stepped from behind Max, though she did not resist when he draped an arm across her shoulders and turned her away. " 'Tis not a pretty sight, Your Highness. But remember, he would have killed you," Max whispered, his mouth near her temple.

"I know." She pressed a hand to his chest. "And you." But there was no time for sentimentality. Max could hear pounding footsteps and guessed—hoped—Kanakareh was coming, with the soldiers.

Releasing Cassandra he took several steps back into the tunnel, relieved when he saw his friend. Few words of explanation were needed before Max and Cassandra, with the stooped Simon by her side, led the way out of the dungeon.

When they reached the palace, Kanakareh and the soldiers fanned out to search for Cardinal Sinzen. Max accompanied Cassandra and Simon to her rooms.

Lady Sophia opened the door to the Queen's apartments and threw her arms around her friend. "Oh, Your Highness, I was so worried. You simply can't imagine. I saw you go through the secret door and tried to stop you, but you wouldn't listen and then, when General Hawke came, I told him. I hope that was the right thing to do." She squeezed Cassandra tighter and looked over her head. What she saw made her eyes grow large and round. "Simon! Is that really you?"

"It is," Cassandra answered as she gently pried herself free. "He's been kept prisoner in the dungeon beneath these rooms for near three years." And all that time he'd been calling to her. Sending forth his visions. Cassandra took a deep breath. "By Cardinal Sinzen and Albert."

Max, who had seated the old man and poured him some wine, glanced up as Cassandra finished her explanation. "They also murdered my father and brother."

"Oh, no." Sophia gasped. "I simply can't believe . . . Oh, Your Highness, how awful. The worst of crimes. How can you possibly punish them enough?"

"Albert is dead." Cassandra's voice was emotionless.

"And Kanakareh is scouring the palace for Sinzen," Max added. "We shall find him, I'm sure. But that won't be the end of our problems, Cassandra."

"I know." Her gaze shifted toward Simon. "There is much to be done. Sophia, summon my maids. I will need a bath and my finest riding habit."

"Wait one minute." Max stepped in front of her, but couldn't stop the motion that sent Sophia off to do her bidding. "What are you thinking here, Cassie? I'm telling you there is chaos in the streets. Everyone thinks—"

"They will be caught in the middle of a huge battle between the French and Prussians. Simon told me when we were in the cell."

"Simon?" Max's gaze shot toward the old man who, with head bowed, seemed innocuous enough. But he didn't bother to ask how Simon, locked away in the dungeon for the last three years could know what was going on. "Well did he also mention that the citizens are probably right? That French and Prussian armies are headed this way?"

Cassandra took a deep breath. "He did. Which is why I need to do something to head off this catastrophe. I shall ride to meet the armies, then—"

"Are you crazy?" Max's hand latched around her upper arm, hauling her toward him so that she was pressed to his side. "I will not allow you to put yourself in danger like that."

"Perhaps you forget I'm the Queen of Breslovia." Anger sparked in her eyes and leaped across the inches separating them.

"Hell, Your Highness, if there's one thing I haven't forgotten it's who you are." His head lowered till he was but a heartbeat from her. "I also remember that you're carrying my child. Or did you think that bit of news eluded me?"

Her lashes drifted shut, and when she opened her eyes the fire was gone, replaced by an expression Max couldn't read. He stared at her a minute, breathing in the scent of her, his own anger cooling. "Were you not going to tell me?"

"No. . . . Yes. . . ." Cassandra shook her head. "I don't know," she finally allowed. "I didn't know until after you were wounded and then—"

"You decided to let Albert think the child his," Max hissed. He straightened, taken aback, when she laughed. "I fail to see what's so funny"

"Max." Cassandra's palm curved up to cup his jaw. The heat of his whisker-roughened skin brought her closer. "Albert would never have believed I carried his seed." She watched as the meaning of her words filtered into his mind. Her smile matched his by the time Sophia returned to announce that Cassandra's bath was ready.

"This discussion isn't finished," Max said as he loosened his grip. "Nor have I changed my mind about— Cassandra—damn it!—will you listen to me?" Max followed her toward the door to her bath. It was Sophia who blocked his way. And though Max was willing to lift the tiny redhead from his path and walk in on Cassandra and her maids, he decided the Queen wouldn't appreciate it. So he glared at the magpie, her friend, then at the closed door.

"Inform Her Highness that I shall return." With that, Max turned on his heel and strode toward the doorway to the hall, pausing only long enough to add, "And tell her not to leave until I do."

Max chose to believe she had obeyed his command, though in truth he was back in Cassandra's apartments before she had finished her toilette. Their eyes met in the beveled mirror of her dressing table when he walked through the open door of her bedroom. She was dressed in a royal red riding habit, trimmed in gold braid. A jeweled brooch, depicting the unicorn seal of Breslovia adorned the front. Her golden hair was braided and woven about her head, set off by the ancient crown of the kingdom.

She'd never looked more beautiful. More queenly. More beyond him.

Cassandra raised her chin. "I *am* going to meet the armies."

Max inclined his head toward her reflection. "As am I, Your Highness." Expecting an argument, he couldn't hide his surprise when she smiled at him in the mirror. She turned, raising her hand toward him, accepting his assistance.

"I see you're wearing your uniform." He looked splendid. The dark blue jacket trimmed in gold accentuated his broad shoulders; the tight-fitting white breeches and tall polished boots did the same for his legs.

"I thought I should, as commander of Your Majesty's army." Max offered his arm. Cassandra accepted. And together they left her rooms in the ancient castle.

Cheers rang on the crisp autumn air as Queen Cassandra and General Hawke emerged from the palace's main entrance. Below them, mounted on the kingdom's finest horses were the Imperial Guards, who'd remained loyal to Cassandra, and the Queen's Regiment of Cavalry.

"These are but a small portion of the men ready to serve you, Your Highness. To help you maintain the peace of Breslovia," Max said. "The remainder of your army awaits us on the edge of the city." He bowed, formally and deeply, ending with a flourish of his plumed hat. "We are yours to command, Your Highness."

Tears stung Cassandra's eyes as she gazed down on his raven curls. Her fingers itched to touch them, to brush aside the stray look she knew would slash his forehead when he stood. But she didn't.

Cassandra turned toward her troops, raising her hands for quiet. The sun sparkled off the polished steel of her soldier's swords, but she no longer worried that she might be overcome by a vision. Now what she should do was clear to her.

When the only noise was the jingle of spurs and the soft whinnying of horses, Cassandra spoke. "Today we undertake a mission from God to preserve the peace that has long been our birthright as Breslovians. As your queen it is my duty and honor to lead you on this most holy crusade. A crusade to save our homeland—our people—from death and destruction."

Again cheers and huzzahs rent the palace grounds. Screams of "God save the Queen" filled the air. "Bless good Queen Cassandra!" others shouted.

Overcome at the exuberance and loyalty of her army, Cassandra looked toward Max. He had stepped behind her and to the side, relegating himself to the background. Yet it was he who had done this for her. Given her the gift of her soldiers' adoration. Love for him filled her heart.

She reached back, taking his hand and drawing him forward. Cassandra could no longer see the future. No longer knew what fate might bring them. But for now she wanted him where he belonged. Beside her.

Again she signaled for silence. "I give you your commander in chief," she announced, her voice clear and bright. "General Maximilian Hawke."

Amid the rousing ovation, Max and his queen descended the wide marble steps. Once mounted, they led the procession through the courtyard and out the palace gates.

Trumpets blared as the Queen and her soldiers nudged their way into the streets. All around them disorder and chaos reigned. People yelled at each other, and horses balked at the heavy loads piled onto carts and wagons.

Max glanced toward Cassandra, wondering how she would handle the demoralizing scene. These were her subjects, but imbued with panic, they ignored the sovereign among them. If he had expected this to drag her spirits down, he was wrong.

Instead, defying the guards he'd positioned around her, Cassandra rode forth, her head held high, her chin at the royal angle. At first there was no response. Children cried, mothers wailed, and men cursed the fate that had sent them riding off, leaving all they'd worked for.

Then, as if by joint accord several citizens glanced up, ignoring their troubles, to notice the calm young woman riding in their midst. "It's the Queen," someone mumbled. Then, "Queen Cassandra rides to meet the foe."

Like pebbles scattered in a lake, the word spread, till more and more of her subjects paused to call out her name. She acknowledged the growing wave of well-wishers with a nod, a smile, a subtle wave of her hand.

Max did his best to stay by her side, but he feared he could offer her little other than the sacrifice of his life if the crowd grew ugly. She'd left the Imperial Guard and the cavalry behind, and though Max could have wrung her lovely neck for putting herself in such danger, he couldn't help admiring her courage.

By the time they had made their way to St. Peter's, Cassandra was trailed by enough people to fill the large tree-lined square. She dismounted, accepting Max's help as she made her way through the crowd toward the stairs.

A hush fell over the crowd as she climbed the steps. At the top of them, near the door, she turned, facing her subjects. "You have all heard rumors," she began in a voice that carried over the square. "Of French and Prussian soldiers."

"Aye, who'll slay us in our beds if we don't flee," yelled someone from the crowd. A smattering of agreement accompanied his words.

Cassandra ignored the man and his prophecy. "I am here to tell you there will be no French soldiers—no Prussian soldiers—on Breslovian soil. We are a free kingdom, protected by the Edict of Liberstein." Her voice rose above the chants of agreement. "I am your queen. And I shall protect you. Go back to your homes. To your families."

As on the palace steps, Cassandra reached back, urging Max to stand by her side. "This is General Hawke," she continued. "We ride with the army to insist that the French and the Prussians uphold their treaty with us."

Now the cheers were too loud to speak over. Cassandra waited, lifting her hands, asking for silence. When it came, she repeated her order. "Go home and pray for Breslovia."

Following her own advice, she entered the cathedral, Max by her side. As soon as the door shut behind them, she let out her breath. Her head fell back against the thick bronze portal.

"You were magnificent, you know," Max took her hand.

"I was frightened." She swallowed. "But I was also . . . I can't explain it." She glanced up through gold-tipped lashes. "My husband is dead. My kingdom in dire danger. Yet I feel as if I'm finally doing what I was destined to do. Does that make any sense?"

Max didn't answer her. He couldn't. Not that he didn't agree with her. She was destined to be queen—to be a great queen. That much was obvious, in her love of her country, in her countrymen's love for her.

But thoughts of her destiny only reminded Max that he was not part of it.

So he merely brushed his lips across hers. "Your Highness has a rendezvous to keep—with two armies," he said, smiling when she looked up at him, her eyes dancing with newfound assurance.

That was a fortnight ago.

Max stood in the parlor of his rooms, staring out the ice-glazed window panes. A light snow dusted the wide avenue below. The first of many as winter settled over the kingdom of Breslovia.

A winter of peace.

Because of his beautiful, intrepid queen.

She had ridden with him at the head of Breslovia's army, then with Max and a few Imperial Guards to meet with the French general. If Valliere had recognized her as the village woman he'd met near the border, he'd had the good grace not to mention it.

Cassandra had spoken candidly telling the general of her husband's treachery . . . and his death. Of the disappearance of the traitorous Cardinal Sinzen. Of her own insistence that Breslovia wanted no part in the European war. No soldiers. And—Max inwardly cringed at this—no weapons.

It had taken more than her request for the French to leave. By this time the Prussian army was camped not ten miles away. And neither general wished to be the first to retreat. But Cassandra was tireless, and persistent, and she didn't return to Liberstein until both armies were on the march back to their respective borders.

Since then life seemed to return to normal for the Breslovians. Without the threat of war hanging over them daily, they laughed and went about their business as before. Joy permeated the land.

It was only Max who could not join in the celebration.

"I thought you were going to the palace."

He turned as Kanakareh entered the parlor. "I am." Holding up a folded parchment, Max took a deep breath. "A post from my father," he disclosed, knowing his friend would not ask. "It seems all is forgiven." Walking toward the hearth on which a friendly fire crackled, Max dropped the missive on a side table. "You can carry this stoicism to extremes, you know. It would show some concern if you asked why."

"I know you will tell me."

Max shook his head, grinning. "I can always count on you, Kanakareh. You are a good friend." He glanced down at the letter, at his father's seal, the Duke of Belmead's seal. "It seems Lord Northford is dead, and the lovely Lady Northford found a journal among her husband's possessions. Apparently the bastard took great delight in describing his successful attempts to ruin my career."

"He had the evidence of my supposed collaboration with the French planted." Unable to control his anger any longer,

Max flat handed the mantel, setting an urn to trembling. "The bastard nearly had me court-martialed—hanged." He took a deep breath. "Luckily the man was a poor gambler who left his wife in enough of a financial bind that she decided to sell this information to my father."

Max glanced down at the letter. "I'm still considered a rogue, simply not a treasonous one. I think Father feels it better I be closer to home." Forcing enthusiasm he didn't feel into his tone, Max glanced around toward Kanakareh. "So, what do you say we leave Breslovia for England?"

"Leave Breslovia?"

"Aye. Queen Cassandra seems to have . . . Well, she doesn't really need us anymore. It never was her desire to expand the military." And the Lord knew she didn't need him for anything else. There had been no word from her since they had returned to Liberstein. Of course, he couldn't blame her. Not really. As he'd told Kanakareh, she didn't really need him anymore.

The letter from his father had been a godsend. Not that he really cared about Lord Northford anymore. Or returning to England for that matter. But at least now when he left Breslovia he had somewhere to go.

"Kanakareh?" Max realized his friend had yet to say anything. What's more, the expression on his face was one Max had never noticed before.

"I do not wish to leave Breslovia."

"What?" Max's brows beetled. "Why not? I know I groused about England, but it really isn't that—" Max clamped his lips together. "It isn't that you don't wish to visit England. It's the little magpie."

"Lady Sophia and I are to wed. The Queen has given her permission."

"That's . . ." Say something, Max chided himself. "Wonderful. Wonderful." His reward was seeing a silly grin crease Kanakareh's handsome face.

"You are not upset?"

"Me? No." Max stepped forward to clasp his friend's shoulder. "I admire Lady Sophia." His grin was wry. "Perhaps I've commented on her chatter in the past, but that was mostly in jest. Cassandra—the Queen—adores her, and 'tis obvious you do as well."

Kanakareh's expression sobered. "What will you do?"

"Hell, Kanakareh, I have an invitation from the duke—from my father. There's no reason to concern yourself about me."

Max waited in an anteroom. Waited to see the Queen. He'd finally sought and received an audience with her, deciding he might never see her if he didn't. And he wanted—needed—to see her before he left.

Max paced the room, hands clamped behind his back, his steps timed by the intricately carved clock on the mantel. What in the hell was he going to say to her? he kept asking himself. He was no closer to the answer when the footman ushered him into the spacious Council Room than when he'd decided he must see her.

She stood facing him, between two windows that looked out onto the wintry garden. Her gown was a deep lavender, reminding him of her mourning. She looked beautiful and lonely, but Max wouldn't allow himself to think of that any more than he would the fact that she carried his child in her womb.

"You look well." She was the first to speak. "Does your wound trouble you?"

Max unconsciously flexed his shoulder. "I hardly know 'tis there."

"That is good." Why were they acting like strangers? Cassandra didn't know. "I . . . I'm glad it no longer causes you pain." She took two steps forward and stopped. He still stood by the door as if he wished to keep as much distance between them as possible.

"I assume you heard of Sinzen's capture?"

Max grinned. "Aye, turned in by the French ambassador."

"Count de Mignard tells quite a tale, of Sinzen coming to

him with a plan to take over Breslovia. Apparently Sinzen wished to regain the province of Melena from Prussia. Centuries ago it belonged to his family." Cassandra shrugged. "The cardinal denies it, of course. Blames his brother and Madam Cantrell for plotting to kill me and set themselves up as rulers. Again with help from the French."

"Do you believe him?"

"I think they were both evil. It is up to the courts to decide Sinzen's fate."

Silence fell between them.

"Max."

"Your Highness."

They both spoke at once, smiling at the occurrence. Cassandra graciously motioned for him to go first.

He might as well get it over with. "I'd like permission to resign my commission with Breslovia's army."

"Resign. But why?"

"I think your commander in chief should reside in Breslovia, and I plan to return to England." It was with great effort that Max kept his tone light. It didn't help when her expression reflected the pain he felt.

"But I don't understand." Fearing she might break down and cry at any moment, Cassandra turned to look out the window. "I thought you were happy here. You seemed to enjoy the military."

"I do. And as for Breslovia, it's a wonderful kingdom. It's just that . . ." Max explained about his father's letter. "So you can see why I wish to return to my homeland."

"Yes. . . . Of course I understand." Cassandra glanced over her shoulder, turning back quickly, but it was enough for Max to see her expression, to note the sheen of tears in her violet eyes.

"Oh, hell, Cassie." He skirted the round council table separating them. "How can I possibly stay here now?" His lashes lowered for an instant. When he opened his eyes she faced him. "You're the Queen and I'm only a soldier."

"I need you." Her hand reached out toward him.

But Max simply shook his head. "You forget, I've seen you handle the toughest general, and an unruly crowd. You don't need me."

"Then I want you."

"Oh, God, Cassandra, don't do this to me. Can't you see I can't stay here? Feeling as I do about you. Watching you . . ." Max swallowed. "Watching you swell with my child and knowing I can never claim you as my own."

Cassandra took another step. "How do you feel about me?"

She heard him moan and moved closer. "Are your feelings anything like those I have for you?" She could touch him now. Tentatively her fingers skimmed down the gold-braided jacket front. "Does the very thought of touching me make you hot and cold at the same time?" Cassandra didn't wait for a response. His tortured expression was enough. "And do you think of me night and day? Remember the way it felt when we lay together, when our bodies joined and sky opened to show us a glimpse of heaven? Do your dreams seem so real that you awaken, your flesh damp and wanting." Her voice was no more than a whisper as she traced the brawny expanse of his shoulder. "Wanting."

"Cassie."

Her skirts swished against his thigh. "Is that how you feel about me, because if it is—"

The pressure of his lips cut off the rest of her words. Her head fell back, her arms wound about his neck, and she gave herself over to the erotic ecstasy of his kiss. She nibbled, she wet the seam of his mouth, she opened for him as he did for her.

Their tongues mated, their bodies strained, and then somewhere in the deep recesses of his mind, Max remembered reality. His breathing rasped in his ears as he separated them.

"You can never be mine," he said, his blue eyes dark with passion, searing in their intensity.

"But I am yours." Her fingers tangled in his hair. "As surely as you are mine." On tiptoe, she brushed his chin with her lips. "You are my destiny for 'tis a prophecy told me by Simon that I shall wed and rule with the man I love by my side. And I shall love only you—only you, for all time."

Epilogue

The splendor of fireworks filled the night sky. Max and his queen viewed the spectacle from the balcony overlooking the palace courtyard. A courtyard filled with hundreds of cheering subjects.

"They adore you," Max whispered, leaning over and brushing his lips across her cheek. "As I do."

Waving, watching the last remnants of exploding brilliance fade into blackness, Cassandra smiled. "I think this outpouring is for you, King Maximilian, as well as me."

Max shrugged as he led her into their private rooms. Today was his Coronation Day, a celebration that rivaled this year's Festival of the Pax. He was now the King of Breslovia. Voted such by the reinstated Diaz after an impassioned speech by his wife.

They were partners in ruling the kingdom, as they were in everything else.

Following Cassandra, Max entered the adjoining nursery where their two-year-old son, Prince Christian, slept. Cassandra touched a dark curl, looking up to smile at Max. "I can't believe he slept through all that noise."

"He was tired," Max let his hand join hers on their son's head. They had taken him with them to the coronation. The child had been cheered wildly as he'd sat in front of his father, astride a large black horse.

Max linked his fingers with Cassandra's, and together they walked back to their bedroom. It was in the new section of the palace. Cassandra had moved there when they'd wed. That was nearly three years ago, and since that time, neither she nor Max had slept in any other place.

They had both wondered how her subjects, how the nobles, would react to their marriage, it coming so soon after the Grand Duke's death. But for their child's sake, and their own, they'd decided they had to be together.

Kanakareh and Sophia were delighted, of course. And as it happened, the decision was met with approval from nearly everyone else as well. Especially after Cassandra began implementing the changes she and Max had planned. Schools were built and hospitals. And the taxes raised by Albert to finance the palace and his army were lowered.

The palace was still grand, but the opulence was now tempered by reason. And some sections, like the old tower where Simon dwelled and the gardens, were open to the public.

Max reached for his wife, who came to him readily, her arms weaving about his neck. The kiss spurred memories of their first touch. Their love ignited fires that warmed their hearts and the hearts of those around them.

Breslovia was once again a happy place. A magical kingdom where a beautiful queen and handsome king loved each other more than life itself.

And where they lived happily ever after.

TO MY READERS

I hope you enjoyed reading about Queen Cassandra and Maximilian Hawke. Writing *SPLENDOR* was great fun. I've always loved fairy tales so you can imagine my thrill when, on the last page of *SPLENDOR,* I typed *And they lived happily ever after.*

Thank you all for your wonderful cards and letters. I'm so pleased that you enjoyed the CHARLESTON Trilogy *(Sea Fires, Sea of Desire,* and *Sea of Temptation)* and the Blackstone Trilogy *(My Savage Heart, My Seaswept Heart,* and *My Heavenly Heart).* And yes, I *am* going to write another trilogy.

The first book of the RENEGADE, REBEL, and ROGUE Trilogy will appear in September, 1996, with *The Renegade and the Rose.* Three men meet amid the death and destruction on the moors at Culloden in 1746. Though enemies, these men find their lives entwined in this life and beyond. The RENEGADE, Keegan Macloud, is a Scottish Highlander, sentenced to hang, who must unite his battered and defeated clan. But not before he has his revenge against Major Foxworth Morgan, the man Keegan feels is responsible for his father's death. Kidnapping the Englishman's sister seems like a good idea . . . until Keegan discovers Lady Chloe Morgan's hypochondria and her ability to make his heart race.

The REBEL (September, 1997) is Padraic Rafferty, an Irish smuggler who despite his best intentions falls in love with his father's young widow.

The ROGUE (Summer, 1998) is Lord Foxworth Morgan, a man living a life of pleasure and debauchery in an attempt to quell the haunting memories of the Battle of Culloden. To heal himself Fox must travel through time and space, to the Scottish Highlands of another century, to the arms of Grace Macloud.

I'm very excited about this new trilogy and hope you, my readers, will be, too. Thanks for all your support and encouragement. For a newsletter please write me and send an SASE care of:

Kensington Publishing Corp.
850 Third Avenue
New York, NY 10022-6222

To Happy Endings,

Christine Dorsey

Please turn the page for
an exciting sneak preview of
Christine Dorsey's newest
historical romance
THE RENEGADE AND THE ROSE
coming from Zebra Books in
September 1996

One

April 16, 1746
Culloden, Scotland

The pipe's haunting tones echoed across the mist-shrouded moor. The sound sang through Keegan MacLeod's blood. He was a Scot, by God, a Scot. As were his ancestors and the clansmen with whom he stood shoulder to shoulder.

He'd nearly forgotten. The gaming halls and perfumed boudoirs of London could do that to a man. That life seemed far removed from the icy sleet and chaos of this April morn on Drummossie Moor. Yet it had been only a fortnight ago when he'd cursed the summons of the MacLeod to return to the highlands . . . to return home.

Cursed yet complied.

For his father wanted all his sons beside him when he fought for his Prince. Charles Edward, grandson of the last Stuart king, had returned from exile in France. He'd landed on Eriskay determined to return his father to the throne of England. The rightful heir many thought, including the MacLeod.

Personally Keegan didn't much care who sat on the throne. At least that had been his opinion till now. But generations of Jacobite blood flowed through his veins, and so he'd come.

His brothers, sons of the MacLeod, were here as well. Angus, the eldest, his red hair plastered to his head beneath his bonnet, to the laird's right. Malcolm, with his soft blue eyes and pleasing voice, beside him. Keegan was to his father's left.

And finally William, fresh from his tutor, and restless with anticipation of the battle to come.

They all wore the white cockade of the Stuarts, five bows of silk in a large knot. Their plaids were kilted, then tied high between their legs. A silver pin bearing the MacLeod crest held the drape free of their sword arms.

" 'Tis a fine day for a fight I'm thinkin'." Angus stomped his feet and flexed his beefy shoulders. He was broader than Keegan, though nearly a head shorter, but he swung his broadsword with an ease Keegan had long admired.

When his father made no reply Angus continued. "I know you've a problem with the field, Da, but—"

"I'll not be second-guessin' the Prince . . . or what happens this day," the MacLeod countered, clasping his free hand on the shoulder of each son in turn. "Nor shall any of ye. We'll stand together as MacLeods, and proud we'll be of it."

"When will they be comin', do ye think? Or will the English bastards turn tail and run at the sight of us?" Arrogant words from William whose cheeks looked more like the downy underbelly of a lamb than those of a full-grown man, Keegan thought.

But all he said was, "Soon enough we'll be knowing."

As if his words were prophetic a loud chorus of huzzahs sounded from the ranks. Across the moor to the northeast, silhouetted against the dark sky, the enemy's first scarlet and white standard topped the rise. It was followed by another, then another. And then the Duke of Cumberland's infantry came into view, three columns of blood red uniforms coloring the gloom.

The shouts and taunts continued, interspersed with the yelled commands to "Close up ranks!" It seemed as if the British troops would do nothing but stand, their numbers stretched across the field, their regimental drums pounding like one giant heartbeat.

Keegan gripped his broadsword, and stood, waiting for the order to advance. He stood thus when the first volley from the British exploded over the field, striking down William at his side. It was as if part of himself were blown away, and Keegan watched in horror as his younger brother crumpled to his knees, then fell face first into the heather.

"Will!" The collective lament roared around him as Keegan dropped to the ground. He knew before he rolled his brother over that he was dead, but Keegan tried anyway to revive William, calling his name and rubbing his palm over the smooth, whiskerless cheek.

It was Angus who took charge, wrapping the body in his plaid and charging two of the clan's humblies to carry the laird's son to safety.

But there was no time to mourn.

"Close up ranks! Close up!" The officer's shouted orders filtered through the thunder of artillery, the screams of the wounded.

All around him men were falling, clansmen and fellow Scots, mowed down like so much harvest wheat as they stood waiting for the command to attack. Waiting. When it finally came Keegan leaped forward, a hoarse cry of "For Will" rushing from his dry lips. His father and remaining brothers were at his side as he fired his musket, then, ignoring the grapeshot hurled his way, yanked one of the claw-handled dags from his belt. But it was the double-edged broadsword he longed to use. To feel the weight of it slash through the faceless soldiers who had killed Will.

The smoke burned his throat and made it near impossible to see. He was within twenty yards of the enemy, he thought, though only infrequently, when a gust of wind cleared the air, could he see the wall of scarlet uniforms. Keegan pushed forward, halting only when he tripped over a body. Falling to his knees, he blinked, then found himself staring into Angus's lifeless eyes.

"God, no!" Keegan scrambled to his feet, wiping his eyes and searching through the mist and smoke till he spotted his father's grizzled head. The older man had lost his bonnet in the fray, yet he still stood, as did Malcolm. But the rebel losses were devastating. Dead and dying covered the field, winnowing from the clans their best young men.

Fury swelled in Keegan's breast. He hurled himself forward, swinging the broadsword like a man possessed. For Will. For Angus. For his fellow Scots littering the moor.

He fought and slashed and somehow avoided the deadly stab of the bayonet, but there was no penetrating the solid wall of the English battalion.

The retreat was called, then called again, and still Keegan ignored it. It was as if another man had possession of his movements . . . of his soul. Not until he felt Malcolm's hand grabbing his arm did Keegan pause in the relentless swinging of his broadsword.

"The laird," Malcolm screamed at him, and Keegan barely heard above the din of battle, though his brother's muddy, blood-spattered face was nearly touching his own. "Da's wounded."

Swinging about Keegan reached for his father, catching him beneath the arm as the laird's knees crumpled. "Take this," Keegan screamed, shoving the bloody broadsword toward his brother. Angered because of Malcolm's hesitation, Keegan opened his mouth to repeat the order. That was when he noticed the glistening fluted tip of a bayonet protruding from Malcolm's chest. Blood gurgled slowly from his brother's mouth before the English foot soldier jerked forward, forcing Malcolm's body to the ground with the heel of his boot.

Keegan had no more time to mourn the passing of this brother than he had the others. He was the only one left. He who had not wished to fight. Had not wished to interrupt his life of fun and debauchery. He who had counseled against supporting Prince Charles more on selfish than patriotic grounds.

These thoughts flitted through Keegan's mind in that briefest of moments when his brother crashed to the ground. Dipping low, Keegan grabbed up his father, tossing the laird over his shoulder, then stumbling away from the English line.

Bodies were everywhere, the dead and dying. Keegan tried to close his mind to the carnage. This was not the time to think on what had happened. He must get his father to safety. Yet two days with little sleep and but a few biscuits to fill his belly were taking their toll. As the sounds of artillery exploded around him, Keegan could not stop the faces of his dead brothers from flashing before him.

Hot pain tore through the arm that dragged his broadsword, and he knew without looking that he'd been hit. Yet he pushed on. He would carry his father to Skye if he had to, to Castle MacLeod. He would.

Yet it was a dry-stone fence that caught his eye. Bordering a sunken road, the fence held momentary shelter. After he caught his breath he'd take his father to the bothy on the rise to the right of the road. This was Cullen land if memory served him, and they'd be proud to treat the laird's wounds. Then they'd be off for the hills of home.

Home.

The word rang, a litany through his heart, as he plodded on over the body-littered moor. As gently as he could Keegan lowered his father, resting his back against the limestones. It wasn't till he straightened that Keegan noticed another using the stone wall as a refuge. A soldier dressed in the uniform of an English dragoon. Despite the chill air, sweat poured down his back when Keegan saw the pistol pointed his way.

Lifting his broadsword Keegan ignored as best he could the pains shooting through his arm. The two men, one wearing a scarlet surtout, the other garbed in plaid, stared at each other without moving. The English soldier was the first to speak and when he did his words were colored by an Irish brogue.

"Be off with ye," he said before letting his head fall back against the rocks. The pistol's muzzle dipped toward the ground.

"I'll be resting my Da if it's all the same to ye." Keegan lowered the broadsword, then dropped to his knees beside his father. The laird's wounds were numerous, but none appeared mortal. At least that was Keegan's uninformed opinion. It wasn't safe to stay there, though, even if the soldier to his right hadn't the strength or inclination to shoot.

"Come on now, Da, we'll be heading home. Give me your—"

At that moment a great huzzah came from the direction of the English. Keegan realized the artillery had stopped, but he could still hear cannon fire from the ships in the bay echoing off the mountains.

"They'll be coming now," the wounded man to his right said. "They're claiming the field as their own."

Keegan stared at the Englishman, then back toward the line of dragoons. As predicted amid shouts and cheers the soldiers began marching across the moor. Then they were running, bayonets fixed, stabbing at any of the enemy that moved.

Keegan grabbed for his father, but in that instant knew it was too late. The wound on his arm dripped blood as Keegan lifted his broadsword, placing himself squarely in front of his father. He thought he heard a mumbled. "Save yourself, lad," but ignored it.

Then he could hear nothing but the clang of tempered steel as he swung the broadsword, fighting off the first three soldiers who came at him. One, then another, dropped to the ground at his feet. But the third soldier had moved to flank him. Even amid the chaos, the click of the pistol hammer sounded frighteningly loud, the report almost anticlimactic.

Keegan waited for the pain to consume him, for the sound came from the wounded Englishman's gun, he was sure. But there was nothing. Jerking around Keegan saw the third soldier crumple to his knees, then slump forward, blood blossoming from the front of his jacket.

"What . . . ?"

Turning, Keegan's gaze met that of the man with the pistol. Their mutual stare held, and for just a moment Keegan could swear there was some sort of link between them, though he was equally sure they'd never met or crossed paths before. Still there it was, a feeling almost akin to friendship. Shaking his head, Keegan again reached for his father. For whatever reason, the Englishman had saved his life, now it was up to him to get his father away.

But there was no escape. More soldiers were bearing down on him, laughing and killing any survivors as they came. Keegan was soon surrounded. His father and the fence to his rear. Scarlet-coated soldiers blocking the front.

Damnation, he would fight to the death.

Keegan raised his broadsword sweeping it in a giant arc, daring the foot soldiers to come at him. Fury raged through him, drowning out the fear. This was to be his death then.

"Halt!"

The shouted command caught the attention of the English soldiers as well as Keegan. He looked up to see an officer, astride a magnificent chestnut horse. Beneath a gold-trimmed hat, the officer's face contorted in anger. The tip of his saber pointed toward Keegan, but it was to his men he spoke.

"I'll have no more senseless killings."

"This thieving rebel is the murderer," one of the chastised soldiers countered. "We be just tidyin' up the field a bit."

"You'll be doing no such thing while I'm about." Now the officer turned his attention toward Keegan. "Surrender your sword."

"And be cut down like a cur. I think not."

"Foolish words from one just seconds away from that very fate."

"I'll die a free man, protecting my father from the likes of you."

For the first time the officer shifted his focus to the old man slumped against the stones. "You'll do him no good with your defiance."

"I'll do him no good by surrendering."

The stallion sidestepped, obviously anxious to be on his way. The officer seemed to share his mount's feelings. "Hand over your sword and I'll see that no harm comes to your father."

"And I've an Englishman's word upon that," Keegan spat, his voice full of contempt.

"Aye, you've Lord Foxworth Morgan's word upon it."

* * *

A word he should never have taken.

With but a few steps Keegan paced the length of his cell, then back, slamming his fist against the heavy wooden door. This was what believing Lord Foxworth Morgan had earned him. A spot in Newgate Gaol; a date with the hangman.

And the memory of watching, helpless, as the soldiers tortured and killed his father.

Keegan shut his eyes against the pain. Four soldiers had grabbed Keegan, pinning his arms to his body, the instant he'd handed over his broadsword. Their laughter still rang in his head. They'd used their bayonets on the laird stabbing and slashing till naught but the bloody plaid remained recognizable.

"Nay." Keegan sucked in his breath on a sob. He would not cry again. Better he go to his death cursing the man he'd cursed as the British had had their sport with his father.

Lord Foxworth Morgan.

Keegan slid to the floor, burying his face in the lee of his bent knees. How much better it would have been to die on the battlefield. For his father. For himself.

Keegan spit into the vermin-infested straw on the floor. In the months since Culloden, he had railed against God, against the Fates, against himself, and even against his father who had championed a cause destined to failure. During those long, lonely days he'd made peace with himself as best he could, then with his father's memory and the God who watched over him.

Forgiveness and acceptance. With one exception. Lord Foxworth Morgan. He should have used his broadsword on the English officer rather than have taken his word on anything. His last regret in a life filled with them was that he couldn't take the British lord to hell with him.

If he ever had the chance, by God, he would.

Keegan's laughter was harsh. He'd have no more chances.

No more options. He'd been judged guilty by the English courts, and as soon as the sun rose over the Thames he'd—

The metallic rattle of key against lock interrupted Keegan's morbid thoughts. He pushed to his feet. So it was time.

"Can't even wait for the dawn, eh?" he said, as the thick-lipped jailor motioned him from the cell. The man carried a lantern in one hand, a pistol in the other. And he said nothing as they walked the corridor, past the spot where a sentry with fixed bayonet usually stood. Keegan's cell was on the third of four stories. He led the way down the stairs into the darkness.

At the bottom he was nudged to the left, down another corridor. Keegan kept walking till he came to the door that marked the end. The silent jailor motioned him aside, then slipped a ring of keys from his belt and unlocked the door. The portal swung open to the blackness of night. And just as quickly Keegan was shoved through it.

"What the hell . . . ?"

The door slammed shut, the jailor disappearing behind it. With Keegan on the outside.

Slowly he turned, trying to focus in the darkness.

"You're safe . . . for now," came a voice from the shadows.

Keegan jerked around. "Who are you?"

" 'Tis of no importance. A friend of a friend. Your freedom was secured . . . for a price. If you feel along near the door you'll find a broadsword." He paused while Keegan searched. "Take it and yourself and get as far away from London as you can. As far away from Scotland too, if you know what's good for you."

"Why? Scotland is my home. My clan is there. . . ." Keegan waited for a response. "You, friend of a friend, answer me. What is going on here?"

But there was no response. Soon Keegan realized he was alone. He clasped the broadsword to his side and sucked in a deep breath. It smelled of rotting food and human waste, but it filled his lungs, reminding him he was alive—and free. But there were those who weren't.

Leave London, the voice in the dark had told him. Stay away from Scotland. But the ghosts of his brothers and his father—of his fallen clansmen—would allow him to do neither.